PRAISE FOR
Sharing Sean

"A Teflon-slick beach read."   —*Kirkus Reviews*

"Pye strikes a balance between the comedic absurdity of three
women trying to juggle one man with the real emotional implications of what they're doing. . . . Once the sharing begins, it
moves to a delicious—and inevitable—conclusion."
                    —*Chicago Tribune*

"An entertaining debut . . . this 'Sex and the City goes London' is
chatty, catty, and downright fun."   —*Booklist*

"[A] wry comedy."   —*Marie Claire*

About the Author

FRANCIS PYE is a writer and journalist. She lives in London with her husband, whom she would be reluctant to share. *Sharing Sean* is her first novel.

Sharing Sean

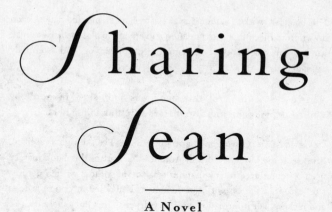

Sharing Sean

A Novel

Frances Pye

HARPER
PERENNIAL

A hardcover edition of this book was published in 2004 by
William Morrow, an imprint of HarperCollins Publishers.

SHARING SEAN. Copyright © 2004 by Frances Pye. All rights reserved.
Printed in the United States of America. No part of this book may be
used or reproduced in any manner whatsoever without written permission except in the case of brief quotations embodied in critical articles
and reviews. For information address HarperCollins Publishers Inc., 10
East 53rd Street, New York, NY 10022.

HarperCollins books may be purchased for educational, business, or
sales promotional use. For information please write: Special Markets
Department, HarperCollins Publishers Inc., 10 East 53rd Street, New
York, NY 10022.

FIRST PERENNIAL EDITION PUBLISHED 2005.

The Library of Congress has catalogued the hardcover edition as follows:

Pye, Frances.
    Sharing Sean : a novel / Frances Pye.—1st ed.
        p. cm.
    ISBN 0-06-054556-9 (alk. paper)
        1. Female friendship—Fiction. 2. London (England)—Fiction.
    3. Divorced women—Fiction. 4. Single women—Fiction.
    5. Sharing—Fiction. I. Title.

PR6116.Y4S53 2004
823'.92—dc22
2003061433

ISBN 0-06-054557-7 (pbk.)

05 06 07 08 09 ❖/RRD 10 9 8 7 6 5 4 3 2 1

for Chris

Acknowledgments

Too many people have helped me with *Sharing Sean* for me to list them all. Every one of my friends has been enormously generous with their time, listening to me talk about my work week after week, but I would specifically like to thank Carol Ann Duffy and Sue Fox for their enthusiastic reaction to my original idea, giving me the courage to put pen to paper; Diana Lovell-Pank and Catherine Marcangeli for their generous support and intelligent advice; Bob Bassing and Carol Jago for their thoughtful comments upon the story; Mary Fenton, Jeremy and Gina Fox, Susan Krajewski, Sarah Lawson and Roshan Tarsky for their encouraging response to the manuscript, and the Stevenson family for allowing me to use their dog, Minnie, in the story.

I owe an especial debt of gratitude to Nena Rodrigue for going far out of her way to help me find my wonderful agent, Christy Fletcher, whom I cannot thank enough for taking a risk on an unknown English writer and finding her book a home. Many, many thanks also to Claire Wachtel, my brilliant editor, both for pointing out my mistakes without ever making me feel stupid and for shepherding me through the entire unfamiliar process of editing and publication.

Finally, a huge thank you to Chris, Holly, and Tom Pye; I would never have been able to do this without your unstinting love and support.

One

one

Jules had put off clearing out the office for ages. Not so much because she expected to find anything, more for fear of reawakening painful memories of her time with Will. But she needed the space; her Chelsea town house was far from large, and keeping one room locked away made no sense. So she steeled herself, inched open the door, and, armed with a vacuum cleaner, dusters, and tons of rubbish bags, she went to work.

Heaps of old letters, of bills and receipts, of ancient yellow, curled faxes and aged theater programs were piled on the floor, against the walls, and on the expensive antique satinwood desk Jules had bought for her then-beloved husband. Even the seat of the matching chair was stacked high with out-of-date catalogs and used checkbooks and grubby bits of paper.

But there were no ghosts. No lingering shades of Will, of his handsome face, his charming smile. No pain. No unhappiness. Not even any memories. Just a dusty, dirty, disused room. And the detritus of a life. Of a marriage.

Jules eased the paper wrapping off a curl of black plastic bags, pulled one from the roll, and teased it open. To begin with, she threw everything away, eager to get rid of it and Will. But as she made her way through it all, she began to look at a letter here and there. Soon she was reading everything, amazed by this new insight into someone she had thought she knew as well as she could know anyone. She'd been aware that her husband wasn't the most truthful person in the world—her girlfriends Lily, Mara, and Terry still laughed at his telling a story about how he had once rescued a party of English schoolchildren who were lost in the Gobi Desert—but reading through the litter of his life she realized just how bad it had been. Truth held as little meaning for him as Egyptian hieroglyphics did for her.

There were dozens of complaints from dissatisfied customers of his interior design company. Letters threatening court action unless he returned deposits paid on jobs he hadn't finished. Jobs he hadn't even started. Jobs he had no intention of ever starting. Will had always insisted that his clients loved him. That the reason he never made any money was because he couldn't bear not to use the best materials, the best fabrics. But in reality it was because he never got around to doing any work at all.

Amazed by the sheer depths of her ex-husband's duplicity, Jules plowed through the heaps of unpaid bills. The stacks of final demands. The endless, threatening notes from creditors.

Then, she picked up a letter from a Mr. Giddes, a fertility consultant based in Harley Street. As she read through it, her body went rigid with shock.

"Bastard. How could he do this to me?" she screamed.

Will had lied to her. He was infertile.

Where a normal sperm count was between 20 and 100 million, his was barely 5 million. That might seem like a lot—after all, it took only one—but Jules knew those kinds of low numbers made fathering a baby almost impossible without the help of in vitro fertilization. Particularly as, according to this, Will also had nonexistent motility. In other words, the few sperm he was producing were going nowhere.

"I am afraid that, given these results, there is no chance of your fathering a child in the usual fashion," the letter clearly stated.

Will's sperm was useless. Inert. Dead.

All those years, he'd let her believe that he was fine, knowing she was going to be devastated every month when she found out she wasn't pregnant. He had watched her ripping open packets of tests, listened to her praying that this would be the day, heard her sobbing as she realized that yet again there would be no baby. He watched her, on the street staring at infants, crying when she saw pictures of mothers and newborns, drooling over the tiny dresses in Petite Etoile. Year after year. Without saying a thing.

She should have known something was wrong when he refused to go for a sperm test. She'd believed his story about the son he'd fathered when he was in his twenties, the son who'd later been killed, with his mother, in an accident. When her tests came back and there was nothing wrong with her, her doctor suggested that that was no guarantee, that the mother might have made a mistake about Will's being the father. Or even lied. So Jules had tried to talk to Will, to ask him as gently as she could to take the test anyway, just to confirm things. And he'd hit her. Hard. She could still hear him yelling at her. Didn't she understand what she was asking? Why did she want to hurt him by dredging up all those old, bad memories associated with children and hospitals and tests? The whole thing was unnecessary, just a stupid whim to reassure her and that old hag of a doctor she'd insisted on seeing. He'd fathered a child. His sperm was fine. If there was a problem, it must be with her.

Now, looking at the letter, knowing the truth, his lies appeared pathetically, painfully obvious. Back then she'd been too worried to think straight. Instead, she had convinced herself that all the two of them needed to do was relax, be patient, and it would happen. There were years of taking her temperature, of rushing home to make love at the right moment, of lying back afterward, giving things time to happen, hoping month after month, only for those hopes to be dashed again and again as every test proved negative. Until, finally, worn out, unable to cope with even one more disappointment, Jules gave up on the idea.

Lily, Terry, and Mara had wanted her to go for fertility treatments, but she couldn't bring herself to do it. She was convinced that it would just mean more of the same: eager expectation followed by bitter disappointment, only magnified a thousand times once doctors and procedures and hospitals were involved.

Jules stared at the letter in her hand, repelled by the musty smell of disuse that hung in the air, struggling to understand how much her ex-husband must have hated her.

She started to cry. All those wasted years. If he had only told her, had just been honest, she would have embraced IVF. She would have given anything, sacrificed anything to make sure it worked and that she and Will had a child together. Part of her knew she wasn't being rational, that their disastrous relationship wouldn't have been saved by a baby. She would've hated being tied to him forever as the mother of his child. And been terrified that if he could hit her, he might do the same to their baby. But she allowed herself to dream, if only for a moment. Their child would have been school age by now, a little son or daughter for Jules to dress and play with and love. The only thing she had ever really, really wanted and failed to get was a child. Instead, she was alone.

Jules crushed the paper she was holding in her hands, hurled it at the wall, then hunted for something more satisfying to throw. Something that might break. There was nothing. She spun around, her white-blond hair flying around her face, her pale green eyes raging, and kicked out at a paper-stuffed black trash bag, sending it soaring across the tiny attic bedroom her ex-husband had once used as an "office." Her mind was filled with dreams of revenge, of wonderful, satisfying retribution, of ways to make Will feel as bad as she had when she'd read the letter.

But then, she stopped short. Wait a second. If he'd lied to her, that meant she was fine. A huge smile spread over Jules's elegant, tanned face. She was fine. She was only thirty-eight; there was still time. She could have a baby. Her smile got impossibly wider. A baby.

two

Terry crossed her hands over the oversize wheel and spun it to her left. Thank God for power steering. Without it, there was no way a hundred-and-twenty-pound, five-foot-nothing like her could do this job. The double-decker bus passed the glassed-over entrance to Victoria Station and made its way unerringly through the crowded bays, then pulled up in an empty space. Terry turned off the engine and heard the heavy footsteps of passengers leaving the upper deck and pouring out of the rear of the bus.

It was lunchtime. They were in the middle of the first warm spell of the year and everyone was desperate to catch some sunshine in case this was the only glimpse of summer they'd get. Just as keen to get a short break from her hot, airless cab, Terry opened the door and leaped the four feet down to the ground.

"You're crazy," came a shout, and a short, round, smiling man in a black serge uniform with a ticket machine on a strap appeared at Terry's shoulder. "One of these days, you're going to break a leg."

"Silly. All these years and I haven't yet, have I?" Terry smiled at Fred, her conductor.

"You're getting on, love. Women's bones, they get brittle, you know."

"Getting on? I'll give you getting on. It's not me who's retiring next year, now is it?"

"Can't wait. It'll get me away from you at last."

"Never. I've told May I'll be round every day for my tea just to annoy you."

"Aagh! Mother of God, what can I have done to deserve that?" Fred grinned at Terry. They'd been together off and on for almost fifteen years now and he both liked and admired her. Maybe to start with, he—along with many others—had had his doubts about a woman driver, but she'd long since won him over. Not only because she was good at her job but also because he genuinely enjoyed her company.

"Something good, of course. See you in a bit." Terry rushed into the station, stopping only to grab a cup of coffee and a sandwich from Pret A Manger before she set out again.

When she'd first seen the ad for trainee drivers in the *Standard*, years ago, she'd been sure they wouldn't want her. But she was alone with her baby son, Paul, and was desperate for a regular job with regular hours so that she could predict when she'd be home, when she could pick him up from the sitter's, when she'd have to take him back. She'd fled her grim, unloving, disapproving family in Liverpool when she was seventeen and after that had skipped from job to job, never staying all that long anywhere. Her usual mainstays—barmaiding, waitressing—were no good anymore since they required being out at night. She didn't want to work in a shop—the wages were low and she'd come home exhausted after all the hours on her feet. She had no real qualifications, so an office job was out of the question. Sitting in a nice warm bus, looking out at the sights of London, with good wages and even a pension plan, that sounded grand. But did they take women? And women as small as she was?

Terry had been amazed when she was given a trial run, and even more amazed when she'd discovered she had a real aptitude for the job. She hadn't fully understood the explanation her first instructor had given her, but it was something to do with depth perception. An inch to someone else was a mile to her. She could turn the huge red double-decker around corners with no worries about hitting parked cars, could drive through the smallest spaces with no concern that she might have an accident. She knew instinctively and absolutely when the bus would fit and when it wouldn't. So she had become one of London Transport's very few female drivers. And she loved it.

She loved the joking with the other drivers and the rapport she had with Fred. She loved driving through the city. Even though she had been on the same route, passing the same bits of London over and over, for years now, there was always something different to see. Different people, different windows in stores, different billboards. Old, sad buildings torn down to be replaced gradually by glassy new ones.

More than anything else, she loved the fact that she had become a recognizable character on the number 73 route. From Victoria to Stoke Newington, people in shops, pedestrians, passengers would see her and remember. As she drove along busy Oxford Street, through fashionable Islington, and up into run-down Newington Green, they caught a glimpse of her diminutive figure behind the wheel, controlling the red monster of a bus, and it made them smile.

THREE HOURS later, her shift finished, Terry walked through the door of her two-bedroom flat that took up the whole of the first floor of a large Victorian house in Stoke Newington. She hadn't known the area until she'd started driving to it every day, but she'd felt at home there immediately. Lots of big, old run-down houses split into apartments, a plain, unflowery park complete with lake and deer, a good mix of people, some truly great Indian restaurants, and, most important, London property she could afford.

A small bundle of tan-colored, high-octane energy came racing down the hallway and leaped into Terry's arms, tail wagging furiously.

"Minnie, you're mad, you are," Terry said, her soft, nasal Liverpool accent still audible despite her years in London.

The dog, an unidentifiable mixture of God knew how many varieties, which Terry had found abandoned in an animal shelter, started enthusiastically licking her mistress's face. "Okay, okay, that's enough. Yes, I love you too." Terry put Minnie down on the floor.

"Paul, I'm home," Terry shouted as she shrugged out of her jacket. The uniform was the only bad thing about being a bus driver.

"Paul!" No answer. It was five o'clock. He should be home from school by now. He was probably holed up in his room.

Followed by Minnie, Terry walked along a narrow corridor lined with photographs of her son, from cute infancy to spotty adolescence, and opened a stripped pine door at the end. Her bedroom was small and almost completely filled by a king-size brass bed that doubled as a wardrobe. Brightly colored clothes, gleaming necklaces, glittering beads, printed scarves, feathers and hats and belts and bags were thrown over its two ends, woven between its curls and loops, hanging from its four posts. It looked as if it was made of clothes, with only the occasional glimpse of gleaming brass giving any hint of what lurked underneath all the cotton and wool and silk.

When Terry got home from work, she immediately changed into some combination of vintage clothing, all of which she'd bought for almost nothing at garage sales or in thrift shops. There seemed to be no method to what she wore; she paid no attention to any rules, ignored what colors should go together, loved things that were supposed to clash but on her somehow didn't.

She was self-conscious about her weight, disliking her lack of height, her curvy frame, and her generous bosom, but few other people noticed. Her quirky, mix-and-match clothes were the perfect complement to her long, curly red hair, her pale skin and light hazel eyes, while her voluptuous build was masked by her narrow ankles and elegant calves. Terry looked like no one else.

Ten minutes later, she walked along the narrow corridor wearing an old blue dress, a mauve cardigan, and some multicolored beads, Minnie at her heels. She went up a set of five steps and stopped outside a door decorated with a skull and crossbones and the words "Death to Anyone Who Enters" painted on a piece of driftwood. "Paul?" she asked.

Silence. Terry knocked on the door. Nothing. She knocked again, louder. A groan.

"Teatime," Terry called through the door. She knew better than to open it unasked. Still no reply. "Hey, it's after five. You've got to be hungry. Come on."

"Don't want anything." His words were muffled by the door but still audible.

"Paul. I bet you had no lunch, did you? And not much dinner last night—"

The door slammed open. Terry looked up at her fifteen-year-old son. Just a few months ago it seemed she had been able to meet him eye to eye. Now he was about a foot taller. Though he was thin and still coltish, his voice had broken and there were definite traces of the man he would become. As well as the acne of teenagehood.

"I don't want anything, okay?" At the sound of Paul's voice, Minnie backed away from the door, her teeth bared.

"You're still growing. You need to keep up your strength."

Paul's sigh and slumping shoulders said everything, but Terry wouldn't give up. He had to eat.

"Come on. I know, egg in the hole. Think I've got some eggs and some bread—"

"Egg in the hole? I'm not a kid. Are you nuts?"

Terry's overly strict, deeply religious grandparents had blamed her for her mother's running off with a man when Terry was only three, leaving them to care for her. They'd expected Terry to repeat this fall from grace and tried to pray the devil out of her morning and night and five times on Sundays, punishing her severely for every tiny infraction of their rigid rules. She could still hear the tirade and taste the week of bread and water she'd endured after she'd made the mistake of telling her grandmother she was nuts.

When Terry had first learned she was pregnant with Paul, she had vowed not to be like her grandmother in any way. In the early years, it had been easy, but recently it had become more of a struggle. Never had she been closer to breaking her vow than in the last few months.

She took a deep breath and tried again. "We'll call for pizza if you like." A huge concession. Terry was yet again trying to lose some weight and pizza was a definite no-no.

"No food," Paul shouted. A low growl came from Minnie.

"You crazy dog. It's Paul." Minnie was a separatist at heart. She hated men. Particularly men in uniform, but knife-thin creases and a load of brass buttons weren't strictly necessary. She also loathed men in general. Any one she saw, if she got a chance, she gave him a nip. She'd been fine with Paul as he was growing up, but recently, when his voice had dropped, she'd become more suspicious of him.

"I'm going out." Paul brushed past Terry and jumped down the stairs in one go.

Terry followed him to the front door. "Hey, love, don't walk out. What's wrong?" She reached out to touch his shoulder.

He jerked away from her hand and stormed out, slamming the door behind him.

Terry sighed and leaned back against the wall. It had been the reappearance of his father that had triggered this in Paul. Until then he'd been occasionally difficult, stubborn, quick to anger, but he was also always quick to apologize and make things right between them. They had been close friends as much as mother and son, but Finn's arrival had changed all that.

Terry hadn't seen Finn since Paul was born. Then, three months before, on a hot summer's night, he'd arrived on her doorstep, leaning unsteadily against the wall outside, scarcely able to walk by himself. Terry's first thought had been not to help him. How could he come to her like that? But then she'd heard the fear and the excitement and the hope in Paul's voice as he came up behind her and asked if the man on the doorstep was his dad.

She'd known then that she couldn't turn Finn away. So she and Paul had helped him up the stairs and got him undressed and into her bed. Hardly able to speak beyond a whispered hoarse, throaty "thanks," he'd fallen asleep. And slept and slept and slept. Terry began to worry when it was more than twenty-four hours. Finally, when the sweetly cloying, old-sweat smell in her room overcame the open windows and the potpourri and the fresh flowers, she called an ambulance. Finn was rushed to hospital, where he lingered another forty-eight hours before dying of cirrhosis. Without ever waking up or saying a word to Paul.

From that moment, Terry's son had been impossible. Unwilling to talk to his mother, to help her, or to let her help him, to do anything other than sulk and brood and lose his temper. It didn't matter what she did. If she left him alone, he accused her of not caring. If she talked to him, he was angry. If she shouted at him, he was furious. Mind you, he was right. She must be nuts to offer him egg in the hole like that as if he were a baby.

three

The sharp, metallic sound of an electronic doorbell echoed through the half-furnished King's Cross loft with its deep, industrial windows looking out onto Regent's Canal, its dark, brick walls, wide wooden floorboards, and bolted iron pillars. The enormous space was virtually empty. Apart from two extra-large burgundy leather sofas, a vast glass-and-wood coffee table, and a tall dark-haired man pacing the floor. Sean Grainger.

He walked to the intercom and, without checking to see who it was, buzzed open the front door to the building. He stood right there, waiting for his guest and mentally crossing his fingers. Hoping that Ball, the latest in a long line of private detectives, would have something this time but fearing it would be more of the same. "You have to be patient, Mr. Grainger." "The trail is very cold, Mr. Grainger." "People are remarkably difficult to find if they want to stay lost, Mr. Grainger." Joe Ball had come highly recommended and had given Sean no reason to doubt his hard work, but months had gone by and still the detective had found no sign of his boys.

A couple of minutes later, Ball was sitting on one of the sofas with Sean opposite him, a cold can of beer clutched in his hand. They were a mismatched pair. Ball was of medium height, balding, and overweight—hanging around watching other people's lives didn't leave a lot of opportunity for exercise—while Grainger was a tall powerful man, his shaggy dark hair unthinned by his forty-five years.

Sean leaned forward, "So? What've you got for me?"

"Not very much, I'm afraid, Mr. Grainger."

"Then, there's something?"

"No. Not really."

"No trace at all?"

"Mr. Grainger, people are remarkably difficult to find—"

"Yes, I know, I know all that." Sean couldn't bear to hear Ball's platitudes one more time. "It's been eighteen months. There's got to be something. The boys must be at school somewhere?"

Ball leaned forward, putting unwelcome strain on the lower buttons of his shirt. "We did discuss this before, if you remember, Mr. Grainger. There is no record of them attending any school in the UK."

"But Canada? What about the detective we hired in Canada? Hasn't he come up with anything?" Isobel, his ex-wife, had been brought up in Vancouver and still had family there. If she'd left the country with the boys, Sean was convinced that was where she would have gone.

"No trace of the boys at all. Or of their mother. I'm sorry."

"What's she doing? Is she teaching them herself, at home?"

"There would still be records. Home education is very strictly monitored."

"Then where are they?"

"The world is a very large place, Mr. Grainger. They could be anywhere. Australia. New Zealand. Europe. South America. And without something to go on, some clue, well . . ."

"The man she ran away with? He's got to be employed somewhere to support them all."

"There are a lot of Steve Joneses, sir. And he could be working anywhere in the world. You're in construction, you know how in demand plumbers are."

"The tax people? No one can avoid paying taxes."

"We've been over and over that. Confidential, I'm afraid. Perhaps if he'd committed a crime . . ."

"He did. He stole my sons."

"Well, sir, not really. The police aren't treating this as a kidnapping, as such." Ball was polite but skeptical.

"I know. I know. Because Isobel took them. But I still don't understand why. She didn't even like being a parent much. Why did she do it?"

"People do things for the strangest reasons, sir. You say she was very keen on Steve Jones. Perhaps she wanted him to think of her as a good, loving mother."

Sean nodded. Ball's theory made sense. Isobel and her lover had been together only a few months when they'd disappeared. He was almost ten years younger than she was, and though Sean had seen them together only a few brief times, it had been obvious that she was bothered by the difference in age. She hadn't been the cool, superior Isobel Sean remembered from their marriage but instead was all over the young, handsome, rather smug Jones, constantly touching him, checking to see that he was happy, as if she were expecting him to change his mind about her any minute and walk out the door. Sean had been surprised by her choice—Jones was rather rougher than Isobel's normal taste—but she had seemed crazy about him. Ball could be right. Even though she hadn't liked being a parent, Isobel hated people to think ill of her and certainly wouldn't have wanted her lover to believe she was a bad mother who didn't care about her children.

Sean couldn't regret his marriage to Isobel—that would mean regretting having the boys—but looking back, he could see that when they had gotten together, he had been in no state to choose a wife. Between girlfriends and still missing his much-loved mother who had died a few months before, he was lonely and vulnerable and eager to find someone to help him blot out his grief. Easy game for Isobel, a failing actress desperate to find herself a successful husband who would keep her in style and allow her to retire gracefully before her sell-by date. His looks, his success, and his newfound financial clout made him attractive to her; her strength, her elegance, her apparent invulnerability made her irresistible to him. Add all that to the natural sexual attraction between two good-looking people and there was only one result. The two were married, on the island of Antigua by a local judge, only three months after they had met.

To begin with, all was well. Sean loved Isobel's style, her ability to charm clients for him, her apparent admiration of him. Isobel loved Sean's kindness, his interest in her, his willingness to listen to her problems. And she adored playing the part of a happily married woman helping her husband with his career. Then, gradually, Sean began to notice that they had little in common. He loved Charlton; she thought football was for idiots. He was happy to spend his time with Ray and Babs; she thought they were dull and staid, and wanted him to cultivate people who could be of some use. He loved his work for itself; she cared only for the money it made. Still, when they couldn't think of anything to say to each other, they could always go to bed. That continued to work despite the lack of sympathy elsewhere.

Then, two years into the marriage, Mark was born. Isobel had thought she wanted children, saw herself in the role of perfect, caring mother. It was only when she was face-to-face with the reality of parenthood, with the vomit on her lovingly chosen designer clothes, the nights spent feeding and comforting a screaming infant, that she realized she had been wrong. But it was too late. She was stuck.

Sean, on the other hand, took to fatherhood with ease. He loved Mark, loved the smell of him, the feel of him, just the fact that he existed, more deeply than he had ever loved anything. His attachment to Isobel, his enthusiasm for his work were nothing compared to his feelings for his son. He wanted another child as soon as possible, determined that Mark should not grow up alone. He had two sisters himself, but they were so much older than he was that he felt he knew what it was like to be an only child and didn't want that for his beloved son.

Isobel was reluctant, but eventually, with promises of live-in nannies to help, Sean persuaded her. And Ben was born. She managed another three years of married life before deciding she'd had enough. Acting star-crossed lover for all she was worth, she dumped Sean for one of his competitors in the construction business, leaving the boys staying with their father.

Sean had been fairly sure that things between him and his wife were over before she left; after three months without her, he was completely convinced. He filed for divorce. A year later, once he had agreed to give Isobel their house in Battersea as well as a large lump sum and had accepted her lawyer's insistence on joint custody, he was free.

The money meant nothing to Sean compared to his boys. And he ended up having Mark and Ben much more than the custody agreement said he should; Isobel wasn't really all that interested in them. As they got slightly

older, she wanted them more—they were good-looking boys, perfect acces-
sories to set off her slowly fading looks, both trained to behave like perfect
little gentlemen, to light cigarettes and open doors for her friends—but still
they spent most of their time with Sean.

Until Isobel began to feel her age. And fell in love with Steve Jones. And
ran away.

In hindsight, Sean could see that his attempt to take Isobel to court to
get full custody of Mark and Ben might have been ill-advised. If he'd done
nothing, maybe she wouldn't have fled with her lover. Maybe he'd still have
his sons. But he couldn't have ignored her leaving them alone while she
went out to a nightclub with Steve Jones. The boys had been by themselves
for five hours. They had been only seven and five. Anything could have happened.

"They are safe, aren't they?" Sean stared hard at Ball, desperate for any
kind of reassurance.

"Of course they're safe, sir."

Sean grabbed his cigarettes and lighter from the coffee table, fumbled a
Camel out of the box, and lit up. "But how can you know that?" Sean
snapped out the words. "Come on, how can you know? If she left them
alone once, why won't she do it again?"

"Mr. Grainger, she wants to stay hidden."

"So?"

"Wherever they are, they'll have neighbors. And the fastest way to be
found is to be reported to the social services. From everything you tell me,
she's not stupid. She'll be aware of the danger."

"Maybe. I hope you're right." Sean ground out his cigarette. He felt useless. But what could he do? When the boys had first disappeared, he'd taken
to driving around aimlessly, praying for any sign of them, knowing that the
odds were infinitesimal. That he had more chance of winning the lottery
and the pools on the same day than of just happening to run across Ben or
Mark or even Isobel. But doing something had made him feel a bit better.
And still, wherever he was, he searched the faces of strangers, hoping that
one of them would be his ex-wife or his boys. But they never were.

He'd even prayed, really prayed, in church, for the first time since he
was a teenager and had decided that all that mumbo-jumbo wasn't for him,
not if it meant he couldn't touch the girl next door's generously tempting

breasts. He'd lit candles, attended Mass, even gone to confession for the first time in thirty years. In his mind, he'd been making his own deal with God. If this is what you want, I'll give it to you, no problem, if you just let me have my sons back. But God hadn't delivered and here he was, eighteen months later, no closer to finding Ben and Mark than he had been when he started. He was fast losing hope. Hell, if he was honest with himself, he'd already done so months ago. A year and a half was a very long time to keep the faith without any new leads or clues.

Sean looked over at the detective, who was waiting patiently. "Do you think I'll find them?"

"Well, Mr. Grainger, miracles do happen."

"And so do alien abductions according to half the population. Don't give me that bullshit. What are the odds? The real odds."

"Normally, if people aren't found within six months of their disappearance, we never locate them."

"Six months?"

"Yes, sir."

"So you're saying it's hopeless?"

"Not hopeless, sir. Extremely unlikely. Unless she wants to be found."

"But you'll go on looking? Ball?"

"It would be a waste of your money."

"It's mine, isn't it? I earned it. I can do what I want with it."

"I'm afraid there's nothing more I can do, Mr. Grainger."

"I need you, Ball. Please. I can't just give up."

"I'm sorry, sir."

"I'll hire another detective."

"That's up to you, Mr. Grainger." Ball's tone spoke more clearly than words; a sixth private detective wasn't going to succeed where five and the police had already failed. "I'm very sorry, sir."

"Very sorry. And how does that help me?"

Ball was silent. There was nothing he could say that would make this any easier.

Sean leaned forward, his head in his hands, and stared at the floor as if the nicks and notches and flat-headed nails in the old boards were the most fascinating things in the world. Finally, he looked up at the obviously uncomfortable detective and took pity on him. After all, it wasn't his fault that Sean's ex-wife had stolen his sons and run off with her lover.

"You can go, Ball." He knew he should thank the man for his efforts but the words stuck in his throat. He got up and stalked across the room to a wide, uncurtained, floor-to-ceiling window that overlooked the canal. He stared out, silent and unmoving, watching the detective's glass-distorted reflection gather up papers and shuffle out of the loft.

He'd already missed a year and a half of his sons' lives. When he'd last seen them, they'd been seven and five. Little, smiling boys, waving good-bye to their dad, thinking they'd see him in a few days. Now Mark was already nine and Ben would be seven in a few weeks' time. Eighteen months was a long time in a child's life. A very long time. They would have grown. And they would look different. Kids that age changed so fast. But he would know them even if they were completely different from the way he remembered them. The arms that had held them as babies, the hands that had soothed away their hurts, the heart that had loved them would know.

However, he could feel himself losing hold of them. He used to carry around pictures of them in his head, but now their little faces had blurred and he needed to look at photographs to remember them properly. Once, he had known all their likes and dislikes, their favorite toys, the clothes they loved or hated to wear, the books they wanted him to read to them over and over again. Even now, when shopping for food, he found himself rejecting things for their reasons: *Not that orange juice, it's got bits in it. Ugh! Broccoli! Daddy. Red cheese, not yellow.* So much time had passed. Maybe now they loved broccoli and yellow cheese and fresh-squeezed orange juice. Maybe everything he thought he knew about them was wrong.

And what about Mark and Ben? What had Isobel told them? Did they think their father was away, or busy, or just uninterested? Did they believe that he'd abandoned them? Or were they waiting for him to call? God, he hoped not. In fact, he hoped that Isobel had done the kindest thing and told them that he was dead. At least that way they wouldn't blame themselves. Losing your father was hard any way it happened but it had to be easier to deal with if you didn't think he was out in the world somewhere, enjoying a life that didn't involve you.

Sean felt resignation setting in. Ball was right. He'd done all he could. There wasn't any point in continuing to go over ground he'd already covered ten, twenty, thirty times with five different detectives. Nor in hiring another. Unless Isobel changed her mind or some billion-to-one chance allowed him to run into them, his sons were out of his life. He'd lost them.

four

"Give me one."

Lily stopped pacing for a moment, reached over Raymond the production manager's shoulder, and grabbed at his pack of Marlboros. The tips of her fingers had just touched the red-and-white cardboard box before Raymond snatched it away from her. "What?" she snapped.

"You've done four days. It's only cos you're drinking."

"I know. I know," Lily groaned, "and once I'm outside, I'll be fine. It's automatic. Drink. Smoke. They go together. I can do first thing in the morning, I can do after dinner, but I can't cope with alcohol. Come on, Ray. Just one." Lily's voice was distinctive, her native Illinois accent tempered by the English inflections she'd picked up during her years in London.

"No." His refusal was reiterated by the other people sitting at their table in the pub, Charlie and Nick, the producers on her surprise-hit TV sitcom, *We Can Work It Out*, about bored mothers trying to cope with fat thighs and families. Jerry, the improbably camp director. Anna, his long-suffering assistant. They were in the middle of making the second series and had been in rehearsal all day, getting the third of seven episodes ready to be taped in front of a live audience next Friday.

"Mean bastards. Then I'll buy my own."

Lily walked over to the bar. Why was she giving up anyway? She was fine, fit and healthy, not coughing in the morning, and although smoking was supposed to make you old before your time, she still looked all right. Maybe there were a few lines here and there, but those were to be expected; she was inching up on forty, for God's sake. And the combination of thick blond hair, long, slim legs, and a gamine little face seemed to please men as much now as it had when she'd first arrived in England.

No, it was just propaganda. Her aunt had smoked thirty a day for forty years and she was still alive, happily puffing away. Besides, what would happen when Lily was writing? When she was sitting at the computer, struggling to invent a character or searching her brain for a gag about treadmills? Or even worse, waiting to go onstage and perform? Like next week when they taped the latest episode of the sitcom? She'd be reaching for the nicotine, that's what. So what was the point of going through this agony now? She should wait until she had a nice, peaceful, empty six months and then give it a go.

The success of *We Can Work It Out* had taken Lily by surprise. She hadn't intended to appear in it herself when she wrote it—she'd been delighted enough to have sold a whole seven-episode series after years of slogging away writing individual comedy sketches for different producers on a variety of shows. But then Charlie, Nick, and Jerry had had trouble making up their minds who to cast as the eccentric aerobics teacher at the gym. Lily had given them a reading to show them what she thought the character should sound and act like, and that had been it. They'd decided that no one else would do. The production company put up a fight to begin with—no one had ever heard of Lily—but they'd given in when Charlie, Nick, and Jerry put enough well-known actors in the other roles.

Even then, the show was one of many. Lily hadn't expected it to become a big hit. She felt blessed enough to be doing what she had always dreamed about. But not only was it funny, it had also hit a nerve with the public, and the first series, broadcast at the beginning of the year, had been huge. Lily had gone from being an unknown writer to being the new face of British comedy.

She smiled as the barman came over to her. While they'd been making the series, the Marquis of Granby had become their local hangout. They'd be in most evenings, lunchtimes too if things were going badly. Close to the office, it was the last unreconstructed pub in Covent Garden. The rest had all been modernized and renamed after unlikely pairs of animals, or closed and reopened as restaurants or clubs. But the Marquis of Granby was as old-fashioned as its name. Dark, antediluvian floral carpeting worn around the edges, wood paneling, chipped ashtrays on the stained tables. Not somewhere Lily would have chosen perhaps, but Charlie and Nick, both expatriate Glaswegians, felt at home there. Said it reminded them of where they'd had their first, underage pint.

She ordered another round, bought her cigarettes, and carried them and the drinks triumphantly back to the small grimy table. To cries of "Lily, don't," she removed the cellophane on the pack, pulled out a cigarette, lit it, and drew in deeply. She leaned back on her stool and exhaled slowly.

"That's better. Oh, fuck." Lily reached into the neck of her shirt, put her hand down her arm, and came out with a nicotine patch. "Perhaps I should take this off first?"

AN HOUR and a half later, a sleek silver Mercedes made its way past the Hampstead tube station, up Holly Hill, and stopped outside a row of five tall, redbrick houses on the far side of a tiny square. The driver, a dark-haired, stiff-backed man, climbed out and strode around the car, toward the back door. Just as he got there, it opened and Lily clambered out. A chauffeur-driven car to take her anywhere she wanted to go was one of the benefits of her recent success. She was trying hard not to get used to it, aware that *We Can Work It Out* could lose popularity as quickly as it had gained it.

"Thanks, Kevin. Okay for tomorrow?"

"Of course, Miss James." Lily had given up trying to persuade Kevin to call her by her first name. He was an old-fashioned sort and it seemed to offend his sense of what was correct.

"If you're sure. I hate to take up your weekends."

"It's no problem, Miss James. I could do with the overtime."

"See you about eleven, then." The producer who'd bought her first comedy sketch was getting married. Weddings weren't her favorite occasions—they tended to raise uncomfortable memories of her own failed marriage—but she was fond of Roger and she'd promised. So she would go to the service and then the reception. If it was a buffet, she'd have a quick drink, a quick congratulations with Roger and his bride, and make a quick escape. Hopefully, no one would notice. She had those two scenes to work on. Of course, if it was a sit-down meal, then she was trapped. . . .

Lily strode over to a pair of wrought-iron gates, pulled one side open, and walked into the long, rhododendron-edged front garden and up the stone-paved pathway toward the bottle-green front door of her beautiful house. She'd bought it two years before but still felt a thrill when she came home to it.

After a messy divorce from her rat of a husband, Clive, she'd wanted a refuge for herself and the twins. Even though Jack and Bella were then six-teen and settled away at boarding school, they still needed a place they could be pleased to come back to and proud to bring their friends. The moment she'd seen the glorious, warm redbrick house in the center of trendy, expensive NW3, she'd had to have it. It had taken every penny she'd just inherited from her much-loved, much-missed mother that was not already set aside for the children's education, but it was perfect. It was not just a house, it was a home. And it had the extra added bonus of upsetting Clive, who'd always longed for a place exactly like that, in exactly that location.

Lily and Clive had fallen in love when she was still a young, eager drama student at Northwestern. She'd taken a trip to the Edinburgh Festival the summer between her sophomore and junior years and she'd met Clive, a BBC producer who was in Scotland doing the rounds of the shows. She'd been knocked out, unable to resist his well-muscled, six-foot-two-inch frame, his black hair and dark blue eyes, his smiling, handsome face. And overwhelmed by his acerbic wit, his smoothness, what she saw as his European sophistication.

Three years later, she'd found herself looking after twin babies in a nice but soulless apartment in a new block of flats on the edges of Hampstead and bored out of her mind, particularly after the kids started school. Not for the first time she'd wondered what it was she'd seen in Clive that made her give up her life, her family, and her dreams of a Lucille Ball–like glittering career and run across the Atlantic to be with him. The husband she'd once imagined to be a man of style, with charm coming out of his ears and talent oozing from every fingertip, wanted by everyone but possessed by her, had turned out to be a small-minded, greedy, work-obsessed cynic incapable of loving anyone or anything very deeply. Apart from himself and his career.

But she'd stuck with him. She couldn't bear to deprive the twins of their father just because he hadn't lived up to her expectations. When she talked to her girlfriends Terry and Jules about their experiences with their men, by comparison Clive didn't seem so bad. Yes, he was a disappointment, but maybe most of them were after the first flush of excitement. At least he didn't hit her. Or drink. Or disappear and never return.

However, she'd been determined to do something more challenging than the laundry to fill the hours between taking the twins to school and picking them up. She'd always dreamed of being a comedienne, but doing stand-up wasn't practical with the kids and she didn't have the confidence or the experience to attempt to be an actress. But she could try to write. Unsure how to go about it, not even certain what form the writing should take, she took day classes at the local community college and read everything she could find that was supposed to be funny, from *Catch-22* to the Marx Brothers, from Monty Python to *National Lampoon*. Finally, insecure and terrified, her head full of other people's ideas, she sat down to write.

It had been impossible at first. Everything she tried was either not very amusing or sadly derivative. She had always, even as a child, been able to make people laugh, but capturing that ability and putting it on paper in some recognizable, sellable form was much more difficult than it seemed. She stopped and started, sometimes leaving the writing alone for months on end. She even came close to giving up once or twice, but encouraged and nagged by her girlfriends, she persevered. And then finally found her voice in observing and writing about the small things in a mother's life, the sometimes black comedy inherent in the stresses and strains of working and shopping, of school runs and potty training, of rushed sex and teenage rudeness.

She got her first piece accepted, a bit in the local newspaper about the indignities of childbirth. Then, using contacts made during her years with Clive, she'd sold a sketch to a late-night TV show about a mother competing with her daughter for everything. And in that way, an inch at a time, she'd begun to build a name for herself as a writer. And to make a bit of money.

But as her career started to take off, Clive's deteriorated. Once, he'd been the golden boy, witty, clever, politically astute, primed to succeed in the Byzantine world of TV. His life had been a steady progression, from researcher to producer to head of department. Everyone had expected it to continue that way, culminating with him as controller of BBC One or even director general. Until he'd been seduced by the independent explosion in the eighties and by the idea of real money. He'd left the BBC to start his own company with Beatrice, a young, ambitious game-show producer, and managed to sell a couple of programs. It was enough to keep him going for a time, but the promised huge financial windfall never appeared. And as the years passed, the debts mounted.

Sensing his desperation and unwilling to see her children's father suffer, Lily had offered to help shore up his business. And he had accepted. She'd handed over five thousand pounds, everything that, over the years, she'd managed to save from her writing. Then, a month or so later, she'd discovered that he was having an affair with Beatrice. And that he'd taken her off to Switzerland on a skiing holiday when he'd told Lily he was going to Scotland to produce a pilot of a reality series. She was furious. Not only had he lied to her, he'd used her hard-earned money to pay for a holiday with his lover.

Boredom was one thing, betrayal another. She threw him out. And was tempted to go home. Her mother was still alive then, her sister married and with two young children. She knew they'd welcome her and Jack and Bella with open arms. But she'd been away a long time. Apart from a few trips to see their relatives, the twins had lived their whole lives in England. It didn't seem fair to tear them away from the only home they knew just to satisfy her own desire to be near her family. In addition, if she went back now, she'd have to start all over again in her career. In a cutthroat, survival-of-the-funniest world where dozens of writers worked together to create and maintain a TV series. Whereas here, she could make a living from her sketches. And if she were to sell a sitcom, it would be hers and hers alone.

In the end, she had had no real choice. She had to stay. For the twins and for herself. And it had turned out to be the right decision. Though she missed her family, she'd been able to spend a month with her mother before she died. And the twins had been happy in England. They'd gone to a boarding school they themselves had chosen, and had been accepted at Durham University, to start in fifteen months' time. Meanwhile, they were spending their year of freedom from education working and traveling in Australia and the Far East.

She let herself into the warm, wood-paneled hall and smiled. Home. Lily had been out every night for what felt like weeks. Script meetings, production meetings, rehearsals, tapings. Until she'd become involved herself, she'd never had any idea how endless making a TV sitcom could be. Particularly if you were both writer and star. She'd imagined a glitzy life full of exciting locations and glamorous parties, not the long, hard slog of gray, faceless offices and dingy rehearsal halls and enormous, echoing studios.

She poured herself a glass of wine and went into her study. Lined with books, the room was a haven, a safe place to be alone, to be quiet, to read and think. Lily sat down by the fireplace, sipped her wine, and sighed happily. A night in. Scrambled eggs, a nice, long bath, early to bed. Pity it wasn't winter. She could have had a fire. Lily stopped herself, horrified by the direction her thoughts were taking. Early nights? A longing to sit in front of the fire? She'd be buying herself a flannel nightgown and slippers next. Maybe it was a good thing she was going to that wedding tomorrow. How long had it been since she'd been to a party? Three months? Six? She hadn't even seen the girls all that much recently. Ah, well, it was their regular monthly lunch on Sunday. She'd see them then.

When her last relationship had crashed a couple of months previously, just before she'd started work on the present show, Lily had promised herself she'd give men a break for a bit. Because none of them, no matter who she chose, seemed to want what she did. Just a bit of fun. A couple of nights a week. Dinner. A movie. Maybe an escort to some of the industry stuff she was beginning to have to attend. And sex. Definitely sex. But no living together. No partners. And absolutely no marriage.

In the last few years, Lily's independence had become extremely important to her. She loved being able to make decisions without reference to anyone else. She loved being able to sleep late if she wanted to, loved not having to cook dinner if she chose not to, loved going where she wanted when she wanted. No way did she need some man in her life who'd expect compromise and sacrifice and conciliation. Even such a simple thing as when to turn out the light required negotiation.

She'd imagined it would be easy enough. Sex without strings—wasn't that what all men dreamed about? Amazingly, she had found that it wasn't what they wanted at all. Once offered it, every single one of them sooner or later—and usually sooner—saw her independence as a challenge rather than a boon and found that they were desperate to settle down with her in blessed domesticity.

They stopped enjoying the time they and Lily had together and started wanting to know what she did on the nights she wasn't seeing them. To move possessions into her house. To settle down. To cling. Lily kept trying, sure that she'd just been unlucky, that her Mr. Right was only around the corner. But he never seemed to be.

So, for the last couple of months, she'd given up. She'd let the work take over. But now she was tempted to look for another candidate. Okay, experience had taught her that she was not going to find what she sought. But she'd been alone for long enough. Without sex for long enough. She was only thirty-nine. And it was time to think of a new lover. After all, even if it didn't quite work out in the long term, she'd have fun searching. . . .

five

"Hello, sweetheart. How about I help you with that?" A balding, round-bellied man pulled away from his friends standing outside the Packhorse and Talbot and fell into step beside Mara.

"No, thank you. I'm fine," Mara said.

"Lovely girl like you. Need something more than this to keep you warm." The man reached for the cat box she was carrying, his hand covering hers.

"Leave me alone. Please." Mara jerked away from him and increased her pace. For a few moments, the man followed her but eventually gave up when she turned off the High Street.

"Your loss, love," he tossed at her as he returned to the laughs and jeers of his friends.

Mara walked on. She'd tried everything. Her clothes were as baggy as she could find in her limited wardrobe. Her full-length black skirt and large, loose gray sweater covered her every curve. She wore no makeup, kept her luminous brown eyes glued to the ground, and had stopped dyeing her rich black hair, almost hoping for bits of gray to come through. And still they tried. She could never understand what it was they saw in her. Yes, she was an attractive woman, but she was thirty-six. A mother with two children. Old enough to walk down the street without being hit upon. She didn't believe it was just because she was Indian. Plenty of other Indian women walked the streets of the city every day and were left alone to go about their business. Lily insisted it was because she was sexy, but that seemed very unlikely when every part of Mara's body was covered in dark, shapeless clothing.

She put down the cat box and moved her shoulders back and forth to ease the strain. She glanced up at the threatening sky, then switched the load to her other side. The parade of shops gave way to a row of small town houses, once workmen's cottages, now sought-after homes close to the center of upwardly mobile Chiswick. Some of them looked freshly painted, their front areas expensively planted. Newly renovated houses for the newly successful. Others still had peeling paint and overgrown hedges. The last surviving remnants of the people who had been there when Mara and Jake moved in eleven years before. Good people. Who were all too often being forced to move, unable to afford the upkeep on their properties or to resist the exorbitant prices being offered.

Mara turned into a neat front yard. She put the cat box down and fumbled in her skirt pocket. She pulled out two sets of keys, picked out one, and opened the door.

"Don't worry, it's only me," Mara called out as she walked into the house. The hallway was clean but the carpet was worn and frayed and the wallpaper looked as if it had been hung before the Great War. "Amy!"

"In here, dear," said a calm voice floating through the door to Mara's left.

"I've brought Joey back. He's had his injections." Mara took the cat box in to Amy Fenton, a tiny, thin-haired fragile old woman in a dark blue dress and thick stockings, who sat in an ancient, shabby armchair in front of a gas fire. Mara had met the lonely, childless old widow the first day she and Jake had moved into their nearby house and had liked her immediately. Since then, they had become loyal friends and Mara had come to rely on her constant support and her unsentimental, no-nonsense attitude toward life.

"Thank you, dear. Now you run along to those girls of yours. What will the Moores think if you're not at home to let them in?"

"Probably just what they think now, that I'm a hopeless mother who shouldn't be trusted with their precious grandchildren."

"Then you don't want to give them any real ammunition, do you?"

Mara smiled and bent over to kiss her neighbor's wrinkled cheek. "The Meals on Wheels people came?" she asked, concerned. Amy's heart was failing and she was finding it harder and harder to look after herself. She insisted on staying in her own house, refused even to think of going into an old-age home, but she could no longer cope with cooking three meals a day. Having dinner with Mara and her girls two or three times a week and her lunch delivered every weekday was an acceptable compromise; it helped her to save her strength but didn't make her feel as if she were completely dependent on others.

Amy nodded. "Very nice. Roast chicken and apple crumble."

"And you'll call if you need anything?"

"Don't worry. Get on with you now. You'll be late. And then you'll never hear the end of it. Go on."

Mara smiled at her friend, then turned and left the room. Once outside, she looked up the street to see two adults and two children getting out of a parked Ford Mondeo. Of course. She should have known. They were early. Just then, a raindrop fell on her hair. She raced along the pavement until she reached her house, ten doors away. Standing in the front yard were her daughters, Moo and Tilly, with their grandparents. Jake's mother and father.

A few more scattered drops of rain fell. The two girls, their smiles wide, ran over to Mara. "Mum, Mum. Look what Pops and Nan have given us." Tilly was often the spokesperson for the two even though at eight she was the younger. Moo, ten, was frequently content to let her sister talk. On the cracked stone in front of the doorstep was a box with the telltale word "Sony" written on the side.

"What is it?" asked Mara, afraid she already knew the answer.

"A PlayStation," said Mr. Moore. "All their friends have them."

"But . . . Thank you, but no. They won't want to read or play outside or anything. They'll spend all their spare time on it."

"Mum."

"Please, Mum, we'll be good."

"We'll work hard."

"Please."

"I don't know, loves. It's your education. Your father would have wanted—"

"I think we're more likely than you to know what Jake would have wanted," Mrs. Moore snapped. Her overpainted face screwed up when talking to Mara, her distaste obvious.

Mara kept quiet. There was no point in saying anything. Jake's parents were what they were and there was no changing them. To some degree, she could understand how they felt. They were jealous of her, they always had been. She'd taken their only child from them. Or so they saw it. And she could appreciate their feeling badly about losing their son.

She was much less sympathetic to their rage at his choice of an Indian wife. All her life she had tried to see things from others' viewpoints, but nothing, nothing could make her empathize with prejudice. And the Moores were riddled with it. Over the years, her relationship with them had been all about dogged, silent resistance. She only wished they wouldn't attempt to interfere in the girls' upbringing.

The rain had been steadily increasing, spatters making kaleidoscopic patterns on the concrete paving. Finally, the downpour that had threatened all day arrived. Mara put thoughts of PlayStations and worries about the Moores and what they were going to see out of her mind. The house was already in bad enough shape without her ignoring the rain. The bowls had to come first.

"Quick, girls." She unlocked the front door and ushered her daughters inside. Leaving Jake's parents to fend for themselves, she ran along a dim hallway and into a small, shabby, but spotlessly clean kitchen, followed by Moo and Tilly. She bent down, opened one of the dark-wood cupboards, and pulled out an assortment of plastic, china, and stainless-steel bowls, stacked one inside the other. She handed a few bowls to each of the girls, keeping the largest pile for herself.

"Tilly, take your bedroom. Moo, my room. I'll do the bathroom."

Ignoring the Moores, who stood in the hallway looking on in amazement, the three raced up the stairs. At the top, Tilly ran straight ahead, followed by Moo. Mara veered off through a doorway on the half landing.

Tilly dashed into a small, twin-bedded room whose walls were covered with colorful posters of interchangeable boy pop groups and glossy models and implausibly young footballers. Without looking up, she began to lay out her bowls on the floor in a well-remembered pattern. At first, nothing happened. But then, gradually, there was the drumbeat of water dripping onto stainless steel as first one, then another leak announced itself. Next door, in her mother's dark-curtained room, Moo laid out her bowls on and around the candlewick-covered double bed. And down in the yellow-and-purple bathroom, Mara rushed to spread out her dishes on the shag-pile carpeting.

As she did so, a drip landed on her nose and then another on her head. She stood up and scuttled out of the room as the pitter-patter of falling water began.

The girls were waiting for her on the landing. "Why do we have to do this every time?" Moo complained.

"You know why, love. Because we may be poor, but . . ."

"We won't live like pigs," the girls chorused.

"But really, Mum, wouldn't it make more sense to leave them out?" Tilly's serious little face was intent, trying to figure this out.

Mara smiled at her younger daughter. She could see both herself and Jake in her physically, but emotionally she was all her father—charming, earnest, curious, and kind. In a way it was like having Jake back. Moo was different. She looked more like him but possessed little of his character; she was a will-o'-the-wisp, a dreamer, impossible to grasp. A leader one day, a follower the next.

"I would have thought it would make more sense to have the roof repaired," Mrs. Moore said, climbing the stairs, toward them.

"I can't afford it at the moment. We cope, don't we, girls?"

"It's fine, Nan. It's fun." Clever Tilly.

"Yeah. It'd be boring to have a proper roof," said Moo.

"Fun. I never." Mrs. Moore turned to her husband, standing behind her on the stairs. "George, tell her."

"You must think of the girls. They can't be expected to live like this. This house is falling down around their ears. You've got to sell it."

"How about a cup of tea?" Mara slid past the Moores and headed down the stairs. This was not something she was prepared to talk about in front of the children. Besides, selling the house was not an idea up for discussion. She and Jake had chosen it together. Lived in it together. Brought the girls home to it when they were babies.

Mr. Moore followed Mara. "How long has this been going on?"

"I've been putting money aside for the roofers." Mara had only managed to save about twenty pounds, and that was earmarked for her mend-the-central-heating fund, but she wasn't going to tell the Moores that. She went into the kitchen, filled the old-fashioned kettle, and put it on the stove.

Mr. Moore appeared behind her. "We think Miranda and Matilda should come and live with us," he said.

"No. No way," Mara said. Her girls were what kept her going.

"It can't be healthy, living in a place like this. It's not just the roof. That wall looks like it's not straight and the plaster's crumbling away in places. You should think of them."

"I am thinking of them."

"We just want to do what's best."

Mara fought down a rising tide of panic. "It's only a bit of water," she said weakly.

Mrs. Moore was standing in the doorway. "In their bedroom. Eight bowls on the floor," she said to her husband. "It feels damp in there. It's not good for them." This was directed at Mara.

She wanted to argue, but she couldn't. Of course it wasn't ideal for the girls to sleep in a damp room.

"Just until you get things sorted out," suggested Mr. Moore.

"We'll drive them to school every day." Jake's mother attempted to soften her abrasive voice into a pleading tone, but her dislike of her daughter-in-law shone through. "No need for you to worry about that, my dear." Mara hated it when one of them called her "my dear." She wasn't anything of the kind. She felt herself gritting her teeth and for the thousandth time reminded herself that there was no point in being angry with them.

For a moment, she considered letting Moo and Tilly go, but she felt her stomach rebel at the thought. Jake's parents had always wanted the girls for themselves. They might promise now that it was only until she had the roof done, but once they'd gotten their hands on Moo and Tilly, once they had them living there, Mara doubted they would ever agree to give them back.

As she pulled the tea bags out of the mugs, dripping hot liquid over the damaged tiles, she tried to reassure herself. The girls were both in perfect health. It was only a bit of rain. People lived in much worse conditions for years and were absolutely fine. She breathed in deeply, fighting for control. She couldn't lose her girls, she couldn't. She got a carton of milk out of the fridge, carefully added some to the tea, and handed two mugs to the Moores.

"Children belong with their mother," she said.

Mr. Moore put down his tea and reached out to pat Mara on the arm in mock sympathy. "My dear, it's for the best, you'll see. You can visit whenever you want."

"No. Moo and Tilly are mine. I'm delighted you care about them, pleased that you want to see them and take them out. They need a family, but they live here."

"Typical," said Mrs. Moore. "Your daughters are at risk and all you can think about is yourself."

"I'm sorry you're disappointed."

"Sorry? Is that all you can say? When Jake's children are as good as living on the streets? My son trusted you to look after Moo and Tilly and you've let him down. In this country, we put our families first. I suppose you frittered away everything he left you on yourself."

"He left me nothing."

"He left you the house. Which you have let fall apart."

"The house was mine. I paid for it. It was mine." Before Mara could stop herself, the words were out. She could withstand Mrs. Moore's racist jibes—she'd been dealing with those for years—but for her to suggest that Mara had betrayed Jake was too much.

"Yours? How could it be yours?"

Mara looked at the Moores, standing in front of her, their faces eager, their eyes alight with curiosity. No chance that they would ignore what she'd just let slip. She and Jake had always allowed them to believe that he'd paid for the house after he'd made a killing on the stock market, when in fact he'd been penniless. Driving limousines earned him enough to pay the bills, no more. He hadn't even been sure he would inherit any money from his parents; the Moores had cut him out of their will when he and Mara married.

"Where would an uneducated Indian girl like you get the money to buy a house like this?"

"I . . ."

"Yes?"

"My . . . my family . . ." Mara blushed. She had never been able to lie.

"Family? What family? You have no family."

"I do . . . I did. . . ." Mara heard the sound of footsteps on the stairs and sighed with relief. The Moores wouldn't pursue this in front of Moo or Tilly.

"Mum, Mum, where's our tea?"

"Here, loves."

"Can we set up the PlayStation? Please?"

They looked so excited that Mara couldn't bear to deny them. They had missed out on so many things others took for granted. "Only an hour a day, promise me?"

"We promise. Don't we, Moo."

"Yes. An hour. Promise."

"Okay, then. Go and set it up."

"Yay! Mum. Thanks." And the girls dashed off into the living room to unpack the box.

Mrs. Moore leaned over to Mara. "Don't think we're going to let this drop," she said.

"Even eleven years ago, that must have been a lot of money," said Mr. Moore.

"And we'll find out where you got it."

"It was my family. I told you." Mara blushed again. Why couldn't she trot out smooth, undetectable lies like Lily and Jules and Terry seemed to be able to do?

Mrs. Moore smiled. "Then you've nothing to worry about, have you? Shall we go and help Moo and Tilly, George?"

six

Lily strolled through the large tent, whispers rising in her wake. *What's she doing here? . . . Don't look now, but Lily James just walked past you. . . . I don't believe it. . . . Is that really her?* Lily walked over to her table. Her newfound celebrity still made her uncomfortable. It wasn't anything she'd actively sought. And it wasn't as if she'd done anything important to get it.

Six of the eight gold-paint-and-red-velvet chairs around the white-linen-covered table were already taken by three middle-aged couples, the men in dark, respectable suits, the women in elaborate, brightly colored hats. All of them were gawking at Lily as if she were covered in green slime.

Ignoring their fixed stares, Lily smiled at the group, pulled out her chair, and sat down. "Hi, I'm Lily James," she said brightly.

For too long a moment, no one spoke. Then, finally, a woman in a froufrou pink hat managed a shell-shocked, "How do you do?"

So that was how it was going to be. "Just fine, thanks. And you?"

No response. The woman's courage seemed to have deserted her. Lily looked forward to an extended afternoon of stilted conversation. Followed by requests for her to be funny and stuttered demands for her autograph for children or nieces. Sighing inwardly, she turned to the small, weasel-faced man on her right. "So, what do you do?"

Sean glanced around. Most of the tables were filled, just a few late arrivals left to straggle in. He studied the elaborate calligraphic seating plan, found his table, and edged his way toward it between chairs and guests. There were eight places, all but one of them filled. He said a general hello, directed at no one in particular, then pulled out his chair and sat down. He turned to the person on his right, a Mrs. Anne Tarsky according to her place tag, and introduced himself. A woman in her fifties in a hideous black-and-green-striped dress, she nodded a greeting at him and then returned to her conversation with the forty-something dark blue suit on her other side. From what Sean could hear, they appeared to be deep in a discussion about breeding otter hounds.

He turned around to investigate his other dinner partner. In a pale gray suit and a tiny hat, more feather than felt, she was sipping a glass of champagne and being talked at by an intent little man on her left. Sean's eyes moved to her face. God. Lily James. She looked amazing. Much better than on TV. The camera smoothed out her features and flattened the planes of her face so you never saw her high cheekbones. Her hair was not the simple blond it looked on-screen but an incredible mixture of beige and yellow and white and tan and brown and gold and ginger and every other color hair could be.

". . . and so I worked out a plan for them to claim all of their honeymoon as a legitimate expense. . . ." Lily nodded and smiled as the bridegroom's apparently very talented accountant went on and on about his latest scam to save his clients money on their tax bill. Still, at least he was talking to her.

She sensed the chair next to her being pulled out and felt someone sitting down. Then a nice, deep, sexy voice said, "I'm Sean Grainger." It was the kind of voice that could prickle the hairs on your arms. Lily waited for the accountant to pause for a second in between Inland Revenue stories and turned to face Sean.

God. The face was even better than the voice. Gray eyes, dark, disheveled hair, a square chin, a wide, infectious grin. Lily stuck out her hand. "Hi. I'm—"

"Lily James. Yes, I know." Sean wrapped her hand in his. "I . . . I love your hat."

"Nice, isn't it? A friend who's into old clothes found it in a weird little shop in Muswell Hill. It's forties, I think." Good. He hadn't tried to pretend he didn't know who she was. For some reason, people seemed to think she'd be more interested in them if they behaved as if they'd been living on another planet for the last six months.

"You must be a friend of Roger."

"I used to write sketches for him when he was a producer. Before he gave it all up to become a landscape gardener. I last saw him leaving the studio after a particularly awful taping, muttering the name of Capability Brown under his breath."

Sean laughed. "I tormented the bride when we were kids."

"Tormented?"

"Slugs featured a lot. Spiders too. I was a horrible little boy."

"I bet you were."

"But I'm safe now. I promise."

"Are you? What a shame." Lily smiled. Things were looking up. On the other side of the tent, she noticed a parade of black-tied waiters marching in time into the tent, trays of food held high. "Dinnertime. Here comes the vegetable terrine," she said.

"How do you know?"

"It's always vegetable terrine at weddings. It's a rule."

"Really? Why?"

"I don't know. It just is. In the last few years, it's sort of taken over the world. First of all, it was weddings, then it started to slip over into awards dinners and christenings and birthday parties. It'll be funerals next. Vegetable terrine—the perfect food. It's safe, it offends no one, and it tastes of nothing."

Sean grinned. "I think you're wrong. Maggie had a lot of imagination as a kid. She'll have chosen something more interesting."

"What do you bet?"

"I don't know. A tenner?"

"No, boring. A kiss."

"Okay. A kiss it is. I'll go for prawn cocktail."

"Pathetic. Too seventies. Too . . . pink."

"Quiche, then."

The waiters were getting closer. "Which one? Quick."

"Quiche. Yes, quiche."

A plate with a green-orange-and-cream-striped slice was set in front of Lily. "I win. I win." She leaned over, kissed Sean on the lips, then picked up her fork, took a taste, and grimaced. "And as bland as ever."

Sean laughed. He was finding it hard to take his eyes off her. It wasn't just that she was a star, although she was certainly that, but she was also fun. And sexy.

"So what do you do? Please tell me you're not an accountant." Surely not, Lily thought. Those muscles weren't developed pushing paper.

Sean smiled. "I'm a builder. I redevelop industrial buildings. You know, New York–style lofts."

"That's great. If I didn't love my house in Hampstead, I'd be tempted. All that space, all that light."

"You should see my place in King's Cross. One entire floor, on the canal, massive windows on all four sides."

"Sounds fantastic. My production manager wanted to get one, only he said the stuff out there now was too small."

"Don't get me going. When I started, it wasn't a loft unless it was at least two thousand square feet. Nowadays, contractors try to call any apartment in a school or factory or whatever a loft. But most of the time they're just open-plan flats with some naked bricks and a bit of stainless steel in the kitchen."

"And yours aren't?"

"I've sort of found a niche in the market. Most companies are fighting over the large projects; I go for smaller stuff I can divide up into four or five large lofts."

"Like?"

"I've just started on an old church hall in Putney. Edwardian building, about ten thousand square feet. It'll split into five. There's even some land attached, so a couple of the lofts can have gardens."

"Wonderful."

Sean had started at sixteen as a laborer on building sites, running errands, making tea, filling in wherever and whenever. After a few years, he could rewire a house, fit a full kitchen, and plumb a new bathroom; by the time he was twenty-five, he knew everything there was to know about construction.

He had always loved industrial buildings, had spent weekends wandering around the London docks out beyond Tower Bridge looking at the few

Victorian warehouses to survive the war, dreaming of converting them into apartments. Eventually, he'd managed to scrape together the financing to buy a small nineteenth-century tobacco warehouse in Limehouse and turn it into four vast, luxurious lofts. He sold them for a substantial profit the moment they went on the market. He had invented a whole new industry.

But he'd learned that not everyone found his business as interesting as he did. And he thought he'd heard a sarcastic tone in Lily's voice. Time to change the subject. "You live in Hampstead?"

"In the most beautiful redbrick house. You must come and see it." Soon, Lily hoped. Preferably that night . . .

AS THE waiters cleared away the dessert plates, Lily watched Sean as he took two cigarettes out of his packet, lit them, and handed one to her. She grinned. "When I first watched *Now, Voyager*, I thought it was the most romantic thing I'd ever seen." She made a grand, sweeping gesture toward the roof of the tent. " 'Don't let's ask for the moon, we have the stars.' I used to long for a boy to light a cigarette for me."

"When I was a teenager, I dreamed of Lauren Bacall asking me to whistle for her."

"I can do that." She deepened her voice, spoke from her throat. " 'You know how to whistle, don't you? Just put your lips together and blow.' "

"At last. At last. Now I can die happy."

"Who said anything about dying?" Lily smiled. She was finding it hard to contain herself. The thought of Sean's powerful body, stripped of its elegant suit and naked in her bed, was mouthwatering. It felt like ages since she'd been with a man and she was ready for it. That body-to-body contact, the touch of skin on skin, of heat and hardness and power. Lily glanced over at Sean as he leaned back in his chair and took a puff of his cigarette. He was irresistible.

An hour later, Sean watched the triumphant lilac-clad bridesmaid catch the bouquet, Lily leaned over and brushed his hand. "How are you getting home?"

Sean's skin leapt at Lily's touch. He turned to look at her as his mind went into overdrive. Why the hell hadn't he got the train? Could he lie and leave his car here, come and pick it up tomorrow? No, she'd never believe him. He glanced down at his best suit. He didn't look like a man who had taken the train. Better tell the truth. Maybe he could ask her out for later in the week? "I brought my car."

"Good. I'll let my poor driver go and you can give me a lift home. You are going back to London?"

"Yeah, yes, of course. Of course I'll give you a lift." Was Lily suggesting what he thought she was suggesting?

Lily smiled to herself. Gotcha.

NORMALLY, LILY loved to show off her house. She'd taken such care with it, choosing the kind of warm, rich colors in the carpets, the curtains, the cushions on the chairs and sofas, even the art she'd recently started collecting that would complement the aged wood of the walls and floors. But she barely allowed Sean to take a peek at the hallway before she put her arms around him and lifted her head for his kiss.

The trip home had been a delicious nightmare. Delicious because of the anticipation of what she knew was to come. A nightmare because she didn't think she could bear to wait for the time it took to get them from Hungerford to Hampstead. She couldn't take her eyes off Sean's hands on the wheel of his Saab, his fingers touching the gear stick, his eyes focused on the road ahead, his mouth slightly open, the tip of his tongue occasionally flicking out to moisten his lips. Then he would turn and look at her and she could sense that he was having the same thoughts.

But Sean was almost too scared to think. Scared to look forward, to presume anything. Lily could just have been flirting. Maybe when they got to her house she'd politely thank him for the lift and go inside. He glanced over at her, saw her staring at him, her eyes on his lips, on his hands. Surely he couldn't mistake that look on her face?

It had been months since he'd been to bed with anyone. When the boys had first disappeared, he'd tried hard to block out the pain of their loss with sex. Lots of indiscriminate sex. He'd gone from date to date, from girl to girl, from bed to bed. But it had given him only temporary relief. After it was over, he just felt worse, the short-lived respite making his pain all the harder to bear.

So he had stopped. He realized now how much he'd missed it. And not only the sex; perhaps even more he'd missed the kind of closeness he had sometimes felt with Isobel after making love. He wouldn't get that from a one-night stand with Lily, he wasn't stupid enough to think he would, but maybe there'd be a ghost of it, a glimmer, a brief hint of real intimacy. If not, well, it had been months and his body was more than ready for a bit of uncomplicated, down-to-earth fucking.

When Lily asked him in and reached for him the moment the door was closed, he didn't hesitate. He pulled her into his arms, lowered his head, and kissed her. Lily pressed herself against him, hard, getting as close as she could, crushing her body against his. Her fingers rummaged in his hair, pulling his head closer, his lips tighter, increasing the pressure between them. Then he felt her hands loosening his belt, unzipping his trousers, reaching in, grabbing him. . . .

SEAN LOOKED down at Lily as she slept. At her large and still-firm breasts, at her long, long legs, her multicolored hair, her strong, odd little face. He couldn't believe her. He'd never been with a woman like her. Hell, he'd never imagined there could be one like her. She was so unreserved, so strong. So free.

As if she sensed she was being watched, Lily opened her dark, sleepy blue eyes. A slow, sensuous smile spread across her face. "Well, if you aren't tired . . ."

Seven

Terry bicycled slowly up Holly Hill, toward Lily's house, standing high in the pedals, straining with the effort. In an attempt to lose some weight, she tried to cycle everywhere she could. But it didn't seem to be having much effect; she was the same size she'd been when she'd bought the old bike a year ago. She consoled herself by believing she must be fitter even if she wasn't thinner.

In an ancient wicker basket attached to the front of the cycle, Minnie sat on her haunches, facing front. As they reached the gate to the house, she lifted her head and yowled her delight.

Terry parked her bike by the door. Minnie leapt out of the basket and hit the ground running. She raced around the side of the house and into the back garden. Lily, Mara, and Jules were sitting around a shaded cedar table, drinks in hand, looking out over a long, smooth lawn and bright flower beds. At the far end, Moo and Tilly were playing on an old rope-and-log swing hung from one of the branches of a huge oak tree.

Lily held out her arms and Minnie jumped into them, lifted up her head, and licked Lily all over. "Minnie, Minnie, Minnie," Lily laughed, trying to hold the little dog off.

"Minnie, you can't eat her." Terry came around the corner of the house, ran over, plucked Minnie off Lily's lap, and set her down on the ground.

Immediately, the dog started to sniff around the door to the kitchen. "Ah. You've got rats, haven't you? She's never wrong."

"I have not got rats. I have not. There's meat in the oven. She can smell that." Lily looked over at Terry. "What're you grinning about?"

"Gets you every time. All anyone's got to do is say anything against your beloved house and you go mad."

"So would you if you'd poured as much money into it as me."

"Is it that bad?" Jules asked.

"You should hear my bank manager." Lily scrunched up her face and put on an affected, whiny voice. " 'Time to tighten our belts, Ms. James. Time to tighten our belts.' All I wanted was enough to redo the kids' bathrooms while they're away. It's not like I'm not earning."

"No. Just hideously overdrawn." Terry pointed at Lily's custom sunglasses and designer jeans. "And with a fashionable spending habit to support." She kissed her friends hello, then reached for the bottle in the center of the table. "Yum, champagne." She poured herself a glass, took a sip, and purred happily. "Ooh, do I love champagne."

"I still want to know where a girl from Bootle learned such expensive tastes," Lily asked.

"It's all Jules's fault."

"No it's not," Jules said.

"Yes it is. If you hadn't brought that bottle to our find-a-flatmate party, I'd have stuck with beer."

"And if you believe that . . . ," Lily started.

"You'll believe anything," finished Jules and Mara.

It was the four girlfriends' regular get-together. Even if jobs and families got in the way at times and stopped them seeing each other more often, they made sure they gathered on a Sunday afternoon at least once a month. They rotated homes, first one, then another. Today it was Lily's turn.

IT HAD been almost twenty years since she'd walked into Connor's Wine Bar and met Terry. It had been pure coincidence; she'd only gone into the bar because it had been freezing outside and she was desperate to sit down somewhere warm for a moment or two. But she hadn't had a lot of money and couldn't afford to be spending any on luxuries like alcohol. Connor's had been heaving with people and she'd thought she could pass unnoticed for a few minutes amongst the hordes of men and women in dark suits celebrating the end of another day.

The wine bar was a connected series of dark, brick-vaulted cellars, lit only by candles. Lily walked through the crowded space until she spotted a small, round, empty table at the far end of one of the shadowy rooms and sat down.

She'd just arrived in London from the U.S., expecting to move in with her boyfriend, Clive. But things hadn't exactly worked out as she'd planned. Sitting in her tiny room at Northwestern, packing up her stuff, saying goodbye to friends, and then confronting her shocked family and telling them she was dropping out of college to live in England with a man, she'd imagined she was going to a world of love and culture, of mornings in bed, of trips to the theater, of weekends spent cuddled up in front of the fire or at sophisticated dinner parties, discussing the latest play or book. Instead, she'd been greeted with an indifference that soon grew into irritation.

During their week in Edinburgh, Clive had raved about the idea of their being together. It was only once she'd turned up on his doorstep, jet-lagged but excited, assuming he'd be thrilled by her arrival, that she realized he'd never imagined she would come. She'd been forced to accept that he didn't want her to live with him in his flat. She wasn't even sure he wanted her to be in London.

When she met Terry, she'd just spent the day wandering the city, trying to decide what to do. And failing to work up any enthusiasm for the famous sights she was seeing for the first time. All over London, she'd run into groups of American tourists, and their happy, would-you-look-at-that excitement had depressed her even more. Of course, she could go home. Her parents loved her, they'd forgive her for messing up her life. They'd even send her the cash needed to pay for her airfare. Only it would feel like such a defeat, to be begging for help when she'd set out only a few days ago so full of hope. But what else could she do?

"What can I get you, love?"

Lily jumped. Then looked up.

A small, pretty, red-haired girl was standing in front of her table, smiling at her. She waited a moment, then repeated her question. "What do you want to drink?"

Lily stared at her, unsure of what to say. Thinking of her diminishing hoard of cash.

The girl leaned forward and put her hand on Lily's shoulder. "Are you all right?" she asked.

"Yes. Thank you." Lily knew she should get up and go, but her fingers and toes were only just beginning to thaw. "Perhaps . . . how much is a glass of water?"

"For you, love, free."

And the girl walked away, weaving her way through the crowded tables. At the far end of the long, low, candlelit room, she went past some ancient barrels and disappeared. Twenty seconds later she was back with a large glass filled with red wine in her hand.

"Here. You look like you could do with this. It's on the house. Only don't tell my boss, whatever you do."

"Thank you. You're very kind," Lily said, smiling.

"You're American."

"Yes."

"On holiday here?"

"Sort of." Lily took a sip of her wine and warmth spread through her from inside out. "That's just what I needed. How did you know?"

"I've been cold and short of the readies myself."

"Readies?"

"Cash. You know. Pounds, shillings, and pence."

Lily blushed. "Oh, yes, that."

"Don't worry. It's happened to all of us." The girl held out her hand. "I'm Terry."

Lily reached out, grasped her hand. "I'm Lily."

"Welcome to London."

"Thank you." Lily felt like crying. This was the first bit of kindness she'd experienced since she'd arrived.

Terry glanced behind her. "I'd better go work. Listen, I get off in an hour or so. Do you want to go for a drink?"

TERRY HAD never been able to work out what it was that had made her take pity on Lily. She'd been in London for two months, working at the wine bar for four weeks, and had seen enough hard-luck cases in that time, but she'd never felt the urge to look after them. Somehow Lily was different. Maybe it was as simple as her being American. Maybe it was the way she had ordered a glass of water, obviously unable to afford anything else. Or maybe it was because Lily reminded Terry of herself when she'd first arrived in town: lost in the midst of a chattering, bustling, indifferent city.

Whatever it was, she'd made a good choice. Less than an hour after they'd walked out of Connor's together, she'd told Lily all about her runaway mother, her martinet grandmother, her restricted life in Liverpool, where even chocolate was forbidden as sinful, and her decision to flee to London two months before. In return, Terry had learned all about Lily's life in America, her ambition of being a comedy writer and actress, and her disappointment with Clive. By the time the two were sitting on cushions on the floor of Terry's tiny studio apartment in Clapham, after retrieving Lily's luggage from Clive's apartment and slogging their way across the city, Terry knew she and Lily were friends for life. They were two of a kind. Both young, both on their own, and both with the ability to laugh at themselves, even in the midst of disaster.

"I've had a fantastic idea," Terry said. "How about we find a house?"

"A house?"

"Yes."

"With what?"

"With our wages, silly."

"I can't work. I've got no permit."

"Dave'll employ you."

"Dave?"

"At the wine bar. He's already paying two girls I know of in cash cos they're on benefit. He likes it. Means he can pay less. Someone'll report him one of these days, but until they do, he'll give you a job."

"I don't know anything about wine."

"Do I look like I do? Nah, it's strictly beer up where I come from. You'll pick it up. Nothing to it. Open the right bottle, pour it out, collect the money. Only took me a few hours."

"Maybe I should just go home."

"You don't want to do that, do you?" Terry saw her new friend disappearing before they'd even spent a day together.

Lily was silent for a moment. "I don't think so. No. I want to stay here.

And make Clive work his little buns off to get me back." Lily grinned. "It's Connor's Wine Bar for me."

"And the house?"

"Sure. Only I still don't see how you and I are going to afford a house."

"Not all of London's expensive. We'll find somewhere cheap. And we'll advertise for a couple of others to share it. What do you think?"

"We'll have to be careful who we choose. You should have seen the slob they made me room with my freshman year."

"We will be. So are you in?"

Lily grinned. The day that had started like a nightmare had ended like a dream. She felt blessed. Who knew what had sent her into exactly that wine bar on exactly that day at exactly that time, but she would be forever grateful. Terry was wonderful. A lifesaver. "I'm in."

MARA HAD seen the girls' ad in *Loot* as fate. She'd been riding around and around on the Circle Line for hours, ignoring all the men who were staring at her—even then, at sixteen, Mara had been stunning looking—while her mind searched for some solution to her problems. And came up blank. She'd run away from home the previous night, fleeing an arranged marriage to a widowed man in his fifties. She'd thought that once she escaped from her authoritarian father, got away from her family's house in Dagenham, and took the night bus into London, all her problems would be miraculously solved. But once in the city, she realized that getting there had been easy. What to do next was the hard part.

She'd never had to fend for herself before. She had a small amount of money—birthday gifts from aunts and uncles over the years—but it wasn't going to last her very long. She needed a job. And somewhere to live. But she had no idea how to go about finding either. Instead, she'd wandered around London since she'd arrived at dawn. Hoping to see something that would give her a clue as to what to do.

At lunchtime, she'd bought herself a sandwich and taken refuge from the cold on the Underground. By four o'clock in the afternoon, she'd done three full circuits on the Circle Line. She knew she should get up, go back out into the city, and find herself somewhere to stay the night, but she couldn't bring herself to leave the warmth and safety of the tube.

Then a young man who had been sitting next to her tore a page out of his copy of *Loot* and got up to go, leaving his paper behind. It was already a few days old but she picked it up and flicked through the ads for second-hand cars and stereos, fur coats and microwaves. Toward the end, she saw a number of notices for rooms to rent. They weren't cheap, but there were a number where she could afford to pay a week's rent. At least that would give her time to look around and find a job.

At the next stop, she got off the tube, found herself a public telephone box, and started calling. But every one she rang had either been rented already or the landlord insisted on references. And she had none.

At first she'd discarded Lily and Terry's ad as too unusual. But then she thought again; maybe unusual was what she needed. "Young, fun-loving, tolerant girls looking for housemates. Must like bathing." Well, she was certainly young, given a chance she might become fun-loving, and her sisters had always complained about the length of time she took in the bathroom. She dialed the number, her fingers crossed.

"I'M VERY fond of bathing," Mara blurted out, then blushed as she saw the two girls standing in front of her glance at each other in apparent amusement.

"That's good," said Lily.

"Yes. I can spend ages in the bathroom. It used to drive my sisters mad."

"Ages?"

"Oh." Mara realized that taking a long time bathing might not be a great recommendation in a house with four girls and only one bathroom. "I'm messing this up, aren't I?"

"No," said Terry. "Of course not."

"Only, I really want to live here. With you." Mara swallowed back tears and forced herself not to beg. "I'm much more fun than this normally, I promise."

"You're doing fine. Calm down. Have another drink." Lily gestured at their makeshift bar.

"Um, thank you." Mara had never had any alcohol before but she felt she couldn't refuse. That wouldn't be fun-loving. She walked over to the table on the other side of the room that held the drinks and a few nibbles. She poured herself half a glass of white wine and then added some sparkling water to it when she hoped no one was watching.

Lily and Terry had chosen a late-Victorian brick town house in Kentish Town, a quietish, unremarkable part of North London that was only a few tube stops out of central London, on a direct line from the station nearest Connor's Wine Bar. The house wasn't large, but it had two twin bedrooms, a huge bathroom with an enormous, old-fashioned bathtub on clawed feet, and even a small garden with a holly tree, its berries still winter red. The area wasn't exciting and the furniture looked like it had been used by generations of previous tenants, but who cared, there was room enough for four. Most important, they could afford it.

Once they'd rented the house using references from Terry's old landlady and Dave at the wine bar, they'd put their ad in *Loot* and waited for the phone to ring. Determined to make the right choice, they'd invited everyone who called to a party, hoping that any prospective housemates would be more relaxed that way than they would have been in a regular interview. But it didn't seem to be working. About fifteen people had called and been invited and only six had turned up.

One of them Terry ruled out the moment she walked through the door because she reminded her of the most sadistic nun at her old convent school. One of them was far too fun-loving; she'd consumed most of a box of wine by herself and then promptly been sick in the kitchen sink. One of them seemed to be interested only in the number of musicians she'd been to bed with. That left three. Mara, whom both Lily and Terry liked despite her nervousness. A tall, black-haired girl who seemed nice enough but appeared to believe that she was doing Lily and Terry a favor by consenting to share with them. And the latest arrival, a slim, blond, conservatively dressed girl clutching a bottle of champagne.

"Hi, I'm Lily. And this is Terry. Is that for us?"

Juliet handed the bottle over. She'd taken it from her parents' wine rack, hoping to be gone before her father noticed it. "Yes. Thank you for inviting me. I'm Juliet."

Terry drew back at the sound of the girl's voice. Lily must have spoken to her when she called and of course would not have noticed the far-back, royal-family accent that denoted wealth, privilege, an expensive education—everything Terry had been brought up to resent. "Shouldn't you be in Chelsea?" she asked.

Lily heard the distaste in Terry's voice and couldn't understand where it was coming from. "Wherever you should be, it's good to see you. And thanks for the champagne."

"You're welcome."

"So you need somewhere to live?"

"Yes. I'm with my parents at the moment and it's not . . . I'm eighteen and I think it's time I was out on my own."

Juliet first realized she had to get a place of her own when her mother screamed at her for having a school friend around for supper without asking first. In front of the friend. Since then, there had been many other arguments, some niggling differences of opinion, some full-fledged rows. Juliet had known there was a good chance that her living in her parents' flat in stuffy, expensive Belgravia would cause trouble. However, she had been so excited at leaving school and getting the job she wanted as a trainee in one of the country's most successful party-planning companies that she'd agreed when her newly elected MP father, Ian Dunne, said that if she wanted to live in London, she ought to stay with them. She'd hoped that perhaps her difficult relationship with her social-climbing mother would improve now that she was grown up. But it hadn't. If anything, Diana Dunne's disapproval of and distaste for her middle daughter had got worse.

She'd had yet another row with her mother that morning, this time about a wild, red flouncy dress she had fallen in love with that Diana considered common. And she'd decided enough was enough. She needed to find somewhere else to live. She wasn't being paid very much and couldn't expect help from her parents, so she was not going to be able to afford Chelsea or Knightsbridge or Kensington. She was going to have to go out into the unknown.

She bought a copy of _Loot_ on her way to work, scanned the list of rooms for rent, and was intrigued when she saw Lily and Terry's advert. There was no trouble with the bathing, and after ten years at strict boarding schools, a bit of tolerance and fun seemed a very good idea.

"Terry can sympathize there. Right, Terry? Terry?"

"Yes. I suppose."

There was silence. The girls all looked at one another. Juliet struggled to think of something to say that might please Lily and Terry. She hadn't been sure before she got there, but now she was convinced that Lily and Terry were just the people who could help her burst out of the armor her parents, her schooling, her background had welded for her. But she wasn't sure how to go about it. She could lay a table for ten courses, she knew all the rules of precedence, and her command of social small talk was extensive, but she had a feeling that Lily and Terry weren't interested in discussing the weather.

"I can understand your need to get away from your mum and dad," Terry finally said after Lily nudged her. "But why here? Why us? Why not some nice, genteel flat in Knightsbridge?"

"I don't want Knightsbridge. I want to get away from Knightsbridge. I want you. I've never met anyone like either of you before."

"Us common folk, you mean," Terry asked.

"No. No. It's only . . . I have been quite . . . sheltered."

"And you want us to help you get unsheltered?" Lily asked.

"Yes, please." Jules took a deep breath before continuing. "I want to have some fun. I've spent all my life doing what I was told. Being good. Trying to please my family. And I suppose in a year or two I might go back to that. But for now . . ."

"For now?" Lily prompted.

"I want to break the rules. Look at me. I could be forty, the way I'm dressed. Nice navy blazer, proper skirt, my grandmother's brooch. I want to wear red and green and turquoise and yellow. Look at my hair. I want to curl it, color it, cut it, anything other than tie it back in a ponytail with a tasteful scarf. I want to go to parties and get drunk, I want to meet real people who don't care about mummy and daddy or doing the right thing or marrying well. I need you. I do. So please, don't take me at face value. I'm more interesting than this. I promise."

Lily smiled. "You sound pretty good as you are. I'll be back in a second. I'll just put this in the fridge." And she headed off to the kitchen, champagne bottle in hand.

Terry was hard on her heels. "I don't like her."

"Give her a chance."

"She's upper class."

"Terry. What difference does that make?"

"Didn't I tell you my father's father was a Communist?"

"Yes, you did. And that he died when you were a year old."

"She makes me feel tense. Like I'm just about to make a huge social mistake. And be laughed at for it."

"She sounded as if she was the one who was tense. And desperate to be accepted."

"Maybe. But she's so . . . groomed. So posh."

"What was that it said in the ad about being tolerant?"

Terry had the grace to look shamefaced. "I can't help it. Put it down to my northern roots."

"Course you can help it. Didn't you like her speech?"

"No. Yes. I don't know."

"She was being honest."

"She's had everything handed to her on a plate."

"Didn't make her happy, did it? Don't tell me you prefer the groupie?"

"No. No. Course I don't. You're right. I'm sure she'll be fine. I'll get over it." Terry smiled at her friend. "But only so long as I can call her something other than Juliet."

"We'll think of something. So it's her. And Mara."

"And Mara."

LILY REACHED behind her and grabbed Juliet's bottle of champagne. She leaned forward and poured the last of the wine into her new friends' glasses. It was late, already past midnight, and they were clustered around the fire in the living room. Mara was half lying on a drab brown couch whose many stains bore witness to decades of other tenants' thrills and spills. Terry was in an ancient armchair that sagged badly in the middle and was spilling stuffing from both arms. Juliet was perched on one of the rickety, mismatched wooden chairs that accompanied the ancient pine table still covered in the debris from the party. And Lily was sitting cross-legged on the scuffed and scarred wooden floor that someone had once painted white in an attempt to make it look fresh and new but that was now an indiscriminate shade of beige.

The other guests had left one by one after Lily and Terry promised to call them and let them know their decision. The moment it was only the four of them, Lily and Terry asked Mara and Juliet to become their housemates and the girls had been talking ever since then. Tentatively to start with, but more and more easily as they discovered that, despite their different backgrounds, they had things in common. They were all young, all just starting out on their own. They were all struggling to cope. And they all needed something to take the place of their lost families.

Lily raised her glass. "To number twenty-four, Bellington Grove."

"Number twenty-four," the girls said, echoing Lily's toast.

"Be it ever so humble . . ."

". . . there's no place like home."

Lily looked around. "I guess 'humble' is the word."

Terry smiled. "Who cares? It's ours."

"It is, isn't it?"

"Once we close the door, no one can come in unless we want them to," said Juliet.

"No one, no one can make us do anything we don't want to," said Mara.

"No one can force us to live their way," said Terry.

"Or tell us off," said Juliet.

"Or tell us off," Terry agreed.

" 'Never go to sleep angry,' " said Lily. "I remember my mom saying that to my sister when she got married, said it was the best piece of advice she could give her."

"Sounds good," said Terry. "Let's make it our first house rule."

"Never go to sleep angry," the girls chorused, and raised their glasses.

Terry took only a tiny sip of her champagne, trying to make it last. "This stuff is amazing. I've tasted what they call champagne in the wine bar but this is something else." She looked over at Juliet. The night's alcohol and the hours spent talking had eased some of her concerns about her new housemate. She might be posh, she might come from the far-right side of the tracks, but she wasn't anywhere near as stuck-up as Terry had thought she might be. "Thank you for bringing it."

"You're welcome. Only you should perhaps thank my father. It's his champagne."

"But you stole it." Terry grinned. "Just like a good working-class Liverpool girl. To Juliet."

"Juliet," the girls replied.

"But you've got to have a nickname. I said to Lils before that we can't go on calling you Juliet, sounds all stiff and poncy," said Terry.

"I know. Every time someone calls me that, I think I'm about to be lectured on my many faults. But my mother insists."

"Well, she's not here. And we are." Lily looked around at her new friends. "What do you think, guys? Jules?"

"I like that."

"Me too."

"Jules it is, then."

"Don't I get a say in it?"

"No," the others said.

Half an hour later, Mara struggled to her feet. When Lily and Terry had made their announcement, she'd been delighted to be chosen, but the longer the evening had gone on, the more concerned she'd become about how she was going to pay her way. She'd tried to ignore her misgivings, tried to join in with the jokes and the laughter, but she couldn't pretend any longer. She was very worried. Suppose she couldn't find a job? Her new friends had selected her over older, better, richer, more employable people. "Can I say something?"

"Of course you can."

"I wanted to . . . to thank you for choosing me. It means a lot. But I . . . I've only got enough for a week's rent and after that I . . . I don't think I can get a job. I'm only sixteen and I've got no qualifications and . . . I'm sorry. I hope you find someone else." She turned away and walked toward the door.

"Wait," Lily shouted. "Where are you going?"

"I . . . I'll find somewhere. . . ."

"At this time of night?" Lily got up, went to Mara, and led her back to the couch and the fire. "Even if you didn't look like Miss India, you'd get attacked. As you do, God knows what'd happen to you."

"But I can't pay. And I mustn't be a burden to you. I mustn't." Mara might have run away from home, but even so she couldn't forget the principle her domineering father lived by and had drummed into his children since they were tiny—neither a borrower nor a lender be.

"Silly. You don't have to be. Terry, what do you think?"

"No problem. She might be too young to be behind the bar, but Dave always needs people for the kitchen."

"There. We've got a job for you."

"You have?" Lily and Terry nodded. "You have!"

Mara stared at her new friends. "I . . . I don't know what to say. There I was, round and round on that tube. And then I saw your ad and came here and met you all and . . . and it's like I've come home. I'll pay you back, I promise. I won't let you down, I won't betray you or be disloyal or anything. If you need me, there I'll be. For . . . forever." Terry, Lily, and Jules looked at Mara, their mouths open in surprise. Mara had been the quietest of them all, always ready to answer questions but never volunteering anything by herself. "I'm . . . I'm sorry. Maybe I shouldn't have said that."

"Yes you should. It was perfect. I think we should all agree to the same things," Lily said.

"To be loyal."

"Trustworthy."

"Faithful."

"Forever."

Lily raised her glass. "To us," she said. "To the beginnings of a long, long friendship."

"To us."

"Us."

"Us."

TERRY WALKED around the cedar table, squinting at the sun in her eyes, and found a seat in the shade. She took another sip of her champagne and grinned. "All right, girls, so what's happening?" she asked.

"Nothing," said Lily. She'd wait a bit to tell her friends about Sean. Build up to it. And get ready for them to tease her about it. They always did whenever she found a new lover.

"Not much," said Mara, her eyes on her drink. She didn't want to mention the Moores' threat to find out about her past; if she did, she'd have to explain to her friends why she was so worried.

Silence. Everyone looked at Jules.

"I need some sperm," she blurted out.

"Sperm?"

"Like man kind of sperm?"

"Yes."

"Sorry. Don't have any on me right now. But we could send Mara out to get some. She's the irresistible one."

"I'm serious, Terry," Jules said, and then explained about Will's infertility.

"What a shit."

"I always hated him."

"How could he do that?"

"It's all right. Honestly. I was furious when I found the letter, but then I realized." Jules looked around at her friends. "I can have a baby." Her smile was as wide as the M25.

"So we need to find you a man," Lily said, beaming at Jules.

"No, no. Just the sperm."

"Just the sperm? What, like cows? With a giant syringe?" Lily was torn between shock and amusement.

"If you want to put it that way. Exactly like cows."

"No man, no father?" Mara sounded doubtful.

"That's right."

"Jules, you can't do this." Instinctively, Terry hated the idea.

"Come on. You all know about me and men. I'm a disaster waiting to happen."

"It's not that bad. I'm sure we can come up with someone for you. Lily, Terry, you must know someone."

"And if he's a good person, I'll reject him. Look at me, I chose Will. I thought he loved me. It took me ages to realize the only thing he loved was the money Dunne Parties was making."

"You made a mistake with Will, but that doesn't mean the right man's not out there for you."

"Will was more than a mistake. He lived off me for seven whole years. And I let him. I believed him when he told me our relationship just kept getting better and better even though I knew inside that it only got worse. And you all know what happened after I stopped paying."

When Jules finally noticed that Will's interior design business constantly lost rather than made money, and refused to continue supporting him, he turned into a different person. A monster. There were no more loving little touches. No extravagant displays of flowers and pricey Belgian chocolates and gourmet candlelit dinners. No more gifts of expensive French lingerie—ultimately paid for by Jules—or classy weekends in the country.

Instead, as long as Jules kept her checkbook closed, Will shouted at her, told her she was worthless, nothing, ugly, impossible to love. If she paid

up—and she did, more than once, unable to stand the insults any longer—
he would become the man he had been when she'd met him. For a time.
A week, a day, an evening. But sooner or later the cold, abusive Will
always reappeared. And it got worse. As Jules found ways to ignore the
verbal battering, he began hitting her until she paid up. In the end, she
always did.

"You're a different person now."

"All that's in the past."

"Will is anyway, thanks to you." Most of the time, Will had been clever,
never hitting her anywhere that might show. And she had been too
ashamed to tell anyone. Until he completely lost it and she ended up in the
hospital with five broken ribs and a badly bruised face. Horrified that they
hadn't realized what was happening before and determined to protect their
friend, Lily, Mara, and Terry had stepped in. With their support and encouragement and love, Jules had found the strength to throw Will out and pay
him off. In return for the more than generous sum of £100,000, he agreed
to a divorce, and had to promise never to attempt to see her again.

"But he wasn't the first. And if I'm not careful, he won't be the last. Apart
from Will, I've had two other abusive boyfriends and the actor who turned
out to be gay and using me as a blind. That isn't a very good batting average.
In fact, it's no average at all. I was twenty the last time I went out with a normal, honorable, honest man. And I turned him down. My judgment is definitely impaired. I only seem to fancy the bad ones. And I'm terrified that if
I go and look for a man, it'll all happen again. Another Will. More humiliation. More broken bones.

"So I'm better off by myself. Besides, I want the baby for me. Not for
some man I don't yet know. I've spent decades trying to please other people.
My family. Will. This is for me."

"This is truly what you want?" Lily asked.

"Yes."

"You're sure?" Mara questioned.

"Absolutely."

"That's not the way to have a kid," Terry said. She understood Jules's
arguments and sympathized, but she knew she was wrong.

"Why not? I want a baby. Why shouldn't I go out and get one?"

"It's not like going shopping, for fuck's sake. You can't just march into Harrods and pick one out, can you?"

"I may be childless, but I'm not stupid. I know that."

"Kids need a father." To Terry, this was a given, and she couldn't understand why Jules didn't see it.

"Why? The world is full of single mothers. Look at us round this table. All mothers. All alone. What's the difference?"

"The difference is, we didn't choose this. None of us set out to be by ourselves. When we had our kids, we thought their fathers would always be round. We didn't know Finn would disappear and Clive would betray Lily and Jake would die, did we?"

"The end result is the same. Well, it is. You've brought up your children by yourselves. And they all seem to be doing well."

"I hate to defend him, but it wasn't only down to me. The twins were teenagers when I threw Clive out," Lily said.

Jules waved this off. "As far as I remember, he was off working most of the time. He didn't exactly go to parents' evenings at school, did he?"

Terry took a deep breath. "Look at Paul. He's not doing well. He's a nightmare right now."

"Poor Terry. He's no better?" asked Mara.

Terry grimaced. "He never comes out of his room, does he? Walks away if I try to talk to him. Slams doors in my face. Take it from me, Jules. Don't do it."

"He could be just as bad if he had a father. Worse. Anyway, it's not the same. I won't even know the name of the sperm donor. You had a relationship with Finn."

"If you call that a relationship."

"I do. You knew him. You spent time with him. He existed."

"Not for long. Jules, he got me pregnant, then fucked off when I was in hospital having Paul. I had to wait on my doorstep in an ambulance for four hours when my baby was only three days old. Four hours. Bloody Finn had the keys, didn't he? Don't you remember?"

"See? I'm better off without all that. At least sperm can't let you down."

"What're you going to say to your baby when he or she asks about their dad?"

"I'll worry about that later."

"Worry about it now, why don't you? It comes round before you know it." Paul had wanted endless stories about Finn. Terry hadn't had many—their relationship had lasted only eighteen months—and so she had made most of them up, talked knowledgeably about Finn's support for Charlton Athletic, his love of brave little terriers like Minnie, his interest in Indian food. And she deeply regretted it. Paul had deserved better than to have his mother lie to him. Maybe the way he was behaving now was just punishment for what she had done. Terry recognized the traces of her Catholic upbringing and made an effort to push her guilt to the back of her mind. "You can't ignore it. The kid's bound to ask. What'll you say?"

Jules shrugged. "I don't know. Do as my friends, I suppose. Lie."

Jules sure knew how to hurt when she wanted to. "Fuck off."

"I'm sorry. That was below the belt."

"Yeah." Terry made an effort to control her temper. Jules's attitude, the way she knew all the social rules when half the time Terry wasn't even aware there were any could still rub her the wrong way. "Jules, think for a second. You say you want this child. That's great. But don't jinx things by lying to it. Please. You can't do this."

"Yes, I can. I can. Don't you understand? I want a baby. I need a baby. It's as if my body was ordering me to get pregnant. And it's an order I cannot refuse. It's all I can think about. When I believed I couldn't have one, I could just about cope. I had to. But from the moment I found out that Will had lied, I just . . . It's overpowering. I can't concentrate on anything else. I've got to do this. I don't know what I'll tell the baby about the father. And I can't worry about it now. I'll work something out when the time comes. Right at this moment, all I can think about is getting pregnant. I don't have all that much time. I'm thirty-eight. And the clock's running down."

"Oh, Jules." Terry ached for her friend. But she knew this wasn't the way to solve her problem. "Lily, you can't think this is okay?"

"Well . . ."

"Mara?"

"If it's what Jules wants . . ."

"Thank you, Mara. At least someone understands."

"Oh, I understand, Jules. I do. I just think . . ." Terry was ready to carry on trying to persuade her friend that she was wrong until a glimpse of the other woman's determined face made her stop in midsentence. Clearly, Jules's mind was made up and no amount of persuasion was going to change it. Particularly not from Terry. She shrugged her shoulders, poured herself some more champagne, and took a long sip.

"So I need your advice. What do you think? Do I get the necessary from a sperm bank? Or the Internet?" Jules looked around at her friends expectantly.

"That's the choice?" asked Lily.

"Yes."

"Both seem a bit cold. Couldn't you find a . . . a donor? Someone you know? I'm sure Jake would have said a baby deserved something more personal." Mara and her husband had had the usual range of good and bad times, the usual highs and lows, but since his death she had suppressed all her negative memories, instead exaggerating everything positive until she saw him as the perfect, irreplaceable man. Whose judgment was to be trusted on all things.

"Who, Mara?"

"I don't know. Someone. Just so it's not so clinical."

"I can see me walking up to some man and asking him to kindly give of his sperm. Or inquiring politely of some woman if I could borrow her husband for a night. It's a lovely idea and I might even get a bit of sex out of it, but it's not practical."

"What's the difference? You know, between the bank and the Internet?" asked Lily.

"The sperm banks vet the men who go to them. They take personal histories and things like that. On the Internet it seems to be about looks. You get a picture and little else. Mind you, they're all gorgeous. Six feet, blond hair, blue eyes."

"They would be." It didn't happen often, but Mara could be acerbic, especially when it came to stereotyping.

"So what do you all think?"

"Sperm bank. Definitely," said Lily. "You get what you want right then and there. No complications."

"If that's the choice. Yes. I would say sperm bank."

The three turned to look at Terry. She shrugged and managed to smile at Jules. Ultimately, this was her call. And if she was that determined to have a baby alone, Terry needed to support her, not quarrel with her. "Sperm bank," she said.

LILY HUMMED softly as she stacked the white porcelain plates in the dishwasher. The kitchen felt cool and shadowy after the bright sun outside.

"Someone sounds happy." Terry was a dark outline against the light flooding through the French windows. She walked into the room, strolled over to the double, extra-wide steel sinks, and put the stack of dishes piled in her hands down on the counter. A second later, she was followed by Mara and Jules carrying glasses and mugs. Minnie dashed in after them and began circling their legs, hoping for a treat or two.

Terry looked over at Lily. "If I was a betting woman, I'd lay money our Lils had a good time at that wedding yesterday."

Lily glanced at her friends, smiled smugly, and said nothing.

"I thought you'd taken a leaf out of Terry's book and given men up for a while." Jules cut up a bit of leftover roast lamb on a plate and put it on the floor for an ecstatic Minnie.

"All boring things must come to an end."

"Lily, you cow, how could you keep this a secret? Why didn't you tell us the moment we got here?" demanded Terry.

"More important, who is he?" Jules asked.

Terry went to the fridge and pulled out a chilled bottle of Möet. "This calls for another drink." She popped the cork, rummaged in a cupboard for some clean glasses, and poured.

"Okay. What's his name?" Terry looked over at Lily.

"Sean."

"To Sean, everyone." Terry raised her glass and took a sip. Jules and Lily joined her. "To Sean." Mara left her glass on the stainless-steel counter where Terry had put it.

"Where did you meet him?" Jules wanted to know.

"What's he do?" asked Terry. Probably another film director. Or, worse, an actor.

"Oh, who cares. What does he look like?" Jules cut to the chase.

"Hey. One at a time. I met him at George's wedding. He's a builder. And he's stunning. Gray eyes. Dark hair. Muscles forever."

"Gosh, you don't suppose he'd like to give me some sperm?" Jules said, laughing.

"Did he go for the deal?" Terry asked.

"Sure did. Couple of nights a week, no more. No commitment. No moving in together or partners or marriage."

"What do you think? Will he last?" asked Jules.

"Yeah, is it going to be thirteenth time lucky?"

"Terry! You've been keeping count? It can't be thirteen, can it?"

"Just a guess. Now, what sign is he?" Terry hoped he was a Sagittarian. Or even a Scorpio. A powerful, freedom-loving man to balance her friend's strong Leo nature.

"You and your astrology. I didn't think to ask him. Hard for me to understand right now, but strangely it wasn't the main thing on my mind." Lily grinned at Terry and her obsession.

"So will it? Work, I mean?" Jules asked.

"Who knows. Probably not. But I'll have fun finding out."

"Poor thing." Mara had been silent up until now. Though she understood Lily's desire to be free, she couldn't help but feel for all the discarded men.

Terry, Jules, and Lily looked affectionately at their empathetic friend. "Now, don't get all softhearted. I never lie to them. And they agree to the deal. If they don't, I don't see them anymore. Simple as that."

"It's just . . ."

"Just sex. That's all."

Mara looked unhappy but said nothing more. She'd tried before to tell them why this all made her feel so uncomfortable but hadn't managed to get her point across. Maybe, if Lily couldn't see why there was no such thing as just sex, there was no way she was going to be able to explain it, no matter how hard she tried.

eight

Mara was in her long, thin, brick-walled back garden, diligently weeding her serried rows of carrots and onions and potatoes. After Jake's death, she'd had very few options. No income, no savings, no qualifications, and so no real prospect of a job that would pay her more than minimum wage. She'd found work five mornings a week as a cleaner—Chiswick was full of wealthy families eager to have their chores done for them—which allowed her to be there for the girls when they came home from school, and with the most stringent economies managed to keep her head above water. Just. But there was no room for luxuries. Keen to conceal her desperate poverty from Moo and Tilly, she had looked for ways to make them see their lack of fashionable clothes and foreign holidays as a challenge rather than a problem, had made a game of the leaking roof, had discovered an aversion to eating expensive meat and dug up the back garden to grow free vegetables.

She was picking the last of this year's string beans when she heard the electronic tones of the first few bars of "Always Look on the Bright Side of Life." It had been Jake's idea and it still made her smile. Even though her supposed optimism often seemed to have died with her husband. She pulled off her ancient gloves, wiped her small hands on a scrap of old towel, and hurried into the house. Who could it be at eleven o'clock on a Wednesday?

She opened the door to see an undersize man in a pale blue short-sleeved shirt holding a pile of letters. The postman. It had been so long

since she'd had anything sent to her that wouldn't fit through the post box,
she almost hadn't recognized him.

"Hello, Mrs. Moore. Long time no see. Got some registered mail for
you. Sign here." He handed her a white envelope and a form. She scrawled
her name at the bottom and passed it back.

"Thanks. Hope it's money, eh? See you." And he was off, whistling, up
the street.

Mara looked at the envelope. It had "Private and Confidential" printed
on one side and the address on the rear flap said it had come from Barton,
Kirkwood, and Ridgeman, a firm of solicitors based in Bedford Square.

What did a lawyer want with her? Worried, she closed the door, tore
open the envelope, and pulled out its contents. There was a three-page,
closely typed letter signed by a John Ridgeman. She flipped through it and
spotted her name. And the Moores'. Now scared, she focused on the letter.
Certain words and phrases jumped out at her: "Gross moral turpitude,"
"Immoral earnings," "Unfit mother," "Unsuitable accommodation," "Appli-
cation for full custody." The Moores were threatening to take her to court to
get the girls.

This was Mara's worst nightmare coming true. She'd always been afraid
it might come to this, but she'd hoped that her letting Moo and Tilly
spend a lot of time with their grandparents would be enough to satisfy the
Moores. But it hadn't been. As soon as Jake's parents had glimpsed a
chance, they'd gone on the attack and found out about her past. It probably
hadn't been hard; if they'd hired a detective all he would have had to do was
find one of her old clients willing to talk. Or speak to any of her old neighbors.

When she'd started on the game, she'd been twenty-one. Living alone in
a bedsit in South London, struggling to afford the rent. Sharing the house in
Kentish Town with her friends had lasted about eighteen months; after that
they had all gone their own ways. They'd still seen each other regularly, had
remained close, but no longer lived together. Lily was married, Jules just
starting her own party-planning business, Terry balancing being a bus driver
with looking after Paul. Mara was the only one who had stayed still. For five
years, she had lived on what she could make from ill-paid jobs. She'd been
a barmaid, a waitress, a cleaner, a chambermaid—all the positions where

qualifications were unnecessary and the wages below poverty level. Then, she'd met Mrs. Grenville.

She'd been working behind the counter of a corner shop, filling in for a few months while the owner's wife was having their third baby. She hadn't thought anything of the middle-aged woman with crimped gray curls when she'd first served her. Just another customer buying milk and cigarettes. But as the weeks passed and she saw her more and more, they began to talk. Later, Mara realized that Mrs. Grenville had been the one asking the questions and she the one answering them, but at the time she was just grateful for what seemed like genuine human contact in the in-and-out, here-and-gone shop.

When the owner's wife was about to return to work, Mrs. Grenville had offered Mara a job. She had jumped at it without asking what it was; anything that would stop her being out of work again, pounding the streets to find another position before the rent was due. When she found out what she was expected to do, she knew she should turn it down immediately and walk away, but she didn't. She couldn't. She was so tired of the gray slog of days spent serving cold, greasy burgers, of evenings pulling pints in stale, smoky pubs, of mornings cleaning grubby rooms in shabby hotels that being a call girl didn't seem all that bad. Mrs. Grenville was offering her security, money, and an unexpected but welcome sense of approval. So long as she did what was asked of her, she was accepted by the madam and even, in an odd way, loved.

Mrs. Grenville found the clients, rich, generous, lonely men who were more often than not charming to Mara. They would take her out to dinner and then on to expensive hotels or luxury flats for the night and send her away in the morning with a large tip on top of what they had already agreed to pay.

Mara's only experience of sex before working for Mrs. Grenville had been when she was raped at fifteen. Though almost every male she'd met since then had asked her out, she'd turned them all down. She wasn't interested in men or sex. And that made what she had to do with her clients strangely inoffensive. Here was no violence, no pain, no struggle fought and lost. Instead, it was a transaction, pure and simple. She had something to sell, they wanted to buy.

She knew it was illegal, that most people would call it immoral, and that in the end, a call girl was no more than an expensive prostitute, but it was so easy. Although she'd never been able to lie with a straight face, after some coaching from Mrs. Grenville, she found she was able to fake desire and pretend enjoyment without any trouble. Perhaps because she had never experienced real lovemaking, what she was doing didn't seem dishonest.

However, she was reluctant to spend the thousands she was earning every week. Making money in that way was one thing, using it to indulge herself another. She rented a small, comfortable one-bedroom flat in Little Venice, looking out on the canals, bought the expensive clothes needed to accompany her clients out to restaurants and clubs, but put the rest of the proceeds in the bank. And she kept her new profession a secret from her friends.

Jake had been the driver for one of her regular clients. One night he'd picked her up from Mrs. Grenville's to take her to his employer and started talking to her. First, she'd ignored him, suspicious of his motives. Men who knew what she did for a living tended to presume she was there for the taking. But as the months passed and he continued to come and collect her for his boss, she was won over. Mostly by his lack of assumptions—he seemed not to expect anything from her. He was charming but never aggressive. He never made a pass. Was never suggestive. Instead, he was a generous and open person. Not particularly bright, not especially handsome, but seriously sweet.

After months and months of talking in the car, Jake asked her out for coffee on an evening off. She accepted. The next time, they went for a drink, then for dinner. And then again. And again. The tenth time, Jake produced an engagement ring and asked her to marry him. Mara was shattered. She'd had no idea that Jake felt like that about her. No one felt like that about her.

She'd thought being a call girl hadn't affected her. But when Jake stammered out his offer, the strength of her shocked reaction told her she'd been wrong. Selling herself to hundreds of men had made her believe that she deserved no better. Now Jake was saying that she had as much right to be happy as anyone else. That she was worthy of love. His love. After she managed to stop crying, she accepted his offer.

They married three weeks later, just a quiet ceremony, only Jules and

Terry and Lily there for Mara and Jake's disapproving parents for him. And then they moved into the little house they'd bought with her immoral earnings. Mara had been worried about the sex, scared that after all her experience, Jake would feel like just another client. But the moment he got into bed with her, she'd known the difference. The years of selling her body had been fake. An emotionless, perfectly tuned, but empty performance with the pleasure all on one side. Jake was real.

Seven years later, Mara opened the door in the middle of the night to two policemen, one male, one female. Her first thought was that they must have made a mistake, gone to the wrong house. Then one of them, the woman, she thought afterward, although she could never remember, asked her if she knew a Mr. Jake Moore. Immediately she understood. She didn't need them to tell her. She knew what a visit from the police in the middle of the night meant. Jake was dead.

He'd been coming back down the motorway after his famous pop-star client decided to stay in Manchester; an SUV had skidded into him at high speed, sending him crashing into the massive lorry in front. The following day, the newspapers were full of the star's miraculous escape. Leather-clad and handsome, he was interviewed on daytime TV, talking about making the decision to stay in the north. About his near-brush with death. A few papers mentioned Jake, in passing, but none of them talked about his wife mourning at home, or his daughters, who had lost their father.

Mara was beyond feeling resentment about that. Or much of anything apart from grief. Every part of her longed to curl up in a small dark place and hide, to try desperately to pretend that it hadn't happened, but she couldn't, she had Moo and Tilly to think about. Someone had to look after them, to love them, to make sure they weren't harmed by the loss of their father. So she just concentrated on moving forward. Doing the next thing that was needed. Telling the girls. Arranging the funeral. The day-to-day business of parenthood.

She clung to the idea of Moo and Tilly. She had loved them before Jake's death; afterward, she needed them. Because despite what had happened, despite her despair at losing Jake, they made sure that there was still joy in her life. How could there not be when she had them? When she had the pleasure of seeing them grow and change and develop into individuals in their own right? When she saw their curiosity about their world and their delight in every new thing they saw or read or experienced? When they both tried so hard to cheer her up?

Shaking, Mara stumbled over to her old, shabby couch and slumped into it, the Moores' letter still clutched in her right hand. She couldn't manage without the girls. She couldn't. They were her connection to sanity, her reason to carry on, her saving grace. Her living, breathing link to Jake.

And the Moores wanted to take them away.

nine

Dressed in her turquoise and gray aerobics teacher's outfit, Lily left the set to the sound of the audience's laughter. Thank God, it had gone okay. Charlie, the producer, gave her a quick hug.

"Pickups?" she asked, wondering if there was anything the director thought needed doing again.

"Not in your scenes."

Lily grinned. That was a relief. Drenched with sweat, she was desperate for a shower. No matter what she did, the lights always beat her. She probably smelled like a ferret with a hangover. With a quick wave at Charlie and a smile for the floor manager as he walked out onstage to tell the audience what was going to happen next, she slipped away, around the back of the set.

Her dressing room was far from the visions of her youth. Then, she had pictured ranks and ranks of exotic flowers, velvet chairs, silk curtains, shaded lights, and elaborate screens. Instead, just like every other one she'd ever been in, it was a dull, uniform space, all cream walls, plastic chairs, and harsh lighting. And, mercifully, showers. Lily pulled off her costume, turned on the water, and stepped into the warm, steady stream. Bliss.

Half an hour later, she was squeaky clean, sitting in front of the room's wide mirror, wrapped in a toweling robe, brushing out her hair. She could hear the other members of the cast trooping past her door, making jokes with each other, discussing their roles, their lines, the audience's reaction. This episode was over. Only two more to go.

There was a knock on the door. "Lily? You decent?" Raymond called out.

"Yeah. Come in." Raymond entered, his round, usually smiling face looking a touch nervous. "What's up?"

"You haven't given up smoking again?"

Lily laughed and pointed out the pack of Silk Cut and the lighter lying on the dressing top in front of the mirror. "You're safe. Spit it out. Charlie and Nick making you do their dirty work again? What is it? Early meeting tomorrow? More new scenes?"

"No. Nothing like that." Raymond paused. Lily wasn't going to like this. "You know Steve? The new security guard at the office? Well, he just came to me, didn't know what to do." Raymond took a deep breath. "It's Clive, Lily, sniffing round again."

"Fuck." Clive was now a leading investigative journalist with one of the major tabloids. His TV company had gone bankrupt just after he and Lily split up; he'd disappeared for a year, only to come back, reborn as a success-ful, sleaze-driven reporter. Since then, he'd been responsible for a string of high-profile scoops, from trapping a member of the royal family's staff into admitting he was selling off official gifts to getting evidence of a top foot-baller having an affair with his head coach's new, young wife.

"What the hell was it this time?"

"Just the usual to begin with. You know, what are you like to work for? How do you behave in the office? Have you tried to fuck Steve?"

"Bastard . . . Hold on. You said to begin with? What else did he try?"

Raymond hesitated. But he had to tell her. "He wanted Steve to tap your phone. Newspaper would pay, lots, apparently."

"Shit."

When Clive had started trying to dig up dirt on her, Lily had decided that the best thing to do was ignore him. He was like a wasp. If she flapped her arms around, she'd get stung. But if she stayed still, did nothing, he'd get bored and fly off home. And so she'd closed her eyes to his activities. Never called, never complained, never tried to persuade him to stop his campaign against her. But he was still buzzing about.

He'd already come up with two unpleasant stories about her. One of her disappointed ex-lovers had been angry enough to talk to him and he'd done a piece on how hard-hearted and selfish she was, gobbling men up and spitting them out as she chose. A disgruntled director who'd been fired from the first series of *We Can Work It Out*—by the producers, not by Lily, but that had made no difference—had given him stuff about how difficult she was to work with. Apparently, he'd called her a vicious prima donna with all the social skills of Saddam Hussein, but Lily suspected that that had been Clive putting words in the man's mouth. It sounded like the kind of snide insult Lily's ex-husband had always specialized in.

Now it seemed those stories hadn't been enough for Clive. He wanted more. More embarrassing dirt, more titillating gossip. It was time for Lily to do something else. To use the flyswatter. The bastard had taken things too far.

Lily looked up at Raymond and forced a smile. "Thanks, Ray. I'll deal with it."

"Are you okay?" Raymond asked. Lily's face looked grim despite the smile.

"Sure. I'm fine. But I've got to do something about that shit I married." Raymond hesitated, concerned. "Go on. I'm only going to talk to him, not poison him. And tell Steve not to worry. He did the right thing."

"Thanks, Lily. He'll appreciate that." Raymond walked out of the room and closed the door behind him.

Lily picked up her new, tiny, silvery mobile phone. She hadn't spoken to Clive since they'd taken Jack and Bella to the airport to get their plane to Australia a couple of months before. Normally, Lily spent as little time with her ex-husband as possible, just enough to hand over or pick up the twins. But that day had been different; their kids had been going traveling on their own for the first time. And it seemed right that they should both see them off. Then, on the way back into London, Clive had suggested they go for a drink. And Lily, missing Jack and Bella already, hating the idea of months and months without any more contact than the occasional phone call, and not looking forward to going home to a now-empty and all too quiet house, had agreed.

It had been a mistake. Over a bottle of wine in an obscure Islington bar, after she'd shed a few tears over the twins' departure, Clive had grabbed her and kissed her. All the rage and the misery she'd felt when she'd first found out about him and Beatrice resurfaced. Sickened, she'd pushed him away as hard as she could and wiped her mouth on her sleeve, back and forth, back and forth, in a gesture of total disgust. He'd stood up, spat on the table in front of her, then turned and stomped out.

His first, failed attempt to win over one of her colleagues had occurred ten days after that. Followed by others. Then there had been the two stories. Clive was out for revenge. And he wasn't giving up. Lily punched a number into her phone. Ignoring him hadn't worked, maybe talking would.

CLIVE WAS sitting at a desk in a large, chaotic, open-plan office, surrounded by the hum of other people on the phone, the whir of computers, the clack of keyboards. Still handsome, his full head of hair only just turning gray at the temples, his smile as charming as ever, there was no sign on his lightly tanned, unlined face of the bitterness that was eating away at him.

He'd been more successful as a tabloid journalist than he could ever have imagined. After a year spent grubbing about at the bottom of the TV market, he'd gotten himself a job as a reporter and through some hard work, a bit of luck, and a previously unrecognized natural aptitude for poking around in other people's private lives, he'd risen right to the top. He was highly paid, esteemed by his peers, wanted by every editor on Fleet Street. But he wasn't happy.

And the way he saw it, there was only one person to blame.

Lily.

Over the years, unable to face the fact that he had failed in television because of his own mistakes and shortcomings, he had persuaded himself that his troubles had all started when his ex-wife threw him out. He'd gone bankrupt, lost his company, lost his lover—Beatrice had dumped him for someone who could help her in her continued pursuit of success—and ended up an exile from the world he had once thought to rule, because of her. Lily's recent achievements had only made his failure that much harder to bear.

Then, his relationship with the twins had never been the same since the split up. He hadn't ever been the most attentive of fathers, only rarely turning up at carol concerts and school plays, choosing work over attending birthday parties, but in his own selfish way he loved Jack and Bella and resented finding himself on the outside of their lives. He saw them when he could, took them out for the day and even occasionally away for the week-end, but he was second choice. And he blamed his ex-wife for that also.

Then Lily had refused him. No, not just refused. She'd snubbed him. When all he'd been doing was giving her a simple little kiss for old time's sake. Ignoring the hurt she'd caused him, the harm she'd done. And she'd thrown it back in his face. Wiping herself clean of his touch as if he were a disgusting piece of filth just crawled out of the sewers.

It had been one crime too many. He wanted revenge. And now that Lily was a celebrity, he had a surefire way to get it. His two recent stories on her had been a start. They'd gotten several people talking for a few days, but they were too soon forgotten, just another batch of tomorrow's cat litter. Clive longed to humiliate Lily, to check that growing reputation of hers, turn the public off their latest celebrity. And make her feel the misery and embarrassment of failure and rejection, just as he had.

The phone on his desk rang. He reached out to pick it up while continuing to type into his computer. "Clive Morris."

"Hello, you shit."

"The famous Lily James." A broad grin split Clive's face. Some response at last. "What can I do for you?"

"You have to ask?"

"It's rare someone of your elevated status calls me. It must be important."

"Yeah, Clive, it's important." Her ex-husband's sardonic, biting tone got up her nose but Lily held back the torrent of abuse she longed to hurl at him. "You can leave my employees alone," she said, emphasizing each word separately.

"And why should I do that?"

"I suppose it wouldn't be enough for me to ask you nicely?"

"Shouldn't think so. You could try though."

"Haven't you had enough of this yet, Clive?"

"No, Lilibet. You see, it's such fun." Clive's old, secret nickname for her. Once it had amused her and made her feel loved; now it just irritated her. But she wasn't going to say anything. If Clive knew how much the name annoyed her, he'd only use it all the more.

"What about the kids? What'll they think?"

"They're away."

"But they'll be back. They'll find out, they'll read what you've written."

"Maybe. But they're eighteen. They're grown-ups. They'll cope."

Lily gritted her teeth. She was not going to lose it. "Look, I'm sorry about what happened in the restaurant."

"Sorry, Lilibet? You, sorry?" Clive sneered.

God, she was stupid. Expecting him to accept her apology without sniggering. But she was sorry she'd rejected him so harshly. "Yes, I am."

"And what is it you're sorry about? Stealing my kids? Fucking up my life? Or just treating me like pond scum?"

Lily's free hand clenched into a fist. Same old Clive. How could he accuse her of stealing the twins when for years she'd struggled to persuade them to see him at all? But there was no point in arguing with him. There never had been. "If I hear of you trying to talk to any more of my colleagues about me, I'll get my lawyers on to you so fast you'll think you're watching the Concorde." There. She'd been firm but not hysterical.

"Aren't you grand. Plural 'lawyers.' Most people just have one."

"I mean it, Clive. Keep away from me."

"Freedom of the press, my dear. Freedom of the press."

"Bastard. That doesn't include bribing people to bug phones."

"You're a star now. It goes with the territory."

"That's crap. What about the Press Complaints Commission?"

"Oh, no, please no. Not the Press Complaints Commission. Anything but that. I'm really scared now."

The conversation brought back bitter memories of hundreds of others over the years, all of them featuring Clive at his nonchalant, cynical, sarcastic worst. Lily had tried but she could hold herself back no longer. "All right. Write what the fuck you like. Do I care? Tell the world I'm giving birth to a vampire baby, why don't you. Who believes that crap anyway?"

"Can I quote you on that?" Clive mocked.

Lily spluttered on the other end of the line. There weren't enough swear words in all the languages in all the world for her to describe just exactly what she thought of her ex-husband.

"Good-bye, Lilibet. Nice to talk to you." Clive smiled with satisfaction and replaced the phone in its cradle.

Lily looked at her mobile, at the crystal display asking her if she wanted to call the last number again. "Never," she shouted at the phone. All too often in recent years, no matter what she decided at the beginning of a conversation, no matter how determined she was not to lose her temper, Clive's annoying, whining voice ended up driving her mad. Hard to believe that she'd found his wisecracks amusing when they'd first been together.

Lily took a few deep breaths to calm herself. She'd been right all along. It was a waste of time talking to Clive. Or shouting at him. If he was determined to pursue her, pursue her he would. Thank God no one who knew her well would speak to him. Best she just got on with her life and paid no attention to whatever he was doing. And made a note to have the office regularly swept for bugs.

ten

Still in her black bus driver's uniform, Terry sat outside the headmaster's office, waiting. She'd been on early shift that day and when she'd gotten home around two P.M., there had been a message on her machine. Immediately, she had started to worry; it was rare for anyone to ring during the day. All her friends knew she was at work. It was either the kind of official call—bank or insurance company or the like—that she hated or something had happened at school. Scared of what she was about to hear, Terry pressed the button.

"Mrs. McKellar. It's Mr. Wallace's office at Newington High School. Could you call us as soon as you get this message?"

Her mind conjuring up hideous images of death and disaster, Terry grabbed the phone and quickly dialed the school. Busy. Why the hell couldn't that place get more lines? She pressed redial, again and again, faster and faster, until she got through. The school secretary's deep voice answered.

"It's Terry McKellar. You called me. What's happened? Is Paul okay?"

"Calm down, Mrs. McKellar. Your son is fine. But there has been an . . . incident. Mr. Wallace needs to see you as soon as possible. Can you come in this afternoon?"

Terry had agreed to go to the school immediately. She'd jumped on her bike and pedaled the mile or so to Newington High, only to sit for half an hour waiting for Wallace to see her, that peculiarly schoolish smell of cheap detergent, sweat, and stale food taking her back to her own nightmare days as a student, ruled by nuns with rods of bamboo.

Finally, after worrying her well-bitten nails to the quick, she was called in. Mr. Wallace was in his fifties, a cadaverous-looking man, thin, long-faced, his eyes deep-set. Terry looked at his grim expression and her nerves got worse.

"Mrs. McKellar? Sorry to keep you waiting. Do sit down."

He didn't look sorry, but Terry was too worried to take much notice. "What is it? What's he done?" she asked, trying to keep calm.

"Your son was caught with a girl, Mrs. McKellar."

"With a girl?" Terry was confused. "Doing what?"

"I don't think I need to say anymore."

"Yes, you do. What was he doing?"

Wallace paused, reluctant to speak. Finally, he barked out, "Having sex. In the boiler room."

"Oh. Is that all." After the phone call, on her way in to the school, Terry had imagined all kinds of things. Bullying. Stealing. Drugs. A few months ago, she'd never have thought of any of those things in relation to Paul, but she wasn't sure how well she knew her son anymore. And compared to selling dope, a quick grope in the boiler room didn't sound so bad.

"This is not something we can dismiss. He is far too young to be thinking of things like that."

"I was relieved it wasn't something worse."

"It is quite bad enough. Not the behavior we expect of boys in this school."

"No. Course not. Who was the girl?"

"I don't see that as at all germane to the issue."

"It might be. If she was older, or . . ."

"She was in his class."

"Oh."

"This is a serious matter. Paul is losing his way. His grades are slipping and his teachers"—the headmaster pointed to a file open on the desk in front of him—"are concerned."

"Yes, I know. I know. But I don't know what to do. I've lost . . . I can't get through to him. I've been hoping it's just a bad patch. That he'll come out of it. But he hasn't."

"If you'd like my advice . . . ?"

"Of course." Terry wasn't sure that she did want Wallace's advice—his condescending, pompous attitude had always annoyed her—but it would have been rude to refuse.

"I believe you're a single parent."

"Yes." Terry sounded wary. "And?"

"Well, Paul's behavior is typical of a teenager without a man in the house. Boys of fifteen do need their fathers round."

"That's cra . . . not true."

"Mrs. McKellar, it's one thing when they're children, maybe just a mother can be adequate then, but once they reach puberty, they need someone of their own gender to show them the ropes, so to speak. To help them understand what is happening to them. Be a role model. An inspiration."

"An inspiration?" Terry couldn't help a small smile ghosting over her face. The idea of Finn as a role model. Although having sex in the boiler room at school was certainly the kind of thing he would've done.

"Yes. If not the boy's father, a family member. An uncle. A grandfather."

"There's no one like that."

"Then a man of the cloth, perhaps."

"No way," Terry snapped. She'd never liked authority figures at the best of times. Particularly "men of the cloth."

"If I may say so, I do have more experience with adolescent boys, and they invariably run wild without the proper influences."

Terry supposed Wallace was trying his best, but did he have to be so self-righteous? She knew she should listen to him, but when he started talking about the benefits of joining the Boy Scouts, she decided she'd had enough.

"The Boy Scouts. That's very interesting. I'll certainly think about it," she said as soon as the headmaster paused for breath. She stood up and held out her hand. "Thank you, Mr. Wallace."

Wallace looked at her disapprovingly. His well-chosen, wise words had fallen on stony soil. "Paul is suspended until the end of the week. Please take him home with you now. Good day, Mrs. McKellar."

TERRY JIGGLED open the front door of the flat. Behind her Paul was scuffing his way up the stairs, hanging back, waiting for her to disappear before he came in. Well, he was out of luck. Even though the chances of his listening were microscopic, she had to discuss with him what he'd done. No question, at fifteen he was too young to be having sex. The last thing she wanted was for him to take after his dad, who had boasted of fathering his first child when just fourteen.

As Paul slunk through the doorway and sidled down the corridor, heading for the steps to his room and sanctuary, Terry called out, "I need to talk to you."

Paul carried on toward his room.

"Don't try and sneak off. Come here!" Terry was trying to sound tough, but even to her own ears her voice rang out as more panicky than hard. She tried to lower her tone. "Paul! I said I wanted to talk to you, didn't I? Paul!" Deeper, but still feeble. And useless. Paul reached his room, sloped in, slammed the door behind him, and rammed home the lock.

TERRY'S KITCHEN was an oddly welcoming room, a mishmash of junk-shop furniture and reconditioned appliances, of old metal signs and ancient posters, of innumerable treasures picked up at countless garage sales. Flower-shaped lamps from the 1950s, chipped blue-and-white china, old biscuit boxes, and bits of wax fruit were scattered amongst assorted glass jars of dried beans and herbs and coffee and oil.

Now out of her uniform and draped in a multicolored, flowery dress, tied around the waist with an old Eton school tie, Terry came in, trailing Minnie in her wake. She walked over to an ancient, half-stripped pine dresser that was held up on one side by a pile of telephone directories and looked at the various jars huddled on the middle shelf. Herbal teas to cope with any occasion. Teas to calm you down. To pick you up. To increase your brain power. To lessen your stress. To ease your digestion. To cleanse your system. To do everything except help you cope with a teenage son who'd been suspended from school and was now closeted in his room, refusing to talk.

Terry picked out a chamomile and ginger mix that its makers claimed would turn even the tensest person into a laid-back, what-me-worry type. Anything was worth a try. She made her brew and sat down at her rickety old kitchen table whose scrubbed surface was half covered with opened mail and newspapers and bottles of vitamins. She took a swig of her tea, reached out for the phone, and dialed a number. "Lils? You busy?"

Lily was slumped in her dressing room. She was taking a ten-minute break from their final rehearsal before taping the penultimate show and she was exhausted. The last thing she needed right at that moment was a conversation with anyone. But then she heard the worry in her best friend's voice. "Terry. I've got a few minutes. What's happened?"

Terry brought Lily up to speed on Paul and the girl and Mr. Wallace. "You wouldn't have believed it. Suggesting the Boy Scouts like it was 1950 or something. I tried to talk to Paul, but he ignored me. God, I have had it up to here with this version of my son. I want my Paul back."

"Patience, sweetie. You'll get him. He's fifteen. It's only a stage he's going through."

"But suppose it's more than that? Before Finn, he was fine. Teenagery, but I could still reach him. Suppose Wallace was right? Suppose Paul needs a man in his life?"

"Well, it wasn't easy for Jack, and he had Clive off and on."

"See. There you are. Wallace was right, the bastard. Hell, it's not like I hadn't thought of it for myself. But I buried my head in the sand. Didn't want to face it, did I? Shit, shit, shit."

"It's not that bad."

"Yes it is. Lils, think. Where the hell do I find a father figure?"

"There's an easy answer to that."

"Easy for you, maybe. I gave all that up years ago, didn't I?"

"Yeah, but you can change your mind. It's not like it's a religious thing or anything. And you're stunning."

"I'm fat."

"Terry. For the thousandth time, you're not. You're stunning. A bit curvy maybe, but guys like that. I can think of hundreds would go for you in a minute."

"I don't want them. I'd have to fuck them, and I won't do that. I know you love it, but it's never done anything for me. Just a lot of sticky mess."

"You really, really have never had an orgasm?" Lily still couldn't quite believe this.

"I really, really have never had an orgasm."

"Even with all those men?"

"Even with all those men. I guess sex is something other people enjoy."

"Like sweetbreads."

"Or Barry Manilow. Yeah."

"There's nothing you miss?"

"The cuddling was nice. But I never got much of that, did I? Either they thought I was a frigid bitch and turned their backs on me, or if I gave my Oscar-winning performance and pretended to come, I was the hottest, sexiest thing, to be fucked, not cuddled."

"I still don't think you should've given up. I said at the time you should persevere."

"It's easier this way. Less stressful. No frustration. No disappointment. And no lies. I was getting so I didn't even know the truth myself. I ever tell you I taught myself to clench my inner muscles in rhythm to fake orgasm? Now, that's sick."

"No. Not sick. Never sick. Sad, maybe."

"Am I being selfish? Should I give up on this celibacy stuff for Paul's sake? Go out and find a man for him?"

"You can't do that."

"Why not? That's what you were suggesting, wasn't it?"

"Only if you want the guy yourself."

"Why not? How bad can it be? It's not like I haven't done it before."

"Okay. One, it's taking good motherhood way too far. And two, could you really hide your feelings for the time it'll take for Paul and this father figure to bond?"

"I'm out of practice, but I could try."

"What if he wants more? In my experience, they always do."

"What, like commitment?"

"Yeah. Pretending to love would be harder than pretending to come."

"I see what you're saying."

"And you don't want to raise Paul's hopes and then disappoint him."

"No, I don't. Not again. That'd be worse than doing nothing."

There was a tap on Lily's dressing room door. "Needed onstage, Lily," a man's voice called out.

"Listen, Terry, I got to go. Don't worry too much about this, okay?"

"Okay."

"Ignore Wallace and his father figure. Paul'll come round, give him time. It's hard to lose your dad before you even knew him."

"I know. I know. Talk later, yeah?"

"Yeah. 'Bye."

"'Bye. Oh, and Lils?"

"Uh-huh?"

"Love you."

"Love you too."

eleven

Jules's town house in Chelsea was her own personal haven. Outside, it was one of a long row of similar properties, each with its own cellar, its own porticoed doorway, its own wrought-iron balcony on the first floor. Inside, it looked more like a pretty country cottage than a hard-edged piece of London. Walls covered in landscapes and paintings of dogs and horses; old, comfortable leather armchairs; chintz sofas; candles and books and photos in silver frames. It wasn't chic, it wasn't even vaguely fashionable, but Jules didn't care. She loved the place, loved the treasures she'd collected to put in it, loved the feeling of peace it gave her whenever she was there.

But that day, the house's calming effect wasn't working. Jules was on edge. Sitting in her pastel-colored, custom-made kitchen, the phone in her hand, she was trying to work up the courage to call a sperm bank. Trying and so far failing. She'd already dialed the number twice and hung up before anyone answered.

She knew she was being ridiculous. If this were for work, she'd have no problem. She'd rung some of the strangest places and asked for some of the strangest things on behalf of her clients and never felt the slightest bit embarrassed. But this was for her.

Through her very successful company, Dunne Parties, Jules organized almost any kind of gathering. Important book launches, opening nights, glamorous weddings, expansive anniversary celebrations, even funerals and memorial services. The more unusual, the more elaborate, the better. For years, problems, and especially complicated, apparently insoluble, last-minute problems, had turned her on. There was an initial sickening panic, followed by a surging rush of adrenaline, a desperate attempt to discover answers to misshapen tents or lost live lobsters or walk-out waiters, and, finally, an enormous sense of satisfaction when she found a way around things regardless of how unlikely that had seemed at the start. It was better than drink, better than drugs, even better than sex.

So why couldn't she treat the sperm bank as just another problem to be solved? Why couldn't she dial a simple number and say the words she'd practiced over and over, "I'd like to make an appointment, please. To discuss artificial insemination." There. It was easy. If she could find five thousand live edible locusts to slap on the barbecue at an obsessed-with-ecology rock star's survivalist party, surely she could make a phone call on her own behalf and arrange a simple appointment?

She took a deep breath, ordered herself not to be such a coward this time, and dialed the number.

"Harley Conception Center. Good morning," a bright, perky female voice answered.

"Um, er, um, I . . ." Jules ran out of steam.

"Can I help you?"

"Yes, please. I . . . I want to make an appointment."

"Certainly, madam. Which of our services were you interested in?"

"Um, art . . . artificial . . . insem . . ."

"Artificial insemination. Of course. One moment, madam. Hmm. We have an opening with the doctor next Monday at three."

"That . . . that'll be fine."

"Good. We'll need you here at two-thirty to fill in some details."

"Yes. Yes, of course. I'll be there."

"And your name is?"

"Juliet Dunne." The last bit of nervousness disappeared as she went through the everyday, reassuring routine of giving her address and phone number.

"Thank you, madam. We'll see you on Monday."

The line went dead. Jules looked at the phone in her hand, amazed that she had made so much fuss over something that people must do every day.

They hadn't even asked her whether she had a partner or not. How times had changed.

She had her appointment despite the idiotic way she had behaved. Now all she had to do was contain her impatience until Monday at three. And dream about her baby . . .

Her thoughts were interrupted by the doorbell. She decided to ignore it. Nobody knew she was here, apart from the office, and no one from there would come around without phoning first.

The doorbell rang again. Whoever it was wasn't going to go away. Jules got up and hurried through her living room to the hallway. She looked through the glass spy hole to see a tall, besuited man of about seventy.

Jules opened the door. "Daddy!" She leaned forward to give her father a kiss on the cheek.

"Juliet. Your office told me you were here."

"What a . . . nice surprise. Come in. Come in."

"I'm glad to see you're well." Lord Dunne walked past his daughter and into her house. He was a handsome man despite his years. His chestnut-brown hair, though graying, still covered his head, his figure was as trim as it had been during the days when he was a commander in the navy, and his raw stare could still intimidate those around him. After resigning his commission, he had become a politician, been elected to Parliament, and five years ago had been given a peerage in the Queen's birthday honors. He now spent his days terrorizing his fellow members of the House of Lords in the same way he had once bullied the sailors on his ship.

"Thank you, I'm fine. And you?"

"Very well, thank you, Juliet. Very well."

"Good. That's good. Would you like some tea? Coffee? No? A glass of champagne, then." She'd have to talk to the girls in the office about telling people she was at home. Although she had to admit that it wasn't easy to resist Ian Dunne when he wanted something.

"Far too early for me. And stop flapping."

"Sorry." There was something about her father that sent Jules right back into childhood. If anyone else had spoken to her the way he just had, she'd have been furious and ready to snap back some clever, acid response. All her early life, she'd been desperate to please him but she just wasn't his idea of a proper daughter. She dreamed of going to university; he thought that a pointless thing for girls to do. She refused to marry the family-approved man-with-a-title who asked her when she was twenty, preferring instead to start her own company and work; her father thought women belonged in the home. When she finally did marry, she opted for someone way beneath her socially and compounded that by splitting up with him; Ian Dunne didn't believe in divorce, regardless of the situation. Everything she'd done had been a disappointment to him. And that wasn't going to change. There was no chance Jules could ever be the woman he thought she should be. Nevertheless, there was still a part of her that longed for his approval and made her jump through hoops whenever she saw him.

Ian Dunne stood in front of the unlit fireplace, legs apart, hands Prince Philiped behind his back, master of all he surveyed. "Now. I'm on my way to lunch with the Lord Chancellor but I wanted to pop in for a moment, to find out when you're going to come and see us."

"Well, I . . . I don't know. It's a bit difficult."

"You haven't been to Bevingdon since you came for tea at Easter."

"I know. I'm sorry. I've been hard at it. Summer's always one of our busiest times." In truth, she'd been avoiding her mother. Diana Dunne could barely manage a civil word to Jules. Apart from one brief period eighteen years earlier, she had never liked her middle daughter, not even when Jules was a child. And as she had got older, Diana's dislike had got stronger. Jules had struggled to understand it; eventually, after much soul-searching and a few expensive therapists, she had given up. Lady Dunne was a force of nature.

"You should always find time for family."

"Yes. Of course."

"It's been some months."

"I know. I'm sorry."

"Philip, Alice, and Elena say they haven't heard from you either."

"They'll understand, I'm sure. I have been very busy." Jules was fond of her brother and sisters—all their lives, they had tried to protect her from Diana, when they could—but they lived in a different world. They'd done what was expected of them by their parents; Alice and Elena were married to wealthy, prominent men and Philip was an up-and-coming Conservative MP. They were invited to parties, not paid to organize them.

"Your mother's missed you."

"Oh." Jules found it hard to imagine a less likely event than Diana Dunne missing her. Intelligent life being found on Mars, perhaps.

"She wants to see you."

"Did she say so?"

"I know she does."

Jules said nothing. There was nothing to say. Lord Dunne had always refused to accept that she and her mother were better off apart.

"So. You'll come for lunch next Sunday?"

"Does Mummy know you're inviting me?"

"She'll be delighted. Next Sunday it is."

Jules knew from long and painful personal experience that there was no point in arguing. Her father refused to accept the word "no." The more she resisted, the more pressure he would put on her to do what he wanted. And she'd end up agreeing anyway, in the vain hope of pleasing him. So she allowed him to believe that she had accepted his invitation. She would send him a note a few days before the lunch, claiming illness. That usually worked. He would be back, of course, but at least she would have postponed the dreaded day.

THE NEXT Monday, Jules hurried along Harley Street, passing door after door decorated with expensive private doctors' brass plates. Finally, she turned into a yellow brick, modern blocky building and ran up the stairs to the second floor. She paused before a blond oak door with a small, very discreet steel sign beside it: "The Harley Conception Center." Taking a long, slow, deep breath, she grasped the doorknob, turned it, and strolled inside trying to look nonchalant, as if she did this every day.

Five minutes later, ensconced in a small, functional waiting room, Jules attempted to concentrate on the detailed questionnaire she'd been handed at reception—Had she ever had rubella? When had she had her last period? Had anyone in her family ever suffered from diabetes? How long had she been trying to get pregnant?—but she couldn't stop herself from wondering about the other people there. Was that nervous couple clutching hands in the corner waiting for the results of tests, hoping for good news? Was that forty-something woman playing with a toddler a happy client, back for another helping?

And what about that group of three young men, boys even, over by the window? Sprawled on a sofa, laughing and joking as one of their number was called by the nurse? Jules watched the short, podgy, spotty young man as he walked toward the door, turning back every now and again to look at his friends and giggle. Was he a donor? A student, here to earn some extra money?

She stared at him, at his greasy, unwashed hair, his acne-flecked skin, round shoulders, and slouchy walk. She was never going to get the handsome baby she'd been dreaming about if someone like that was the father. A young, grubby, uncouth kid wasn't what she'd had in mind at all. She hadn't expected George Clooney, but she had hoped for tall and reasonably presentable.

"Juliet Dunne?" A pretty, young nurse holding a sheaf of folders appeared in the doorway. Jules got up and followed her down a cheerless beige corridor and into a bleak colorless room. There was a modern desk with two chairs placed in front of it, a long, waist-high, black-vinyl-covered table, one end raised, the other fitted with shiny chrome stirrups. A swivel chair for the doctor. A kidney-shaped dish holding speculum and syringe.

The nurse pulled a roll of paper over the table, handed Jules a blue throwaway gown, and gestured at a screen placed across one corner of the room. "If you could get undressed and put this on, please. Take everything off. Dr. Cotton will be with you in a minute." With that she left, closing the door behind her.

Jules took off her favorite navy designer suit, which she'd worn for luck, slipped out of her Italian silk underwear, and put on the large, stiff paper gown. She held the two edges of it together behind her, walked to the table, and perched on the edge. She tried to look away but couldn't stop staring at the stirrups. The dish. The speculum. The reality of the place was hitting her hard. She was desperate for a baby, but this was so . . . crude. So businesslike. So unromantic.

She thought she'd grasped what the words "sperm bank" implied. But she hadn't. Not really. Not until she'd been faced with the boys outside, the room here, the implements of Dr. Cotton's trade. She was proposing to have a stranger, a complete stranger, father her child. She'd never know anything about him apart from the barest medical details. Never know what he looked like, never be able to search for him in her baby, never know what part of her child was her genetic heritage, what part his.

The door swung open to admit the nurse, followed by a middle-aged man in an expensive three-piece suit. He was perfectly turned out, with matching tie and handkerchief, monogrammed cuff links, silk socks, and handmade shoes.

"Miss Dunne?" He held out his hand. "Hello. I'm Dr. Cotton."

"Hello."

The nurse handed the doctor a buff-colored file and he flipped it open. Inside, Jules could see the questionnaire she had filled out. "So you want a baby? Well, good, babies, that's our business. I see you were tested for fertility some years ago, but I need to examine you, make sure there's no new problem. Take some blood, check your hormone levels. Then we can talk about arrangements, times, what you need to do to prepare. Okay? If you'd just lie down here . . ."

Jules stared at him as he went to the bottom end of the table, positioned himself between the stirrups, and turned on a small light that was on the end of a flexible steel arm.

"Miss Dunne? If you could lie down, put your feet in the stirrups?"

Jules didn't move. Her fists were clenched, her nails biting into her palms, her body as stiff and unyielding as the cold, metal speculum the doctor now held in his hands.

"Are you all right, Miss Dunne?"

Jules burst into tears. She wanted a baby so much. But not here, in such a cold sterile environment, with the father a person she'd never met and the doctor a dispassionate, workaday man whose prosaic attitude was better suited to giving her an enema than a baby. There was no love, no romance, no beauty here. "I'm sorry. I can't do it. I can't. Not like this."

twelve

Sean tugged at his collar, took a deep breath, and walked onto the stage. Lily, dressed in jeans and a sweatshirt, her thick mane still slightly damp, was standing talking to a striking woman with shoulder-length white-blond hair. It was the wrap party for *We Can Work It Out*. An hour before, the cavernous studio had been filled with the audience's laughter. Now the seats were empty and the stage, with its sets of reception desk, juice bar, treadmills, and dance studio, was filled with cast and crew and caterers.

It was the first time Lily had asked Sean to meet any of her friends or colleagues and he was nervous. Terrified, in fact. He was desperate to make a good impression, to make Lily's friends and, through them, Lily think well of him. They'd been going out for the last month and she'd changed his life. Seeing her had helped him to stop thinking about the boys all the time, to put his troubles aside for an hour or two and concentrate on her.

He crossed the stage, stopping only to pick up a glass of red wine and take a quick gulp on the way. He came up behind Lily and laid his hand on her shoulder, gently caressing her. She looked up at him and grinned. He bent down to give her a quick kiss.

"I thought you'd got lost. Here, this is Jules. Jules, Sean."

"Hello."

"Hi. It's good to meet you at last. Lily's told me a lot about you."

"Oh."

"I better mingle. See you guys later." Lily moved off to join some other cast members who were huddled in a group, gossiping.

Sean tried hard to think of something interesting to talk about. And came up empty. At first sight, he'd been impressed by Jules's cool good looks. Then he'd heard her voice. Only a childhood of Norland nannies, exclusive finishing schools, and lots and lots of money bought a voice like that. What on earth did he have to say to a woman like her?

"Did you see the show?" Jules asked.

"No." Was that the best he could do?

"It was one of Lily's finest. She's an amazing writer, don't you think?"

"Yes." Useless.

Jules smiled. "Do you say anything other than yes or no?"

"Yes, I mean, of course. I just . . . Excuse me. Nice to meet you." Deeply embarrassed, Sean shuffled off to the other side of the stage.

Mara came over to Jules. "Is that him?"

"Yes. Lucky Lily. All that and shy too."

"He looks nice. Kind."

"Mara, Mara, Mara. Open your eyes. He's not nice. He's gorgeous."

SEAN HUGGED the side of the juice-bar set, trying hard to look as if he were enjoying a moment's respite before plunging back into the party. In reality, he was standing by himself because he'd mucked it up. His nerves had gotten the better of him. After his monosyllabic disaster with Jules, he'd been introduced to all of the cast, most of the crew, and Lily's friend Mara and he'd not done much better with any of them.

He gazed around the room. Everyone looked happy chatting to someone else: Lily was laughing with her production manager, Raymond; Charlie and Nick, her two producers, seemed to be attempting to drink the bar dry; Jules and Mara were with a small, redheaded woman wearing an extraordinary pale-green, black, and ecru 1920s dress, and there was a tall, thin, sulky-looking teenage boy hanging about in the far corner. He looked as uncomfortable as Sean felt. Poor kid.

Sean strolled over to him. "You look like you're hating it as much as me."

"Stupid bloody party. Don't know why Mam made me come."

"I don't even have that excuse." Paul looked puzzled. "No one forced me to come," Sean explained. "I'm here all of my own accord."

"If I was grown up, no way I'd be within a million miles of here."

"I know. You're right. I'm a real fool."

Paul looked at Sean speculatively. Then decided that this wasn't a trick. "Yeah." He grinned.

TERRY HAD had Sean pointed out to her by Jules and Mara the moment she arrived. Now she was amazed to see him deep in conversation with Paul, who was smiling and chatting away as if he were an ordinary good-tempered, talkative child rather than the teenager from hell. And he'd been like that for at least ten minutes. Desperate to find out what Lily's latest's secret was, Terry walked over to them.

"You really think we'll make it this time?" Paul asked.

"Sure. The manager's learned from last time. We've all learned. Wait and see. In May we'll all be looking back on a successful season in the Premier-ship."

"What's it like, you know, at the Valley?"

"Great. Like you've come home. I can't describe it."

"I've only seen the stadium on TV. I wish I could go."

"Go where?" Terry asked.

Paul's eager, smiling face collapsed back into its habitual scowl as he spun around to face his mother. "Nowhere," he snapped, then stomped off.

Terry watched her son wend his way through the guests to find a quiet spot safe and uncontaminated by his mother. She turned to Sean. "God, I'm sorry. I ought to have left you alone. It's the first time he's said more than two mumbled words to anyone over the age of fifteen for months."

Sean smiled down at the woman he'd seen talking to Mara and Jules. Her pretty face, her soft, Liverpool-accented voice, and her disarming can-dor made him realize that there was no need to be nervous about talking to her. "Having a hard time with him?"

"Are they all like this?"

"So they say. I certainly was."

"And me. Oh, no, this is a punishment for the way I was at his age. If only I'd been nicer to my grandmother . . ."

"I think I detect a Catholic upbringing."

"You too?"

"Yeah."

"No matter how much I deny it, it's always there, even though I left years ago and I hate the whole idea of it. Oh, shit. I've put my foot in it, haven't I? You're still going, aren't you?"

Sean was tempted to tell Terry about the boys and his recent attempt to make a pact with God. Something made him want to confide in her despite the fact that he didn't even know her name. He was close to opening his mouth and pouring it all out, but he held back. She wouldn't want to hear all that stuff. "Not really," he said.

Terry glanced over at Paul, huddled in his corner on the far side of the stage. "What's your secret?"

"Nothing. I like kids. They like me. I don't know. Don't panic, he'll get over it soon enough. You're a parent. You're embarrassing. That's all it is."

Terry was sure it was a bit more complicated than that but she wasn't going to tell this guy all her problems, nice though he was. "So what were you talking about?"

"Football. We're both Charlton supporters."

"Oh. Right."

"He said his dad supported them."

Terry felt the familiar guilt tug at her. Finn hadn't known what shape a football was, let alone anything about Charlton Athletic. Then something else hit her; Paul had mentioned Finn for the first time since he died. That jerk Wallace had been right; Paul did need male company. If a few minutes at a party with this guy could make him open up this much, what would a real relationship with an adult man do for him?

"He talked about his dad?"

"Yes."

"Only Finn died a few months ago and Paul hasn't mentioned him to anyone since."

"I'm sorry. That must have been hard."

Terry didn't know how to answer him. Whether to tell the truth or let it go. So she changed the subject. "Is that where he wanted to go? Charlton?"

"Yeah."

"Maybe I should let him. I guess I'm being too protective, but, you know, football. . . ."

"It's not like the eighties. I go every time they're playing at home and I haven't seen a fight in years."

"I don't know. He's still very young. To be going alone . . ."

Sean looked over at Paul, still holed up in his corner, and had a glimpse of himself at that age. Prickly and tongue-tied, still not comfortable in his own skin, he had come to life at the Valley, where he'd been able to forget his shyness and cheer for Charlton. "Umm, I suppose I could take him. If you like?" After all, why not? Paul seemed like a nice kid and Sean wasn't going to be taking his own sons.

"You wouldn't want to do that, would you?"

"I'd be going anyway. Besides, all the kids now are Manchester United crazy. It's great to meet a teenager who cares about a local team. And he says he's never been."

Terry watched her son glowering at them from the other side of the set. Maybe a treat like this would cheer him up a bit. Make him easier to live with. "Are you sure?"

"Course. It's no big deal. Honestly. I'll call you when I can get tickets."

"Thank you. Thank you. You're a real star. I'm Terry, by the way."

"The third musketeer." Terry raised a dark red eyebrow at this. "Lily's three friends. Jules, Mara, and you."

"Oh."

"I'm Sean. I'm . . . I'm seeing Lily."

"Hi, Sean." She held out her hand and smiled. He seemed much nicer than any of Lily's others. Terry supposed he'd be for the chop soon enough, but she couldn't help hoping he and Lily would last for a bit so he could deliver on his promise to take Paul to Charlton.

JULES SAT on one of the stools at the juice-bar set, alone for a moment amid the noise and laughter. She'd done well, she thought. No one there had any idea of just how miserable she was. It wouldn't have been fair to Lily to droop through the evening. And she could wait to talk to her friends about her problem; tomorrow or the day after would be soon enough.

But she couldn't help thinking about it herself. Of the cold, bleak, workaday sperm bank. Of her instinctive refusal of its services. And of where she could go from there. Of course, there was always the Internet, but she didn't like the sound of that. Yes, she'd have a picture of the donor, but as Lily had said, who could guarantee that the website was telling the truth? Besides, how was she supposed to conceive? Inseminate herself? Or get one of her friends to help with a piece of kitchen equipment? Jules didn't know whether to laugh or scream at the mental pictures that idea conjured up. It was definitely the very, very last resort. No, Mara was right. She was going to have to look for a donor. And one who would be prepared to give his sperm without wanting anything in return. Except perhaps for a bit of simple sex. Jules wouldn't say no to that.

It had been a long time since she'd been to bed with anyone and she did miss making love. But she wasn't interested in becoming a nuclear family, a mother-father couple. Or in the power games and risk of further abuse that went with all that. Regardless of what Terry might say, Jules was determined to do this on her own.

She started to make a mental checklist of her requirements. She needed a man who was interested in someone else and thus unlikely to fall for her. A man who would be prepared to do her a favor but who was not on the lookout for a relationship. And who wouldn't expect to have contact with the child. She'd have to be clear about that from the start. This baby was to be hers.

The donor would need to be a proven breeder. Preferably, she would like someone who was reasonably good-looking. If she was going to go to bed with a man, she might as well find him attractive. Besides, one of the how-to-get-pregnant books she had read years ago had said orgasm was supposed to aid conception. And there was little chance of that if the man was a Quasimodo. Plus, she'd like there to be a better than even chance that her baby would be pretty or handsome. There was no harm in trying to get it right. . . .

She gazed across the room to where half-drunken producer Charlie was trying to persuade Lily to write another series of the show. No, not him. Too single. Too tough. Her eyes carried on skipping over the male guests, trying to imagine one of them as her donor. It was difficult. There was a problem with every one of them. Too annoying. Too ugly. Too hard. She attempted to fantasize about a couple of the marginal ones but got stuck at the point where she asked them for their sperm. Then, her eyes lit on Sean.

Sean. Was he a possibility? She conjured up fantasy images of him naked. She could definitely go to bed with him. But what about Lily? Would she mind? After all, she only wanted a bit of Sean for herself. And it wasn't as if Jules intended to steal him. All she needed was a few milligrams of sperm. With luck and a friendly ovulation test, no more than one or two nights. Well, she could only ask.

But first, the most important question. Jules walked over to Sean, who was propping up the reception desk, listening to Lily finish her conversation with Charlie.

"Hi."

"Hi."

Jules thought about how to bring up the subject of children. Mentally, she tried out various hopelessly clumsy opening gambits and then had an inspiration. "Have you met the girls?" she asked, pointing at Moo and Tilly, happily playing on the gym equipment.

"Yes." Keen to recover lost ground, Sean cast about for something that would keep the conversation going. "They're very cute," he managed.

"Aren't they. Do you have any kids?"

"Yes. I did. I mean, I do."

"That's nice." Jules smiled. This was looking better and better.

thirteen

It was four in the morning. Sean woke to find himself alone in bed. "Lily?" he asked softly. He looked around her bedroom. It was all about self-indulgence. Rich velvet; warm, age-polished wood; deep, thick carpet. The bed itself had been Lily's greatest extravagance. She had slept on one like it in the Four Seasons Hotel in Los Angeles and had immediately bought one for herself, mattress, Daz-white linens, duvet, and all. Sean loved that about her, that ability to decide what she wanted and go for it. Just like she had with him.

LILY HAD had trouble sleeping ever since she'd first had the kids. Something to do with the acquired habit of waking in the night. When alone, she'd just read for a while or watch TV and eventually drift back to sleep. With Sean there, she had got up and was in her study, in the middle of the latest Martin Amis.

Sean stood in the doorway, watching her curled up in the deep armchair by the fireplace, her feet tucked underneath her, needing to keep them warm despite the sticky summer night. He smiled at the sight of her.

"I missed you." Sean's deep voice echoed through the late-night room.

Lily jumped. "I didn't see you there."

"Sorry." Sean walked over to kneel in front of Lily. "You weren't in bed."

"I couldn't sleep."

"You should've woken me."

"Why would I do that?"

"So I could keep you company."

"I'm not that cruel."

"I'd have liked it. We could've talked."

"You were asleep. And I wanted to read."

"I was worried about you."

"No need. I often wake in the night. It's nothing." Lily struggled not to snap. If she wanted to get up in the middle of the night in her own house and read, was she not to be allowed to do so without people worrying about her?

"But things are different now. You've got me."

"That I have." Sean's behavior, his possessiveness, was sounding a loud warning bell. He was starting to want more than she was prepared to give. It might be time to cut him loose.

"Come on, come back to bed." Sean leaned forward and put his hand on her knee. "I can think of something to send you to sleep." He pulled her close to him and kissed her.

Lily thought about having it out with him then and there and decided against it. Their next date would be soon enough. And she might as well enjoy what was on offer now.

"TWENTY MINUTES late. I could set my watch by you. That is, apart from the times I expect you to be late. Then, of course, you're early." Sean got up to give Lily a kiss.

"Keep 'em guessing, that's what I always say." Lily sat down. She'd heard Terry say the same thing about her often enough—why did it irritate her when it came from him?

Craxos, the newly opened upmarket Greek restaurant Sean had chosen, hoping it would please Lily, was already buzzing and it was barely eight o'clock. Located in trendy Belsize Village, just down the hill from Hampstead, it had bright, low-voltage lighting, minimal decor, and echoing wood floors.

Lily looked over at Sean. God, he was sexy. She didn't want to finish with him. Until the other night, everything had been working out fine. He hadn't shown any of the usual symptoms. No desire to know what she did on the nights she wasn't seeing him. No attempts to move his CD collection into her house. No yearning for romantic weekends together. But when he'd appeared saying he was worried about her, it felt as if he were beginning to get involved. If he was like the others, he'd want to change the rules. And she'd have to say good-bye.

Unless it was just her paranoia. Maybe she'd had so many bad experiences she saw commitment-philes everywhere. Maybe he was happy with what she had to give, maybe he didn't want more. Deciding then and there to try to ignore her worries, Lily smiled at him across the table, "I'm ravenous. Lunch in that pub isn't fit to eat."

An hour and a half later, Lily was sipping the remains of her red wine, enjoying an after-dinner cigarette. She was looking forward to a night in bed with Sean when she was horrified to hear him ask to move in with her.

"What?"

"I'd ask you to live in my place, but somehow I don't think you'd want to move to King's Cross." Sean reached out to hold Lily's hand, his expression earnest, his eyes intent. "Lily, I want to be with you. To live with you." He held his breath, waiting for her answer.

"Sean . . ." Lily pulled her hand away from his.

"You're everything I want."

"And that is?"

"What?"

"You said I'm everything you want. I just need to hear what that is."

"You want a list?"

"Please."

"Well." Sean paused to collect his thoughts. This had seemed so easy when he'd rehearsed it in front of his bathroom mirror. "Sex, of course." That shouldn't be a problem. He knew Lily liked sex.

"Okay. Go on."

"Companionship. Friends. Mutual support. You know, helping each other with, um, with problems and . . . and that." Sean was losing confidence by the word. "Er, children, perhaps. And . . . and love, I suppose."

Even though she'd feared that something like this might be coming, Lily was still disappointed. Another failure. And so soon. Not even a couple of months. "Sean. Remember when we first met? We talked about no commitment? Just two or three nights a week?" Lily's voice was soft as she tried to let him down gently.

"Um, yes. Sure I do. But I don't see—"

"I asked you if that would be enough and you said yes."

"But things have changed since then."

"No. They haven't. Not for me."

"But it's good with us."

"Yes, it was."

Sean didn't hear the end in Lily's "was." "Well then? Come on, Lily, we could be happy. I know we could. You just need to let go of this idea of yours that all you want is sex. There's so much more I can give you . . ."

Lily sighed. He hadn't heard a word she'd said.

". . . and you're not too old to have another kid. You've got years and years. My plumber's wife was forty-five when she had her latest."

She'd tried the kind way. And as usual it hadn't worked. She was going to have to be strong. And blunt. Time for the speech. "Sean, I've got two grown children. I don't want any more. I'm happy being single. I don't need help with my tax return or my insurance. The outside of my house needs a lick of paint, but I can hire someone to do that. I can change my own lightbulbs, mow my own lawn, take out my own rubbish. I don't need companionship. I've got my girlfriends for that. As for love, in my world, it's just another word for possession. I'm sorry. I did tell you. I wanted sex. Without strings. No commitment. And you agreed."

"But that was then. I didn't know I was going to fall for you."

Lily knew from long experience that once it had reached this point, there was nothing she could say to make things any easier. Best to get away, leave him alone. She picked up her bag from the floor and stood up. "I'm sorry. It was good with you. And I promise I'm flattered. But you don't want me. Truly, you don't." She leaned over the table and kissed him on the cheek. "Good-bye, Sean. Good luck."

LILY WOKE up in the middle of the night. Her feet were cold again. It was the height of the summer, the nights were nearly as warm as the days, but that made no difference. Her feet were always cold. The rest of her could be boiling hot, she could be lying on top of her bed naked, desperate to catch any breeze that came through the open window, and still her feet would be icy. Unless she had a man to warm them on. It was virtually the only thing she missed about having one sleep through the night with her. Almost without exception, they seemed to generate heat. Like huge living, breathing, self-refilling hot-water bottles. Sean had been particularly warm. And had never once complained about her putting her feet on him.

Men were so unrealistic. No woman she knew was up for the full monty anymore. Jules, for instance. She'd be happy with Sean's sperm. Or Terry. She was only looking for a friend for Paul and perhaps a bit of help with the bureaucracy of life. No one wanted that love-marriage/horse-carriage stuff. Why couldn't men accept that? Why couldn't Sean accept it? Lily put her feet one by one behind her knees in an attempt to warm them up. Damn him. They were freezing.

fourteen

"I dumped him."

"You didn't!" Terry exclaimed.

"Lily. I had plans." Jules was horrified.

"Shit. What am I going to say to Paul?"

Lily and Mara and Jules and Terry were sitting around Mara's old kitchen table, the fragrant remains of a vast Indian meal in pots and pans and dishes on the cracked counter behind them. From the living room drifted the sounds of Tilly and Moo playing a game on their new PlayStation.

This time, it was Mara's turn to provide the location and the food for Sunday lunch. It had come as a welcome distraction from her worries over what to do about the Moores and their threats. She'd been in the kitchen, roasting spices, chopping herbs, and slicing vegetables since dawn.

Mara knew that while she didn't have an expensively decorated, handsome house like Lily or Jules or a quirkily furnished and blessedly waterproof flat like Terry, she could cook better than any of them. Lily could manage only roast lamb, Jules had been known to have her lunch catered, and Terry's idea of good food veered wildly, from bacon sandwiches to tofu and salads without dressing, depending on the state of her feelings about her weight. And her willpower. The others looked forward to going to Mara's—it was better than a restaurant. Water might come in the roof, but no one cared, the food was wonderful: sag paneer, bhindi bhaji, aloo gobi, channa dal. No one even missed the meat.

"Hey, hey, what's all this? You guys only met him once."

"Once was enough. I wanted ... I was going to ask ...," Jules stammered. What had seemed so simple a few days ago now felt shockingly bold.

"What?" Lily asked, puzzled. It wasn't like Jules to be worried about telling them anything.

"It doesn't matter now."

"Come on. What were you going to ask?"

"Nothing."

"Don't you hate it when people do that? Say it's nothing when you know it's got to be something. Just makes me all the more curious," Lily said, grinning at Jules.

"Yeah. Come on, Jules. Inquiring minds want to know," Terry said.

"Whatever it is, it can't be that bad," Mara's quiet voice chimed in.

Jules looked around at the three interested faces. "Oh, okay. If you all insist. I thought Sean could, you know, solve my problems. . . ." She ground to a tense, quaking halt, unsure how to continue. Her friends stared at her blankly. "All right. All right. I wanted his sperm."

"His sperm?" Lily laughed.

Jules relaxed back in her chair. She should have known Lily would react like that. "He was a perfect donor. He has children, he's proved to be fertile, he's interested in you so he wouldn't fall for me, and you aren't in love with him and so wouldn't be jealous. Besides, you're my friend, so you would want to help. Perfect."

"Until you dumped him," Terry said, her disappointment obvious.

"Hold on. Why are you so upset? You're not interested in sex or sperm."

"Paul talked to him. He liked him. He even mentioned Finn to him."

"And? I mean, it's nice and everything. . . ."

"Sean was going to take him to a football game. He's been looking forward to it. I was hoping—" Terry stopped. It all seemed so stupid when she tried to explain it. Of course Sean wasn't the answer to all her prayers.

"Hoping what?" Lily coaxed.

"Oh, that you'd stay together long enough for him to maybe have a bit of influence over Paul. You know, talk to him about man stuff. Silly, huh?"

"No. He can still do that. Ask him. He's a good person. He just wanted too much of me."

"I can't. Not now. He'll think I'm making a move on him. He's bound to, isn't he?"

"She's right, you know," said Mara, trying not to sound shocked. Even though she'd known Lily, Jules, and Terry since she was sixteen, they could still come up with ideas that surprised her. She was yet to recover from Jules's revelation about using Sean as a donor.

"Yes. He's a man. It doesn't matter how good he is, he'll see it that way," said Jules. "Just as he would with me if I were to ask him to donate his sperm now."

"So that's it." Terry gave a hollow, theatrical moan and slumped dramatically, her head in her hands. "Fucked."

"Me too."

Lily was silent, lost in thought. Listening to her friends' complaints, she'd had a revolutionary idea.

It would give them all what they needed. Lily her two or three safe, uncommitted nights a week with a man she enjoyed, Jules the healthy, happy, handsome sperm she desired, Terry a thoughtful, warm father figure for Paul. And maybe even Mara would join in. It was four years since Jake died and time she learned that there were other men in the world. Sean would be a good, unthreatening place to start. She could spend time with him without worrying about him demanding sex—he'd be getting enough of that from Lily—and so get used to male companionship again. And ease herself back into the idea of dating. Maybe he could even help her with her house. It was way past time she got the roof fixed. She wouldn't think of allowing Lily or Jules to pay for the repairs—they'd offered often enough—but if she got to know Sean, maybe she'd let him do the work for free? He was a builder, after all. Just what she needed.

Together, they could be his perfect woman. What was it he'd wanted? Sex: Okay, Terry and Mara would have none of that, but Lily certainly would, and Jules might also if she fancied getting pregnant the traditional way. Friends: Well, they were definitely friends, and if they did this, Sean would, in a way, become a part of their group. Even though he wouldn't know what was going on. Mutual support: No one needed a bit of mutual support more than Mara and Terry. Children: Well, he'd be giving Jules one and he'd be inheriting Paul and perhaps Moo and Tilly. Love: True, maybe none of the four would love him, but they were an affectionate, caring bunch. Who needed love? Anyway, four out of five wasn't bad. Not bad at all. Better than he'd get in one lone woman.

Lily looked around at her friends and grinned. This could work. Sure, it was shocking to begin with, but the more she thought about it, the more it seemed the ideal way out of all of their problems. Four friends. One man. Sean.

"Okay. Okay. I think I've come up with the answer," Lily declared, taking a deep breath. "We share him."

"What did you say?" Jules couldn't believe her ears.

"How about we share him? You know, each take the bit we want."

Silence. Three shocked faces stared at Lily.

"The bit we want?" Terry finally asked, her voice shaky.

"Sure. None of us is in the market for the whole package. We've got other things in our lives—other people, kids, jobs, whatever. So why don't we agree to share? That way, we all get what we need without having to put up with all the things we don't want."

"You're mad, you are," Terry said.

Mara shook her head, then laughed. This must be one of Lily's jokes.

"Completely crazy," Jules agreed. "Besides, he would never agree to it."

"He'd never know. Think about it. It's a great idea. We all need a man, right?"

"I don't," Mara said.

"But you do. Maybe not need, but wouldn't it be nice? Someone to take you out? Pay you a bit of attention once in a while? Maybe even help with the roof?"

"I couldn't—"

"Think of it like this. Sean wants a woman who can be lots of things to him. Who can give him companionship and children and friendship and support and sex." Lily decided not to mention the love. No need to scare her friends off. "But he also wants me. And I can't give him all that. But we can. All of us together. He needs us."

"That's it. Call the men in the white coats. My best friend is insane."

"No I'm not. I'm the sanest I've ever been. Hell, I'm a genius. Don't you see? If we do this, everyone gets what they want. Everyone wins. Terry, listen.

You said it yourself. If you ask him to help with Paul, he'll think you're coming on to him. You too, Jules. But if he's with all of us, he'll be too busy to
think. Too happy."

"Lily, this is not for me." Mara sounded deeply troubled. "Jake wouldn't
have approved."

"Sweetie, I know how much you loved Jake. I know how much you miss
him. But it's been four years. Be practical. Sean's a builder, he can help you
with the house, be a friend for the kids, a friend for you. You don't have to love
him. You don't have to go to bed with him. Give it a try. I know you're lonely."

"I'm not."

"Mara . . ."

"I'm not. I've got my girls, my memories. Anyway, this is wrong. It's . . .
it's just wrong."

"Why is it wrong? Okay, people haven't done it before, but that's no reason to dismiss it out of hand. You can't hold back progress. And who's to say
this isn't the way of the future? Helping each other, giving everyone what
they want, forgetting jealousy. We'll be pioneers, setting a new standard in
human relationships."

"Pioneers, Lily? As a child I always did dream of being an intrepid
explorer." Jules loved the idea. It would give her what she wanted and, ultimately, she couldn't see the difference between this and what she had
already intended. Apart from the labeling. Lily was suggesting a more formal
arrangement than she had planned, but the end result would be the same.

"Setting off into the unknown, risking all on a new venture. I suppose it
does sound exciting." Terry's doubts were unspoken but definitely there.
She couldn't help but be concerned about Sean—how was he going to feel
about being shared, like some birthday cake?—but she was also reluctant to
turn down her friend. She had to do something about Paul. And where else
was she going to find a role model for him without her having to get
involved?

"I couldn't, I'm sorry, I just couldn't." Mara was on the verge of tears.
The mere idea of spending time with any man other than her beloved Jake
made her deeply miserable. "You . . . you don't know me at all if you think
I'd join in." Mara's head slumped down, her shoulders shaking with sobs.

Terry reached out to put her arm around Mara. Lily got up and went to
kneel next to her.

"Babe, I'm sorry. I'm stupid. It was just an idea. Take no notice."

"But how could you believe I'd do that?"

"I got carried away. Typical me. Convinced I'd had a genius notion and getting so enthusiastic I didn't think it through. Of course I don't think you'd be interested," Lily said, doing her best to comfort her upset friend.

"None of us do." Jules leaned over the table to squeeze Mara's hand.

"Come on, love. No harm done. It's just Lils, off on one of her mad jaunts. Take no notice of her." Terry looked over at Lily and very deliberately winked.

"Quite right. Ignore her." Jules smiled and gave Lily a quick thumbs-up sign.

Mara looked up. "You . . . you aren't going to do it?"

"Let's forget all that, talk about something else," Jules said, hoping to change the subject. "You will never believe who called me on Friday after-noon, wanting me to arrange a dinner party for fifty for the same night. . . ."

fifteen

Lily grabbed the handle of the corkscrew and yanked backward. The cork flew out. She poured two glasses of ice-cold Chardonnay, handed one to Jules, who was perched on the side of the desk, and took the other herself.

"You're in."

Jules nodded. "I'm in. Mara was so upset yesterday I didn't want to say anything, but I definitely want to . . . um . . . share Sean." Jules hadn't even had to think about the idea. Sperm was what she wanted and sperm she was going to get.

"Share Sean. I like the sound of that. It's almost poetic."

"You haven't changed your mind?"

"Hell, no. I was expecting you." Lily grinned as the doorbell rang. "And there's our other sharer."

She padded away down the corridor and in a couple of minutes was back with Terry. She handed her a glass of wine and said, "You look terrible. Been up all night trying to decide what to do?"

"Waiting for Paul, more like. You won't believe this. He was out until four in the morning. Four. And when I asked him where he'd been he said it was none of my business, didn't he? Well, actually he said, 'Get a fucking life.' I can't cope with this much longer."

"So you need Sean?"

"I need something. And Sean's the best idea anyone's come up with yet." Sitting at home the night before, waiting for her son, having called the police and the hospitals, Terry had struggled to decide what to do about Lily's idea. Part of her was very, very tempted, but at the same time something inside her shied away from the notion of them all parceling Sean out as if he were a wheel of cheese. But when Paul finally returned, swore at her, and slammed himself into his room, she had managed to force her concerns to the back of her mind. Paul and her need to rescue her disintegrating relationship with him had to come first. "Count me in."

"Okay. That's three of us."

"I think we have to forget Mara, at least for now," Jules said.

"Maybe I shouldn't have mentioned it to her. Only I'd hoped she'd see reason for once."

"Poor Mara. What are we going to do? Her obsession with Jake is ruining her life," Terry said.

"We could tell her the truth," Lily suggested.

"No way!"

"It would destroy her."

"Then, what? I don't think we should just give up. Sean would be the perfect first step for her."

"Possibly we can persuade her later? When she's more used to the idea?" Jules suggested.

"Yeah. When she's seen how well it's working for us."

"If it does." Terry was going ahead, but she wasn't stupid. She could see potential problems everywhere.

"Pessimist. It'll work fine. I guarantee it."

"Hmm. We'll hold you to that."

"What I don't see is how you're going to set it up. What are you going to say to Sean? He wants you, not us," Jules asked.

"Well, for a start, I'm not going to tell him we've talked about this. It needs to seem spontaneous, almost as if he's thought of it himself. But first, I've got to get myself back with him. . . ."

Two

sixteen

Sean closed the job specs he had been working on, leaned back in his chair, and moved his head from side to side in an attempt to loosen his board-stiff neck muscles. It felt as if he'd been in front of the computer screen for days.

He got up, strolled across his plain, functional office, and looked out of the window at the quiet, shadowy yard beneath. At the trucks parked for the night, at the shrouded piles of lumber, sand, and gravel ready to go out the following day. At the neon chip shops and off licenses and darkened funeral homes of Askew Road.

Everyone had gone. Everyone but him. He had been spending more and more time at the office since the split with Lily; at least when he was concentrating on work, he wasn't thinking of her and alternately regretting losing her then railing against her selfishness. He glanced at his watch, saw that it was almost ten o'clock. He supposed he should leave too. If he was going to feel sorry for himself, he'd prefer to do it lying on a sofa with a beer in his hand.

Sean picked up the keys to the office, grabbed his cigarettes from next to the computer and his leather jacket from the back of his chair, and was about to walk out when his mobile phone rang. He looked at the display to see who was calling but the number had been withheld. He pressed the button and held the phone to his ear. "Sean Grainger."

"Sean. It's Lily."

Sean tensed at the familiar voice. God, she sounded good. For a second, he was elated. She'd called him. She must want him back. Then, anger took over. The anger that had been accumulating ever since he'd sat in that hideous trendy restaurant and listened to her dismiss his feelings. The anger he'd nurtured through many a long night, the anger that he still used as a painkiller. "Fuck you," he said, and disconnected her.

Almost immediately, the mobile rang again. Sean didn't answer and the rings went on and on, seemingly forever, until finally his voice mail picked up. He slumped in relief. He'd resisted the temptation to talk to her. Then, the phone rang again. And again. He reached for it, was about to answer, then, in a last, desperate attempt to stop himself, threw it across the room. The ringing stopped. Silence. Another moment and he'd not have been able to stand it. He'd have forgotten his hurt, rolled over onto his back with his paws in the air, and answered. He thought for a second about calling her back and dismissed the idea, horrified by his lack of pride. All this would pass. Soon, he'd be fine. Lily would be a memory. The ending would fade and he'd be able to think back on the good parts and smile. . . .

Lily was curled up in her den, her phone in her hand. She'd expected Sean to be angry, hurt, even furious, but she'd never thought he'd refuse to talk to her. In her ear, his voice-mail announcement ended and she hung up without saying anything. What would be the point? She needed to speak to him, talk him around, not leave an easy-to-ignore message. Maybe it was time to quit, make another attempt in the morning, but Lily hated admitting defeat. She decided on one more try and hit redial.

Hoping that Lily had now given up, Sean walked across his office to pick up the tiny mobile lying in the corner of the room. Halfway there, it started to ring again. He raced over, grabbed the phone, and pressed the button to answer.

"Please don't hang up," Lily said quickly.

"I should."

"Don't. Please. Just let's talk for a moment."

Sean struggled with himself. And lost. "What do you want, Lily?"

"I want to say I'm sorry."

"What for?"

"For the restaurant. I was too hard, too tough."

"Yes. You were."

"But that's cos I didn't want to say good-bye."

"It was your choice, not mine."

"I know. But I've missed you."

Some warmth crept into Sean's voice. "Have you?"

"Yes. A lot. More than I imagined. Much more."

"That's . . . good to hear."

"And?"

"And what?"

"And how about you?"

"What about me?"

"Sean! You're driving me crazy. Have you missed me? Have you missed me?"

"Of course I've fucking missed you, idiot."

Lily laughed. "Maybe I deserved that."

"Maybe you did."

"So are we pals again?"

"Yes. Pals."

"Then can we see each other?"

"Maybe."

"Only maybe?"

"Lily, are you asking to be my friend? Or my lover?"

"Lover, please."

Sean couldn't help smiling at her words. There was no one like Lily for saying what she meant. "And as we're being so honest with each other, just so I get it right, are we talking about two or three nights a week here? No commitment, just fun?"

"Yes."

"Lily, I don't think—"

"Come on. We got on well, didn't we? Had fun? Enjoyed each other? Missed it when we stopped? Let's forget all that stuff in the restaurant, pretend we never went there, that none of that was said. You'll be happy, I know you will. I'll make you happy. So happy you won't have the energy to want more."

"That happy, huh?"

"Yup."

Sean was sorely tempted. He was desperate for Lily, but if he said yes, he was setting himself up to be hurt again. Because he was sure to want more from her than two or three nights. On the other hand, he'd been miserable without her. And why should he deny himself something he wanted just because he knew he wasn't going to get as much of it as he'd like? Did that make any sense? Don't eat one chocolate because you can't have the whole box?

At least this time he was walking into things with his eyes open. No illusions. No lingering dreams of domestic bliss. After that speech in the Greek restaurant—which he would never forget, even though Lily suggested he should—he knew exactly where he stood with her. And if two nights were all he could have, well, two nights with Lily would be better than seven with anyone else.

"Doing anything tomorrow night?" Sean asked.

THE SOHO bar was heaving with people, the Thursday night, it's-almost-the-weekend crowd spilling out onto the pavement outside, clutching their ice-frosted glasses, looking for some relief from the summer heat. Terry and Jules, the former in a frothy white Victorian petticoat and low-cut violet chemise, the latter in crisp, beautifully ironed Ralph Lauren shorts and polo shirt, sat at a tiny wrought-iron table, watching Lily inch her way through the multitudes.

"How do you think it went?"

"Hard to tell. She doesn't look very happy, does she?"

Lily's mouth was a thin line, her eyes blank, her shoulders drooping beneath her green linen shift. She reached the table, sat down on the chair her friends had saved for her, poured herself a glass from the bottle of wine the others had bought, and sighed. Terry was dying to ask her what had happened with Sean the previous night but held off. If it had been a disaster, maybe Lils wouldn't want to talk about it yet.

Jules had no such scruples. "So? What happened? Don't tell me you messed it up?"

Lily looked up from her drink. Slowly, a tear formed in her left eye, fell from her lashes, and ran down her cheek.

"Oh, Lils!" Terry reached for her friend's hand. "I'm sorry."

"What did you do? I thought it was all arranged?"

Lily looked at both women, the muscles in her jaw working, then burst out laughing, unable to contain herself any longer. "Gotcha."

"Lily, how could you?"

"God, I was sure you were really down."

"But you cried. I saw you."

"Yeah, me too. You cow. How'd you do that?"

"An old soap-opera actress taught me. You just tighten your throat for a minute, like you're continually swallowing, and you cry. Clever, eh?" Lily lit a cigarette and took a drag. "It was great. We're back together, two, three nights, just like it was before. Hell, it's hot out."

"Eight o' clock and it feels warmer than it did at noon." Terry pressed her cold glass against her forehead in an effort to cool down. She found it hard to deal with the summer. Her skin didn't like the sun and she tended to wilt anytime it was over seventy degrees.

"It's being in the city. Someone told me the concrete soaks up the heat all day, then lets it out again once the sun goes down."

"You mean it's nice and cool out there in the country? That's it, I'm off. I hate this. Look at all those people, happily sweating away. Ugh."

"Only a few weeks to go, babe, and it'll be September and back to the rain."

"Can't come soon enough for me."

Jules was unable to restrain herself any longer. "Can we forget about Terry's endless problems with the weather? And talk about what matters?"

"Being hot matters to me."

"It's the summer. It's only a little warm spell."

"And I suppose I'm exaggerating, is that it?"

"Don't be so touchy. I just meant I want to talk about Sean and the plan."

"Okay, girls, enough. Come on, you love each other really. And we do need to decide how it'll all work."

"Yeah, Lils. I know." Terry took another gulp of her drink. There was no point in her getting annoyed, she was aware of that, but the way Jules seemed to stay perpetually cool when she was too hot to think about anything other than a cold shower drove her crazy.

"Now, I think we should leave it a couple of weeks, give him a chance to relax into things again. Then, we'll persuade him that three is better than one."

"How'll we set it up? Who'll get first choice of nights?"

"Me. Then you guys get to pick. There shouldn't be a problem. He's got time enough for all of us. And he doesn't tire easily, so no need to worry about overuse."

"Good. Because I have plans," said Jules.

"You're not going to fuck him, are you?"

"Of course. So long as Lily doesn't mind."

"No problem with me. He's got more than enough to go round."

"You only wanted sperm. That's what you said."

"Why not harvest it the natural way?"

"Organic sperm," Lily said, laughing. "The best."

"And enjoy myself at the same time. I will enjoy myself, won't I?"

"You will, babe. You will."

"Yummy. I can't wait."

"But . . . won't you be jealous, Lils?"

"Of Jules? I don't think so. I mean, I only want Sean for my nights, so why would I mind him being with Jules on some of the others? Anyway, I love the idea of us all sharing him. It sort of feels like an extension of us being friends. We share lots of other stuff, like secrets and problems and things, so why not him?"

"Are you sure?"

"You're not thinking of joining in the sex?"

"God, no. I just . . . I don't know. So much can go wrong. It could get very messy."

"Well, it won't. We all know what we want. And we're all going to get it. Don't worry so much."

"I can't help it, can I? You know me, I'm a worrier. Always have been."

"Well, there's nothing to worry about here. A perfect solution to a tricky problem."

Terry looked at her best friend, still concerned that this could end in tears but aware that there was no point in continuing to argue. Lily had always been the kind of person who barreled ahead without a lot of thought; once she'd decided that something was a good idea, that was it. She'd go on with it, regardless of what people said to dissuade her.

"And Mara?" asked Jules.

"What about her?"

"When do we tell her we're going ahead with it?"

"She's not stupid, you know. She'll have figured out we were interested."

"Has anyone heard from her?"

"Not me."

"Me either."

"See. She knows."

"And she's not talking to us."

"She's just shocked. You know Mara."

" 'Jake wouldn't have approved.' "

"Balls to that. When it's all set up, we'll call her, get together. Let's just give her some time. She'll come round."

seventeen

Mara knelt over the bowl, scrubbing brush poised, breathing in the acrid smell of strong bleach. No question, cleaning other people's toilets was the worst of her job. Generally, she liked the families she worked for. They were good payers. They passed on things they didn't need anymore—dishes, clothes for the girls, food past its sell-by date—and they never left any hideous messes for her to clear up. But she still hated the lavatories.

She held her breath and dove in, trying to distract herself with thoughts of Jake and a picnic they'd had in the Chiswick House park the first year they were together, when she was pregnant with Moo. It was one of her favorite memories. But even that failed to block out what she was doing. She gritted her teeth and scrubbed.

Ten minutes later, she was out of the bathroom and on to the master bedroom, tossing the clean linen high over the bed, letting it fall through the air to settle on the mattress. She tucked the sheet in, hurried to put the duvet into its cover, and waved the duster over the dressing table. She was going to have to skimp on her work today if she was going to make it to Chelsea to drop in on Jules.

She needed a lawyer to find out how good a case the Moores had against her. And to do that, she needed money. She'd made a few calls, found out that even the cheapest solicitor would charge her hundreds of pounds to give her his advice and write a response to the Moores' letter. Hundreds of pounds she didn't have.

But she was going to have to find it somewhere. Jules and Lily would help her if she asked, but she hated the idea of borrowing from them. Partly, it was a hangover from her childhood. Growing up, she'd had the idea of operating with only cash dinned into her for so long that her family's taboo against being in debt had taken very strong root. But mostly it was that she felt her relationship with her friends would never be the same if they were to lend—or even give—her money. She and Lily—or she and Jules—wouldn't be equals anymore, no matter what they might claim to the contrary. And she valued their friendship far too highly to put it at risk.

Perhaps she could have forced aside her scruples in this case, given what was at stake. Only, her friends had offered to help in the past and she'd always refused. They knew how she felt about borrowing. They'd want to know what was so important that she would change the habits of a lifetime. And she didn't want to tell them about the Moores' letter. Because then she would have to explain about her past.

She couldn't bear to do that. It wasn't that she thought Jules and Terry and Lily would stop being her friends if they knew she'd been a call girl. Of course they wouldn't. They loved her, and that wouldn't change. But she hated the idea of them knowing. She needed her friendship with them to remain untarnished by her past, needed them to see her as she wanted to be seen: Mara, friend, wife, and mother. Not Mara, ex-prostitute. Of course, if they ever asked her if she had been on the game, she'd have to tell them. But she prayed they never would.

Besides, Terry never had any cash to spare and Lily had been talking only a few weeks ago about how buying and doing up the house had nearly bankrupted her. She couldn't have asked them even if she had nothing to hide.

But she could approach Jules. Not for a straight loan, but for a job. Jules was always talking about how hard it was to find responsible temporary staff to help with her parties—surely she'd hire her friend. Amy could look after the girls; even the Moores would approve of her as a baby-sitter. And if Mara worked three or four evenings a week, it should take her only a month to accumulate what she needed.

Or she could ask Jules to advance her the money. Just for a short time while she worked to pay off the debt. There would be no need to mention the true reason for such need—she could tell Jules that she had gotten behind with the bills. Which was true. She was always behind. And as she was going to work to redeem the loan immediately, Jules should accept the excuse that it wouldn't be true borrowing. Mara couldn't deceive herself—a debt was always a debt—but she was getting desperate. Who knew how long she had before the Moores made their next move?

"SHE WON'T be long now. Are you sure you don't want anything to drink?"

"No. Thank you. I'm fine." Mara tried to smile at Claire, Jules's efficient, smartly dressed assistant. But it felt more like a grimace. If only she didn't feel so out of place. Her secondhand T-shirt and threadbare cotton skirt didn't exactly complement Jules's plush outer office with its pale wood furniture and huge vases of lilies. She shoved her hands under her thighs to stop herself fidgeting and hoped her nerves didn't show. She'd only been waiting for ten minutes or so but it felt like hours. She knew she should have made an appointment, but she hadn't wanted to explain her visit over the phone and so had decided to drop in. Of course, Jules was busy, having a meeting. Claire had offered to interrupt her, but Mara insisted on waiting; as she'd come to ask a favor, she didn't think she should be getting in the way of her friend's business.

The door to the inner office opened. A tall, blond man in his forties carrying a stuffed leather briefcase and a couple of box files came out, Jules behind him.

"Claire, Dennis is coming back next week for another couple of hours." Jules walked up to her assistant's desk. "Tuesday, you said, Dennis? How are we in the afternoon?"

"I'll have to postpone Lady Ruffington. . . ."

"Do it. Maybe I can see her for a drink later. We've got to sort out the books or I will be in trouble."

Dennis leaned down and kissed Jules on the cheek. " 'Bye, love. See you then."

" 'Bye." Jules turned to go back into her office and saw Mara perched on an overstuffed ottoman in a corner of the room.

"Mara! How wonderful! Claire, why didn't you tell me?" Jules rushed over to Mara and put her arms around her. "You haven't been waiting long? Come on, into the inner sanctum. Claire, can we have some coffee?" And, chattering away, Jules led Mara into her office.

The small, discreet, laptop computer sitting on her desk was the only concession to contemporary living in the room. Jules had always hated the sterility of modern offices and the moment she could afford her own had been determined to make it an appealing place to be. After all, if she was going to spend the greater part of her life there, she might as well enjoy it. And gray machines, cream walls, and neutral carpet made her feel depressed. The moment she could manage it, she had bought some stylish patterned sofas, some fashionable 1920s lamps, and a beautiful Victorian keyhole desk. Added to the original nineteenth-century flower drawings on the walls, and the collection of antique wine bottles and corkscrews scattered around the shelves, and she had a handsome, relaxing room in which she loved spending time. And which impressed her clients. The general consensus seemed to be that a woman who chose to work in an office like that must be good at creating the kind of party mood desired.

Jules waved Mara to one of the sofas, sat down opposite her, and fell back against the cushions. "Gosh, what a relief. It's a wonder I can still see straight after all that."

"I'm sorry. You're tired. I shouldn't have come."

"Silly. Of course you should. You're a very welcome sight. I needed cheering up. And here you are. The answer to a businesswoman's prayer."

"A bad day?"

"The worst. Three hours going over the books. And he's coming back next week. Sometimes I wonder what possessed me to start a company."

"Jules! You love it."

"Not today, I don't. A meeting with Dennis isn't pleasure, it's duty." The mention of pleasure made Jules think of Sean. And wonder if she should mention Lily's scheme to Mara. But her friend had been so upset by the idea when it was first mooted. . . . "He's a pest with all his forward projections and revenue flows and tax assessments."

"Everything's okay, isn't it?"

"Oh, yes." Well, it would be when Sean had agreed to give her what she wanted.

"Dunne Parties is doing well?"

"We're doing ama . . ." Jules ground to halt, realizing that it would be unkind of her to go on about the astounding year she was having and the stunning number of bookings that had already been made for the next one when Mara was so broke she was forced to wear clothes Jules wouldn't have used as rags. She chose her next words carefully. "So-so," she said. "We'll be all right."

Mara was shocked. Jules's company had always seemed to be thriving. "But I thought . . . A few years ago, when Jake was . . . You were doing so well."

"It's a hard business. Lots of competition." All of which was true. If not really relevant.

"Jules. I'm sorry." Mara had little knowledge of businesses and books and accountants. But she could read between the lines and it was clear her hope of help had vanished. She couldn't ask Jules now, not when she was in trouble herself. "Will you be all right?"

"Course I will. These things never last forever. Trends change." Jules looked at Mara's concerned face and wished she hadn't started with this. But she couldn't change things now, she'd have to explain why she'd minimized her success in the first place. And that would be more hurtful than her boasting about her bumper year could ever have been.

"Can I do anything to help?"

"That's so sweet of you, but I'll be fine." Jules was mortified. Here was Mara offering to help her when she was raking in the profits and Mara was the one who needed assistance and would never accept it. Guilt-stricken, she moved to change the subject. "Now. Tell me what you're doing in Chelsea. I thought you never left Chiswick during the day."

Mara tried to think of something she might have had to do in Chelsea. That Jules would believe. And that wasn't a lie. "I . . . I . . . Moo needs a new pair of shoes. And . . . and they've got a sale on . . . in King's Road. . . ."

eighteen

"Well, I suppose someone's got to start this. Here goes." Terry, remarkable in a glam-rock-era shimmering gold shirt over pale, patched jeans, looked across at Sean, standing about twenty feet away just outside the French windows, keeping an eye on the meat on the barbecue.

Despite Lily's efforts with a hose, her garden had that dried and dusty, end-of-summer look. A month of heat had left the last remaining flowers drooping, the trees brown at the edges, and the lawn more like a yellowing, grassless cricket pitch than the smooth expanse of green it had been at the beginning of the season. It was Saturday and Lily had organized a small party. Ostensibly just for fun, to take advantage of the last warm days of the year. But really to give Terry and Jules a chance to advance the plan.

"Would you like me to go first?" Jules said, smiling at an ill-at-ease Terry.

"Will you? I'm no good at this. Look at me, I can't stop shaking." Terry held out a far from steady left hand. "You'd think I'd been on the ale."

"Ale? You? I'd adore to see that. Don't worry. I'll start." Jules drew herself up, pasted her society smile on her face, and strolled across the garden, winking at Lily as she passed her.

The smoke from grilling sausages and burgers hovered over the barbecue. Eyes watering, Sean leaned in with his tongs and started flipping.

"Could you do with some help?" Jules sounded unhurried, calm, as if this were nothing more than a toss-away conversation, unimportant and meaningless. When underneath she was a desperate, seething mass of apprehension and fear, terrified by the thought that this might all go wrong. That she might not get her sperm.

Sean swung around. "No. I mean, thanks, it's almost done."

"Good. So we can get to know each other a little better. I'm delighted you and Lily are seeing each other again." No need to explain why. At least, not yet.

"Me too."

"You look like such a nice couple. Gosh, listen to me. I sound like my mother. But you know what I mean."

Sean grinned. He was beginning to see past the facts of her background and the oh-so-confident manner and relax. Maybe it was the casual shorts and T-shirt she was wearing. "Thanks. Is there a Mr. Jules?"

Jules laughed. "That's a funny way to put it. No. No Mr. Jules."

"You don't sound too sad about that."

What a great opening. "I'm not. Only . . ." Come into my parlor said the spider to the fly.

"Only what?"

This was too easy. "Oh, nothing. I just need to find a man to help me with a little problem."

FOUR HOURS later, the barbecue was ashes, the guests had all gone, and Lily and Sean were in Lily's outsize bath, Lily lying back against Sean's chest, between his legs, his arms around her.

"I saw you talking to Terry."

"She's a great girl."

"That she is. My best friend."

"She told me all about her problems with her son."

"Paul. He's a nightmare."

"Sounds like it."

"Yeah, I think she needs some help there. Did you get to talk to Jules too?"

"Yes."

"And?"

"She's not what I thought. You know, her being upper class and all that.

She's very open, isn't she? She was . . . she told me stuff. . . ." Sean's voice petered out.

"The sperm search?"

Sean was pleased that Lily couldn't see the blush that spread over his face. "Yes."

"Hmm. Were you embarrassed?"

"A little, maybe. It seemed an odd thing to be telling a stranger."

"I suppose they both think they can talk to you cos you're with me. A friend by extension."

"Maybe."

"So did you offer to help?"

"What, me? Me? I never thought . . . I . . ."

Lily turned around to face Sean, ignoring the water sloshing over the side of the bath and onto the mottled gray marble floor, and swam up his body until her face was level with his. "Just an idea." She kissed him, hard on the lips. "Now, to more important matters . . ."

LILY SAT back in bed, coffee in hand, Sunday papers spread out in front of her, watching her lover as he took his toothbrush and shaving stuff out of a small, leather holdall and walked into the bathroom. She smiled. It had been a great night. Sean was getting better and better at knowing what she wanted before she even asked. Part of her was tempted to ask him to stay for the day. The idea of them lazing around together, reading the papers, going out for lunch, then back to bed in the afternoon was enticing. She almost opened her mouth to suggest it, but stopped herself in time. No. Fun though it might seem now, it would only encourage him. And he'd been so good since they'd got back together. Besides, she had other things to talk to him about.

"I wouldn't mind, you know," Lily said as he reappeared, face smooth, teeth gleaming.

"Wouldn't mind what?" Sean sat down next to her and reached out to touch her lips. God, even first thing in the morning she looked sexy. "You're not ready for more?"

Lily turned her head into his hand and licked the center of his palm. "You helping out my friends. You know, giving Terry a bit of assistance with Paul and Jules some sperm."

Sean laughed. "I suppose I asked for it, going out with a comedienne." He leaned over, kissed her on the lips, then got up. "So, Wednesday, then?"

"I'm serious."

"Lily . . ."

"I am. You could be the answer to their not-so-maidenly prayers. They need a man. And you've got time. And the equipment."

"Lily, I like your friends—"

"And they like you."

"That's nice, but—"

"More important, they need you."

"No. They need someone. Not me."

"But you'd be perfect."

"I wouldn't. I couldn't."

"Course you could. Paul already likes you, and we know there's no problem spermwise."

"I'm not a one-man solution to all their problems."

"Why not? You wanted more of me than I could give, maybe they can fill a few of those holes?"

"So they're to stand in for you, is that it? What the hell do you think I'm about? It's you I wanted, not some committee."

"I know. I put that badly. I'm sorry." Stupid, stupid. She'd gone far too close to the truth there. She pushed covers and papers aside, got up, and walked over to Sean, who was slamming razor and toothbrush and yesterday's shirt into his bag. She touched his arm, turned him around to face her. "It's just that I can't help worrying about them. They're my friends. They've helped me through the worst bits of my life. I want to do something for them, you know, help them too. But I shouldn't expect you to feel the same way. I'm sorry."

Sean looked down at Lily and smiled. "I'd like to help, of course I would, they're your friends, I like them, only . . ."

"Don't worry. It's not your responsibility. Forget we talked about it. Okay?" Lily reached up and smoothed Sean's hair away from his eyes. "Okay?"

"Is it important to you?"

"Yes. Yes, it is."

"Okay. Then I'll think about it. All right?"

"Of course it's all right. Thank you."

"I'm not promising anything."

"I know. Whatever you decide is fine." That had been a close thing. She was going to have to be more careful. Lily put her right arm around Sean and let her left hand trickle down his chest and grasp the front of his jeans. Better send him away happy.

LILY HEARD the front door close behind Sean and reached for the phone.

"Terry?"

"How'd it go?"

"I almost fucked up, big time. Went way too far, told him you two could give him what I couldn't."

"Shit, Lils. Did he go ballistic?"

"He wasn't happy."

"What did you do?"

"Talked him round. Told him how important helping you was to me but that of course he couldn't be expected to feel the same. He said he'll think about it, but who knows what he'll decide? If I had to bet, I'd go for yes, but it's close."

"God, I wish I still prayed. When we first talked about this, I had major doubts, did you know? But now that you tell me it might not happen, it's becoming the thing I want most in the world. Isn't that weird?"

"No. It's human nature. How's Paul?"

"Holed up in his room. Not even a grunt when I tried to talk to him. It's getting worse. How the hell am I going to wait till Wednesday?"

"As patiently as you can."

"Patient? Me?"

"Yes, you. I'd better call Jules, give her the news. Love you."

"Love you too."

SEAN WAS outside his church hall in Putney, watching as four of his workmen detached the ornate, cast-iron Edwardian guttering from the building and handed it down to be packed away, stored, and put back in place after the renovations were complete. All around him was a wilderness of thistle and nettle, of waist-high grass and overgrown yew. It was a strange property, stuck as it was in the middle of streets and streets of turn-of-the-century town houses, but it was an impressive building in a very good area and he had been lucky to get to it before anyone else. He had already sold three of the five lofts it would make before he had even started retiling the roof or thinking about doing the plumbing.

It had been a long wait, but finally all the necessary planning permits had come through. This was the first day they'd been able to work. Normally, it was Sean's favorite moment, breaking ground on a new project, imagining how the place would look once it was finished, but today he was finding it hard to concentrate on what was going on. He couldn't stop thinking about Lily and what she had asked him to do for her friends. And whether or not he should agree.

God knew, he had sympathy with someone wanting a child. Maybe he should donate his sperm to Jules. He liked her; he'd found her a tad intimidating to start with, but it was hard to be afraid of someone who was so needy. Would his giving a helping or two of sperm hurt anyone? Maybe Mark and Ben might be upset to discover that they had a new brother or sister, but they were just as likely to be delighted. That's if he ever saw them again. No one else he knew would care. And going ahead with it would make Jules very, very happy.

From Sean's own point of view, though a new baby wouldn't, couldn't make up for the loss of Mark and Ben, the idea of having another child was tempting. He wasn't worried about Jules's insistence that she intended to raise the baby alone, as he couldn't believe she meant it. She was only saying it because she thought that was the way to persuade a potential donor to give his sperm. That most men would refuse her if they thought they were expected to take responsibility and be real fathers. As far as he knew, it was something sperm banks guaranteed, complete anonymity. But he wasn't most men. And once Jules realized that at least one potential donor would be more than keen to be involved, he was sure she'd want the father of her baby to be around.

And how about Terry? A bright, independent woman having trouble with a teenage boy. Well, he could help there also. He'd got on well with Paul at Lily's wrap party, and had liked Terry the moment he'd set eyes on her. Why shouldn't he act as a surrogate father for the kid? What harm could it do? They both supported Charlton, that was a starting point, and they could go from there. Yes, Paul wasn't his and could never, ever be so, but if he could fill even a tiny bit of the gigantic, gaping hole Mark and Ben had left . . .

Okay, the whole thing seemed a bit odd. But then Lily herself was a bit odd. And she definitely wanted her friends helped. She would be pleased with Sean for having done so, but did he want to get that involved with people he hardly knew? It was a huge commitment, fathering a child. Even if Jules was serious about not needing contact afterward, he was not about to donate his sperm and then just disappear. And what if Paul became attached to him? Then it wouldn't be a matter of only a few trips to see Charlton, would it? He'd have to be around for ages. Paul was what, fifteen? It could be years and years and years. That or end up hurting the boy and destroying any effect he might have had . . .

"Hey! Hey! Boss?" A hand touched his arm. "Boss?"

Sean turned away from the contemplation of a pile of rust-reddened chains, old tires, and rotten wood and focused on his foreman on the job. "Sorry, Joe. Dreaming. What is it?"

TERRY STOOD on the corner of the street, in the shadow of an enormous horse chestnut, early conkers scattered on the ground under her feet, and stared past the small triangle of garden, down the hill. Where the hell was Jules? It was almost nine o'clock; Terry had been waiting for at least twenty minutes and there was no sign of her. The two were supposed to arrive at eight forty-five. Lily would be going crazy.

"Here I am." Jules's voice came from behind Terry. "Sorry. Traffic was a complete nightmare." Jules kissed her friend on the cheek.

"I was beginning to think you weren't coming."

"I'm here now." She nodded toward Lily's house. "Anything happening?"

"Not really."

"How do you think it's going to go?"

"No idea. If I were him, I'd refuse."

"Why?"

"It's a hell of a lot to ask."

"No it isn't. Besides, it's what he wants. Lily said so."

"Maybe."

"Please, please, please may he say yes."

"Well, Lils has been softening him up. They were in the bedroom for ages."

"You little voyeur."

"I am not. Anyway, you can't see anything from here."

"Then you did look?"

Terry ignored this. "Ready?"

"Do you want to go over your story?"

"God, no. I've been practicing all evening."

"Then it's time you started crying. Come on, tighten up your throat. . . ."

Inside the house, Lily and Sean were lying on a sofa in the drawing room, the remains of a picnic of charcuterie and cheese and salad spread out on the large, square, bird's-eye-maple coffee table. They had finished one bottle of South African red and were making inroads into another when the doorbell rang.

"Don't go." Sean was comfortable, he was happy, and he didn't want to lose any of his time with Lily.

"Probably a delivery for next door. I'll get rid of them. I won't be a sec."

Lily left the room. Sean could hear the sound of her footsteps on the parquet floor in the hall, then muffled voices, and then multiple steps coming back. Damn.

"It's Jules and Terry." Lily came in first, followed by the girls. As she went toward Sean, she mouthed the words, "Sorry. Terry's upset," at him.

Sean glanced at Terry and saw tears glistening on her cheeks and shadows of run mascara around her eyes. His irritation faded. He was a complete sucker for tears. "Maybe I should go?" he asked.

"Course not. You can help. We're going to cheer Terry up a bit. Come on girls, a drink, a drink." Lily disappeared to get glasses. Jules sat opposite Sean on another sofa. Terry hunkered down on a warm-brown-and-red Persian rug in front of the fireplace. She tightened her throat and squeezed out another tear or two.

Jules reached over and touched her shoulder. "It'll be all right. He'll change, grow up, honestly he will."

"Yeah, but when? People've been saying that for ages, but nothing seems to happen, does it?"

"It's teenage behavior. They all do it, I'm told," Jules said, delivering her lines.

"They all stay out till four in the morning? Then abuse their mothers when they come home?"

"That's what he did?" Sean asked.

"Yes." Terry turned to him. "I mean, a bit of rebellion is normal, I know that, but does he have to be so hurtful? I thought I'd be pleased he was speaking to me again, but now I think I liked it better when he was all silent and grumpy."

At that, Lily reappeared, glasses in hand. "Talking has to be better," she said. "Doesn't it?"

"I don't know." Terry buried her head in her hands. "I just don't know what to do," she said between sobs.

Sean looked at her bent head, her shaking shoulders. She was crying out for his help and he felt selfish for having ever thought of withholding it. Then he glanced at Jules, who was kneeling next to Terry, her arm around her, trying to comfort her. Suddenly, he wondered why he had agonized so much over Lily's suggestion that he assist her friends. The answer was simple. Both women needed him and it would be cruel to refuse either of them. He could help and therefore he should. Tentatively, certain that neither of them knew that he and Lily had discussed his getting involved, he said, "Perhaps . . . perhaps I can help."

Terry looked up, her eyes highlighted by the growing black smudges around them. "Wh . . . what do you mean? Help? How?"

"I just wondered, maybe contact with an older man might be what he needs? Because his father's dead? And he and I seemed to get on well at Lily's party, and then there's the Charlton thing and . . ." Sean ran out of steam. God, maybe Lily had gotten this wrong. Maybe Terry would see this as him butting in on something that was none of his business.

"Sean. That's really nice of you. I never thought . . . But he did seem to get on with you, didn't he? Yeah, he even mentioned Finn to you."

"I think it's a great idea," Lily chimed in.

"It could be exactly what he needs," Jules said, adding her support.

"A father figure."

"A role model."

"Well, I'd try. I'm not sure how much of a role model I can be. Aren't they supposed to be footballers or movie stars or something?"

"Who cares? You'd be an older man, taking an interest in him. Giving him a little of what he never had from his father. Like I said, it's a great idea," Lily added.

"I don't know. It's a lot to ask. Sean hardly knows me or Paul." The group had agreed that one of the two women had to seem a bit reluctant when Sean offered his help—presuming he did—in case he smelled a large and long-dead rat. Terry had volunteered.

"No. But I like him. And I like kids. It'd be fun."

"Maybe."

"Look, it's up to you. The offer's there. Okay?"

"Thank you. Really, I'm very grateful. Can I just think about it for a day or two?"

"Of course. Of course you can."

"Now, I'm taking you upstairs to get you cleaned up. You look like a panda. Come on." Lily led Terry out, leaving Jules on her own with Sean. The non-waterproof mascara had been a stroke of genius.

"You know, you're a very nice man," Jules said as she poured herself some wine and then refilled Sean's glass.

"Because I offered to help Terry?"

"He's a difficult boy."

"Not really. He reminds me of me. An only child missing his dead father. And I was just as spiky."

"I find it hard to imagine you being as rude to your mother as Paul is to Terry." Jules smiled.

"Maybe not. But I was a handful, believe me. And I bet my mum would've been delighted if someone had come along and taken me off her hands every now and then."

"She must be proud of you now."

"She died twelve years ago. Poor Mum."

"Sean, I'm sorry. . . ."

"It was just after I'd finished my first building. She was very proud of that. Her son, his own boss. She insisted on having my headed notepaper framed and hung by her bed. 'Sean Grainger Construction.' Bless her."

Sean raised his glass as if in tribute, took one sip, and then stared into the remaining wine, half smiling at the memory. Then he made an effort to shake off the past. Lily and Terry would be back any minute and he'd prefer to offer his services to Jules in private. But how to bring the subject up without embarrassing them both? "How're things with you?" he asked.

"Okay. Summer party season's almost over. There's a bit of a lull at the moment."

"Right." Well, that hadn't helped. He was going to have to be more obvious. He cast around for some tactful way to introduce the subject.

"And of course, if I mention the words 'sperm donor' to anyone, they run a mile."

"That's . . . that's terrible." He sighed with relief. Jules had done his work for him.

"To be honest with you, I'm finding it hard to think of anyone else to ask. It's not exactly an everyday kind of request."

"No, I suppose not." Sean took a deep breath. "Um . . . would you consider me?" he asked.

And Jules's body pushed him back against the sofa cushions, her two hands holding his head while she deposited quick kisses on his cheeks, his lips, his forehead.

"Hey! Hey," he spluttered, "hold on."

Jules climbed off him. "I'm sorry. I'm afraid I got a bit carried away."

"Do I take it that's a yes?" Sean asked, smiling.

Jules beamed back. "Oh, yes. Yes. Yes. Yes."

TERRY SAT in her cluttered kitchen, cup of ginger tea in hand, Minnie on lap, telephone waiting in front of her. It was two days since Sean had made her his offer and she was still trying to understand her feelings in all this. When she'd thought she couldn't have Sean's help, she was desperate for it; now it was on offer, she kept going over and over the possible pitfalls. What if Sean found out the girls had made a deal among themselves and manipulated him into sharing himself? What if Paul discovered that his mother had arranged for Sean to be his friend? What if on meeting Sean again Paul decided he didn't like him? What if Lily got jealous and called off the scheme? What if Sean again asked for commitment from Lily and was once more dispatched into the ether? What if he decided that he preferred Jules to Lily? What if he fancied Terry?

Okay, a number of these were unlikely, but that didn't stop Terry from worrying about them. And she was a talented worrier, capable of descending into a vortex of anxiety over the smallest thing. Deep down, she wanted to back out of the whole Sean deal, but Paul had either refused to talk at all or had shouted insults since the night he'd stayed out until four A.M., and she was close to the end of her tether. She had to do something—and Sean was her only option. She couldn't ignore her son's unhappiness because she had a few worries about taking up a solution to his problems. Quickly, before she could dither anymore, she reached out, picked up the phone, and dialed a number.

"Sean? It's Terry."

nineteen

"You look tired." Lily leaned against Mara's cracked counter and watched her friend scuttle about, making tea for the two of them.

"Do I? Oh. No, I'm fine." Mara had no intention of discussing the recent sleepless nights, the problems with Jake's parents, her need for money. The trouble was, that didn't leave her very much to talk about.

"Are you sure?"

"Yes, of course. Really."

"Okay. If you say so." Lily sounded doubtful.

To avoid any further questions, questions she wouldn't and couldn't answer, Mara tried to change the subject. "So where are you filming?"

"Nowhere. I was just passing."

Mara handed over a mug of strong-looking tea. "Lily, love, you don't just pass Chiswick."

"I might. If I was going to the airport."

"Yes, you might. But you aren't."

"Well, no. There is that."

"What is it? Problems?"

"No."

"You came all this way for a cup of tea?"

"Would you believe me if I said yes?"

"Of course I would."

"You're a saint. I'd be lying."

"I had a feeling you might be."

Lily laughed. "I came to tell you something."

"That you've decided to go ahead with your scheme."

"Hell, I told Terry you'd've worked it out. You're not still shocked?"

"I was, when you first mentioned the idea. But you can't keep up shock for weeks."

"You disapprove, though."

"Nooo." Mara smiled to hide her continuing dislike of the plan. No point in debating something if they'd decided. "Not really. It's fine. If you're all pleased, then that's good."

"Really?"

"Really. I want my friends to be happy." No need to mention that she hardly thought this was going to make them so.

"So have you thought again about joining in?" Lily looked around her, at the dilapidated house, at her proud friend who refused all offers of help and yet still somehow managed on so little to keep herself and her daughters going. Who deserved something better than being alone, struggling to make ends meet, dreaming about her dead husband. "You could do with someone—"

"No."

"Are you sure? It doesn't feel complete without you."

"I'm sure. Totally, totally sure. Jake would hate it."

"Sweetie, it doesn't matter what Jake would feel. He's dead."

"Not to me."

"It's been four years."

"That makes no difference. It's kind of you to think of me, but I don't want this. Truly, I don't."

"Okay. But I hate to see you missing out."

Mara couldn't help but smile. No one could ever accuse Lily of not trying. Or persevering. "Has it all started? How did you persuade him?"

"Jules has her first date with him tonight. . . ."

twenty

Rules had been around for over two hundred years. Inside, it looked more like a gentlemen's club than a restaurant. Well, what Sean imagined a gentlemen's club would look like. Personally, he'd never been in one. He didn't come from the right part of town for all that. But he liked the look of Rules: discreet lighting, old leather, heavy curtains, and very private tables. And it felt like the kind of place Jules would enjoy. She'd certainly seemed pleased with her dinner, eating her steak with every evidence of genuine delight.

But she was perhaps less pleased with her companion. Apart from all the business of ordering, Sean had been worse than uncommunicative. He hadn't said a word unless prompted. The question of his sperm and exactly how Jules was going to extract it was hindering his efforts at dialogue. Visions of syringes, turkey basters—or the more traditional method— were blocking out all attempts to concentrate on what was being said. He couldn't quite forget those kisses Jules had rained on him when he'd offered his sperm that night at Lily's. Had that been natural enthusiasm? Or was she expecting him to have sex with her?

It wasn't that Jules hadn't tried to get him to talk. So far, she'd touched on Lily, work, the weather, the traffic, the wine, and the food, all to little effect. Now she was attempting to discuss the merits of sea over ordinary salt.

"I believe chefs prefer sea salt, but I find it can be a little crunchy when scattered on food. How about you?" Jules was running out of ideas. She hadn't thought it would be this difficult. Why wouldn't he say anything?

"I'm sorry. I'm not much fun tonight, am I?"

"Well, no. Not much."

"It's only, you see, I can't stop thinking about the . . ." God, this was difficult.

"The what?"

"The . . . the insemination," Sean finally managed to get the word out. "About how you'll do it."

Jules heaved a massive sigh of relief. Was that all. Thank God, she'd thought he'd been having second, third, and even fourth thoughts. "Don't worry. It's very simple."

"I'm sure. Only . . . I sort of need to know what I'll be expected to do?"

"Nothing. Absolutely nothing. You see, sperm stays alive outside the body for three or four minutes. You just have to provide it. And I'll do the rest." Oh, he was embarrassed. It was so sweet. At first, Jules had seen sex with him as a nice added extra, but she was beginning to look forward to it for its own sake as well as for the expected result. She could almost wish she didn't conceive the first time so that they could do it again.

"No syringes?"

"No syringes. Leave all that to me."

"God, what a relief. I don't know why, but I had to know. I'm not normally all that imaginative, but I kept seeing snapshots of . . . of . . ."

"Forget it. Please. You're the donor. You only need to donate." Rather more than he knew, but time enough for that on the night. He might be mad keen for Lily, but he was a man and therefore eminently seducible. Jules had yet to hear of one who could resist a concerted effort at seduction. She leaned back in her chair, picked up her wine, and took a sip. Yes. He'd do. He would very definitely do.

"We have to get the timing right. I'm afraid I'll have to ask you to jump to whenever the ovulation test tells me I'm at my most fertile. There's a small window, twenty-four, forty-eight hours, when conception's most likely to happen. And I'll need you then."

"No warning, then?"

"I can give you a vague idea, but no. No real warning. Will that be all right?"

"Sure. It's fine. I'll try to be ready. Let's just hope there's no one desperate for my attention those days. Course, with my luck, I'll be supposed to meet with someone like Freddie 'I'm Paying' Hecht."

"A customer?"

"You could call him that."

"Bad?"

"You have no idea. He bought a loft off me last year. It was a reasonable price and well renovated, but he wanted more and more and more. Wouldn't speak to any of my staff. It always had to be me. And with the smallest complaints. A missing nail. A minimally loose floorboard. A tiny section of not-quite-perfect paint. In the end, he threatened to take me to court over an improperly aligned radiator."

"And did he?"

"No. I fixed the radiator. Moved it two millimeters. A nightmare."

"He sounds bad. But nowhere near as bad as Leticia Smallwood." When Jules said the name, she put on a doom-laden voice.

Sean laughed. "A difficult woman?"

"The absolute worst. Nothing is ever right. And she always knows best. I once organized a ball for her daughter. She was adamant, she wanted a tent made of pink silk and net. I tried to make her change her mind. This is England, after all. All I could see were yards and yards and yards of soggy material falling on the guests. But she was immovable. Of course it rained. And I somehow had to find a real tent and get it erected in four hours. Even then she blamed me for not managing to find a colored one in time. It just wasn't good enough for her perfect little daughter."

Sean laughed again. Jules wasn't stuck-up at all. In fact, she was lots of fun. At last he could see the connection between her and Lily, could understand what it was that made the two friends. For the first time since he'd agreed to help Jules, he began to think that he was going to enjoy spending time with her.

twenty-one

Terry walked into the latest coffee-shop addition to the High Street. She could remember when the first of the frosted-glass-logo and zinc-tabled cafés had opened a few years before; everyone had been so excited about tasting the cappuccinos and the lattes and the espressos. Real coffee at last. Now they had become as commonplace as rats: you were never farther than seventy-five feet from one wherever you found yourself in London.

She ordered a nonfat, decaf latte and sat herself on a tall stool in the window so she could see Sean coming. Her shoulders were tight with tension and she had that heavy, pre-headache feeling in her neck. She had hoped that, having made the decision to go ahead with the share scheme, she would have stopped worrying about it. But she hadn't. Maybe once it had all started, she would be able to relax more.

She looked over the road to see a metal-gray Saab reverse easily into a narrow parking space and Sean get out. She smiled. He could have been a bus driver.

As he crossed the road, Terry began to mumble mantralike phrases to herself. Please may this all work out. Please may it be the right thing to do. Her horoscope appeared to be favorable—for the last few days, there had been lots of talk about positive new starts in both the *Mail* and the *Mirror*—but she couldn't help crossing her fingers just in case. She saw a spill of sugar on the counter next to her and quickly tossed some over both her shoulders. Okay, it was supposed to be salt, but maybe it worked with sugar too.

"Hi."

"Oh. Hi."

Sean got himself a double espresso and sat down next to Terry. "You look terrified," he said.

"No. Not terrified."

"But nervous."

"A bit."

"Don't be." Sean reached over to squeeze Terry's hand for a moment. "I have a feeling this is all going to work out okay."

"Well, Peter Watson in the *Mail* insisted that this is a good time for me to try and solve long-standing problems."

"See. And Jonathan Cainer in the *Mirror* was convinced that I should get involved in something new.".

"You read your stars?"

"I know. I know. You should hear the girls in the office laugh at me."

"Why?"

"Astrology's for women."

"That's crap."

Sean grinned at Terry. "What are you?"

"Aquarius. You?"

"Virgo."

"Earth and air. Good combination."

"See. We're friends already." Sean took a gulp of his coffee. "God, that's hot. So what do we do? What do you want to tell Paul?"

"Only that you're a pal. If that's okay? Nothing about the arrangement and that. I mean, if he knows this is a setup to provide him with a father substitute, he'll go all stubborn and say no."

"Okay. I'm a friend. You've invited me back for . . . ?"

"Dinner?"

"Sounds good. I'm ravenous. We builders need feeding often."

"Bless. All that paper pushing must be exhausting." Terry smiled at Sean. He already felt like a friend. It wasn't just his reading his stars in the paper—although that was a wonderful discovery—it was his whole attitude. His lack of machoness. If there was such a word. Lils would know. He just didn't feel threatening. There was never a hint that he was about to make a move. No lingering glances, no flirtatious looks, no tension.

"It is. It is. So is there any need for him to know more than that?"

"No. You're a new friend I met at Lils's party at the same time he did. And maybe we ought not to mention you're with her? In case, you know, he figures it all out. He's very bright."

"Yeah. And I wouldn't talk to a fifteen-year-old," Sean looked at Terry, who nodded, "about my sex life, would I? Not likely, is it?"

"No. Anyway, this is about him finding a friend, isn't it? Helping him get over Finn." Terry thought for a moment, a slight frown shadowing her face. "Sean? If this works . . . well, you know, when he's happier, you won't . . . um . . ."

"I won't what?"

A long pause. Finally, Terry mumbled, "Disappear."

For a moment, Sean felt hurt. What did she think he was? A complete jerk? Then he reminded himself that she didn't have much reason to trust men. Lily had told him all about the vanishing Finn. "No way. I'll be round if he needs me. Okay?"

Terry nodded. "Yes. Course. Only it's asking a lot, I know, and you hardly know us and—"

"Now, don't start worrying again. This is going to be fine. Come on. I want that dinner you promised."

PAUL WAS lying on his bed, the room vibrating to heavy, beat-driven music, when Terry burst in, Minnie in her arms, and thrust the little dog at her son.

"Keep her with you, will you, love?"

Curiosity won out over rebellion and Paul's "Fuck off" died unsaid. "Why? Who's here?"

"A friend. No one. 'Bye, Min." Terry hustled out of the door, leaving Paul staring after her, clutching Minnie.

Half an hour later, she and Sean sat at the kitchen table, eating Terry's bean-heavy minestrone soup. She'd been reluctant to offer it to him; in her mind, she pictured the heaped plates of all-day breakfasts, the sausages and beans and eggs and fried bread that she presumed all builders ate, and was concerned that her simple soup would be found wanting. But there wasn't anything else; she had recently convinced herself that giving up meat and dairy products was the key to losing weight—she couldn't remember the last time she'd seen a fat vegan—and her fridge was full of fruit and vegetables and hummus. It turned out she'd had no need to worry; Sean had tucked in with all evidence of delight and no complaints about the lack of meat.

Terry, however, had barely picked at hers, too worried about where Paul was to think about food. "Where is he?"

"Relax. He's a teenager. His mum's having dinner with some man. He won't be able to resist coming to take a look." At that, there was the sound of a door slamming elsewhere in the flat and clumpy footsteps coming nearer and nearer. "See?"

The door to the kitchen opened. Paul stomped in.

"Hey," said Sean.

"Oh. It's you."

"Yeah. How're things?"

Paul shrugged.

"Have some dinner. Here, let me get you a bowl." Terry jumped up and headed for the stove.

"D'you see the team on TV the other night?"

A long pause before Paul answered sullenly, "Don't have a satellite."

"Then next time come watch at mine."

Silence. Terry leapt in to fill the gap. "I don't think that's a good idea. You don't want Paul bothering you when you're trying to watch TV." Terry might have been emotionally involved, but even she could see that if she didn't want Paul to do something, he would immediately find that something the most attractive option in the world. What had Lily said? It was human nature.

"I'm not a baby."

"He wouldn't bother me. Would you?"

"Here. Here's your soup." Terry put the brimming bowl down on the table. Paul stayed where he was, leaning against the dresser.

Sean finished his food. "It's very good," he said to Paul.

Again, the boy said nothing, before bursting out with, "You said you'd take me to the Valley."

"And I will. I promised, didn't I?"

"I didn't hear anything."

"Paul. It's only been a few weeks." Terry was embarrassed by her son. It was one thing to have him misbehave when there was just her around—after all, she was his mother and would love him regardless of what he said—but another to have to listen to him be rude to a kind man who was only trying to help.

"Who the fuck asked you?"

Terry stiffened. No matter how many times he was nasty to her, she still found it difficult to dismiss it as teenage rebellion. It hurt. It hurt a lot.

"Paul, I don't think . . ."

"I'll be back in a bit." Terry got to her feet and walked out before Sean started to defend her and so made Paul see him as her ally, not his.

"Can you really get tickets?"

Sean debated talking to the boy about the way he was treating his mother but decided not to. It was way too early. "Should be able to. It's a small ground and people are crazy for football right now, but I've got a few contacts."

"I'd be . . . I'd be . . ."

"Pleased? Grateful? Made up? Over the moon?"

"Yeah. All of them. It'd be like when I saw Eminem. Cool."

"Eminem, eh? Maybe you can explain something to me."

"Sure." Paul sat down opposite Sean, picked up the spoon that Terry had left there, and began to tuck into his food, showing every sign of being a starving fifteen-year-old who hadn't eaten anything in an hour or so.

"Rap."

"Hip-hop."

"That's what it's called nowadays?"

"Well, yeah. And no. It's kind of hard to explain."

"Go on. Try."

"They're sort of the same. Only rap's just the music and hip-hop's the whole thing. You know, dance and clubs and clothes and stuff."

"The whole subculture?"

"Yeah. I guess. Course, 'rap' is the word for old people who read news-papers."

"Like me?"

"Well . . . maybe."

Sean grinned. "Okay, being an old person who reads newspapers, what I want to know is, what is it about it? Why do you all like it so much?"

Paul smiled. At last. An adult who didn't say things like "Where's the melody?" or "That's not music," or "It's just talking." He took a deep breath and set out to preach the new gospel.

TERRY INCHED open the door to the kitchen, hoping to be able to listen to what was happening before she was noticed. Paul's portable CD player was pounding out a hip-hop track, so she was sure no one would hear her. She would have left them alone for longer, only she thought it might seem a touch odd to have deserted her dinner guest for such an extended period of time. Through the crack in the door, she could see Paul and Sean sitting at the table, opposite each other, eating fruit salad and ice cream straight from the bowl and the tub. Finally, the track ended and Paul reached out to turn the boom box off.

"Yeah. That helps. Thank you. I always got that it was your rock and roll but I never could see why you would like it. Apart from the fact that your parents didn't, of course." Sean grinned at Paul.

He grinned back. "But that doesn't hurt."

"No. I'm sure." Sean couldn't believe how nice Paul was. Anyone seeing him with his mother would think him a monster. But in fact he was a bright kid who thought hard about things and cared deeply. Maybe that was why he was being so difficult. The long lack of a father, followed by Finn's sudden arrival and immediate death, must have hit him hard. Sean hadn't been sure that Terry was right about the reasons for the kid's problems, but now, seeing how Paul had opened up when an older man showed a little interest in him, he was convinced.

No question, the two of them were getting on well. To begin with, Sean had played it safe and gotten Paul talking about stuff he knew about, but now he decided to try and risk a little more. "Okay, so you love music. You love football. What else? Home?"

Paul looked over at Sean. "Home? What do you mean, home?"

Oops. Too far too fast. Sean tried to recover his error. "Um, you know, the area round here. Stoke Newington. North London. It was just a question, okay? Nothing sinister."

Terry thought it was time she made her presence felt. "Hey! Hey! You're supposed to use bowls. Not eat from the dish."

Paul pulled back. His shoulders slumped over, his arms wrapped his stomach. His mother was here. He stood up and slammed out of the room without saying anything.

"God, I ought to have stayed out. I am so fucking stupid."

"Course you're not."

"You were getting on so well."

"And we'll continue to get on well."

"But I interrupted you. Now he's back in his room and there's no way we'll get him out and—"

"Relax, will you? This is just the opening round. I'll call him next week, talk to him about football, that kind of thing, you know? Then maybe I'll suggest we do something together in a couple of weeks. It'll be fine."

"It will?"

"It will. Give it time. I like him, he's a good kid under all those bristles." Sean smiled his reassurance at Terry. "Now, do you think I could finish that ice cream?"

twenty-two

"How're you doing, Tilly?"

"Finished, Mum."

"Me too. Can we use the PlayStation now?"

"Yes. But it's dinnertime in half an hour."

"Okay, Mum." Moo and Tilly left their completed homework on the kitchen table and disappeared through the door to the hallway. Standing at the stove, frying some onions and ginger in a pan, Mara smiled at the sound of their excited voices as they turned on the machine and decided what to play. She'd been reluctant to sanction the PlayStation, but she couldn't help getting pleasure from her girls' continuing excitement about it. And although she didn't like the source, she was happy that they had something new for once. And something that was their very own.

Mara added some cumin, some coriander, and a chopped potato or two as she looked through the kitchen window at the darkening sky. It had been mercifully dry for weeks, but she knew what was coming. With the autumn, there would be rain. And lots of it. The roof would get worse. And it would get cold.

She was going to have to go back to collecting wood. Last March, the central heating had gone. For the next month or so, still needing to heat the house but unable to afford expensive smokeless fuel, she had started walking in the nearby grounds of Chiswick House every day, collecting enough fallen branches to keep a fire burning while the girls were home. She'd hoped over the summer to be able to think of some way to raise the £1,200 she'd been told it was going to take to get the heating repaired. But she hadn't been able to. And now it was September and she could see no alternative to her daily trips to the wood.

Since her visit to see Jules at her office, Mara had tried to ignore her own problems. To tell herself that there was no way a judge would tear Moo and Tilly away from her because of her long-past life as a prostitute and a few drips of water coming through the roof. Deep down, of course, she knew she couldn't just let things slide forever, but while the weather held as the summer petered out into fall, she allowed herself to bury her head in the sand. And pretend things were all all right.

The doorbell rang. Mara glanced at the clock. It was five-thirty and all the girls' friends would be at home. It must be someone for her. She pulled the food off the burner and went to the door.

A tall, bespectacled man in a three-piece suit was waiting outside.

"Mrs. Moore?" he asked.

"What is it?" In Mara's experience, no one who called her Mrs. Moore boded well.

"John Ridgeman." Mara looked blank. "From Barton, Kirkwood, and Ridgeman?"

"I'm sorry. . . ."

"We represent Mr. and Mrs. Moore. Can I have a word with you?"

What did they want now? "It's not a very good time. My daughters—"

"It won't take long. If you don't mind?" And the man walked straight past Mara and into her living room. Leaving her no real option but to shut the door and follow him.

"Moo! Tilly! Upstairs, please. To your room."

"Mom, I was at the fourth level!"

"You can try again later. Now go on."

The girls got up and inched toward the stairs, their faces alive with curiosity about their mother's visitor. They couldn't remember any man coming to call on her, let alone one in a suit, carrying a briefcase.

"Girls. I said to your room. Quickly."

Moo and Tilly heard the serious note in Mara's voice. And disappeared upstairs.

"May I?" Ridgeman asked before dusting off one of Mara's dilapidated chairs and sitting down. Clearly, he didn't think his question needed an answer. "Actually, I'm glad to have seen the two Misses Moore. Their grandparents wanted me to check on their welfare."

"As you can see, they're fine," Mara said through gritted teeth. What a nerve. Check on their welfare indeed.

Ridgeman put his briefcase on his knee, opened it, and pulled out a sheaf of papers. "Now. To business. Mr. and Mrs. Moore are sure you won't want to go to court. It is always a long, messy, expensive business, and I gather you have very few resources. And the press are bound to get involved. Given your previous, er, occupation. So my clients have empowered me to offer you a deal."

Mara moved to sit opposite the lawyer. A deal. Well, if the Moores were suggesting it, it was bound to be to her detriment. But if they were willing to talk, surely they could sort this out. No need for courts or lawyers or summonses. Or press. "I'd be more than willing to talk to them, arrange for them to see more of the girls, perhaps. I am aware of how important grandparents are in a child's life and I know that Moo and Tilly enjoy seeing their Nan and Pops." Mara prepared herself to make a major concession. But it was worth it if it stopped them pursuing their claim for full custody. "I would even consider sharing them. You know, letting the Moores have them every other weekend. That sort of thing." Mara's voice drifted off into silence. The lawyer continued to rustle through his papers. Either he hadn't listened to a word she'd said or he was completely uninterested.

Finally, he looked up, a document in his hand. "Ah. Right. Now. Mr. and Mrs. Moore will go no further with their suit if you will voluntarily give them full custody of," the lawyer paused and flicked through the document he was holding, "ah, yes, Miranda and Matilda."

"They must be joking." That wasn't a deal. That was victory for them. Total and utter victory.

"Now, should you agree to do this, they will allow your daughters to visit you, unsupervised, once a week. And for one weekend in every four."

"But they're my children. Mine. Not theirs. They can't do this." Mara was dumbfounded. Couldn't the lawyer see that this was not right?

"They are concerned about letting you continue to see your daughters with no one else present, considering the moral issues involved, but feel their generosity is justified if it stops their granddaughters being dragged into court."

"Generosity! Moral issues!" Mara couldn't believe what she was hearing. The Moores seemed to think she should be grateful to them for letting her see her daughters once a week.

Ridgeman ignored her outburst and carried on, unmoved. "If, however, you refuse their offer, they will continue with their case and ensure that you are only allowed to see, ah, Miranda and Matilda under supervision for an afternoon every two months."

"They can't expect . . . You can't expect me to agree to this. It's horrible. I'm their mother."

"If you'd like to take a look at this?" Ridgeman handed Mara one of the documents he had taken out of his briefcase. "The place where you are to sign has been marked." He pointed to a yellow plastic clip placed on the side of the paper, toward the end of the sheaf. He reached into his inner pocket, pulled out an expensive-looking marbled fountain pen, unclipped it, and held it out to a stunned Mara.

"This is wrong. Wrong. Surely you can see that?"

"If you'd like to take a look at the contract?"

"How can you come to my house and try to get me to sign something like this?" Mara's shock was beginning to wear off.

"I have also been authorized to offer you a substantial sum of money." Ridgeman delved into his briefcase again and came up with a check for £25,000.

Mara lost her temper so very, very rarely that the world believed her to be the most placid of people. Few knew that underneath all that serenity and calmness, she could mix it with the best of them. It might be only once or twice a year, but when given real cause, she could and would erupt.

"You bastard. You want me to sell my children."

"Of course not."

"No? You want me to take money in return for their company."

"I wouldn't put it like that."

"How would you put it, exactly?"

"The money is a . . . contribution."

"Is it? A contribution. And who thought of that? You? Or the Moores? Because I'd call it blood money. For twenty-five thousand pounds, you want me to sign my daughters over to them. I thought that slavery had been abolished in this country. I thought buying and selling human beings was illegal. Clearly, I was wrong. You bastard. Get out of here." By now, Mara was standing over Ridgeman, her arms akimbo, her face flushed with rage.

"Mrs. Moore. Please. There is no need for this. Your parents-in-law just thought the check might help." Ridgeman made an attempt to calm things down.

"I hope for your sake you believe that. But I don't think you do. I think you're another sleazy lawyer raking in money off other people's misery."

The lawyer was beginning to look as if he'd been caught in some very high-powered headlights. He slithered out of his chair.

"I assure you, no one intended to upset you." He closed his briefcase, then picked it up. He put the contract and check on a small, junk-shop bamboo table. "In case you change your mind," he said, and walked away.

"You must be deaf. For the last time, I won't sell my children!" Mara ran after him and thrust the papers at him. He ignored them and they fluttered to the floor. "Go away!" Mara shouted as Ridgeman reached the door and opened it. "Get out!"

The door closed softly behind the lawyer.

"Who was that, Mum?"

"Why were you shouting?"

Mara looked around in a panic. The girls were hanging over the banisters, looking down into the living room. She'd forgotten about them in the heat of her anger. She forced herself to calm down. "Nothing. Just a . . . a salesman." She didn't want the girls to know about the Moores and their threatened lawsuit. So far, she'd managed to head off any questions about what had happened to their Nan and Pops by telling Moo and Tilly that they'd gone on a long holiday, but sooner or later the girls would find out something was wrong. And she wanted it to be later. Whatever happened, she didn't want Moo and Tilly hurt.

"What was he selling? You sounded really mad."

"Yeah. You told him to get out."

"Er . . . meat. Pork chops. And . . . and lamb."

"Ugh. Disgusting."

"What are those papers?"

"Just . . . leaflets. I'll throw them away." Mara rushed to pick up the

thick, detailed contract and the thin insult of the check. "I'm late with dinner, girls. You can use the PlayStation for an extra half hour."

"Yay!"

"Cool!"

The girls dashed to the console. Mara walked into the kitchen and ritu-
ally ripped both check and contract to shreds before slumping against the
counter. All the energy her rage had lent her had drained away. The Moores
were not going to give up. She had to find some money, get a lawyer of her
own. And stop them. Or she might lose the girls.

THE FOLLOWING afternoon, as Mara took Amy's weekly shopping into the old
lady's house, she was no closer to finding a solution to her problems. She
couldn't even decide where to start. She'd tried to reassure herself that if the
Moores thought they could get the girls, they'd have gone to court already,
but it didn't help. The glass-half-empty side of her kept insisting that of
course a judge would decide against a woman who'd been an expensive
prostitute, and for Dorothy and George with their churchgoing respectability and their power to feed and clothe and house the girls without needing
to grow their own food or collect wood from the local park to make a fire or
clean other people's homes. Even Mara's job might prejudice a judge
against her—she had no idea. And wouldn't unless she consulted a lawyer.

She walked down the dim hallway, into the old-fashioned, cream-and-
green kitchen. Amy hadn't changed anything since she'd moved there in
the 1940s. The sink was wide, shallow porcelain, the stove ivory enamel,
the floor cold flagstones. Mara set the shopping bags on the wax-cloth-
covered table and started to put things away.

"Mara? Mara! Is that you?" The old lady sounded terrified.

Mara rushed into the living room, horrified that she'd forgotten to say
anything when she'd come in. "I'm sorry, Amy. I don't know what I was
thinking. Of course it's me." Mara's voice was distorted by unshed tears.

"Are you all right, dear?"

"Yes . . . no . . ." Mara started to cry. The pressure had been building
since the lawyer's visit last night and she could hold it in no longer.

"Come here." Amy was in her usual armchair. Mara staggered over and
knelt at her feet. The old lady reached out and stroked her hair. Mara buried

her head in her neighbor's lap and continued to sob. "That's right. Get everything out."

Finally, Mara lifted her head. She swallowed and wiped her face with a tissue her friend handed her. "I'm okay."

The old lady snorted. "What is it, dear? Is there anything I can do to help?"

"I'm not sure anyone can. It's . . . it's Moo and Tilly's grandparents. They're trying to get the girls. If they win, they'll only let me see them once a week, if I'm lucky. Once a week. How can they do that? How can they want to steal all the joy in my life from me?" Mara sounded close to hysteria.

"You're Moo and Tilly's mother. They can't take them away from you, it wouldn't be right."

"They sent this lawyer." Mara looked up into her neighbor's kind, generous face and decided to tell her. She couldn't hold all this in any longer, she had to talk to someone, and Amy often felt more like mother than friend. Plus, she had always been tolerant of others' sins. "They found out about something I did before I met Jake. Something they think means I can't be a good mother. A proper mother."

"Rubbish. You're the best mother I've ever seen. Whatever it was you did, dear, it can't change that."

"I . . . I was . . . a call girl."

"Were you? Did you enjoy it?"

"You don't understand. I was a prostitute."

"Does that make you an unfit mother?"

"Amy! I sold myself to men for money."

"I know what a call girl is, dear."

"And you aren't shocked?"

"I went with U.S. servicemen for nylons and chocolate and cigarettes during the war. We all did. And I can't see why that's so different. Just money instead of things."

"Oh, Amy." Mara burst into tears again. "You're wonderful."

The old lady let Mara cry for a bit, then offered another tissue. "Dry your eyes, dear. Yes, that's it. Now, you need to be practical. You need a lawyer."

"I know. But it'll cost hundreds and hundreds of pounds."

"How much exactly?"

"About five hundred."

"Hmm. That is a lot. What about those friends of yours? Lily, is it, and the others?"

"They're all struggling themselves at the moment."

"And so you can't ask them."

"No. Besides, even if I could borrow the money from Jules or Lily, how would I ever pay it back? On what I earn?"

"No, I see. I do see. You need a fairy godmother, dear."

"And I'm all out of them." Mara saw the concern in her friend's face and forced a smile. "Don't you worry about this. I'll find a way out of it."

"I only wish I could do something to help."

"You have. You've listened to me, let me pour out all my woes. Not judged me like other people might have." She leaned over to kiss the old lady on her cheek. "Thank you."

"Anytime, dear."

Mara got to her feet. "I better finish putting away the shopping. The girls will be back from school soon. Don't you worry. Something will turn up."

twenty-three

Sean looked up at the dilapidated old factory. Hidden away off the A4 in Brentford, it had not been used for years. The downstairs windows were boarded up, the grounds were a mess of weeds and overgrown shrubs, and the gates had almost rusted away.

But it had definite possibilities. First of all, it was small. That and the fact that it hadn't been easy to find had stopped its being snapped up by one of the bigger companies. Second, he had worked with the same council before and knew a lot of the planning-applications people. And third, it was fabulous. Or it could be. Erected sometime between the wars, probably in the 1920s, although he couldn't be sure, it still had its original windows, was built of redbrick rather than the unattractive yellow London stock, and looked, from what he could see between the boards on the windows, to have some amazing iron beams and pillars supporting the floors. And it was all due to Terry that he'd found it.

He'd not been looking forward to spending the day with her. He loved his occasional Sundays wandering through London alone and wouldn't have chosen to take a companion, but Terry had persuaded him to let her come along. She'd wanted to spend some time with him to encourage Paul's belief in their pretense of being friends. And Sean had ended up enjoying it more than he could have imagined. They had crisscrossed the city, going from Battersea to Dalton, from Hackney to Hounslow, looking at the list of potential properties. The other places they'd seen had been completely unsuitable. Either too small or too large for his purposes, or just too dull to be likely to attract the kind of young, trendy, turned-on-to-industrial-architecture people who went for lofts. But Terry hadn't complained once. In fact, she'd been more eager than he had. When he'd wanted to ignore the last place on his list and go for a pizza instead, sure that Brentford was all postwar tower blocks, 1960s houses, and square, one-story warehouses, she'd insisted on their going to take a look.

"You're a star, you are, Terry."

"All part of the service."

"I mean it. I'd've given up. I had given up. And then this."

"Will it work?"

"Yeah. For definite. Have to see how much it costs, of course. But everything else is right. Look at it. It's fantastic."

"That it is."

"Thank God I had you with me."

"Even though you didn't want me to start with," Terry teased.

"That's not true. I did want you."

"Liar. When you told me what you were doing today, I know it was supposed to put me off. You should have heard your voice when I asked to come."

"I was a bit surprised. That's all." Sean looked worried. He hadn't meant to be nasty.

"Don't worry. I'm only teasing. And now that you know I'm interested and I won't want to stop for a drink every five minutes or complain that I'm bored all the time, will you let me come again?"

"Let you? I'll make you. If it means I can find something like this again." And Sean went back to staring at the factory longingly. "God, I can't believe it. It's perfect."

twenty-four

Sean and Paul both revved their go-carts, ready for the off. They were two in a group of six, all racing against each other. And Sean was feeling very insecure. He'd always imagined he was a good driver, able to handle anything, but Paul beat him hands-down. The kid was amazing. A natural. He could judge speeds and distances, the spaces between go-carts, like a pro. They'd had nine races so far and he'd won every one. Sean told himself that because Paul was so much smaller, younger, and more flexible, it made it easier for him to fit his body into the ground-hugging go-cart and allowed him to do things that the tall, solid Sean couldn't. But he knew he was only making excuses for himself. Paul was better at it.

It had been an odd three weeks. Fun and strange and fascinating all at the same time. Things with Lily were better than he had ever imagined; he had been very, very careful not to tread on her oversensitive toes, and the longer that went on, the more she loosened up with him. The previous weekend, she had even felt relaxed enough to suggest that they go away together to a pretty inn in the Cotswolds.

He'd had another dinner with Jules whilst waiting for the big day and had found himself liking her more and more now that he'd seen past the intimidating, glossy surface to the vulnerable, child-hungry woman underneath. He still found her desire to have a baby in this way eccentric, but he was flattered that she wanted his sperm and determined to be as good a father as possible.

And in Terry he felt he had found a real friend. It was not just the things that they had in common—a working-class Catholic background, the astrology thing, a mutual love of London—but also that he felt no need to pretend with her. She didn't care that he preferred beer to wine. That he would choose the *Mirror* over the *Times*. Or that his favorite meal was fish and chips followed by apple dumpling. With her, he didn't have to feign the sophistication that he felt he had to assume for many of his clients. And for Lily and Jules. He could relax.

Paul, though, had been and still was a challenge. Sean was making progress, but it was slow. He had called him a couple of times the first two weeks. To talk about Charlton and keep him up to speed on the search for tickets. Then he had suggested the go-carting trip. Paul had been cool on the surface, unwilling to admit to being excited by the idea. But he had said yes. And here they were. Sean looked over at him, intent in his go-cart at the far end of the row. Whatever the kid might say to his mother later, he was having a great time.

The owner of the go-cart track stepped up to the line, carrying a black-and-white-checkered flag. "Ready, steady," he shouted above the noise of the engines. Then he dropped the flag to the ground and shouted, "Go." They were off. And naturally Paul was first to the corner. . . .

twenty-five

"Amy! Where did you get this?" Mara stood in her shabby living room, a cardigan draped around her shoulders against the chill of the evening, and looked down at the wad of notes her friend had just handed her. She had hideous visions of the old lady robbing a bank in order to help her. Amy had no savings as far as Mara knew; there was only her weekly state pension, and she practiced the strictest economies to make ends meet.

"I sold Archie's clock. To a nice man from that antiques emporium in the High Street."

"His retirement clock? You can't do that."

"I already have."

"But he'd turn in his grave."

"He was cremated, dear."

"You know what I mean. He loved that clock. You told me."

"I was glad to have an excuse. It's been annoying me for years. All that chiming."

"But it was his. Your husband's." Mara shook her head and tried to give the money back. "I . . . I can't accept this."

Amy ignored the outstretched hand trying to hand her the cash. "Yes you can, dear. I've got lots of other things to remember Archie by. And it's not a loan, so none of your scruples about borrowing. It's a gift."

"Amy. It's too much. You must spend this on yourself, not give it to me."

"What would I buy for myself? I'm an old woman. I've got what I need. It's for you. And the girls."

"I don't know. . . ." Mara looked at the money, more cash in one place than she'd seen since her call-girl days. She knew she should refuse it, knew that Amy shouldn't be giving her all this, but she so wanted to say yes.

"No more arguments, dear. If I want to give you a present, I will. Put it away now and you can arrange to see a lawyer as soon as possible."

"Amy. I don't know what to say."

"Say nothing. Come on, put it in your purse." When Mara showed no signs of moving, Amy made her slow way across the room to the table beside the front door where Mara had left her black leather bag, a hand-me-down gift from one of her clients the previous Christmas. The old lady picked it up, brought it back, and opened it for Mara to put the notes inside. "There you are."

Mara was still flabbergasted by Amy's gift. "No one's ever, ever, ever done anything like this for me. How can I thank you?"

"No need. I was pleased to do it. But I do want to talk to you for a moment."

"Of course."

"Sit down, dear. I've been thinking about you and the girls. What you should do. The money will be enough for now, but there'll be other problems, other emergencies. Winter's coming, you know, and your heating's broken." Amy hesitated. "I don't know how to put this quite. . . ."

"Please. Anything you think might help."

"You can't manage all on your own, dear. You've done marvelously but it's too much to ask. You and the girls and this rickety house. I think . . . I think it's time you found another man."

"Anything but that."

"I know how much you loved Jake, but it's been four years, and the girls would love to have a father."

"No, no, no. No way," Mara screamed. And was ashamed of herself almost before the words left her mouth. Shouting like that at the woman who'd just done so much for her. "I'm so sorry, Amy, I didn't mean to yell at you. But you don't understand. I can never replace Jake. There isn't another man for me. He was ideal in every way."

The old lady took a deep breath. She knew Mara didn't want to hear what she was about to say, but she owed it to her to try. Even if she was bellowed at. Surreptitiously, she turned her hearing aid down a bit. There. "Are you sure about that, dear? When he was alive . . ."

"What awful words those are. 'When he was alive.' "

"Yes, dear. But you used to quarrel a lot. I recall you telling me that you locked him out of your bedroom on occasions. After he didn't come home all night."

"He never judged me. Loved me even though he knew what I was."

"I know. That was wonderful of him. But he also used to annoy you. Remember how you wished he'd let you drive the car?"

"I loved him. From the first moment. He was perfect."

"Mara, really. Nobody's perfect."

"I still dream about him. I wake up smiling from visions of him laughing at the TV or playing with the girls or leaning over in bed to kiss me . . . and then I look round and see his empty shelves in the wardrobe, the spaces where his hairbrush and pile of books used to be."

"I know you miss him."

"He's still with me. Every day. Whatever happens, I know he's looking down, proud of me, loving me. If I'm in doubt about anything, I think of what he'd've done. And I have my answer."

"Yes, dear. Very nice. All I'm saying is, it might be time to move on."

"I said I'd love Jake forever and I will. There's no question of anyone else. Not ever. No question."

twenty-six

"You haven't?"

"I have. A week on Sunday, four o'clock, Stamford Bridge."

"That's . . . that's . . ." Paul spluttered to a halt.

"Nice?"

"Brilliant. Cool." Paul let out a whoop, ran ahead of Sean down the quiet, Sunday-afternoon street, swung around a lamppost, and then ran back. "Really? Chelsea?"

"Yes, Chelsea." Sean had expected Paul to be pleased but hadn't been ready for him to go through the stratosphere. He watched the boy jump up and down with excitement. At times, he could look almost grown up; at others, he was still a little kid, unable to contain himself or his feelings.

Once back at his house, Paul raced up the stairs to the flat. "Mam, Mam," he shouted. Terry emerged from the living room. "I'm going to see Charlton," Paul said. "I'm going to see Charlton." He took the stairs to his room two at a time and disappeared inside with a final whoop.

Terry looked at Sean as he came through the door. "You must be a magician, you must. That's the first time he's spoken to me, unforced, in months." She went over to him and gave him a hug. "Thank you, thank you."

Sean smiled down at Terry. "Hey, hold on. If that's what happens with one sentence, what'll you do when you have a conversation?"

"I know, I know, it's way too soon. But he was smiling, wasn't he? I haven't seen him smile for, I don't know. It feels like forever."

Ten minutes later, the two were sitting at the kitchen table, Terry with chamomile tea, Sean with strong, dark coffee.

"How come you're so good with him? Paul, I mean. You sort of seem to know what'll make him happy."

"I was a difficult teenager myself. And I haven't forgotten what it was like."

"Do your kids know how lucky they are to have you as a dad?"

"I don't know." Sean tried to shrug the question away.

"How old are they?"

"Mark's nine. Ben's seven."

Terry could hear the hollow misery in Sean's voice when he mentioned his sons. "I'm sorry. I didn't want to . . . I mean—"

"Their mother ran away with them. I have no idea where they are."

"God. I'm sorry. Stupid me. I should have realized that there was a reason you didn't talk about them. I just didn't think."

"It's strange how you miss people. To begin with, it's all the time. Then time passes, you manage not to think about them for a minute here or there. Then maybe you can manage an hour. Two. Three, even. But they're still there. You're only blocking out the pain. It doesn't go away."

To Sean's amazement, he found himself telling Terry all about the boys, about Isobel and Steve. Describing his frantic searches, the desperate hunt for clues here and in Canada, the various hired detectives, his bitter disappointment when they came up with nothing. And his eventual decision to give up looking. "I had to stop. I couldn't deal with the hope anymore. Every week, I'd see the detective, I'd look forward to it, I'd think, This week, this week there'll be something. And there never was. And after eighteen months of that, after seventy-eight weeks of anticipation always being followed by misery, I gave up. And I know it was the sensible thing to do. But I still feel I've betrayed my boys." Sean leaned over to hide the tear he wiped away from his eye. He hadn't cried since he'd first learned Isobel had taken Mark and Ben; he wasn't about to start now.

Terry couldn't think of what to say. She might rant on about Paul but she couldn't bear the idea of losing him. She reached out across the cluttered table and touched Sean's hand. "I'm so sorry."

Normally, Sean couldn't bear talking to anyone about his boys. Somehow he felt that his keeping them to himself allowed him to maintain a last, slender hold on them. Over the months since Isobel had taken them, he'd learned how to answer people's questions so as to discourage any further interest. But some unexpected, irresistible impulse had driven him to spill his guts to Terry. He was glad he'd done so—though she'd said very little, he'd been able to sense how deeply she sympathized—but he hated the idea that she might discuss what he'd said with the others. "You won't mention all this to anyone, will you?"

"Not if you don't want me to."

"I don't. Lily and Jules wouldn't . . ." That was not the relationship he had with them. "I'd just rather you didn't. Is that okay?"

Terry couldn't help but be flattered that he had chosen to tell her, that he trusted her. People often did tell her their secrets—she didn't know why, she must look trustworthy, she supposed. "Course I won't tell anyone."

"I hate the idea of people talking about my boys. When I'm not even sure what they look like anymore."

Terry's stomach lurched in sympathy. Not to recognize your own children . . . Maybe to pass them by on the street and never know. She couldn't imagine a more painful situation. And Sean had to live with that for the rest of his life.

If only she could think of some way to help. But there was nothing concrete she could offer him. Not even any consolation. How could she comfort someone who had lost his kids? "Of course I'll not tell anyone," she repeated softly. It wasn't much, but if he didn't want her to tell Jules or Lily, that was the least she could do.

"Thank you. You don't mind that I told you?"

"No way. I'm pleased. Not that it happened, God, not that. That you wanted to tell me. You know."

"You're a great listener." Sean attempted a smile. "Lily's a lucky girl to have you as a friend."

"She's been pretty good to me too."

Paul came into the kitchen, leaving the door ajar. "I'm hungry. When's lunch?" he said to his mother. Who beamed from ear to ear. It might not have been the essence of politeness but it was a lot better than silence. Or insults. "I'll get something together. Sean, you want to stay?"

Before he could answer, a small bundle of tan-colored electricity dashed into the room. "Paul! You let her loose. Quick, grab her before she can get to Sean!" And mother and son started to chase Minnie around the room, reaching down to try to capture her. But she was small and supple and very elusive. And determined. She darted through Paul's legs, skipped around Terry's attempted blockade, and went straight for Sean.

"Minnie!"

"Stop it! He's a friend! Friend!"

Minnie leapt off the ground, toward Sean. She landed in his lap, reached up to lick his face. And settled down on his knees as if he were Lily or Mara.

"That's incredible."

"She's never done that before."

Sean laughed and scratched Minnie's back. She raised herself toward him, accepted the caress, and then curled up in her chosen spot.

Terry leaned over to look at Sean more closely. "Are you sure you're a man?" she asked.

twenty-seven

"Hi, it's me."

"Lils. What've you been doing? You're almost purring."

"Mmmmmm. Sean, of course."

"Good night?" Terry smiled to herself, leaned back in her chair, phone in hand, and settled down for a good, long gossip.

"Great night. If he's as fab with Paul as he is in bed . . ."

"God, Lils. He's amazing, isn't he? They get on so well. And it's had a massive effect. Paul hasn't told me to fuck off in three days."

"A major improvement."

"Don't laugh. It is."

"I know, babe. I didn't mean to laugh. It just sounded so odd."

"I guess it did. But trust me, this is a real step forward. Okay, he still isn't talking much, but I'd rather nothing than being shouted or sworn at."

"And if all that took was three weeks, think what'll happen in three months."

"You know, I did have my doubts, but this was definitely one of your better ideas."

"Paltry. One of my best, you mean. You're happy, I'm happy, and Jules is beside herself with excitement."

"Any idea when?"

"She's always been an off-and-on girl. Any week now."

"She's still going ahead?"

"You know Jules. If she wants something . . ."

"She gets it. Yeah. You heard from Mara?"

"No. You?"

"No."

"I'll call."

"No, I will."

"Let's all call. Tell her how well it's going. See if she'll join in."

"She'll never. Not Mara. Didn't you see her face when you first mentioned it?"

"Yeah, but she's had time to think about it. Get over the shock. See the advantages."

"Lils. This is Mara you're talking about."

"I know. I know. I just hate to see her still worshiping that bastard."

"So do I. So does Jules. But you don't want to tell her?"

"No. Yes. I don't know."

"We agreed we'd keep quiet, didn't we? That there was no need to hurt her."

"That was years ago. The guy had just died. She didn't need to know he wasn't the ideal husband. We thought she'd gradually get over him, then move on. Instead, she's made him into a saint. When he was anything but. She's ruining her life cos of him."

"No. Not ruining. Missing out on stuff, maybe."

"And living in that tumbledown house. Keeping it as a shrine to her lost, perfect love. When all the time they were together . . . Fifteen women, was it?"

"Well, there were letters from seventeen. Might have been more, of course."

"We should have shown them to her."

"Lils, we couldn't do that. Remember what she was like?"

"If she'd just felt up to clearing out his things, she'd have found them herself."

"It'd've destroyed her, wouldn't it?"

"I know. I know. But I can't bear to see her stuck in that place, alone, damp, and broke. When she could be sharing Sean with us. Spending time with a man other than Jake. Learning how to date again."

"She'll never do it."

"Maybe not. But I refuse to give in this easily. We're going to have another go."

"We?"

"Yup. We all call, we rave about the share deal, Sean, you know. Put some gentle pressure on her. Let her know what she's missing."

"She'll say no. I can hear her now. 'Jake wouldn't like it.' "

"Then we do something else. Get her to meet Sean again, see how great he is. Okay?"

"It won't work," Terry warned.

"I know. But we've got to try. Okay?"

"Okay."

twenty-eight

Jules stood over the plastic glass, staring at the dipstick, willing it to change color. But it remained stubbornly the same. Just as it had for the previous seven mornings. She was on tenterhooks, desperate to get started, to try to make her baby. And get into bed with Sean. But she had no clear idea when she was going to be fertile; she'd always been irregular, and the best she could do was give herself a two-week window. She was now seven days in, and nothing. Surely it had to happen soon.

The testing kit had said to wait for two minutes. If nothing happened by then, it meant the time wasn't right. Jules had been giving it first four, then five minutes, but it hadn't helped. The dipstick still detected no change in her early-morning urine. Now she had to wait a full twenty-four hours until she could try again.

She looked out of her bathroom window at the gray light of dawn and yawned. She wasn't sleeping well. She kept waking up to check the time, hoping the night was over so that she could do the test.

She threw the dipstick down the toilet, left her immaculate, navy-blue-and-white-tiled bathroom, and started to rummage through the clothes closets that covered two walls of her pretty, feminine bedroom. There was no point in her trying to go back to sleep, she was far too wide-awake. Besides, it would give her a chance to get some paperwork done before the workday began and the telephone started ringing.

She was going to have to wear something that would go all day and into the evening; she had a lunchtime function her company had arranged that she'd have to attend, then meetings all afternoon and an early-evening drink with a possible client before hurrying around to Lily's for dinner.

She yawned again and rubbed her eyes. Normally, she enjoyed the dressing-up aspect of her job, but today she would have liked to be able to slop around in an old pair of jeans and a loose sweater. Still, that was out of the question. Her clients expected a certain standard from her. And Sean would be at Lily's; she had to make sure that he saw her as an attractive woman, not as a shapeless mother type. But she mustn't overdo it; it was supposed to be Mara's night.

Jules moved past a red, flouncy cocktail number—way too blatant—thought about and discarded her much-loved navy blue suit—too sedate—and finally settled on a black, form-hugging but not overtight designer dress that she'd had for three years and worn over and over again. It was one of her favorite outfits. Attractive but not obvious, the vee neckline was just the right length to suggest a great deal and show very little. It was stylish, sexy . . . but understated. Perfect.

twenty-nine

Mara had had a bad feeling about Lily's dinner party. When she saw the seating arrangements, she knew why. She was next to Sean. On his other side was Jenny, one of the costars of Lily's sitcom. Mara had talked to her only once but she remembered her perfectly; she was possibly the world's most self-absorbed person and refused to pay the slightest bit of attention to anyone unless they were likely to help with her career. Sean was certain not to fit that bill, but just in case Jenny might have been tempted to talk to the builder, Lily had put her next to Danny, a film producer who had just signed a big deal with a major studio. And who would be irresistible to an ambitious, determined actress.

It was a setup. Mara was supposed to sit with Sean, talk to him, be charmed by him. And then give in. Her friends still couldn't accept the fact that she didn't want anything to do with their scheme. She made a face at Lily, who grinned and shrugged as she took her place at the opposite end of the long, oval table. Jules, who was three people around from Mara, leaned over and smiled encouragement. Terry, diagonally opposite, mouthed, "Go for it." Why wouldn't they leave her alone? What she'd longed to do that evening was stay at home and get a good night's sleep, in preparation for tomorrow, when she was going to meet with a family lawyer that one of the women she cleaned for had recommended. But of course her friends knew nothing about that, and she wasn't going to tell them. So here she was, stuck for what she imagined would turn out to be a long, long evening.

To begin with, Mara shrugged off all of Sean's attempts to start a conversation. But when she saw how isolated this left him as the laughter and noise swirled around them both, she took pity on him. After all, it wasn't his fault.

Two hours later, she was sitting back, sipping her glass of very expensive claret, toying with some mouth-numbingly strong cheese, and smiling at Sean, who was listening openmouthed to Jenny's increasingly desperate attempts to convince Danny she was a massive talent just waiting to be discovered. Mara had found it impossible not to like the builder. He was friendly and kind and was almost the only man she'd met—apart from Jake—who listened. Who didn't just wait through her part of the conversation for the moment he could jump in and start talking again. More than that, he saw through her face. Treated her as a person, not a trophy to be won or a body to be chased. Often, men made her feel uncomfortable. They stared so. But sitting with Sean, for once she was able to forget the way she looked. In short, she liked him a lot.

Having failed to persuade Danny by personality alone, Jenny had apparently decided to take another tack and had started trying to seduce him. She was leaning on his arm, her hand caressing his neck, her breasts pressed against the table to accentuate her pushed-up cleavage. Sean turned back to Mara. "God, I feel sorry for that guy. I think he's going to have to kill her to get away. Is there anything she won't do, do you think?"

"Lily told me she's notorious for it." She looked over at Jenny, who was now whispering in Danny's ear. "A real career woman. Think what I could do with even a tenth of her drive."

"No ambition?"

"Just to see my girls happy and well."

Sean smiled at Mara. When he'd first met her, he'd seen her as arrogant and reserved, one of those women who believe that their incredible beauty gives them a right to behave as they wish. The drab clothes, the lack of makeup, even tonight at Lily's dinner party, all seemed to confirm this belief; she was so sure of her attractions, she didn't even bother to dress up. Instead, he'd found she was quiet and rather shy. And very warm once you got beyond her reserve. "Nothing for yourself?"

"If Moo and Tilly are fine, so am I."

"And are they?" Sean couldn't help being drawn to Mara's maternal instincts. God, if only Isobel had felt a bit like that.

"They're great. Everything a mother could want in her daughters. Good at school—Tilly's even joined the choir—fun at home, understanding when I can't quite manage to buy them what they'd like. And so beautiful, both of them. I just wish Jake could see them. He . . . he . . ." Mara's voice trailed off into silence.

Sean was quiet for a moment, giving her some room. Then: "I know how saying the words somehow makes it more real."

Mara looked up at Sean in surprise. People usually didn't get that. He must have lost someone he loved. "Even now I have trouble. If I have to, I can manage things like 'I lost him' or 'He had an accident,' but I still can't say it straight. Silly, I know."

"Not silly at all. You must have loved him a great deal."

"I do."

Sean looked at the tear snaking its way down Mara's beautiful face and cast around for something else to talk about. Something to distract her from her grief. "Lily said you're having problems with your roof?"

"Did she?"

"Does it need replacing? Have you had some quotes done?"

"No. I'm afraid I . . . It's fine. Just a leak or two, a few tiles need replacing. Nothing major."

"Lily thought I might be able to help."

Mara said nothing, just stared at Sean. Why couldn't Lily keep her mouth shut?

"I could come round some weekend, take a look, see what needs doing. If it's just a small leak or two, it'd only take me a couple of hours."

"Thanks. That's very nice of you. But I can manage."

"Are you sure?" Sean had seen too many experienced men fall off roofs not to be concerned by the idea of Mara trying to mend hers herself. "It can be dangerous. You will be careful?"

"Careful? You didn't think I was going to do it myself? No, no, there's a local handyman, he's done my neighbor's." Mara stumbled through the unaccustomed falsehood. Her friends would have seen through it in a minute, but Sean didn't know her well and maybe he wouldn't realize she was lying.

Sean did notice but ignored it. He wasn't about to start accusing her of telling porkies. Ultimately, the roof and what she did with it was her business. "Okay. Whatever you say. Just call if you change your mind."

"Thank you. But honestly, I'm fine. Lily worries about me too much."

"She's a good friend. I can see how much she cares about you all." Sean beamed up at Lily, who was leaning over Jenny, pouring out some more wine. "She's so happy about me helping you guys. Terry with Paul. Jules with . . . well, you know. Now you. I think it's wonderful that she wants to share whatever she has like that."

Mara was surprised. Lily had said that Sean wasn't aware of the friends' arrangement, but he seemed to know exactly what was going on. "You don't mind?"

"What's to mind?"

"Nothing, I suppose." Was she the only person in the world who thought sharing a man among women was a bad idea? No, a wrong idea?

"I sense a 'but' in there."

"Not really. No 'but.' Only . . ."

"Only what?"

Mara couldn't keep quiet any longer. She just had to know. Maybe Sean could explain it all to her so she'd be able to accept it. "You don't think it's wrong?"

"No. Course not. Why would I?"

"I just think there are some things shouldn't be shared."

"Like what?"

"Like . . . like men."

"Not even if it helps everyone?"

Mara was confused. Maybe she was the one who was wrong. It seemed as if everyone else thought so. "But don't you mind them dividing you up between the three of them like that?" she blurted out, anxious to understand.

"Dividing me up?"

"Yes. You know. Like a presliced pie. One serving for you, one for me. According to how much they want."

"Presliced? What do you mean, presliced?" Sean's normally easy voice was sharp, urgent, testy.

"Um, well . . ." Mara stammered. Oh, no. She'd made a mistake. He didn't know.

"What did you mean?" Sean's face was intent.

"Nothing. Nothing, I promise. Just a figure of speech. You know." Oh, why, why had she said that? Yes, she believed Lily, Terry, and Jules ought to have been honest with Sean about their scheme, but in the end, that was their business, and she certainly didn't want to betray them.

"Exactly how am I being divided up?"

"Just . . . you know, like . . . like you are with Jules and Terry and . . ." What could she say?

"She means the way you do stuff for the girls," Lily said, leaping in. "Here, finish this." She poured the last of the bottle of wine into Sean's glass. "You know, helping my friends." She looked along the table. "And me. Could you bear to go to the cellar? We're out of red. And I've got to get the dessert. Come on." Lily led Sean out of the dining room. In the corridor outside, once out of sight of the door, she backed Sean up against the wall and kissed him hard and long. Then she tilted her head to look up at him.

He was staring down at her, his face immobile, his expression severe. "Couldn't wait?" he asked sarcastically. He might have left school at sixteen, but he was not stupid, he knew when he was being deliberately distracted.

"No. I couldn't. You're irresistible." Lily reached up for him and tried to pull his lips down to hers again. But he resisted.

"What's all this about slicing pies?"

"Pies? What pies?"

"Mara says you girls have some kind of deal. To divide me up between the three of you."

"It's nothing. You know Mara. She's not in this world all the time. Like she said, a figure of speech." Lily peeked up at Sean, who was not convinced. His mouth was grim, his eyes stern.

"Have I been set up?"

"Set up how?"

"Me, you, your mates."

"I don't know what you mean."

"You said they could give me what you couldn't. Fill holes you couldn't."

"When did I say that?" Lily was beginning to panic. She was just batting his questions back at him while she flailed around trying to think of some way to convince him he was wrong.

"When we first got back together. Did you and your friends manipulate me into this? Set up your own agenda and get me to agree?" Sean had images of the four of them, sitting around, laughing at his expense, planning to make a fool of him.

"Hush," Lily said. Sean's voice was getting louder and louder. "Come here." She took hold of his hand, dragged him into her study, and tried to put her arms around him, but he pulled himself away from her.

"I need answers, Lily. Did you and your pals set me up? Get together and plot to use me?"

"Of course not." All she could do was deny it. And do her best to convince him. "Sean, listen to what you're suggesting. It's madness. Sure, I want you to help the girls if you can, but to think that's a plot against you? That we all got together and conspired to use you? That's paranoia, pure and simple."

Sean forced himself to look at things as dispassionately as possible and he couldn't help but see the force of Lily's argument. After all, why would they plot against him? Okay, Lily had encouraged him to help her friends, but that was far from being a conspiracy. She'd done it from the best of motives. And looking back to the night when he'd offered to help Terry and Jules, there'd been no hint from either of them that they'd expected him to put himself forward. Their surprise and delight had looked completely unfeigned. He thought of Jules leaping on top of him, raining kisses on his face. He couldn't imagine even Bette Davis in her prime carrying that one off if she'd known what was going to happen in advance. His face lightened somewhat but he was still wary. "Then why did you pull me out of there so quick?"

Lily felt her hard, tense stomach muscles unclench. Thank God. He was going to go for it. He just needed one more push. "It's . . . well . . . I hate to admit it . . . I love Mara, but she's so beautiful and you were so intent on her. . . ." Please may he take the bait. Men usually responded well to a suggestion of jealousy.

And Sean was no exception. Jealousy he understood. The hard, cautious look left his face. "You have nothing to worry about," he said as he leaned down and kissed her. Then he lifted his head up, looked into her flushed face, and grinned. "I suppose you want to nip up to bed for a quickie?"

Lily breathed a metaphorical sigh of relief. That had been close. She looked longingly toward the stairs before a shout of laughter from the dining room made her remember her guests. She shook her head. "Better wait and take our time later. They can't stay forever."

thirty

"This seems quite straightforward." Robin Heath, a well-groomed, beautifully dressed man, his hair in perfect place, his clothes immaculate, put down the letter from the Moores. "Unless there is something else to come out."

"Something else?"

"Yes. About your past, er, experiences?"

Mara blushed at this reference to her history. It had been the most difficult thing about the meeting so far, letting a complete stranger in on her most closely guarded secret. "No. Nothing."

"Or your present situation, your relationship with the children in question . . . ?"

"The Moores know everything there is to know."

"No trouble at school?"

"No."

"No . . . discipline problems?"

"They're the best girls. They never give me a moment's worry."

"No, of course not. But if they were to be badly behaved, shall we say, what might you do?"

Mara looked at the lawyer, confused by this constant questioning. What was he getting at? "I don't know. Stop them playing their video games for a day, perhaps?"

"Nothing physical?"

So that was it. "Mr. Heath, I can assure you that I have never, ever hit either of my daughters."

"In that case, their position is not a strong one. Courts nowadays are very reluctant to separate children from their mothers if they can find nothing incorrect in the situation."

"My past doesn't matter?"

"Mothers have done many worse things than you, Mrs. Moore, and been allowed to keep their children."

"And the house?"

"Again, there are any number of children living in far worse conditions."

"Then . . . then I'm safe. They can't get my girls." Mara had to stop herself from jumping up and embracing the man on the other side of the desk. "They can't get my girls."

The lawyer held up a lightly tanned, perfectly manicured hand. "Of course, there is no guarantee. If your parents-in-law are determined to pursue this further, there is nothing to stop them. And once a case has reached court, no one can say for sure what will happen. There is always a chance that the judgment will go against you."

Moments ago, Mara had been ecstatic, thinking it was all over, that she could go back to living her life without the threat of losing Moo and Tilly hanging over her head. But her relief had been fleeting. The threat was back. And somehow redoubled in strength now that her own lawyer had confirmed it was there. "So . . . so what do I do?"

"Let me see. Do you have family of your own?"

"Yes. I mean no. Not that I've seen in twenty years almost."

"Get in touch with them. Make some kind of rapprochement. There's nothing the courts approve of like a large, close family. Grandparents, aunts, cousins, that kind of thing."

Mara swallowed hard at the daunting idea of seeing her father again. "Anything . . . anything else?"

"Put your house in order. Mend the roof. Repair the central heating. Redeem any debts you might have. Or at least make arrangements to pay them off gradually. Perhaps some extracurricular activities. Gymnastics. Ballet. Music. Things like that. Show the courts you are serious about looking after your children. That you understand the responsibilities."

"But . . . but . . . I don't have . . . I can't . . ." Mara's voice was getting higher and weaker as panic took hold. She couldn't do one of those things, let alone all of them. It would take thousands and thousands of pounds. And once she'd paid the lawyer's bill, she'd have only a hundred pounds left of Amy's gift. Which might pay for a course of ballet lessons for the girls, she supposed. That was if she could persuade either of her pop-music-listening, break-dancing daughters to be interested in anything as traditional as ballet.

The lawyer ignored Mara's rising panic, got to his feet, and held out his hand. "Very nice to have met you, Mrs. Moore. I'll send you a copy of my response to the Moores' letter. Hopefully that will deal with the issue. I'll be in touch. I'll be in touch."

thirty-one

"It's happened." Jules couldn't hide her excitement. Ever since the pink blush had appeared on the dipstick at five-thirty that morning, she'd hardly been able to contain herself.

"Jules, that's great."

"Yes, after all the waiting. I'd almost given up. I was terrified I'd skipped a month. And then there it was. I'm fertile."

"That's wonderful."

"Now all I need is Sean. I've left a message at his office, but he's out at his site. I hope he's not busy."

"You want him tonight?" Lily's voice sounded tight.

"Well, yes. Today. Tonight. As soon as possible."

"But we've got plans. We're going to the Comedy Awards. He's my escort. I've been nominated, remember?"

"Oh, Lily. You can find someone else, surely?"

"I can, I suppose. . . ." But Lily couldn't see why the hell she should.

"You're a star. I knew you'd understand."

"What happens if you wait until tomorrow?"

"Very funny. Waiting for the test to be positive has almost killed me. Any longer and I'll go mad."

"What happens if you wait until tomorrow?"

"Lily, don't joke about this."

"What happens if you wait until tomorrow?"

"You're serious. I can't believe you're asking me. We agreed. Whenever the time was right, I would get Sean."

"What happens? . . . What fucking happens?"

"You know what happens. I can still conceive. I told you at the start of all this. There's a two-day window. So yes, I could wait until tomorrow. But the more often you do it, the more likely it is to happen. I need him tonight."

"I'm sorry, Jules." Hell. This was supposed to be easy. Fun. Sharing her man with her friends. She hadn't expected there would be a clash. Nor that she would feel so possessive. But it wasn't that. No, course it wasn't. It was only that she needed Sean herself. She was up for an award for the first time and was already feeling terrified with over ten hours to go. God knew what she would be like when the show started. She couldn't imagine going through with it without Sean's support.

"Two nights, that's all I want. If I'm lucky, that's all I'll need. It's not so much to ask. After all, you've been with him all these weeks, whenever you wanted."

"He's mine, Jules. Mine to give. Mine to withhold." This was unfair. Why should she have to give up her night? She'd been thinking about these awards, worrying about them, for weeks. What to wear. What to do if she won best comedy actress. If *We Can Work It Out* won comedy of the year. What to do if she lost. She needed Sean. Jules could just as easily do it the following day, she'd admitted that.

"This whole thing was your idea. You thought of it. You planned it all. And now, at the first opportunity, you're pulling out." Jules started to cry. She had to have Sean. Why couldn't Lily see that?

"I'm not pulling out." The sound of Jules sobbing made Lily feel a bit guilty. No, a lot guilty. What was one night? She'd be fine. After all, it was only a lousy awards show. She'd call Raymond or Charlie or Nick. One of them would be free. "I want you to have him. I do. You're right. I'll find someone else."

It was Jules's turn to feel uncomfortable. Sean was Lily's. This was an important night for her. And if she wanted him to escort her, she should be able to have him do so without some desperate-for-a-child friend crying in her ear and trying to take him and his sperm away. She'd always thought how hard it must be to go to one of those things, particularly alone. To run the gamut of all those photographers going in, then sit and wait for some-one else's name to be announced and pretend you were happy to have lost . . . "No. Of course you must have him. Tomorrow will be just as good. I'm sure it'll make no difference. The books say forty-eight hours and they can't be wrong, can they?"

"I don't know."

"Well, I do. They can't."

"Let's not find out. He's yours."

"No, yours."

"Crap. Yours."

"Lily. Yours."

"Yours."

"Yours. I insist."

"Of course, we could do both."

"What?"

"Well, he could come to the awards with me and then go on to you."

"Would he?"

"Why not?"

"Well, it'll be late. Won't he be tired?"

"Tired? Sean? He, I'll have you know, is always up for it. I'll leave right after the comedy of the year thing, get the car to drop him at your place. Okay?"

"Lily, are you sure?"

"Course I'm sure."

"Then, thank you. Thank you, thank you, thank you. You are the best friend."

"No I'm not." The best friend would have given up the evening immedi-ately. The best friend wouldn't be feeling slightly queasy at the idea of Jules and Sean in bed together. "I've got to go. Enjoy yourself, okay? Call me in the morning."

thirty-two

Jules walked from one hot, crowded, smoky room into another. The overblown fragrance of lilies mixed with the musk of expensive perfume and the aroma of hot canapés. Another very proper, quail's-egg-and-vol-au-vent drinks party. What on earth was she doing here? When she could be tucked up at home, waiting for Sean? Coming to her old school friend's gathering had felt like such a good idea only half an hour ago when the minutes until midnight and Sean's estimated time of arrival seemed endless. She needed something to distract her, to make the time pass a bit more quickly, and the party had seemed perfect. She would have a couple of soft drinks—alcohol made it more difficult to conceive—see a few old acquaintances, stay for an hour or two, then go home and get herself and the house ready for Sean. Simple.

Instead, she had already run into three people she would have been pleased never to have seen again. The rooms were overfull and everyone was tipsy. Happily swigging back glass after glass of champagne. Apart from her. And there was nothing worse than being the only sober person in a room full of drunks.

"White shoes!" Jules heard a familiar, booming woman's voice. "I tell you, the girl was wearing white shoes. In May!" She looked around and saw Jocelyn Hannesford-Jones gesturing her disgust to someone. A tall, solid, horsey woman with a deafening voice and all-weather skin, Jocelyn had been one of Jules's first-ever clients. When she had been an eager twenty-three-year-old, struggling to make a name for herself, she had arranged a christening party for Jocelyn's first child. It had been a big success and Jocelyn had recommended Dunne Parties to all her friends. Jules hadn't seen her for ages, but she couldn't help smiling at the sight of her. She was older, rounder, and much more leathery, but still the Jocelyn of fifteen years ago.

Jules snaked her way through the guests. "I was just standing there, regretting having come. And then I saw you." Jules reached out and hugged Jocelyn. "How are you? How's Christopher? And Annabel?"

"We're fine. All fine. How are you? I hear great things about Dunne Parties."

"Thanks to you. I don't know what I'd have done without your wonderful recommendations."

"Rubbish. You were bound to succeed. Anyone could see that." Jocelyn stepped aside to reveal a tall, handsome man who was graying at the edges. And scowling. "Do you know Michael Hungerford?" she asked.

Jules took an involuntary step backward. Michael. It only needed that. Why, oh why, had she come? In an attempt to cover up her instinctive retreat and seem normal, Jules forced a smile, stepped forward, and held out her hand. "Michael. How are you?"

"Juliet." He touched the tips of her fingers, no more.

If Jocelyn hadn't been there, Jules would have turned and walked away. It was how she had always dealt with Michael on the few times they had met in the last eighteen years. Polite greeting followed by disappearance. But this called for something more. Jocelyn clearly hadn't heard the old story—it had all happened a few years before the christening party and people had stopped talking about it by the time they met—or she wouldn't have introduced them. And the last thing Jules wanted to do was embarrass Jocelyn. So she cast about for a topic of conversation.

"I was sorry to hear about you and Rose." No, no, why did she say that? It was completely wrong. What on earth had made her mention his divorce?

Michael stared at Jules. Then turned to Jocelyn. "Good to see you, Jocelyn," he said, then stalked off.

"What? Michael? What was that? I didn't think he was so touchy about Rose. I was talking to him about her a few minutes ago."

"It's not Rose, Jocelyn. It's me. He and I . . . I was engaged to him. Eighteen years ago."

"Come with me." Jocelyn took Jules's arm, led her over to an empty couch, sat her down, and stood over her. "Now. You are not getting up until you tell me."

"It was nothing."

Jocelyn frowned down at Jules. "My dear, I am quite sure it was not nothing. The way Michael reacted to you was not like him at all. What on earth did you do?"

"I broke it off. I don't think he was very pleased."

"You broke it off."

"Yes."

"That's all you did?"

"Well . . ."

"It seems a long time for him to carry such a grudge."

"I'm afraid I didn't tell him as early as I might have done."

"Jules. You left him standing at the altar."

"No. Well, yes. A bit. I told him in advance of the wedding, but it was only a day before."

"My dear! No wonder he won't talk to you."

"He was so keen. I was only twenty, I didn't want to get married. But everyone was so pleased with me." Everyone being her family. For the first time in her life, Jules's family had approved of her. Loved her. Her mother, Diana, delighted in the fact that her daughter—*her* daughter—was going to marry the heir to an earldom, had lavished all the love on her that she had previously withheld. Jules became the apple and orange and pear of her mother's ice-cold eye. Nothing was too good for her, nothing too expensive or precious or special.

She'd known she wasn't ready to marry, that she needed to work, to have a career, to do things before she settled down. She didn't want just to wed a powerful, wealthy man and spend the rest of her life bringing up his children, choosing her hat for Ascot, and opening church fetes. But the effect her engagement to Michael had on her family was too seductive. All her childhood she had longed for her mother's approval and love; suddenly she had it. And it felt so wonderful she thought it was worth giving up her life to keep it. Until, the day before the wedding, she realized that she couldn't go through with it. She was making a terrible mistake. Michael genuinely loved her and he deserved more than a woman who was marrying him to please her mother. He deserved someone who loved him back. And while Jules liked him a lot, she was not ready to marry anyone.

So she had walked out on him and the wedding. Her mother had never forgiven her. And it seemed that Michael hadn't either.

"But you must have seen him since? You move in the same circles, know the same people? Surely you've talked before tonight?"

"Hard to believe, isn't it? But we haven't. A polite greeting once in a while, no more. A 'how do you do' and that's been it. Of course, he hasn't been round much, particularly since he married, had kids, and then inherited. I've seen him no more than three times since I stood him up. Until tonight." Jules's face crumpled in on itself. "Gosh, why, why did I have to mention Rose? After all that expensive education, you would think I could manage a bland comment or two about the weather. I'm so stupid. I could at least have been polite. The last thing he deserves from me is to be upset. Or insulted."

"He won't think about it for more than a few minutes. It was so very long ago. And he's been through so much since. He was just being sensitive. Men's pride, you know, my dear."

"I know. But I think I'll slip out nonetheless. He doesn't need to see me again." Jules stood, kissed Jocelyn on the cheek, and quietly edged her way to the door, through the crowds. Jocelyn watched her go, a thoughtful expression on her face.

Michael Hungerford was standing by himself in a corner, his eyes following Jules as she passed through the guests and into the next room. When she disappeared from view, he reached out, grabbed a glass of champagne from a passing tray, and drank it down in one go. It might have been a long time, but he couldn't forget.

thirty-three

Clive Morris stood in the foyer of the LWT Building, watching the celebrities arrive for the evening's festivities. Awards shows had become dull, unexciting occasions in recent years since the organizers of the various events had begun to postpone dinner—and drinks—until after the awards were all handed out. Sober celebrities made for polite, repetitive, and very boring evenings. The one exception was the Comedy Awards. There, the wine flowed freely from the moment everyone sat at their table. And there was always some kind of scene. Heckling nominees, a hurt presenter, even a fight on-screen one year. The PRs were not in charge for a change . . . and the journalists loved it.

Clive was particularly interested because of Lily. Her first Comedy Awards, her first nominations, she'd be bound to be nervous, and with any luck she'd get drunk, behave badly, make a fool of herself. The fates couldn't be so unkind as to deny him everything in life he wanted.

He looked at his watch. She was leaving it a bit late. Most of the usual suspects were already inside, the executives all correct in black tie, the stars ranging from a glittery Cilla to a T-shirted Chris Evans. Just a few stragglers left now. Ah, there was Lily. Tall, blond, and chic in a skintight black designer dress. And her escort. Now, he was something new. Since her recent rise to fame, Lily had often been escorted to industry events by one of her colleagues—those two producers of hers, that Raymond, the production manager—but Clive had never seen this one before. Tall, broad, and weathered, he didn't look as if he spent his life in neon-lit TV studios. It wasn't like Lily to bring a boyfriend to a show—as far as Clive could discover, few of them lasted long enough—but this one seemed to be just that. The body language was right—Lily was holding his arm, he was leaning over her, protectively or possessively or both.

Hey, maybe she was in love? Lilibet, in love? Clive rubbed his inner hands together in glee. What fun he could have with that. Stolen pictures of them together—he knew just the man—preferably with clothes missing; deep background on the hunk—please may he turn out to be something sensational like a bigamist or a con man; humiliation for Lilibet. Okay, maybe that was a little far-fetched, her date was probably a grip she knew who liked sunbeds, but a man could dream, couldn't he?

LILY CAME offstage, clutching her award—a sort of plastic scrolly thing with a joker inside—and couldn't stop herself giving a little skip of joy. Two nominations. Two awards. She found it all hard to believe. Three years ago, she'd been another anonymous writer, fighting to sell sketches to producers. Two years ago, she'd been doing the rounds of the production companies with her sitcom. A year ago, she'd been thrust into the limelight. And for some reason had been taken to the public's heart. Now here she was, best comedy actress and the writer of the comedy of the year. She knew she was supposed to be cool about it, not to show how excited she was, but that was impossible. She'd just been given the greatest compliment of her life. People thought she was funny.

An improbably tall woman draped in a Grecian-style costume escorted Lily into the press room. Massed rows of photographers flashed at her as she stood, holding her joker, smiling and smiling and smiling. After what seemed like a year, when her jaws ached with the pressure of constant beaming, the statuesque woman led her on to face the press proper.

Lily looked out at a host of semifamiliar faces. Men and women she had talked to off and on over the last months. Some she liked, most she felt indifferent to . . . and then there was Clive. Lily noticed his smirking grin somewhere toward the back and prepared herself for a few snide, unpleasant questions. He'd be bound to have something prepared. He'd probably been working on it all week just on the off chance that she might win.

"How do you feel, Lily?" a voice called out. She identified Peter Bourne. The *Star*. She settled down to the business of answering questions.

"What did Steve Martin say?" the man from the *Mirror* asked. The famous American comedian had presented her with the award.

"Were you surprised?" the *Express* asked.

"Which award means more?" from the *Mail*, on Sunday.

"Is it true you've signed to make a movie with Hugh Grant?"

"Are you making more episodes of *We Can Work It Out*?"

"Who's that hunk you came with?" Clive waited until the end of the session, when the questions had slowed down almost to a stop, then jumped in.

So that was the direction he was going to go in. He must have thrown away his ready-prepared attack after seeing her with Sean. "He's a friend," she said. "Okay, guys, if we've finished—"

"Where'd you meet him?"

Lily gritted her teeth. No point in refusing to answer, it would only make Clive worse. And tip him off that there might be a story. "At a wedding."

"And are you in love?"

Some of the other journalists roused at the mention of love. "Yeah, Lily, is it wedding bells for the two of you?"

"When's the happy day?"

"Where's the honeymoon?"

Lily laughed. "Only you guys could get from friendship to marriage in three short steps. Don't tell him, will you?" And with that, she swept out. The press pack, reassured that they weren't missing a story, settled down to wait for the next lucky award winner.

Clive was disappointed. Lily had turned out to be a good actress, true, and could still be hiding something, but the easy way she dealt with his and others' questions didn't suggest that it was anything worth his pursuing. She was probably having sex with her escort—knowing her, he'd say it was almost certain she was—but he wasn't interested in another story about an occasional lover. Lily wouldn't care; she'd just laugh and move on. She was unattached, and chances were the hunk was also; he'd have to be extraordinarily stupid to take a well-known woman out to a televised awards show if he were married or engaged. Or a con man. And Lily didn't usually go for stupid.

No, Clive was after a bigger story than a short-term fling between two consenting adults, regardless of background. Let the other papers worry about Lily's latest beau if they cared; he wasn't interested. He wanted something much more spectacular. Something for the front pages. Something that would linger in people's minds, tarnish Lily's glittering career, and make her want to hide from the shame of it all.

LILY WALKED away from the press room feeling sure that she had convinced the pack that Sean was just another celebrity escort.

Apart from Clive. She couldn't help feeling a touch worried about Clive. If he got hold of the story about her and the girls and Sean, it'd be spread over the front page of his newspaper with the truth twisted to make the sharing scheme appear the worst, most heinous sin in the world rather than a good-natured deal between three old friends.

For a moment, she thought about calling it off, forgetting the pact she had with Terry and Jules and just enjoying Sean herself. He certainly seemed satisfied this time with what she was giving him. Perhaps he'd come around to seeing things her way? After all, if there were no sharing, she could go home with him right now.

But then there was Jules, sitting in her little house, fantasizing about nappies and carry cots and building blocks. And Terry, whose relationship with Paul was so bad she was grateful he wasn't swearing at her anymore. She couldn't wave the possibility of a solution to their problems in front of them and then snatch it away to suit herself. So Clive had asked a few questions. Clive was always asking questions, it didn't mean he was going to find out anything. No one apart from Terry, Jules, Mara, and herself knew. And they wouldn't talk.

LILY CUDDLED up to Sean in the back of their limo. He put his arms around her and kissed her quickly. "I think it feels the same," he said. Then kissed her again. "No, I'm not completely sure," and lowered his head once more before pulling back and looking at her, weighing her up.

"What is it? What's the matter?" she asked.

"Just testing to see if it's different, kissing the comedy actress of the year," he said.

Lily laughed. "Wait till you try fucking her." She was tempted to lean forward and pull the blind down between their compartment and the driver, but before she could do so, the limo drew up outside Jules's little mews house. Damn. She was going to have to wait. Sean was Jules's now. That was the deal to which she'd agreed. "Okay. We're here. Ready?"

"As I'll ever be," Sean said, kissing Lily. "Wish me luck."

Lily saw the door to the house open. Jules was standing there in a lacy wrap, her figure silhouetted against the light. "Of course I wish you luck," she said. "Not that I think you'll need it." The sight of Jules, primed for seduction, was having a strange, unwelcome effect on Lily. If she didn't know herself better, she'd have said she was jealous. Now desperate to get away, to forget about Sean and Jules and what they were about to do, Lily leaned over Sean and opened the door on his side. "Go on," she said, "Jules is waiting."

thirty-four

Sean stood in the shadowy, candlelit living room, a glass of champagne in his hand. Jules was sitting in front of him, her lacy robe giving him tantalizing glimpses of skin in spite of the fact that she had it pulled decorously around her. He took a sip of his drink, then another. It had all seemed so simple when they had talked at Rules, but now he realized that they hadn't really discussed details. He'd been embarrassed and so had been happy to leave it all to Jules, once she'd reassured him that he wasn't needed for the actual insemination part, but now he wished he'd been braver and found out exactly what he was supposed to do. And when. And into what. Instead, he was standing here, like a lemon about to be squeezed, waiting to be instructed by Jules. And she didn't seem to be in any hurry.

"You look terrified," Jules said.

"I'm okay."

"Sean."

"Well, I suppose I am a little nervous."

"Please don't be. This is such a special night."

"Special?"

"Of course. Can't you feel it?"

"I don't know. . . ."

"We're about to make a baby."

"Yes. Yes, we are."

"The most wonderful thing that two people can ever do together."

"A baby."

"Yes."

"A baby." And Sean felt himself get caught up in the magic of the occasion. He'd never known the exact time he and Isobel had conceived either of the boys. The week, maybe, but not the hour, the minute, the second. Tonight would be different; he would know precisely, and the sense of strength, of potency that gave him was indescribable. He felt as if in some small way he was going to be part of creation itself.

"We're going to create another human being," Jules said, echoing Sean's thoughts.

"A miracle."

Jules stood up and moved toward him. "You hadn't thought about that before?"

"Not until just now. It didn't feel real. You know. It was just an idea. Not this." He looked around the room, at the glowing embers in the fire, at the flickering candles, the warm, welcoming feel of the house, and was overcome with a sense of wonder. He was going to make a baby.

Jules took Sean's glass from him, put it down on the invitation-cluttered mantelpiece, then placed one hand on his sleeve. "Do you think . . . ?" She let her question hang in the air, unasked.

"Do I think what?" Sean asked softly. He felt very, very close to her at that moment.

"I've . . . I've got all the necessary things, but . . . Do you think we could do this the old-fashioned way?" Jules reached up and kissed Sean gently on the mouth.

Sean knew he should have been shocked. But he wasn't. Somehow, any scruples he might have had, any loyalty to Lily, had been overtaken by the enormity of what they were about to do. What Jules was suggesting felt right. He wanted to take a true, full part in what was going to happen. To be there at the moment of conception, a real father, not an adjunct sitting in another room while Jules did whatever she needed to do.

She was waiting for his answer. He put his arms around her and hugged her to him for a moment. Then he pulled back and lifted her chin with his hand.

"Yes," he said.

· · ·

SEAN LAY back, his eyes fixed on the four-poster bed's embroidered canopy. Jules was motionless beside him, her back turned, the occasional soft snore confirmation that she was still asleep.

Unlike him. Oh, he had dozed off for a short time after their lovemaking, feeling happier and more fulfilled than he could remember. It wasn't that being with Jules had been so good, more that he had lost himself in the wonder of the act, in the purposefulness of making a baby. At the moment it was happening, it had felt as if that was what sex was for. Perhaps there was more of the Catholic left in him than he had thought. Or maybe it was an echo of all those years of training and catechism. What was it the Jesuits said? "Give me a child until he's seven"? Well, part of them still had part of him.

But it was a small part. Now, without all the candlelight and the beauty and the excitement of the moment, he didn't feel as if he were God's instrument of propagation. He felt like an asshole. He'd had sex with his lover's friend. A vulnerable woman, too desperate for the evening to have the right result to be held accountable for her actions. He should have stopped it. But he hadn't. Instead, he had jumped right in. He hadn't needed to be persuaded, one suggestion from Jules and he'd agreed. And betrayed Lily.

Jules stirred. Sean realized that he hadn't heard a snore for a few minutes.

"Are you awake?" she whispered. Sean said nothing. Jules turned over. Though lots of the candles had gone out, sputtering in their own wax, there were still enough lit for her to be able to see that his eyes were wide open. And staring into space. Looking anywhere but at her. "Sean?"

"I better go."

"You don't want to do that. It's the middle of the night. It's raining." Wind was blowing the drops hard against the window. Behind that, there was the faint rumble of approaching thunder. "And there's a storm coming."

"Still. I think I should."

"What's the matter?" Jules waited for an answer. There was none. "What is it?" Still nothing. "Lily?" she ventured.

"I can't believe I did that. I love her. I don't know how I could have . . . With one of her oldest friends. I'm sorry."

Jules, who had woken up eager for another go-round with Sean, wasn't in any mood to indulge his wallowing in guilt like this. The way she saw it, they'd done it once, they might as well do it again. And again. Time enough for him to regret it tomorrow or the day after.

"Don't be sorry. I'm not."

"But Lily . . ."

"Is fine. Sean, look at me. Look at me." Sean didn't move for a moment or two, then finally turned slowly onto his side. His face was a foot away from Jules, their eyes on the same level. "She's at home, fast asleep. She's got no idea about this and there's no need for her to ever know."

"You won't tell her?"

"Why would I?"

"Well, she's your friend and . . ."

"What should I tell her? What have we done?"

"You know. She thought we were just going to . . . I was only a donor and now . . ."

"Now we've gone a little bit further. It's nothing. I wanted your sperm. You were prepared to donate it to me. We changed the method of delivery. That's all."

"I suppose that's true."

"Of course it's true. Now, stop worrying about it. There's no problem. I promise."

Sean sensed that Jules was putting something over on him but he couldn't quite put his finger on what it was. Her reasoning seemed soundish, if unusual. But this whole situation was unusual. No point in relying on old rules in a new world, he told himself. It was true that Lily had wanted him to do this, just not perhaps in exactly this way. But if she never knew, who was hurt? Jules was right about that.

"Don't tell me you didn't enjoy it."

"No."

"I thought not."

"But that makes it worse."

"Does it? Why?"

"I don't know. It just does."

Jules sighed inwardly. If only he wouldn't make it so difficult. She supposed she was going to have to go back to her original approach. "Hopefully, we made a baby. We didn't hurt anyone, we didn't use or abuse anyone.

We did a wonderful thing. And I for one refuse to apologize for it. And I'm very disappointed that you seem to want to."

"I don't, truly, I don't," Sean said. And he didn't. Looking back, even though he felt guilty about what they had done, he wouldn't change things. Their baby-making efforts had been very special. And he couldn't help preferring the idea of a child conceived in pleasure to one created by artificial means.

"Good." Jules smiled. "So you won't mind making sure?" As she leaned forward and kissed him, her right hand snaked its way down his body. "You know what they say about sheep and lambs?"

thirty-five

Lily sat huddled in her favorite chair. The thunder had passed over, leaving that eerie, clean, after-the-storm silence behind it. There was no noise from outside apart from the occasional echo of a passing car. No sound from the house apart from the odd creak of old, settling timber. She had tried to sleep, but after hours lying looking at the ceiling, trying to keep her mind off what was going on across town, she had given up and decamped downstairs. Normally, she had no problem getting to sleep, she just tended to wake up in the middle of the night and have a hard time dropping off again. But then, normally she wasn't haunted by images of her lover and her friend in bed together.

If anyone had asked her before that night how she was going to feel about sharing Sean with Jules, she'd have said that she was sure she'd be pleased and proud. Pleased for Jules, who so desperately needed someone like Sean to help her; proud of herself for being such a generous, thoughtful, inventive friend.

But it hadn't turned out that way. Lily could think of nothing else apart from Sean making love to Jules, enjoying it, maybe more than he did with her, getting things from Jules he couldn't get from her, maybe deciding that he no longer wanted her but wanted Jules instead. No matter how hard she tried to concentrate on something else—since moving to her study she'd had a go at watching an old movie on TV, reading, working, listening to her favorite CD, anything she could imagine would be an effective distraction—visions of the two of them kept flooding into her head. Of them in bed, in the bath, lying in front of the fire, of them in each other's arms, kissing, cuddling, touching, fucking . . .

She couldn't understand why she was so obsessed. She was the one who didn't want commitment, after all. What could it matter to her what Sean did in his spare time?

Hell, she was dying for a cigarette. When she'd gotten home, she'd had ten to last her until the following morning. It should have been no problem. Of course, she hadn't planned on being up half the night, puffing away, agonizing about her feelings. Desperate for a comforting hit of nicotine, she got up and started rummaging through her desk, hoping that there would be an old pack she'd forgotten. Ah. There. Right at the back of the top middle drawer. An ancient, soft packet with one very old, very dry cigarette left. She pulled it out and lit it. It was way past its sell-by date, and staler than week-old bread, but it was still heaven.

She settled back in her chair to carry on where she'd left off. And decided that whatever other dire faults she possessed, she'd never been unwilling to share. So why was she so upset? Was all this noncommitment stuff self-delusionary? Deep down, did she want love and—ugh!—marriage? Surely not. She'd been doing the twice-a-week thing for years; if she was faking it, she'd've found out way before now.

So what was it? First-time nerves? Yes, that made some sense. She was just having a bit of trouble getting used to it. Nothing that needed all this soul-searching. Once she'd spoken to Jules, once she'd seen Sean and been reassured that the two of them weren't in love, that she wasn't going to lose her sometime lover to her friend, she'd be just fine.

thirty-six

"He called her a what?"

"A f . . . fucking bitch." Paul's headmaster, Mr. Wallace, stammered out the unaccustomed word.

"Oh."

"The school views this kind of thing very seriously, Mrs. McKellar, very seriously indeed. We have standards to meet. Abuse of the teachers is completely unacceptable."

"I'm sure he didn't mean it. . . ." Terry didn't know what to say. Deep down, she had some sympathy for Paul. Mrs. Stroud, his maths teacher, was a fucking bitch. The kind of stuck-up cow who looked down her nose at the likes of Terry. The way the woman held on to her handbag whenever Terry was near made it look as if she believed that Terry was about to steal it.

"It was not the first time he has caused this particular teacher problems in class," Mr. Wallace went on.

"But he's been improving recently. Really he has. You must have noticed."

"I would not call this improvement. I'm sorry. I'm afraid I have no alternative but to suspend Paul for two weeks. Any more trouble when he returns and we will have to consider expulsion."

"Expulsion? For two little words?"

"For those two little words."

"But you can't do this—"

"I'm afraid I can, Mrs. McKellar. I'm sorry, but I do have the other pupils and parents to think of. Good evening." And Wallace rang off.

Terry was shocked. Things had been going so well. Okay, Paul hadn't been exactly loving, but he had stopped slamming about the house so much and occasionally even exchanged a few voluntary words with her. And now this.

Even if Mrs. Stroud had been the worst bitch in creation, Paul shouldn't have said she was. He was in deep trouble. Expulsion. God. She hated to upset the delicate balance their relationship seemed to have reached, but she had to do something that would bring the seriousness of this home to him. And she could think of only one thing that might do that. The long-awaited trip to see Charlton play Chelsea was this weekend. Terry didn't want to forbid his going. She couldn't bear to deny her son his treat. It meant too much to him. But if she were to say she was thinking about canceling it, maybe he'd be shocked into realizing the gravity of what he'd done. And be frightened enough not to do it again. She was going out tonight; if she told him now, then gave him the evening to think things over . . .

"Paul," she called as she climbed the stairs to his room, dreading his reaction to what she was about to say.

thirty-seven

"You were right, Lily. He is marvelous. Absolutely marvelous. We must have done it three or four times each night." Jules beamed at her friends. Once Sean had gotten over his attack of guilt, he had been everything she had expected. And more.

"God. You've got to be exhausted." Terry drained her half-full glass of white wine and refilled it. Perhaps alcohol would help her get into the spirit of the evening.

"But nicely so. Very nicely so. Very, very nicely so."

"He's that good?"

"Definitely. If not better."

"Fuck. If twenty years of failure hadn't finally managed to drum some sense into my thick head, I'd almost be tempted to try again." Terry made a pathetic stab at a grin. The scene with Paul had been even worse than she had imagined and she was having a hard time thinking of anything else.

"Not with Sean," Lily blurted out. She, Terry, and Jules were sitting in a little Italian restaurant around the corner from Jules's house, getting together for dinner to discuss the last few days. It had been Jules's idea; she was so full of what had happened between her and Sean that she couldn't wait to tell her friends, sure that they would share her feelings.

"What's this, Lils? Getting possessive?"

"No, no, of course not. If you fancy Sean, be my guest." Lily forced the words out. What the hell was wrong with her? First it was Jules, now Terry. She stiffened her inner upper lip and told herself sternly to behave. These were her friends. She loved them more than any man.

"Go on, Terry, it's your turn."

"No, I don't think so."

"You'd love being with him. I can vouch for it. He's so considerate. It was the first time for me, you know, since Will, and I was worried I might be scared. Or have flashbacks to . . . to all that. But there was nothing. I couldn't have imagined him hurting me. No question, you'd love it."

"Yeah, but I'm not sure she would," Lily said.

"Why on earth not?" Jules asked.

"I just think . . . Ter, you always said one of the things you hated about sex was the way men ground away at you. And you might need someone a little more gentle than Sean if you're going to try again."

"More gentle?" Jules asked. "I'm not sure that'd be possible."

Lily stared at her friend, shocked. "He . . . you thought he was gentle?" Sean's aggression in bed was one of the things she liked about him. Most men she ran across nowadays thought all women wanted hearts and flowers, wishy-washy, tender sex, and it was rare to find one willing to be as in your face as Sean.

"Don't you? But he was wonderful. Never a rough moment. Even the, the"—Jules searched for the right word—"the penetration was lovely. Slow and easy and kind. He'd be perfect for Terry. Perfect."

"Thanks. But no thanks. I'm happy as I am. Celibate to the death, that's me." Terry glanced down at her watch. The more the evening went on, the more her thoughts were with Paul, at home. And whether her ploy had worked.

Lily slowly relaxed. Of course there was no chance of Terry wanting Sean. Plus, she'd been reassured by Jules's use of the word "kind." Kind didn't imply heat or sweat or excitement. Kind was nice. Sweet. A task undertaken out of compassion. Not the sort of hot encounter that Sean would be eager to repeat. Not her Sean.

She smiled at her friend. "So when will you know?"

thirty-eight

The house was dark.

Terry fumbled for the switch. She was sure she'd left a light on in the hall. "Paul," she called out.

No response.

She went up to the door of his room and listened for a moment. No music, no computer games, no snores. "Paul? Are you asleep?"

Nothing.

Gingerly, Terry opened the door to his room and peeked inside. It was empty. Where was he? Had he ignored being grounded and gone out?

She made a quick search through the flat.

There was no one in the living room. Or in her bedroom. The kitchen too was empty. In fact, it looked just as it had when she'd left a couple of hours before. Except for one thing. The table was covered with every bottle of alcohol she could remember having in her possession, even the hideous half bottle of peppermint Mintu Lily had bought as a joke gift when on a trip to Finland. And every single one of them was drained.

He couldn't have drunk it all, could he? She went to the sink and sniffed, hoping to find traces of port and cherry brandy and Mintu. But all she got was a vague, underlying scent of bleach, left from when she'd cleaned the kitchen the previous day.

God, that much alcohol might kill someone who was unused to it. Where was he? She'd tried everywhere, kitchen, lounge, bedrooms. . . . She rushed to the one she hadn't yet searched. The bathroom.

To find the door locked. He had to be inside.

"Paul? Paul? Are you in there? Are you all right?" She rattled the handle, pushed against the door, put her shoulder to it, and tried to force her way in, getting more and more frantic. But it held firm. What the hell was she going to do? She had to get him out of there, and quickly. She was going to have to get help.

She rushed to the phone, completely panicked. And rang the one person she was sure would understand.

Sean.

Twenty nerve-racked minutes later, he was at the door.

"How much was there?" he asked as he ran down the corridor to the bathroom.

"I don't know. I've been trying to work it out. Most of the bottles had only a bit in them. Stuff left over from parties, you know?"

"Yeah. The last dregs of a bottle of Amaretto you never throw away unless you move. I have lots myself. Stand back."

Sean turned his shoulder to the door, ran at it, and battered it open. Inside, Paul was lying on the floor, surrounded by vomit, moaning softly. Sean bent over, picked him up, propped him up in the pink bath, and turned on the shower. Cold water rained down on him and Paul together.

Terry leaned against the sink unit, her hands gripping the tiles in an attempt to hide the shaking she was unable to control "Is he . . . will he be okay?"

"Don't worry. He's gotten rid of most of it. A cold shower, a lot of water, and a long sleep, and all he'll have is a monster of a hangover."

"I'M SORRY about your clothes."

"What, an old pair of jeans and a sweatshirt? Water won't hurt. But please don't tell anyone you saw me like this. 'Specially not any of the men on the site. God, I'd never hear the end of it." Sean smiled. He was dressed in an old, dark red, embroidered chenille robe that Terry had found in a shop in Covent Garden. Luckily, she liked her flopping-around-the-house clothes extra, extra large. Even so, it gaped over his chest and reached only to just below his knee.

"I can't even offer you a drink."

"After that, I'm not sure I'd fancy one. Tea will do just fine."

Terry put the kettle on. "Did he say anything?"

"Not a lot. And what he did say didn't make much sense. I think he was embarrassed."

"I shouldn't have gone out."

"Course you should. For all you know, he'd have done something worse if you'd been here."

"But I told him I was thinking about forbidding him the one thing he most wanted and then I walked out and left him alone. And look what happened."

"Terry. Don't beat yourself up about this. Kids have tantrums."

"That's all it was? You're sure?"

"I'm sure. He's a teenager. Hormones are rushing around his body at the speed of light. He was worried and angry and he wanted you to know it."

"I thought it was the only thing that would get through to him."

"Perhaps it was. For all you know, it was just what he needed. Maybe he'll never swear at a teacher again."

"Maybe."

"You aren't going to stop him going to the Chelsea game? Not after all the trouble I had getting tickets?"

"Oh, no. I didn't know it was so hard. We shouldn't have asked you."

"And I shouldn't be teasing you when you're like this."

Terry tried to smile. "Sorry. Sense of humor failure."

"Don't worry about it. It's natural. You're upset."

"I've no idea what I'd've done tonight without you. Rushing round here in the middle of the night."

"It was only ten-thirty."

"Still. You came. I'll never, never forget it." And Terry burst into tears as the realization finally struck her. Paul was fine.

Sean moved to put his arm around her shoulders. "It's okay. It's all right. He's safe." He repeated the words like a mantra as Terry sobbed out her relief.

After a few minutes, she pulled herself away, grabbed a piece of kitchen towel, and wiped her eyes.

"I didn't mean to do that."

"It's no problem."

"You've already done enough for me for one night."

"It was nothing."

"It wasn't nothing. You were wonderful. You are wonderful. Thank you, thank you, thank you. God, that's not enough."

Sean held up his hand to stop Terry's words. He was close to tears himself. It had been an emotional evening and any more might push him over the top. "Please, Terry. I like Paul. I was glad to help, okay?"

"Well, okay. But if you ever need me . . ."

"I'll be sure to call. Now, the tea?"

thirty-nine

Sean wasn't sure what he was going to do right up until the moment he walked into the fashionable Moroccan let's-all-sit-on-overstuffed-floor-cushions-to-eat restaurant in the center of town and saw Lily, wearing what looked like a new and very expensive suede jacket, huddled under a low-lit brass lamp.

He'd spent the previous few days struggling to decide what to do about her. Should he tell her the truth about what had happened with Jules? Or carry on as normal? Part of him felt the honest thing to do would be to call and cancel their prearranged dinner date. And end their relationship. However, though he wanted to atone for his own disloyalty, he wasn't sure it was fair to make his penance Lily's also. To make her pay—presuming she would miss seeing him—for his sin. Nor was he sure what his leaving Lily would do to her friendship with Jules. Because if he ended things right after he'd been a "donor" for Jules, Lily would be bound to ask some difficult, probing questions about what had happened between him and her friend. And he didn't know Jules well enough to know whether she would be able to lie as easily by commission as omission.

Hoping to clear his mind, he had spent a day in Putney, using a sledge-hammer to break up the old concrete floor in one part of his building. But it hadn't helped. His thoughts continued to go around and around as he veered from one course of action to another. Until, finally, it was too late to do anything other than meet Lily and see what would happen.

He walked across the dimly lit room toward her, curled in opposite, and pecked her on the cheek.

"Hello."

"Hi."

"Sorry I'm late."

"Don't worry, I've only been here a few minutes. Bad day at work?"

"No."

"Traffic?"

"No."

Lily realized that this was going to be harder than she had imagined. "The menu looks amazing. Stuff I've never even heard of, and I took the twins to Morocco on holiday a year ago."

"Oh." God, this was difficult. She was being so matter-of-fact.

Lily reminded herself not to push too hard. Naturally, he was feeling guilty about Jules. Give him time and things would be fine. "Let's order. I want those aubergines and the salad and definitely the lamb and apricots. What do you think?"

"Fine."

"And you?"

Sean pushed the menu away unread. "I'll have what you're having."

"No, come on, have something different. Don't you want to taste stuff?"

"Sorry. Of course." Sean quickly chose, at random, hummus and a strange sweet chicken pie.

The food was ordered and the starters came, but Sean still couldn't decide what he ought to do. Should he keep quiet and in essence reward himself with Lily's continuing presence in his life? Or tell her the truth and in so doing hurt her badly?

Lily wiped her plate with her bread and finished off the last of the spiced aubergine. "That was absolutely delicious. No question, Jonathan Meades was right about this place." She would have to work extra hard in the gym the next day to pay for this evening's indulgences, but right now she felt in need of the comfort food could bring. Her failure to drag more than a few monosyllables out of Sean had shaken her confidence and she'd been horrified to find herself longing to ask him for reassurance. She wanted to hear him say that he preferred her, that he wasn't still thinking of Jules, that he wouldn't choose her kind of sex over Lily's. Instead, gritting her teeth, she carried on pretending that everything was just as it had been.

Then a waiter decked out in fez and tunic brought them Sean's choice, an eat-with-your-fingers sort of pie called a *bistilla*, made out of chicken and phyllo pastry and covered with confectioners' sugar, and left it with them uncut. Lily had seen the people at the table next to them pulling theirs apart with their hands and reached out to do the same. She ripped off a section and put it in her mouth. "Come on, this is great."

Sean took a minuscule piece.

"Pathetic."

"Sorry. I'm not all that hungry."

"All the more for me, then."

She reached out again, this time taking more. But the phyllo pastry separated and the chunk fell apart, spilling confectioners' sugar and bits of chicken all down her chin and over her new jacket. Lily looked startled, then burst out laughing.

At the sight of her covered in food, giggling, Sean started to laugh also. He leaned over to try and help her wipe away the mess but succeeded only in spreading the sugar farther over the black, velvety suede.

Which made Lily laugh all the more. "I must look like I've been snowed on," she gasped.

"Frosted. Like some cereals. And very attractive it is too."

Lily grinned. Attractive, eh? That was more like it. "We could take the remains home and try it out in bed."

"Good idea. Lily pie. Sounds delicious. And there'd be a snack handy in case we got hungry." The two laughed again. And with the laughter, all the tension between them evaporated and everything was as it had been.

A couple of hours later, in the middle of making love to Lily just the way he knew she liked it, Sean looked down at her lying naked beneath him and murmured, "I've missed you." Because he had. And because it felt as close as he would get to apologizing for what had happened with Jules.

Lily moved against him, eager for more, all her remaining doubts about him and her friend wiped away. She had the reassurance she wanted. And without having to suffer the humiliation of asking for it.

By the time she left the house to go to work the following morning, feeling tired and very pleasantly stiff, she had convinced herself that now that she was sure Sean preferred her, she would be fine about lending him out to Jules again.

Although she would be happier if her friend were pregnant at the first try.

"CAN WE ring her?"

"Hell, Sean, what time is it?"

"I don't know. Six, maybe?"

Lily groaned. "Six?"

"So can we call her?"

"Are you mad? It's the middle of the night."

"It's not. It's morning."

Lily squinted at the gray light outlining one of the bedroom's large, curtained windows. "Only just. And no, we can't."

"But today's the day."

"I know today's the day, you know today's the day, if Jules has been as bad with everyone else as she has with us, the whole of SW3 knows today's the day. She'll call when she has something to tell us. Sean, it's only six o'clock. Every sensible person is unconscious right now." Lily turned over to face away from him, hoping to catch another hour of sleep. But it was too late. Maybe if she were alone, she might be able to drop off again, but Sean was here and she was awake. She might as well get up.

"All right, all right, I'll make us some tea." Lily climbed out of bed, grabbed her robe, and set off downstairs. Normally, Sean would have offered to make the tea himself, or at least to help, but today he was far too preoccupied even to notice Lily leaving the room.

Downstairs in her stainless-steel kitchen, she puttered about, putting together a breakfast tray for the two of them. Earl Grey tea, warmed croissants, French butter, her favorite imported quince jelly. If she had to be up this early, she was going to indulge herself. After all, she deserved it. The last couple of weeks had been hard work. First there had been her initial, edgy meeting with Sean after his nights with Jules. Then there had been the need to talk to Jules an ever-increasing number of times each day in an attempt to calm her down, to smooth away her mounting anxiety as the moment she could take a pregnancy test and trust its results approached. And finally, there had been Sean's own growing excitement over the possible baby, which she had begun to find a tad annoying. Touching, in a way, she supposed, but irritating nonetheless. The sooner Jules was pregnant and this was all over, the better.

UPSTAIRS, SEAN lay on his side, his eye on the red-light numbers of the clock radio. It was still only 6:20. How was he going to wait until seven or even seven-thirty, when Lily would agree that he could call Jules? The last weeks had crept by increasingly slowly as the day of reckoning approached. He wasn't sure that he could manage to wait the eons that forty minutes now seemed to represent.

Lily, he knew, thought he was so on tenterhooks because he wanted to find out if he had been successful or not. A sort of male need to prove his potency. And he let her believe that. But it wasn't true. Oh, once Jules was pregnant, he'd be able to think of the child and be delighted about it, but right now what he wanted, what he longed for, was to be free of the obligation to return to her for another try. Because he knew that he was weak. Whatever he intended beforehand, he would succumb the next time, just as he had the first. He would end up back in bed with Jules. And he would be faced with the same dilemma again. And again. Unless the result was positive now.

He heard Lily's slow, tray-laden steps as she started the climb to the bedroom. The clock read 6:40. God, another twenty minutes.

ON THE other side of London, Jules looked across her canopied bed at the brass carriage clock. It was 6:40 on the first day her period could be due. And so the first day she could take a pregnancy test. And yet here she was, still lying in bed, her ClearBlue kit still sitting beside the toilet, waiting for her to pee on it and discover the answer.

Yesterday, she'd been desperate to find out whether she was pregnant or not. Today, she'd been awake for a good two hours but had held back, too afraid of failure to take the test. For the last few days, she'd been able to hope and it had been wonderful. But now it was reality time.

The alarm would go off any minute. Then she'd have to get up. No more huddling in bed like a hibernating bear. No, that was too generous. She wasn't hibernating, she was hiding. Annoyed by her own feeble cowardice, Jules jumped up and turned off the bell. Time to find out the truth. After all, there was always next month. And the consolation of another marathon session with Sean . . .

In the bathroom, Jules shimmied out of her dark blue silk pajama bottoms, opened the foil wrapper, removed the test stick, and took off the cap. She held the stick over the toilet and peed on it. After five seconds, she pulled it away, replaced the cap, and prepared to wait the minute to see if the blue line appeared in the tiny square window.

Slowly, she counted. "Mississippi one, Mississippi two . . . Mississippi fifty-nine, Mississippi sixty!"

The minute was up. She took off the cap.

"Yes! Yes! Yes!" she cried as she leapt about the room, waving the test stick in the air before looking at it again and then again, needing to confirm that it had indeed been positive. And each time she looked, the clear blue line was still there, in the right place. "I'm pregnant, I'm pregnant." Jules jumped up and down with delight. Until a thought struck her. She stopped moving, put her hand protectively over her stomach, and sat down on the side of the bath. She shouldn't be hopping around like this. It might hurt the child.

"I'm going to have a baby," she said softly to herself, still finding it hard to believe. "A baby."

Three

forty

Mara hustled the girls into their coats and out of the smoke-filled house. The wind was blowing from the north again. Worse, it had rained the previous day, so the wood was wet and the chimney, unswept for so long, its stack half fallen to the roof over the summer, couldn't cope with the amount of smoke the fire produced when it was first lit. After a few minutes, once the flames had had a chance to take hold, it was fine, but until then they either sat around in clouds of smoke or took refuge outside. But there was little else she could do. Her free wood worked fine when the weather was good, but if it was rainy she needed to give it a chance to dry out before using it and she never could manage to do that. It was hard enough to gather sufficient branches for their immediate needs.

However, she had little choice but to continue. Moo and Tilly had a small storage heater in their bedroom for the coldest nights, but Mara didn't have the money to pay for costly electric fires. Even when the cheaper gas heating had been working, she'd had to be careful with it or she struggled to pay the bills in winter. The free fires were a financial godsend, but they carried their own risk; there was always a chance someone would see the smoke and she would be arrested for burning wood in a smokeless fuel zone. She kept telling herself she was safe—if they didn't have enough police to stop old ladies from being mugged in the High Street, they wouldn't have an anti-wood-burning fires squad—but she couldn't help worrying nonetheless. That would be all she needed, a criminal conviction.

Coughing, she wedged the front door open to get some fresh air blowing through the house and walked outside into the chilly October night to check on Moo and Tilly. There they were, huddled against the outside wall.

"Mum, Mum, is it okay now?"

"Can we go back in?"

"Let's give it a few minutes."

"I'm cold."

"Me too."

"Come here, then." Mara put her arms around her two daughters. "That better?"

EVER SINCE Mara had seen the lawyer and heard his advice, she'd been operating more out of habit than anything else, going through the motions of everyday life whilst underneath, her mind struggled to come to terms with what Robin Heath had said she should do. She kept hoping she would find some other way out of her problems, kept praying every night to Jake to help her see some alternative, but her prayers remained unanswered.

She was going to have to get in touch with her father. A man she hadn't spoken to in almost twenty years. Not since she'd fled the family house in Dagenham, near London, one icy night when she was just sixteen. Running from an arranged marriage to an elderly man.

The lawyer had said she could do with some close relatives. Aunts and uncles and cousins and grandparents. And her family were all under her father's iron control. Plus, she needed money. She was living on borrowed time with the chimney and she had just received a wake-up call. If nothing else, she had to get the central heating fixed. What if the Moores found out she was breaking the law and burning wood? They'd make sure she was charged and convicted.

Even if she wanted to continue running that risk, sooner or later the rest of the stack would fall, the flue would close up, and she wouldn't be able to make her free fires anymore. With no way to heat the house, she would either have to run up an electric bill she would never be able to pay and so end up being cut off or be forced to ask Amy to have Moo and Tilly every night until Mara could find a solution to her problems. Not only would that not look good if the Moores insisted on going to court, but it would also mean Mara imposing on a friend who was far from well. And spending every night apart from her girls. Just like Mara's own, Amy's house had only two bedrooms.

Mara hadn't thought about Shama Mattajee in ages, hadn't even known if he was still alive. Until a few months ago, when she had seen an article about him in *Metro*, talking about his chain of electronic superstores, his luxurious house in an exclusive suburb of London, his millions in the bank. All proudly achieved without borrowing a penny from anyone. At the time, she had felt nothing more than a mild sense of disappointment— he didn't deserve that kind of success—before dismissing it from her mind. But now it all came back to her and she couldn't get the picture of his house, his cars, his money out of her head. He could afford to help her, if he chose to do so.

Could she go back now? Could she bring herself to beg for money and attention from the man whom she had first loved, then hated so much? Could she forget the way he had blamed her when she'd staggered home, a fifteen-year-old girl raped by a gang of youths? The way he had seen what had happened as his shame, a loss of family face rather than a devastating attack on a young and vulnerable girl? The way he had begun to shop her around to anyone who might take her as soon as it was clear that she was not pregnant? He hadn't cared about age, prospects, financial situation, history, anything. All he'd wanted was someone to take her off his hands as soon as possible. And so wash clean the stain she had brought to the family.

He'd found that person in Anil Patel, a fifty-five-year-old widower with grown children, a thin, desiccated-looking man with a leering eye and wandering hands. And a yen for some juicy young flesh.

Apart from Mara's younger brother, Roshan, who before Mara ran away had been occasionally—and secretly—supportive, her other siblings and even her mother all followed the line set by her father. Obedience was second nature to all of them. They were terrified of him. They shut Mara out, acted as if they also believed that she was something dirty, to be kept out of sight and then disposed of as quickly and quietly as possible. Mara was sixteen. Her family was everything to her. So, though she hated the idea of Patel slobbering all over her, she tried to go along with her father's wishes.

She sat quietly while the old man pawed her, while the betrothal was agreed upon, when all the way through, somewhere inside she was screaming her refusal. That night, lying in bed, imagining how it would feel to have Patel next to her, his hands reaching for her, she knew she could never go through with it. She had to get away. Immediately. She wasn't sure she would be able to hide her disgust for another minute, and once her father found out how she felt, he would make sure she had no chance of escape.

She waited until it was late, until everyone was asleep. Then she crept down and out of the house. When she paused at the corner of the narrow street on which she had lived her whole life, to take one last look back at the family house, she'd seen a figure leaning out of an open window, waving. Roshan. Softly he'd called out, "Good luck," before quietly closing the window. And Mara had turned and walked away.

Her family had long since moved on. Her father had made a fortune from his electrical stores. Her brothers and sisters were all married, with their own kids. And all of them, even Roshan, had refused to have anything to do with her ever since she'd walked out that night. Mara's father had forbidden it. She was to be treated as if she were dead. As far as he was concerned, she was. They had obeyed him, seemingly without question. To begin with, she had tried to contact her family, but had soon given up. Even Roshan, even her mother were too afraid of Shama Matterjee to have anything to do with her. And so she had tried her best to stop thinking about them. First her friends and then Jake and the girls had become her family. Most of the time, she had been happy with that. When Moo was born, she had longed briefly for her own mother and attempted to get in touch, but she had gotten no reply to her letter and soon forgot her longing in the excitement and worry of her first baby. By the time Tilly arrived, she was too involved in her life with Moo and Jake to want anyone else. Her family had become as dead to her as she was to them.

But now it was time to try and bridge the chasm that had existed between them for nearly twenty years. It had been a long, long time. And they said that space, distance, and age transformed people. Perhaps her father had mellowed. Tilly and Moo were innocent of Mara's own crimes against him; maybe he would want to help them, even if he were still furious with her. After all, he had always cared deeply about his family, if in a medieval, overly controlling sort of way. Yes, it was a slim chance—she never remembered her father changing his mind about anything—but she had to try. It was what Jake would want her to do.

forty-one

"To Jules." Lily raised her glass of champagne and took a sip.

"And the baby," Jules added.

"Of course. And the baby," Lily agreed.

"Congratulations, Jules," said Terry, buttoning her lip. Now was not the time to say anything. The baby was on its way, there was no changing that. And it was her job to be supportive. If she could. Hiding her feelings wasn't one of her strong points—God, how much easier her life would have been if it were—but for her friend's sake she needed to try and conceal her continuing worries about Jules's plans.

"Jules and the baby," Mara said, thankful that in the general melee of greetings and coat taking and the getting of drinks no one had noticed her being subdued.

"Us." Jules was radiant, her happiness shining out of every pore.

"And I just want to say that none of this would have happened if not for me and my brilliant idea." Lily smiled around at her girlfriends. This was what she had envisioned when she'd had her brain wave all those weeks ago. Each of them benefiting—well, three of them anyway—and none of them being hurt.

"Yeah, yeah, yeah. You're a genius, we all know."

"Laugh all you like. But that baby is part mine."

"I'm not laughing. Without you, there'd be no child." Jules raised her glass of fizzy water to her friend. "Thank you," she said softly. "I'll never forget it."

Lily blushed. "Hey, it was nothing. Thank Sean."

"I will. But without you, he would never have done it. And done it so well." Jules grinned. "Imagine, all that and potent too. Pregnant on the first try. Although I wouldn't have minded having him again."

"Well, there's nothing stopping you." Lily felt able to be generous. She was confident Jules wouldn't go to bed with Sean again.

"Thanks. But no thanks. That might just complicate things. I've got what I wanted."

Mara watched her friends discussing Sean, their lives, their scheme, and felt almost as if they were characters in a movie. Lily's pride in her plan, Terry's banter, Jules's excitement barely registered with her. She was in a scary, isolated world of her own. Tomorrow she was going to make a surprise visit to Roshan in the hope he would help her see her father.

She'd been sorely tempted to back out of Jules's celebration. She knew constant worry had rubbed her emotions raw and that there was a chance she'd break down if she were challenged in any way. It was going to be hard to convince her friends that all was well. But she'd left the girls with Amy and forced herself to go. The night was for and about Jules, not her. And she was delighted for her friend. So she had come, trusting to the occasion to distract the others from her lack of animation.

Terry searched for something to say to Jules that was suitably nonjudgmental. "So who gets to be godmother?" she asked.

"Me."

"Ahh, Lils. I thought of it first."

"But I deserve it. Me. Me. Me."

"Calm down. You can both be. You can all be."

"Yes." Lily pumped her fist in the air. "I've always longed to renounce the devil and all his works."

"I'll do my best to be a good one. And that's a promise," said Terry.

Three faces turned to look at Mara. Who didn't respond.

"Mara?"

"Didn't you hear what Jules was saying?"

"Are you okay?"

"Sorry. I was dreaming." Mara searched for something to say to explain her inattention. "I . . . I've not been sleeping well." It was true, after all. No need to say why.

"Poor thing."

"You do look exhausted, sweetie."

"Are the girls all right?"

Mara looked at her girlfriends' concerned faces and burst into tears.

"Mara?" Terry went over to her friend and held her. "Mar? What is it?"

Mara burrowed into Terry's shoulder. "It's nothing," she said, sobbing.

"Like hell it's nothing." Lily sounded deeply concerned. It was not like her friend to break down like this just from tiredness.

Mara made a superhuman effort and managed to stop crying. It felt as if she'd only skimmed the surface, that if she really let go she'd be bawling for weeks. "It is. Tilly's fine. Moo's fine. We're all fine. I'm just tired. Promise."

Lily and Terry still looked doubtful, but Jules was prepared to take Mara at her word. If she said she was just tired, she was just tired. After all, everyone knew she didn't lie. "What you need is some fun," Jules suggested.

"Fun?"

"Yes, fun. It's about time you gave yourself a present. And I have the perfect thing."

"I don't think . . . I'm a bit broke at the moment." She could barely manage to buy the girls something for Christmas. She was hardly going to give herself a present.

"Ah, but this gift costs nothing. And it comes complete with hammer and nails."

It took Mara a second or two to work out that Jules was talking about Sean. Then she was annoyed by the suggestion. Wouldn't they ever give up? "No. I've said no. Why can't you accept that?"

"Right. I agree. If Mara says she doesn't want to have a part of Sean, she should be allowed not to do so." Up until a few moments ago, Lily had believed that she wanted Mara to take part in the scheme. She'd been convinced that it would be the making of her, in fact. But as Jules mentioned it, she'd seen a flash of Mara and Sean together. Of Mara, beautiful, sexy, irresistible Mara, in bed with her lover. And she was shaken by just how much she hated the idea. No way did she want those two to get together. If Sean was once with Mara, what chance he'd return to her?

"Yes, Jules. Leave her alone, why don't you?" Terry said. She was starting to feel uncomfortable about the way they were treating Sean. Though she'd always had some doubts, when she hadn't known him, when she hadn't realized what a great guy he was, when she'd been unaware of the tragedy in his own life she'd allowed herself to believe it was okay. A bit of innocent fun for them all. But now, particularly after the other night, it felt sort of degrading. Both to him and to them.

"But . . . but . . ." Jules was amazed by her friends' reactions. "I thought we all agreed. Sean and Mara should get together."

"That was then, wasn't it?"

"Ages ago. Anyway, you can see Mara isn't interested. We should stop pestering her."

"I wasn't pestering her. I was just suggesting. *Like we agreed.*" Jules looked from Lily to Terry, hoping for some kind of understanding. The last time she'd spoken to the two of them about it, they'd wanted Mara involved. What had changed?

"Don't get worked up about it. I don't want him. Please, please, will you believe me? I can't bear all this pressure to join in. I'm fine as I am. There's only one man I want and he's . . . gone."

"That's absolutely ridiculous. I think we've all had enough. It's about time you were told—"

"How much we all care about you," Lily jumped in to finish Jules's sentence. She glared at her friend. Maybe the time was coming for Mara to find out the truth, but not now. Not unless they all concurred. And had planned it in advance. Now Mara was tired and emotional and not ready to hear that her sainted husband had been a complete shit. "We just want you to be happy, that's all."

"Yes. Happy," Terry echoed.

Mara smiled. "I know. And I can't believe how lucky I am to have friends like you all. Even when I ruin Jules's celebration by crying over nothing, you still love me. Jules, forgive me."

"Of course." Jules couldn't believe she'd been about to blurt out the truth about Jake. She'd lost control there for a moment. Maybe what they said about rampaging hormones was true? "I shouldn't have pushed you. I'm so sorry."

"It's okay. Only . . . can you all please leave it alone from now on? I promise you I don't want him. Please."

"If that's what you want," Lily said. "Of course."

"It is. It is. Thank you."

"Well, we've just seen one of the effects of single motherhood," Terry said.

"What's that?"

"You're always, always tired."

"I don't care if I'm exhausted for the next eighteen years," Jules said, smiling around at the group. "Am I really, really going to have a baby?"

"You are really, really going to have a baby," Lily said, grinning back. "In about thirty-seven weeks and six days."

"Yippee!"

forty-two

Sean stood outside the door to Jules's little house. It was the first time he'd seen her since their two nights together. He'd spoken to her briefly, to congratulate her, but he'd been getting most of his information about her through Lily. He had to admit that he was nervous; he didn't know how to treat Jules, what to say to her. They'd been to bed together—would you call what they had done an affair?—he was the father of her child, and yet they were almost complete strangers. A couple of dinners and two nights of baby making didn't tell you much about a person. And they needed to know each other rather well. They were going to be mother and father. Sean had no intention of stepping on Jules's toes, wasn't expecting to move in with her or have joint custody or anything like that, but he wanted to be involved as much as possible. He yearned to spend time with a child of his own again, to have a new son or daughter to love.

He wasn't trying to replace his lost sons. That was totally impossible. Mark and Ben were Mark and Ben and no one could take their place, ever, ever. But he didn't only miss them as individuals. He also missed the fact of having a child around. Their noise, their mess, their laughter, even their tears. It was one of the reasons he was so enjoying being with Paul.

So tonight had been his idea. To celebrate, of course, but also to bring some normalcy back into his and Jules's relationship. The sex—thank God—was over and they needed to put it behind them. Forget it if they could and concentrate on being coparents. Sean had asked Lily for the name of Jules's favorite place to eat—the Dunmore—and had made a reservation. He had a large bunch of flowers clasped in his hand along with a book about pregnancy and a minuscule white-and-yellow sleeping suit for the baby.

He reached out and rang the bell.

THE DUNMORE was not one of the newer, hip additions to London hotels. It had been around since Victorian times and the decor hadn't changed since the thirties. But it was still the hotel of choice for many celebrities who preferred its old-world charm and traditional service to the more modern, trendy atmosphere of the Metropolitan or the Sanderson.

It was eight o'clock. The plush restaurant to the left of the marble-and-gold lobby was three-quarters full with diners and hovering, black-tied waiters. To the right, the pink-and-gray bar was empty. Apart from Martin, the barman, famous for his martinis, who was polishing glasses, and Clive Morris, who was lurking at the far end, sipping from a half-empty pyramid-shaped goblet.

It was Tuesday. And on Tuesdays Clive always visited the the Dunmore bar to talk to Martin. To find out just who had arrived that week. And, if he was lucky and Martin had been able to get a look at the reservations, who was expected. The two had had an agreement for over a year. Clive paid Martin a small retainer for his exclusive services and a series of substantial bonuses based on information received. It suited both of them.

It had been a quiet week. An older American film star had been expected but had canceled due to illness, and a famous literary lion from South America was ensconced in the Presidential Suite. Not much of interest for Clive's readers.

He drained his glass and put it down. Time to move on. He had been romancing the concierge at the Lanesborough for some time, hoping to tempt the man to the same deal as Martin. Maybe he'd hop over there, give it another go. Last week, he thought he'd sensed the man wavering.

"That's it, Martin. I'm off. Same time next week?"

"No problem. May be a better slate then. October's often slow, though."

"Yeah, yeah. Excuses, excuses."

Clive stood up and put on his coat. Outside, in the lobby, the doorman swung open the front door to the hotel to let Sean and Jules in. Clive walked out of the bar just in time to see them disappear into the restaurant. And his nose for a story gave a little, preliminary twitch. What was Lily's escort at the Comedy Awards doing here with Jules?

Concealed by a pillar, he watched them being seated in the center of the dining room, then walked up to the middle-aged man on the restaurant's front desk and asked for a table behind and to the side so that there was little chance of Jules seeing him. He'd prefer Sean not to see him either, just in case Lily had pointed him out at the awards dinner, but given a choice between the two, he'd definitely take Sean. There was only a slim chance he'd know Clive, whereas Jules would recognize her friend's ex-husband immediately. And wonder what the hell he was doing there. She'd know he wasn't the Dunmore restaurant type. Hadn't been even in his successful TV period.

He looked at the menu, ordered the least expensive things he could find, and settled down to watch.

SEAN MOVED the dry, unappetizing pieces of meat around on his plate. They were now on their main course and he had yet to see what it was that made this Jules's favorite restaurant. The food was, well, "ordinary" was the kindest adjective he could think of. Everything was a touch overdone, and it all somehow tasted alike, as if it had been cooked in the same all-encompassing giant pot. He decided that he had had enough of his chicken, laid down his cutlery, and looked up to see Jules watching him with a smile.

"That was delicious," he said.

"Liar. It was dry, overcooked, and not all that tasty."

"Damn Lily. She told me this was your favorite restaurant."

"It is. But not for the food. They do great breakfasts and teas here, but almost everything else is a bit dull. I love the room, the decor, the way it feels. The tradition of it. My grandfather used to bring me here for lunch when I was a child. I loved him, so I love the Dunmore."

"I didn't do wrong, then, bringing you here?"

Jules touched Sean's hand for a moment. "You did very right. As I said, I love it. And the desserts make up for the rest of the food. Come on, let's make pigs of ourselves. I'm eating for two, you know."

Sean laughed. "No. Really?"

"Yes. Really." Jules's face softened. "And I owe that to you." She leaned over the table and reached out to stroke Sean's face, to run her fingers from his cheek to his chin.

Sean blushed. "It was nothing."

"No it wasn't. You gave me what I've always wanted. A child of my own to love. And you did it in the way I wanted even though I know you felt bad about it afterward. But you didn't complain or presume anything from it. You were the perfect donor." She leaned over the table and kissed Sean full on the mouth. "Thank you for my baby."

"I don't know what to say."

"You don't need to say anything. Now, let's get on with choosing our puds. I definitely want pavlova. And something chocolate."

HALFWAY THROUGH his roast lamb, Clive had begun to regret staying on. Sean and Jules had been friendly enough with each other but had done nothing out of the ordinary. Nothing intimate. They could be and probably were just two mates out for dinner. His nose for a story had never steered him wrong before but he was starting to think that this could be the first time. After all, what did he know about Sean? He'd been seen out with Lily, acting as if he was much more than a mere escort to her. Now he was having dinner with Jules, one of Lily's best friends. Big deal. Nothing major in that. Maybe they both knew him. Maybe Lily had met him through Jules. Maybe he was just part of their social circle.

Clive pushed his meal aside and was about to wave for the waiter and ask for the bill when he saw Jules reach out and touch Sean's hand. A moment later, she stroked his cheek. And he appeared to blush. And then she leaned over the table and kissed him.

Clive's nose twitched again and more strongly this time. Something was going on. He had no idea what was happening, or why, but he intended to find out. Maybe it wasn't the kind of thing he was looking for, but it was worth investigation. Just in case he'd found, by pure luck, the story he'd been seeking for months.

forty-three

Mara stood huddled in a phone box opposite an enormous electrical goods store. It was eight at night but the lights were still on, the doors still open, the customers still emerging with large boxes containing all the compelling morsels of modern technology. Computers, mobile phones, fax machines—you name it, Techno World sold it. And sold it.

When Mara had been living at home, her father had had only two bargain shops, both in low-rent areas, both cluttered with small stuff like toasters and clocks and kettles. Since then, he had specialized, concentrated on the growing communications and IT business. He'd kept the low prices, kept to the less-expensive areas, and every time he had had some spare capital, he had expanded. Now, there was a Techno World in every city in the UK. And Shama Mattajee owned them all, outright.

This was the London flagship, recently opened in a blaze of publicity in a modern, warehouselike building in Mill Hill. And managed by Roshan, Mara's baby brother, now grown into a tall, handsome, fashionably dressed man according to the article she had read and the picture accompanying it. She looked over at the store through the dirty glass of the telephone box, hoping to spot him. She was sure he would be there somewhere—their father had always been a tough taskmaster and would expect the family to work as hard and as long as he did. But there was no sign of him. Just hordes and hordes of happy customers. Roshan was probably holed up in an office somewhere, counting the profits. She would have to go in and find him.

Crossing her fingers and asking Jake to watch over her, she exited the telephone box and walked into the store. Her eyes blinked at the bright neon lights and she stared around in amazement. The place appeared large from the outside, but from the inside, it was absolutely huge. And filled with the latest in modern technology. Ranks and ranks and ranks of hulking, pale grayish-cream computers, standing at attention, screens at the ready. Of tiny mobile phones, many no bigger than a business card. Of printers and faxes and discs and software. Her father had come a long way from remaindered fans and out-of-date electric razors.

She looked around. No sign of Roshan. She needed to ask someone. The staff all seemed to be wearing red-and-green-striped hats so that they were identifiable from a distance. She spotted one standing idle for a moment. "Can you tell me where I'd find Roshan Mattajee?"

Five minutes later, she was outside a faceless, brown, Portakabin-like door. The salesman she'd spoken to had been very helpful once she'd mentioned that she was Roshan's sister. She reached out, her hand shaking, and knocked on the door. Please, oh please, may he be nice. . . .

"Come in."

Mara opened the door and stepped into the plain, MDF office. Roshan was sitting at a utilitarian desk, working on a computer. "Problem?" he asked without looking up, presuming that she was one of the store's sales staff.

"Yes, er, a little," Mara said in her soft voice. This was even more difficult than she had thought.

Roshan's head snapped up. To see a strangely familiar woman swaddled in an outsized black sweater and long, loose skirt. "Who are you?"

"I'm Mara . . . your sister."

"Mara?" Roshan got up from his desk, walked around it, and peered into his visitor's face. "It is. It's Mara." He put his arms around her and hugged her hard.

Mara laughed. "Hold on. That hurts."

Roshan pulled back and looked up at a closed-circuit camera in the corner of the room. "Come with me. Quick, come on." He hustled Mara out of the office, down the corridor, and out of the building through an emergency exit. Once in the open air, he led her behind a pair of half-full Dumpsters. "Okay. We're safe here."

"Safe?"

"Dad. There are cameras everywhere."

"He can't watch them all, surely?"

"No. But he's reputed to look at every tape to check up on us. Me especially."

"Still the rebel?"

"That's you. Anything I do couldn't come close to you running away."

"He's not still angry about it?"

"Your name is never mentioned."

"So I'm a pariah?"

Roshan shrugged. "We were all commanded not to talk to you after you left. And he's never said anything about revoking that order."

"But it was almost twenty years ago."

"You know Dad."

"He's not mellowed with age?"

Roshan laughed. "Not likely." Mara's face dropped. "What is it? What are you doing here anyway? Years of nothing and then you turn up in my office." He stared at his sister. "Were you hoping for something from him?"

"It's my daughters." In a few simple, short sentences, Mara described the trouble she was in to her brother. "So I need a family. And money. For the central heating. And the roof."

"I don't know."

"They're his grandchildren."

"But they're yours."

"Yes."

"And you were banished from the family."

"I have to see him, Roshan. I have to at least ask."

"It won't be nice. Even if he does give you the money, he'll expect something for it. And it's bound to be something you won't want to give. You know Dad."

"Whatever it is, it'll be better than living without my girls."

"What did you want me to do?" Roshan looked scared. "Support you?"

"No. Don't worry. I don't want to mess up your life. All I need is his address. I won't tell him where I got it, I promise. I'll say I saw the house in the newspaper and did some research."

"When are you thinking of going?"

"Sunday? After lunch? He was always at his mellowest then."

"I don't know."

"Please, Rosh. I don't have time to find out on my own. Please? I promise I won't betray you."

forty-four

Jules closed the door behind the Harrods delivery man. She walked through to her living room, sat down, and started to open the package. No doubt it was another gift from Sean. When they had first started arriving, she'd been delighted. She loved getting presents. But a giant teddy bear, two stuffed seals, a pair of tiny Nike sneakers, and three books on motherhood later, and she was getting tired of the endless stream of baby-related deliveries. Tired and worried.

She pulled a hand-carved, hand-painted mobile, to hang over a crib, out of the package. A ring of bright planets and stars. It was beautiful. And expensive. And not the gift of a disinterested party.

At Lily's barbecue, when Jules had first told Sean she was looking for a donor, she had explained that the baby was going to be hers and hers alone. That she would not expect or want anything from the father apart from the initial sperm. She could not have been more clear. But when she'd called him to say thank you after the first gift arrived, he'd spoken about the baby as if he were going to be around when it was born. As if he'd have an important role in its life. As if he already loved it.

Over the last week or so, she had tried gently to remind Sean of their original deal. But it seemed he hadn't heard her. Otherwise, why all the packages? A dinner, a small farewell present, that would have been accept-able, but the growing pile of gifts seemed to indicate that Sean was thinking of himself as a father. And if that were true, she needed to dissuade him. And quickly. She didn't want to hurt him—without his contribution there would be no baby—but she needed to make it plain to him. The child was hers to love and be loved by. No man was going to come between her and it.

She picked up the phone and dialed his mobile. He answered after one ring.

"Jules! Did you get the mobile?"

"Yes. I wanted to talk to you about it."

"Did you like it? Great, isn't it?"

"Of course I liked it. It's beautiful."

"I thought it'd look great over the baby's crib. We need to give him something to look at. Keep him interested in his world."

"Him? His?"

"Well, for now. Until we know. I can't go around calling our baby 'it.'"

Oh, no. Our baby. He did believe he was going to be a part of this. "Sean, I don't think you should be buying so many things for my baby." Listen to me, Sean. The word is "my."

"It's okay. I can afford it."

"That wasn't what I meant."

"And I'm loving looking for things. I saw the most wonderful new buggy the other day. Triangular, very light, folds up very small. I got all these brochures. I thought I'd go and get one next week."

"Please don't. I want to get my buggy myself." My buggy, Sean.

"Do you? Fine, of course you do. Maybe we could go together? The shop's a bit of a trek, in Barnes, but I could pick you up?"

"No, no, no. I want to do this alone."

"Okay."

"Sean, the baby's mine."

"Course it is."

"And I need to prepare for it in my own way. I want to choose my own things. It's part of the pleasure of it all. Planning the room, buying the clothes. The crib. The car seat. And the buggy."

"Okay. Okay. I just wanted to help."

"I know you did. And the gifts have all been lovely. But they've got to stop. All right?"

"Yeah. All right."

"It's not that I'm not grateful, but I've been looking forward to doing all this for years. I want to buy the things I'll need for when it's just me and my baby, by ourselves." There. She couldn't be clearer than that unless she actually told him to go away.

"I suppose I just wanted to feel part of things."

"I know. But this is my time now."

"Your time."

"You do understand?"

"Yes. Yes, course I do. Your time."

"But thank you for the mobile. The baby'll love it, I know."

"You're both welcome."

Jules put down the phone. Sean seemed to have understood, but something told her that this was not the end of it. Looking back, she thought he'd given in too easily. She hoped she was wrong. She hoped he'd taken what she said on board and was now ready to accept his nonexistent role in her baby's life. If she was right . . . well, she would just have to be more forceful next time. Much more forceful.

forty-five

"This is amazing."

Terry spun around, her eyes having a hard time taking in what she was seeing. In her world, football games were played on dull, cold days, in dank stadiums. In her world, the fans were young thugs wearing huge boots and kicking the crap out of each other. In her world, people ended up in hospital or even dead when they went to a game.

But this wasn't anything like the news footage of chasing mobs, of kicks and punches and thrown bottles that everyone was familiar with from the TV. It was more carnival than riot. Okay, the fact that it was a brilliantly sunny autumn day helped, but she had never imagined it would be so colorful. The scarves, the banners, the gigantic homemade hats, the songs echoing around the streets as they walked toward the stadium . . . No wonder Paul had so loved his previous trip to Stamford Bridge to see Charlton play Chelsea. No wonder he'd been so desperate to go again.

Terry looked around for her son. Just as he'd been doing since he'd first set eyes on her, he was hovering around Sally, the very pretty, very perky fifteen-year-old daughter of Sean's best friend, Ray. The game was at the Valley, Charlton's home stadium, and Sean had taken them to meet Ray and his family beforehand. The two had been friends since they were kids. They'd lived on the same street, gone to the same schools, known the same people, dated the same girls. Until Sean had moved uptown. But they'd stayed friends and it was obvious that their differences in wealth and position—Ray was a greengrocer and still lived on the street where he and Sean had been brought up—had never come between them.

Terry couldn't help smiling. She felt like a lucky woman. A good-natured son, a sunny day out, and a nice man to spend it with.

Sean ran off into the crowd and reappeared a moment later with a red-and-white Charlton scarf. He wound it round Terry's neck.

"Can't come here without your colors."

"Thank you. This is great. Really great."

"No thugs throwing bottles, no fights, no riot police?"

"How'd you know?"

"It's what everyone who doesn't come thinks it's like. Come on, in here."

Sean led the way into the ground, through metal turnstiles and concrete corridors, and then they were out, high up, looking down on the brilliant, unexpected green of the pitch. Ray and Sean looked at each other, their sense of community unspoken but clear. Paul took a moment away from Sally to stare around, then turned to Sean and Ray.

"Like coming home."

"Yep."

"Every time."

THREE HOURS later, walking back to Ray's house through the crisp evening, the trees' bare branches Etch A Sketched against the sky, discarded newspapers swirling around her feet, Terry thought that it had been a perfect day. Though she wasn't and would never be a mad-crazy football fan, there was something magical about being part of twenty thousand people who all wanted the same thing. Sean was right. It made you feel you belonged. And when the desired thing happened and Charlton scored, once, twice, then three times without giving up a goal themselves, it was incredible. The sudden rush of excitement, the sense of unity, of kinship with all those other people, of strangers not being strangers but long-loved friends. Best of all, Paul had hugged her. Not once, but three times.

The smell of frying fish drifted through the air. Terry realized she was ravenous. Almost as if she had said something, Ray stopped outside a neon-lit chip shop.

"Okay. Who wants what?" he asked.

"We always stop here, get ourselves some dinner. Take some back for Babs and the kids," Sean explained.

"Great. I'm starving. I want lots and lots and lots of thick, fatty chips, some pieces of thin, unhealthy white bread covered in tons of butter, and a full bottle of brown sauce."

"Mam!"

"Chip butties. The greatest treat of my childhood."

"But . . . but . . . ," Paul stammered. For as long as he could remember, his mam had been watching her weight. And failing, veering from her normal all-embracing strictness to occasional extreme indulgence. He would have bet his new Jurassic 5 tape he knew all her treats—ice cream, bacon, chocolate, cheese—but he'd never heard her mention chips, let alone chip butties.

"I'm a cruel parent. I've deprived you of one of nature's best inventions." Terry grinned at her shocked son. "Paul'll have the same," she said to Ray.

"THAT WAS delicious." Terry licked her fingers with obvious relish. She'd forgotten just how wonderful a meal that consisted of nothing but fat and carbohydrates could taste.

The group were sitting around Ray and Babs's kitchen table, all happily eating out of paper, all drinking either beer or Coke out of the can. Ray, Sean, Paul, and Sally were rehashing the game, going back over the goals, over the incidents that had amused and pleased and amazed them. And complaining that, yet again, it was Manchester United headlining *Match of the Day*. All Charlton versus Middlesboro merited was a brief glimpse of the goals and—if they were lucky—a short sound-bite interview with the head coach.

As Babs cleaned up her two young sons and sent them off to play, Terry watched Paul. Watched his intent expression, his enthusiasm for the conversation, his smiling response to something Sally said. And watched as he took his last bite of his chip butty, looked over at her, and grinned.

"Good, eh?" Terry said, grinning back.

"I'm calling Childline. You knew about these all this time and you never gave me any. That's abuse."

Terry laughed. "Guilty. It's true. I can offer no defense."

"Do you promise to rectify the matter?" Paul deepened his voice to sound like his idea of a pompous, powerful judge.

"Yes, m'lud. Certainly, m'lud." She didn't know where to put herself. She had thought the school suspension, her threat to ban him from the Chelsea game, and his subsequent tantrum would have set them back months, but instead it seemed to have cleared the air. Here they were, talking, laughing, teasing each other just as they had before Finn.

Of course, this was today. Tomorrow, things would probably be difficult again. Her son would retreat to his room once more and she would hardly see anything of him for days. But she didn't care. He was changing. It was slow, but it was there. And she could live for weeks on this one glimpse of the old Paul. Because it proved what everyone had been telling her: that the rude, crude, hateful teenager she'd had to endure the last few months was nothing more than a passing phase. The moment Paul started to joke about the chip butties, Terry had felt mental muscles she hadn't even known she was clenching relax. It was going to be all right. With a bit of patience on her part and a tad more help from Sean, she would get her son back.

"See that you do," Paul said mock sternly, and turned back to Sally.

Terry smiled. Having a girlfriend wouldn't hurt either. The two teenagers could hardly manage to keep their eyes off each other.

forty-six

The smell of frying onions, of garlic and ginger and cumin, of coriander and cinnamon hung in the air as Mara walked up the gravel driveway. She had been surprised to find the gates open but delighted not to have to ring the intercom set outside the grounds; so much easier for them not to let her in if she were a hundred grass-, tree-, and flower-filled yards away rather than right at the front door.

The house was enormous. Built of gray stone, it looked more like a palace than a place where her family might live. There must be five, no, six windows on both levels on either side of the main door. A main door heralded by a grand cupola and imposing marble pillars and furnished with an impressive solid brass knocker in the shape of a mobile phone. Specially made for Shama Mattajee, Mara presumed.

She reached out, grasped the phone, and heard the deep knocking echo through the inside of the house. The door opened almost immediately. Mara's sister Meera stood in the hallway. She was fifteen years older than Mara and she looked it, her face deeply lined, her sour mouth more turned down than ever.

"Mara."

"Meera." Mara held out her hand and attempted a smile. She and Meera had never gotten on as kids and Meera had appeared to enjoy rejecting her the last time she had attempted contact, but lots of time had passed, and anyway, she was trying to mend bridges, not keep them broken.

Meera looked at the hand, appeared to think about it, and decided against it. "Come with me," she said, and marched off across a spacious entrance hall, circling a large, round, highly polished table complete with elaborate flower arrangement.

Mara followed her, staring wide-eyed at the expensive glass chandelier, the broad double staircase, the domed roof. And this was just the hall. It was a very, very long way from the tiny family house she had left all those years before. Meera opened a pair of double doors on the other side of the hall and ushered Mara in before her.

In the middle of a long drawing room sat Shama, surrounded by his dutiful family, all of them arrayed on elaborate brocaded couches and chairs, all facing the door, as if posed for a photograph. Or as if they had been expecting her. Hold on. This was very odd. The open gates. Meera's immediate recognition and lack of surprise at seeing her. The family waiting.

Mara looked over at Roshan, who was huddled behind their father. He turned away from her but not before Mara noticed the guilty cast to his face. He must have told on her. Said she was coming and when. Protecting himself, just in case she let it slip that he'd talked to her. Making sure that he looked good. Getting ahead in the age-old family race to be Shama's favorite. Or the closest thing he had to that. His least blamed, perhaps. Least likely to be picked on or bullied.

"What do you want?"

It had been nearly twenty years since Mara had heard that voice, heavy with the assumption of complete authority. She couldn't help shivering. He had the same effect as always. He had aged, put on weight, lost a lot of his hair, but that was only cosmetic. He was still the father she had always been terrified of. Mara resisted the temptation to slump forward, to avoid looking in his eyes, to make herself as small as possible. She wasn't going to be bullied. "Hello, Papa. How are you?"

No answer. Mara looked beyond him, at the rows of her family, at her scowling siblings, at strangers she presumed were in-laws and youngsters who must be nephews and nieces, hoping for some sign of welcome. But there was none. Only her mother, older, grayer, withered by the years, smiled at the sight of Mara and stretched out a hand toward her daughter.

It was slapped down by her husband. "I will deal with this," he said. Mara's mother shrank back, her smile dying, her eyes leaving her daughter's face. "What do you want?" Shama repeated.

So it was to be like that? "Didn't Roshan tell you?" Mara asked.

"I want to hear it from you."

Without mentioning her time as a call girl—if her father found out about that, there was no chance he'd help—Mara explained her problems, telling him that the Moores were claiming the girls on the basis of Mara's supposed inability to look after them. She put it all as simply as she could, trying to appeal to a grandfather's natural desire to see—and hopefully help—his granddaughters. Finally, she came to a stop. She'd done her best. If her father wasn't moved . . . but he had to be. He had to be.

"Your . . . husband?"

Mara nodded.

"Is dead?"

Mara forced herself to ignore the way he'd questioned her relationship with Jake. "Yes. Four years ago."

"He didn't provide for his children?"

"As much as he could. We weren't wealthy. But we were very happy. Jake was a truly good man."

"Hmm. Happy."

"We were."

"Are you bringing your daughters up as Hindus?"

"I . . . I haven't talked to them about religion."

"I thought not."

"But I would be pleased to start." Anything if he would help. She hardly had kind feelings toward any religion, but she was sure she could counterbalance any influence she didn't like.

"Hmm. And how are you intending to support yourself and them?"

"I have my cleaning."

"Which clearly does not bring in enough."

"I'll get myself a real job."

"You left school at sixteen."

"I . . . I could go back. Go to college. I've always wanted to. I . . . I'd like to train to be a therapist. To help people with their problems, their marriages, their children."

"And I am to pay for that too?"

"I don't know. I hadn't thought." She hadn't. She'd just blurted out her longtime fantasy.

"You will return home, of course."

"Home? Here?"

"I never gave permission for you to leave."

"I don't . . . the girls . . ." Mara was stunned. Never, never had she imagined he'd ask that. Yet how could she refuse? She was desperate for his help. She couldn't turn him down. But she couldn't say yes. She was an independent woman. Not an unpaid servant bound to obey all orders on the double. "I don't know what to say. I've been away a long time. Surely you wouldn't want me here?"

"Still disobedient, I see."

"No, I'm not. I just . . . I need to think about it."

Shama stood up. "No need to think. This is what I expected. As always, you want for yourself but do not give in return."

Mara heard the refusal in his voice. "No. Please, Papa. Wait. I was just surprised. If that's what it takes, of course I'll come home."

Her father carried on as if he hadn't heard her. "As selfish as always. A disgrace to your family. Getting yourself attacked, shaming your mother and me."

All the hideous nightmare of the days and months after her rape came flooding back to Mara. Roshan had been right. He hadn't changed one little bit. He still blamed her for something no one in their right mind could imagine had been her fault.

"You forfeited all right to my help when you ran away. I gave you some time, to think better of it, to come back and ask my pardon, but you did not do that. And now, after almost twenty years, you come asking me to pay for roofs and central heating and colleges and suchlike. To be a family for your children. Well, my answer is no. I did not work hard all my life to support someone who has no idea of duty or loyalty or obedience."

Mara looked at the old man, in shock. She had prepared herself for his being difficult, for his refusing to help at first, but not for this complete and utter rejection. Part of her longed to march out and away from this nightmare. But she needed his help. Without it, she might not be able to keep Moo and Tilly warm this winter. Might have to send them to Amy's. And if the girls were already living apart from their mother, with a stranger, that could give the Moores the ammunition they needed, could tip the law in their favor. Mara imagined being able to see her daughters only occasionally, pictured her home without their noise and clutter and laughter, and shuddered. Anything was better than that. There was no point in her trying to cling to her last remaining vestiges of pride. Her father, her quarrels with him, his persecution of her, that was the past. The girls were the future. And Jake would expect her to sacrifice whatever was necessary to keep them.

"Surely you want to see Tilly and Moo? They're such lovely girls, they're bright and clever, and pretty, and everything you could want. Please. I'm begging you. See, I'll get on my knees. See?" Mara lowered herself to the floor. "Forget about me, think about the girls. They're your blood. Your kin. And they need you." Mara threw herself to the ground, her face level with her father's shoes. "Please, Papa. Please. Please. I'll do anything. Please."

"Get her up." Shama snapped out the order at Raj, his eldest son, a small, plump, balding man, who picked Mara up by the waist and lifted her. When he tried to let her stand alone, she moaned and fell forward, all the stuffing knocked out of her. "Rahul. Help him." Another taller, thinner man raced to do his father's bidding, propping Mara up on her other side.

"These are my final words. I will not help you. Nor will I help those children you try to foist on me as my grandchildren. My blood. They have nothing to do with me or my blood. Nothing. These people gathered here are my family. You are a stranger. Now and always." Shama sat down and gestured to Rahul and Raj. "Get rid of her."

The two brothers turned Mara around and tried to shepherd her out of the room, half leading, half carrying her. She struggled out of their grasp. Maybe she had collapsed in there but she was not so weak that she couldn't manage to walk out unaided. She turned back to look at her father one last time. "I feel sorry for you," she said softly. At last she could see Shama for what he really was. Not the ogre of her childhood. Not even frightening. Just a sad, stubborn old man, a classroom bully still trying to scare everyone into submission.

Before the two men standing on either side of her could stop her, Mara went to her mother, took her thin, heavily veined hand from where it was clenched in her lap, and kissed it. Her mother looked up at her longingly. "I love you too, Ma," Mara said.

"Get her out of here!" Shama shouted. Mara turned away from her mother, evaded Raj and Rahul's attempts to grab her, and walked out of the room without looking back. Tomorrow she would worry about the money. Tomorrow she would try to think of something else to do. Today, she was going to feel good about herself. Shama believed that he'd humiliated her, and yes, she'd given away all pretence of dignity when she'd begged him to help, when she lay on the floor at his feet, but she refused to feel ashamed. She had done everything she could to try and help her girls. And whatever her family might think, Jake was proud of her.

forty-seven

"Terry!"

Sean stood in the narrow hallway of Ray's house, watching Paul and Sally huddled in the corner near the front door, whispering to each other. He was holding Terry's coat, waiting for her to appear from the kitchen, where she'd been closeted for the last hour with Babs. He had no idea what the girls had been talking about, but, judging by the giggles coming from the two of them, it must have been hilarious.

No question, the day had been a major success. Charlton had won, Paul had been great—he wasn't even complaining about leaving, although Sean wasn't all that surprised by that; he'd overheard the boy making an arrangement to meet Sally the following day—and Terry had fit right in. She'd got on fine with Ray, had become instant mates with Babs, and had even played with the kids.

Unlike Isobel. Sean's ex-wife hadn't liked Ray and Babs. Had thought them boring and dull, too wrapped up in family and children and home to have a good time. For a moment, he wondered how Lily would get on with his friends and then dismissed the thought; though she'd have charmed Ray and Babs, a Saturday night spent eating fish and chips, talking, and playing cards didn't feel like her idea of fun either. Besides, meeting a lover's childhood friends probably broke those strict relationship rules of hers.

More laughter came from the kitchen. Ray tilted his head toward the door at the end of the hallway. "You've got a good one there." He sounded pleased. He'd never said anything against Isobel but Sean had always known that he hadn't liked her.

"It's not like that."

"Why not?"

"She's just a friend." Or would you call her a friend of a friend? Sean wasn't sure, but he didn't want to explain to Ray about Lily and Paul and everything.

"You're an idiot if you let her get away. Even more of an idiot than I thought."

"Idiot? Me? The only kid in the street who passed maths O Level?" Sean deflected the conversation away from himself and Terry.

"You cheated."

"Did not. You can't cheat at those exams."

"There was no way you knew enough to pass that."

"Did."

"Did not."

The door to the kitchen opened to let Babs and Terry into the hallway. "God, no, you're not arguing about the maths O Level again, are you?"

"Not arguing, love, no. Discussing."

"Have we got to the point where Sean insists you can't cheat?"

"We're past there, Babs. Ray's about to claim they mixed me up with another student."

Babs turned to Terry. "It's a ritual conversation. They've got lots of them. For some reason, they have to have one every time they meet. Okay, then, boys, get on with it. Some of us want to go to bed."

Ray grinned at his wife. "You couldn't even spell 'algebra,'" he said to Sean. "Go on, spell it."

"A-L-J-A-B-R-A."

"Wrong. See. They must have got you mixed up with another Sean Grainger."

"Couldn't have."

"Come on, admit it. You cheated."

"Did not."

"Did."

"Okay. Okay. That's enough. It's late and I need my sleep even if you boys don't. 'Bye, Terry." Babs leaned forward to kiss Terry. "See you soon, yeah?"

"Very soon."

Terry couldn't keep the smile off her face. It had been a fantastic day. In fact, the best she could remember in a long, long time. Not only had she seen more than a glimpse of the old Paul, but she'd also met a new friend. Terry already felt as if she'd known Babs for years rather than just one evening.

The good-byes over, Sean held open the door for her. She walked out into the street, where a slight fog misted the lights. Back at the house, Sean was laughing at something Ray had said. And Terry realized what else it was that had made the day special. It was Sean. Here, with his childhood friends, he'd dropped the veneer of the charming, urbane builder-with-taste. Part of that was still there, of course—she wasn't accusing him of living a lie—but today she'd seen the real Sean. Not the one her friends saw, not the one his clients saw, but the unvarnished, undisguised truth. With Ray and his family, Sean was different. Relaxed. Himself. And Terry was deeply flattered that he'd trusted her enough to invite her into his private world.

With a final laugh, a tease, a pretend punch, Sean left Ray. He put one arm around Paul's shoulders, another around Terry's. "Come on. Home time." And the three of them started to walk together up the street, Sean's arms still around the other two.

"What a great day," he said.

With a final wave, Ray closed the door.

And from under an overhanging porch on the other side of the road, a tall, well-built man wrapped in a dark overcoat, baseball cap pulled down over his eyes, materialized out of the shadows. And furtively followed Sean, Terry, and Paul.

It was Clive.

forty-eight

"Lils. Guess what?"

"I don't know. Tony Blair resigned. David Beckham went to Barcelona. Guy Ritchie made a good movie."

"No, silly. Paul and I laughed together."

"Ter! That's fantastic. Where? How? When?"

"We went to a football game with Sean's friend Ray, then had dinner with him and his wife and kids. And Paul was fine all day and we joked together and he met Ray's teenage daughter and I think he's in love and he's holed up in his room now but it's a different kind of holed up. If you know what I mean?"

"Yes, I know."

"And I loved Babs, Ray's wife. She's funny and down-to-earth and friendly and everything. . . ."

Lily tuned out as Terry babbled on about her great day with Sean's old mates. The wonderful Babs and the fascinating Ray and the precocious Sally and the charming younger kids. Yet again, she found herself with that clawing feeling in her gut that reminded her uncomfortably of jealousy.

She knew she had no right to be hurt that it was Terry whom Sean had taken to meet his friends, not her; she'd laid down the ground rules and they didn't include nice social evenings with his pals. She had insisted that she didn't want to get involved in Sean's life . . . and she didn't. But she didn't appear to want Terry to do so either. And that was what confused her. Why wouldn't she want her best friend to meet her lover's friends? What on earth could it mean to her? She had no desire to go to Woolwich or Charlton or wherever it was and spend a day at a football game followed by an evening eating fish and chips and playing cards. It sounded like utter tedium. So why was she upset that Sean had taken Terry? Unless she was, indeed, jealous?

It was only later, when she was waiting for Sean to arrive for the evening, that she realized what was happening. It wasn't him she was jealous about. She had only begun to feel bad when Terry had started going on and on about Babs. Of course. This was a throwback to life in the playground. She was jealous of Babs. She and Terry had been best friends forever, and for a moment she'd started to see Babs as a rival. That was all it was, a knee-jerk reaction to old school memories of friends made and lost in a day. Nothing to worry about.

"SO DID you watch it? All those weird characters hopping around on one leg? Grimacing and drooling. Gnawing on bones and mumbling at the same time. I think it must be an actor's fantasy. They get the contract from the BBC and they pull out their pens and sign, dreaming about pockmarks and limps and the public's openmouthed admiration when they demonstrate their talent for pulling faces. It drives me crazy. All of them imagining they're giving a richly comic performance when we can't understand a word they're saying. God, I hate Dickens adaptations."

Lily had been walking up and down in her living room as she'd delivered this speech. Now she looked over at Sean, slumped in an armchair opposite her, unmoving and unmoved. She supposed she should be grateful that he wasn't heckling her.

She'd been talking to a concert-promotion company about her doing a stand-up/sketch stage show. She wasn't sure it was a good idea—if she was scared before a taping, with a nice, tame, nonpaying audience who laughed when they were told to, she'd be hiding under the table if asked to go onstage in front of people who'd paid their money and expected to be entertained in return—but she'd agreed to think about it. It was true that over the years she'd collected a lot of material that wouldn't fit in a sitcom or a short sketch, but stand-up? She'd never done any, and even the best comics took time to learn how to do it. But it was tempting—the money was outrageous, and though she was earning more than she'd ever imagined she could, she'd also acquired some expensive tastes and cash seemed to exit her bank account as quickly as it came in.

So she'd decided to try out a routine on Sean. And had bombed. Okay, maybe it still needed a bit of work here and there, but she'd been expecting at least a laugh or two. A smile. But she'd got nothing. A big, fat zero. If Sean was anything to go by, she'd be better off staying at home. Lily saw her new career die before it was born. Then she looked at Sean more closely. And realized from the faraway look in his eyes that he hadn't been listening.

She should have been pleased. Her routine wasn't a complete washout; Sean hadn't even heard it. But she wasn't. She was peeved. Just a couple of weeks ago, it seemed he had hung on her every word and now he was daydreaming his way through her performance and their evening. . . .

"Sean?" She snapped her fingers. "Hey! Anyone home?"

"What?"

"I guess I must be one of those interminably dull people who just blather on and on and on while no one listens. Ah, well. What do they say? You're always the last to know."

"Sorry, Lily. I was miles away. Big meeting tomorrow. I'll find out whether or not I've got the building Terry and I found. Remember?"

"Um, yeah." Terry again.

"So what was it? What you were saying?"

"Nothing. I was just trying out a new idea."

"Great. Let's go. I'd love to hear it."

"You already did."

THREE HOURS later, Lily wasn't peeved; she was worried. When Sean hadn't appeared as interested in her and her material as he once had, she'd been disappointed; when he'd attempted to excuse himself from sex with her, she'd been stunned. They'd been seeing each other for only a few months. In total they'd spent about twenty-five nights together. Maybe thirty, but no more. And he was bored with her already?

Oh, he'd claimed hard work and tiredness and all the usual things, but she'd not believed him. A man claiming tiredness was like a woman claiming a headache—a sure sign that the person involved was losing interest. And that was something Lily was not used to. Her men were normally clamoring for more, not making sad, old, unimaginative excuses to get out of their duty.

She looked down at Sean gently snoring away beside her. Why wasn't he as keen as he had been to start with? Was he just one of those people with a short attention span? Or was he ready to move on? At the beginning, he hadn't been able to leave her alone. He'd arrive at the house and within a few minutes the two of them would be fucking away. She'd never had to cajole him into making love to her in the way she had tonight.

So what was it? Was it just accelerated entropy? The end that comes to all relationships, arriving early? Or had the years caught up with her? Was she beginning to look old?

She'd have sworn no one would have guessed she was only a few months off forty. Okay, close inspection revealed a few small lines around her eyes and mouth, a slight sag to her underarms, and traces of cellulite on her thighs. But a naturally spare frame, no heavy sunbathing, and hours and hours in the gym had done their job. Lily looked ten years younger than her age. Or so she had thought.

She jumped out of bed, naked, and stalked into the bathroom. She switched on all the lights until the room was ablaze, and then stood in that unforgiving glare in front of the mirrors, banked, three-sided, around the Starck freestanding bowl-like hand basins. She twisted one way, then the other, subjecting first her body, then her face to minute scrutiny. Hating herself for not being able to give the finger to her thirty-nine years, for caring so much about a few wrinkles, but unable to stop.

She was fine. Her tits weren't those of a young girl—hell, she'd breast-fed twins—but they weren't around her ankles either. Her jawline was slightly blurred . . . but only very, very slightly. No one would notice unless they were specifically looking for it. Her thighs were chunkier than they had been when she was in her twenties, but her height allowed her to carry that off. Okay, nobody would mistake her for a teenager, but nor would anyone take her for thirty-nine. Whatever Sean's problem was, it couldn't be that.

Perhaps she'd overreacted and he was genuinely tired. Some percentage of the men who claimed that must be telling the truth. Five, maybe ten percent, say? Perhaps Sean was one of those. Perhaps he did have a major meeting the next day.

Or perhaps it was the scheme. Perhaps he'd lost interest in her because he preferred one of her friends. Jules or Terry. Or even Mara. As far as Lily knew, she wasn't interested, but the two had seemed pretty close at that dinner party. Perhaps . . .

She stopped herself right there. She was being silly. This was just middle-of-the-night, can't-sleep paranoia. Her friends were not plotting to steal her lover from her. She had lent him to them. And not one of them was interested in having more of him than they were already taking. The fact was that she hadn't managed to spend this much time with any of the men she'd seen in the last few years. She'd always had to get rid of them long before this point. It was perfectly possible that this was the way of things nowadays. That three months was the limit for anyone at any age and it was all downhill after that.

forty-nine

Jules clicked off on the last of her e-mails. Unfortunately, she could communicate this way only with suppliers: caterers, tent people, booking agents, and the like. Most of her clients were the old-fashioned sort who would no more mess with e-mails than they would consider going to church without a hat. A handwritten note demanding a similar reply was much more likely. Or a phone call. Or a visit to the office. All of which were far more time and energy consuming than a blessed two-minutes-and-then-gone e-mail.

The door to her office opened. Jules didn't look up, expecting it to be Claire. Her capable, unflappable assistant had been with her for five years. And Jules lived in fear of losing her. Particularly now that she was going to spend more and more time out of the office. She needed Claire's composure, her dedication to the job, and her way with a file if Dunne Parties was to continue to run smoothly in her half absence.

"Juliet!" Jules's father's voice rang out.

She jumped up. "Daddy!"

"I'm sorry, Jules. He insisted."

Jules smiled at her assistant. She couldn't blame her for the force of authority that was Ian Dunne. "It's fine. Don't worry."

Claire slipped out of the room. Jules looked at her father. "Hello, Daddy. It's nice to see you."

"And you, Juliet. And you. Are you well?"

"Yes. Yes, I'm fine."

"Good. Now, get out your diary."

"My diary?"

"Yes. Is that it?" Lord Dunne pointed to a large, black leather book, the word "DIARY" embossed on it in gold, that was lying on the desk. It was clear he'd come intending to set up a date for a lunch or a dinner with him and her mother. For a moment, Jules contemplated pretending it was next year's, that she'd left the relevant one at home. But it was pointless. He'd never believe her.

"Yes."

"Then open it. Open it." As always, Jules obeyed. Sometimes she felt just like a wayward ensign. Her father must have been a wonderful officer. He had such a commanding way with orders.

"I suppose you're going away for Christmas again?" Jules nodded. She'd not stayed in England for Christmas for the last couple of years; arranging to fly off to the Caribbean meant she got a bit of sun when she most craved it and at the same time avoided pressure to go home for the holiday. Dunne took a calfskin-bound notebook out of his pocket and consulted it. "Then what are you doing on the twelfth December?"

Jules flipped through the diary. "It is our busiest month, Daddy. Yes, here we are. There are two parties that night, one in Chelsea, one in Little Venice."

"Then, the tenth?"

"No, I'm sorry. I'm sure we're booked up every evening in December."

"Then November. November the tenth. Or is that one of your busiest months also?"

Jules decided not to answer this one. She prayed that there would be something written in the diary for that night. She found the page. They were busy. A midweek anniversary party in Wiltshire. Phew. "I'm afraid not."

Lord Dunne returned to his list. "November twelfth?"

A weekend. It was unlikely. Jules flipped two pages forward. "No."

Her father didn't seem bothered by her refusals. It appeared he was prepared to suggest dates until he found one when she was free and couldn't refuse. "The fifteenth, then?"

It was a Monday. There was little chance she'd be busy; Mondays weren't the day of choice for high-profile parties. She could hope for a book launch or a birthday. She turned the pages. There it was. Monday, November 15. A blank page.

"Capital. We'll agree on that, shall we? Dinner at my club. All the family. Eight sharp."

Jules could see no way out, for the moment. "Fine. Of course. Er . . . thank you, Daddy."

"And Juliet? I do not expect to receive one of your little notes calling this off. I will accept no excuses. Understood?"

"Yes, Daddy. Understood."

When her father had gone, Jules tried hard to think of a way out of the dinner. But short of her being in hospital, she couldn't. And she wouldn't put it past her father to come and drag her out of the Cromwell or the Lister or wherever it was she'd managed to persuade someone that she needed to be taken in overnight. Or, worse, to convene the whole family around her bed. Without the distraction of food and drink. No, unless she had some major inspiration between now and then, she was going to have to go. And endure her mother's constant barbs. She wasn't even likely to get a good meal out of it. The club specialized in return-to-boarding-school dinners. Overcooked meat and veg and steamed suet puddings with thick, lumpy custard. Yuck.

Still, it sounded like her brother, Philip, and his wife, and Jules's two sisters, Alice and Elena, and their husbands would be there. Maybe that would protect her a little. And it was only one night. A few hours to be borne in silence before she could escape. And if she were lucky, that would be it. Once Diana learned Jules was having a baby by herself, not even Ian Dunne was going to be able to persuade her to have anything to do with her black-sheep daughter. Briefly, Jules wondered how her father would feel, whether he would disown her also, but then pushed the thought to the back of her mind. No point in worrying about it now. Having a baby, that was what mattered.

The door opened and Claire walked in, looking harassed. "I'm sorry, Jules. I couldn't stop him."

"No one can. Honestly, don't worry about it. He trained for years to learn how to make people do what he tells them. Listen, I'm ravenous. Do you fancy lunch?"

"I'd love it. Only you've got another visitor."

"Not Mrs. Pilkerton again?"

"No. He says he's a friend. Tall, good-looking, well built . . ."

"Oh, pooh. It must be Sean. What on earth does he want?" Jules had had a feeling that she hadn't heard the last from him. But she had been hoping that he'd got the message. She opened the door to the outer office a crack and looked out. He was sitting, looking very pleased with himself, a large, unwieldy package on the floor by his side. What was it this time? "I'd better see him. It'll only take a few minutes."

Jules walked into the outer office. "Sean?"

"Jules. I'm sorry to interrupt you here, only I was so excited."

"Come into my office." Sean picked up the bulky parcel. "Can't you leave that?"

"Not really. It's for you." He maneuvered his way into Jules's inner office. "Well, for the baby."

"I thought we agreed."

"I know what you're going to say, but it isn't something like a buggy or a car seat or anything. It's special. And I'd ordered it before we talked." Sean put it down next to her and then stood back, smiling expectantly. Jules ignored the parcel. "Aren't you going to open it?"

"No. I'm not."

"Why not? Are you saving it for later?"

"No. I don't want it."

"But you don't know what's in it."

"I don't care what's in it."

"It's great. Go on, take a look."

"No thank you. Take it back to wherever you got it. Or keep it yourself. Whatever you want. But get it out of here."

"It's a rocking horse. Handmade. A friend of mine does them in his spare time. I thought you'd like it. I know our baby would—"

"Fucking hell," Jules exploded.

And Sean took a step backward, surprised by her language. Normally, she never used anything stronger than "damn." And more often she favored schoolgirlish words like "drat" or "rats" or "pooh." "Jules? Are you okay?"

"It's not OUR baby. It's MY baby."

"I know it's your baby."

"No, Sean, you don't. You say you do, but you don't. All right. I didn't want to have to do this, but you leave me no option. Putting it bluntly, you were a wonderful donor and of course I'm deeply grateful—"

"You don't need to be grateful. I was thrilled, you know that."

"—but I don't need you anymore."

"You what?"

"I don't need you."

"And that's it?"

"Yes."

"But I'm the father."

"No, Sean. You're not. You're just a man who provided me with some sperm. And you knew that. Right from the first moment we talked about this, I told you why I wanted a donor. That I wanted my own baby, with no man involved."

"But—"

"You heard me say that. I know you did."

"I thought you couldn't be serious. And then after the way we made the baby—"

"That was just sex. Nice, fun, and a means to an end. But it changed nothing. I meant what I said when I said it, and I mean it now. You have no further place in my or my baby's life."

Sean was staring at Jules as if he could not believe what he was hearing.

"Is that clear?" she asked.

It was. It was hideously, horrendously clear. For the last few weeks, he had been blocking out Jules's denials, convinced that there was no way she could mean what she'd been saying. But she did. The bubble that had been shielding Sean from the truth burst. This was all real. Another woman was stealing a child from him. And this one not even born yet. "You monster. You fucking bitch. It's my sodding baby too."

His voice rose in volume with every word. Terrified, Jules backed away from him. Sean followed her, unsure of what he intended but desperate to do something to stop all this. "It's going to be my child too, not just yours. Mine," he shouted, his voice getting still louder.

The door to the outer office burst open and Claire came rushing in.

"What's going on?" she screamed at Sean.

But he didn't hear her. Lost in his rage, he continued to yell at Jules, who was shrinking farther away from him. Panicked, Claire picked up an ornate walking stick that had once belonged to Jules's grandfather and brandished it at Sean.

"Get out," she shouted. "Leave her alone."

It was enough to shock Sean out of his fury. Horrified by his behavior, he turned and ran out of the room.

"He's gone, Jules," Claire said as she heard the sound of the outer door slam through the building. "Are you okay?"

Jules nodded. "Yes. He didn't touch me." She made an effort to pull herself together. Nothing had happened. Sean wasn't Will, although for a moment she had felt herself slip back into the old nightmare. She was fine. And Sean had certainly gotten her message.

Outside, Clive stood in the deep shelter of a porch, looking down the street at a rapidly disappearing Sean. What was it with this guy? First Lily, then Jules, then Terry, now Jules again. And this time Sean was seriously upset. He had come racing out of the building, slamming the front door shut behind him, obviously deeply troubled by something. Or somebody. Whatever all this was, it wasn't a gentle social friendship. There was passion here and rage and heat. And where those were, a scandal was often lurking also.

fifty

Terry walked up the street, toward her house. The wind, heavy-laden with rain, blew full in her face. She pulled her uniform jacket closer around her. Even she was going to have to admit that it was time to get her overcoat out. She resisted it every year; for some reason, she could never find a normal coat that was bright or colorful or had her kind of style. The cold weather seemed to bring out the undertaker in the English—black, black, and more black. She had a gorgeous red velvet cloak from the 1920s, but it was old and getting worn and so she used it only on special occasions. Until the fur lobby went crazy, she had worn a shaggy, antique wolflike coat, but she'd had to put it away. People had started threatening her on the street.

A young boy passed her, oblivious to the rain, twirling a spluttering sparkler in his hand. If this kept up, he and lots like him were going to be very disappointed. Terry didn't want to wish for that—guaranteed bad luck to want others to be unhappy—but a Guy Fawkes night free of fireworks would be a great break for poor, terrified Minnie, who tried to hide in the bookcase the moment the bangs and whines started.

Terry reached her house and turned off the street, to find someone sitting on her steps. The porch light wasn't on and she had trouble making out who it was. She peered through the growing gloom.

"Sean?"

"Terry. I'm sorry, is it okay? I needed to talk to you."

As Terry got closer, she noticed the desperation written plain on Sean's face, the empty cans of beer lying on the step, and the scattering of cigarette ends around his feet. It looked as if something had gone badly wrong. She had been looking forward to lying in a hot bath with a large mug of strong tea, but Sean was unhappy. And she owed him.

"Course it's okay. Come on in. I'll just get out of all this and you can tell me what's happened."

Ten minutes later, the two were settled in Terry's mix-and-match living room. Sean was sitting on a large old sofa, the holes in the upholstery covered with a variety of multicolored throws. He had a bottle of beer in his hand and Minnie was coiled on his lap. Terry, out of her drab uniform and dressed in pale-blue-and-yellow 1930s lounging pajamas, was on the ancient tiger-skin rug on the floor in front of him, her legs curled beneath her.

"Are you okay?"

"I'm fine."

"I don't think so. You don't look fine, do you? You look terrible. Like you've just heard your moon's coming into Saturn. What's happened?"

"I . . . nothing." Sean was beginning to regret having rushed around to Terry's. It had seemed so obvious to him at the time that she was the person he needed, but now that he was here, in her house, he wasn't so sure. After all, Jules had been her friend for ages.

"Sean."

"Really. I just thought I'd come and say hello."

"And the beer? I suppose you always have six cans before dinner?" Sean looked embarrassed. Terry leaned over and put her hand on his knee. "Come on, love, what is it?"

"I don't think I should tell you."

"Why on earth not? I'm trustworthy. I promise."

"That's not it. I know you keep secrets. You didn't tell anyone about the boys."

"God, it's not them, is it?"

"No. I've heard nothing."

"Work, then? Has something happened at the office?"

"No."

"Lily?"

"No."

"I'm running out of ideas here, Sean. Is it me?"

"No. Never."

"Then what? Jules?"

And it all came rushing out. "Oh, God, Terry. I lost it with her. I never thought I was the kind of bloke would do that, but I just attacked her." The words rushed out, uncheckable. Sean gulped down some beer. "If it hadn't been for her assistant, I don't know, I might've throttled her." Sean's head dropped and he held on to Minnie, racked with guilt.

"What happened?"

"She's stealing my child from me. Just like Isobel. Only I'll know where this one is and still not be able to see him."

"Stealing?"

"She won't let me see the baby when it's born. Says I have no further place in his life."

"Oh, Sean. I'm sorry."

"She just used me. Picked me up, exploited me, and then threw me away. She even said that. 'I don't need you anymore.' Just like that. She was completely cold. Like what we did never happened." Sean realized that Jules had reminded him of Lily when she gave him her speech at the Greek restaurant. Just as cool, just as determined.

"When did this happen?"

"Lunchtime."

"You've been here since then?"

"How could I have threatened her like that? You should have seen her, she was terrified. I'm a monster. I said she was one, but it's me. It's me."

Terry reached for Sean's hand. She knew why Jules had been so scared, but she wasn't about to tell. It would mean breaking a confidence, and besides, it wouldn't help him to be compared to Jules's abusive ex. She wasn't all that surprised to find her sympathies were mostly with Sean. No question, he'd been used. And she could imagine just how hard and unfeeling Jules would have appeared when telling him he was unwanted. She could be a very determined woman. Though there was no excuse for his behavior, Terry found herself understanding how and why Sean had been pushed to that point and almost beyond. But the most important thing was that he hadn't crossed that line, that he'd pulled himself back when on the brink.

She squeezed his hand and tried to reassure him. "Nothing at all happened. You lost your temper. And you came to in time. You didn't touch her."

"But if the assistant hadn't been there . . ."

"She was. And even if she hadn't been, you would have stopped yourself. I can't see you hitting a woman."

"No. No, you're right, I didn't touch her. I didn't. And I'm not going to let this go. I have rights. I'm the father. I won't just lie down. I'll take her to court, make sure she allows me to see the baby. It'll need a father. All children need a father. Don't you think?"

And so it went on. For hour after hour. With Sean veering from abject depression about his loss of another child to overwhelming guilt about his attempted attack on Jules to defensive belligerence about Jules's theft and what he was going to do to counter it. Terry sat with him, got him a fresh beer when his was empty or flat, listened to him rant and mumble and apologize, then tried to persuade him that he was no ogre. He'd only done what 99.99 percent of people do when pushed to the edge.

Gradually, as it got later and later, she managed to calm him down a little. Helping to make her lucky seven-vegetable couscous for dinner, then discussing Charlton with Paul while the three of them were eating it allowed Sean to recover some sense of equilibrium; it was hard to maintain real misery when faced with such normal domesticity. Trying to calm Minnie down when the rain stopped and the yearly November fifth fireworks started in earnest, pressing a vet-prescribed tranquilizer into a bit of soft cheese and attempting to get her to swallow it took his mind off his own troubles for a bit. In the face of such desperate, uncomprehending fear, it was hard to worry about himself. But eventually the pill took effect and the little dog collapsed, exhausted and calmed, on Sean's knee, the whines and screams and thuds of the rockets no longer sending her wild with fear. And he was free once again to go back over and over his own misery, his own anger, his own guilt.

Finally, after they'd been talking for hours, Terry felt that she'd managed to get him to stop accusing himself. Jules was fine. He hadn't hurt her. That was the bottom line.

The next bit was harder. Much harder. He also needed to let go of the baby. Terry didn't expect him to forget about the child, of course she didn't, or even to give up all hope of getting to know him. Who knew what would happen in the future? Hopefully, Jules would come to her senses and welcome Sean's involvement, for everyone's sake. But for now, he had to back off. Otherwise his next few years would be as miserable as his last had been.

And so Terry chipped away at his determination to fight for the child, encouraging him to accept reality. To admit that he'd gone into donorhood with his eyes open. That Jules had told him right from the start that she intended to raise the baby alone.

At last, around midnight, he acknowledged it. "Yes. All right. She did tell me. Of course she did. I just buried my head in the sand, I guess. Pretended it wasn't said. Or that she couldn't have meant it. Not now the baby's a reality. Silly, huh?"

"No, not silly."

"But a deal's a deal? That it?"

"Maybe later, when it's older, the baby'll want to meet you. Maybe it'll insist. And Jules'll have to give in, won't she? But, for now, yeah, you've got to let go. I don't know the law. Maybe there isn't one. But I do know suing Jules only helps the lawyers. And the press. I'm sorry."

"I can't take her to court?"

"You can, but . . ."

"I shouldn't."

"No."

Terry's no was softly spoken, but for Sean it carried all the unambiguous certainty of a five o'clock football result. And with it he felt the last, tiny traces of long-lingering hope disappear. The baby wasn't his. Had never been his. Would never be his. And he couldn't bear it. Desperate for some consolation, for contact and warmth and comfort, he slipped from the couch to the floor, put his arms around Terry, and, before she could say anything, do anything, kissed her.

If you'd asked him even half an hour before, he'd have said he had no interest in Terry that way. That he liked her. Trusted her. Saw her as a good pal, no more. But right at that moment, he needed more than a friend. He needed someone to hold on to, someone to help him block out Jules, the baby, everything. And Terry was there. And so he reached for her, unprepared for the shock that roared through him. For the crazy desire he felt. To touch her, take care of her, make love to her over and over again.

If Sean was unprepared, he had nothing on Terry. She'd resigned herself to a celibate life. Accepted that sex was not for her, that no matter how hard she tried, with no matter how many different people, she just wasn't made to enjoy it. Then, at the first touch of Sean's lips, she was overcome with what she supposed was desire for him. A galloping pulse, a somersaulting stomach, a desperate need to get closer and closer . . . things she'd only heard and read about before.

And she was immediately rocked by hope. Hope that she'd been wrong about herself, that she wasn't completely frigid. That maybe Sean was the one man capable of unlocking her body for her.

After allowing herself to fantasize for a few seconds, she forced herself to stop. She mustn't think like that. She'd been down that road too many times before and the only thing it offered was frustration and regret. Maybe her attraction to Sean was stronger than she remembered feeling for anyone else, but she would be nuts to imagine that it would turn out any differently. Hadn't all those years of disappointment taught her anything?

"What the fuck do you think you're doing?" Terry blurted out, her voice hard and angry. She was cross more with herself than with Sean—she thought she'd gotten rid of that particular useless fantasy eons ago—but it sounded as if she was furious with him.

Confused, both by Terry's abrupt, angry rejection and his volcanic reaction to the kiss, he backed away from her, still on his knees. "I'm sorry. I didn't mean . . . I'll leave you alone."

He stood up, grabbed his coat, and went to the door. "Good-bye," he said.

A FEW minutes later, Sean was walking through Stoke Newington. Taxi after empty taxi streamed past him, splashing rain puddles over the pavement, all on their way back into town to pick up another fare, all of them happy to take him home, but he ignored them. He needed to walk. To let the now-dry, cold air blow away the beer and allow him to try and make some sense of what had just happened.

He wanted to call his reaction to the kiss an aberration. The result of an emotional day, a late night, and too much to drink. But he couldn't. Okay, he wouldn't have reached for Terry if he hadn't been drunk, but no beer he'd ever heard of turned a simple comfort kiss into a sudden need to carry a female friend off to bed and not emerge for days.

No, it had been real. He'd touched her and he'd exploded. And for a moment there, he'd thought she felt the same. Until she pushed him away and ordered him to leave her alone. Of course, he could've been mistaken. It could've just been him, overtired and far from his most perceptive, reacting to what had not been there. And even if he hadn't made a mistake, even if she had responded, it made no difference. Whatever she had felt, she didn't want to pursue it. And it would be best to forget all about it himself.

But he couldn't. Those few seconds were acid-etched on his mind. He kept playing them back, over and over, as if he had a VCR in his head. Only this video came complete with memories and sensations and touch and feel as well as pictures. . . .

But she didn't want him. That was the bottom line. She'd not said it in so many words, but she had as near as damn it told him to fuck off. It was clear that he had to stay away from her. He didn't want to drop Paul, but he could arrange to see the kid separately from his mother. And if he ran into her when he was with Lily, then he'd be polite and keep as far away from her as possible.

Lily. Hell. No wonder Terry had pulled away from him like that. He was going out with Lily. Terry's best friend. God, she must despise him. He was a real shit. He couldn't keep his hands off his lover's best friend. No wonder she'd been so angry. He'd betrayed Lily. And with her.

He'd always thought of himself as a decent guy. No saint, but no major sinner either. Okay, he'd slept around a bit after the boys disappeared, but he'd been free to do so and he'd hurt no one. He'd been faithful to Isobel when he'd been married to her, even though he hadn't loved her, at least not toward the end. But now, when he was with a woman he did claim to love, he had gone out and slept with one of her closest friends and made a move on another. All in the space of a month. It was obvious he had been deluding himself all these years. He wasn't the faithful, honorable man he'd imagined he was. Instead, he was a chancer, without any true sense of loyalty or commitment or principle.

By now, Sean had reached the upper limits of Islington. Hardware stores began to give way to chic little bistros and posh fish shops and expensive knickknack stores. Cabs were still speeding past, but he continued to ignore them. He wasn't ready to go home yet.

He couldn't change what he'd done, couldn't take back the kiss. But nor could he ignore what had happened. He had to apologize to Terry. Not now, not tonight, not tomorrow even, but sometime soon he had to pick up the phone and call her and tell her how sorry he was. Sorry that he'd upset her, sorry that he'd betrayed her friend, sorry that he wasn't the person he'd thought he was. Hopefully, she wouldn't notice that he didn't apologize for the kiss. But he didn't feel he could do that. Because despite how bad he was feeling, despite the unwanted insights into his weak character and the gut-clenching pangs of guilt, if he was honest with himself, he had to admit that he wasn't sorry. He wasn't sorry at all. The kiss had been wonderful.

BEEP.

"Hi, Terry, this is, er, Sean. Just wanted to say hi. I'd love to talk to you, er, explain the other night. So give me a call if you get a chance. Um, well, 'bye, then."

From the moment Terry walked in the door from work and heard the annoying, off-rhythm beep of the answering machine, she had known who it was going to be. As she'd listened to Sean's fumbling, embarrassed voice, half of her had been delighted, half scared.

Delighted to hear his voice. And scared of the effect it might have on her. Because she'd been having a hard time fighting off the urge to call him herself, to tell him she'd made a mistake, that she did want him. The temptation to believe that there might be one last chance for her was almost too strong to resist.

She hadn't even dared tell Lily about the kiss. Not because she believed her friend would be upset by what had happened but because she thought Lily would encourage her to go for it. And it was hard enough stopping herself calling him without her friend egging her on to do it.

Terry had tried to make herself hate Sean. She'd tried to tell herself that any man who would attempt to seduce his girlfriend's best friend wasn't worth even a tin of beans, but it hadn't worked. Because, when she thought about the way the group of friends had used him, his kissing her when tired and emotional didn't seem like anything at all.

No, they were the more likely villains. She, Lily, and Jules. They'd manipulated and exploited him with no real thought to his feelings. Now that she looked back, she wasn't sure they'd ever even discussed how he would feel. They'd just taken it for granted that their needs were paramount. And he, what had he done? Only taken her out, introduced her to his friends, saved Paul's life, that's what. Even Minnie, who'd never liked a single adult male in her entire life, loved Sean.

Terry was going to miss him. A lot. She looked longingly at the telephone, even reached out for it, picked up the receiver, and got halfway through dialing Sean's number before she managed to pull herself back. No. She was not going to call. She was going to stay well away from him until she could be sure that she'd managed to block out all memory of that night. Until her life was back on its usual even, passionless keel. She would be happier that way. She was sure of it.

fifty-one

"Things have changed a lot, pet, I'm afraid. You're still beautiful, I'll say that for you, but you're . . . thirty-three?" Mrs. Grenville put down the delicate, flower-painted porcelain teapot and handed Mara a matching cup and saucer. "Sugar?"

"No, thank you. I'm thirty-six."

"Always so honest. That's retirement age nowadays." The tall, angular, conservatively dressed woman offered Mara a plate of chocolate Bath Olivers. It had always been that way. Mrs. Grenville might have made her money selling flesh, but she insisted on living more like a society matron than a successful madam. If you saw her before five, it was the formal tea, complete with napkins and tiny plates and finger sandwiches. After five, it was sweet sherry in minuscule glasses.

It had been eleven years since Mara had sat in just this chair, sipping tea out of just this cup, telling Mrs. Grenville that she was finished. Yet the room felt and looked the same. There was the same dark, heavy, prewar furniture, the same gas fire lit even on the warmest day, the same shelves cluttered with the same little multicolored glass animals and pillboxes and antique dolls. And the place still positively glowed with respectability. There was absolutely no hint as to Mrs. Grenville's profession. Or what went on day and night upstairs.

"Thank you." Mara took a biscuit and put it on the plate she was trying to balance on her knee. "I was always very popular. You remember. You said I was your best earner."

"That was then."

"Things can't be that different?"

"There's no call for older. So many babies pouring in from all over. No need, you see."

"Please, Mrs. Grenville." Mara knew that going back on the game was potential disaster if the Moores found out—she had made sure that no one would follow her on her way to her old employer's house, jumping on and off tube trains as they were about to depart and doubling back on herself like an experienced cold war spy in case her in-laws had hired someone to watch her—but her options were limited. The Moores had written back to Robin Heath saying that they intended to take Mara to court as soon as possible. She had to do something. She couldn't deliver the warm, close family the lawyer had advised her to find; she had to improve the house. The roof was perhaps asking too much, but she had to find at least the £1,200 needed to get the central heating fixed or she ran the risk of losing her daughters for good.

"Not down to me, pet. It's what the customer wants. Why d'you want to start again anyway? When you left, you said nothing would make you come back."

"I know. I need the money."

"There are easier ways."

"I've tried. Don't you think I've tried?" Mara heard the desperation creeping into her voice and struggled to pull herself together. She had enough strikes against her; Mrs. Grenville wasn't going to employ her if she weren't calm and professional. "Of course I'd prefer not to do this. But I need a lot of money. And soon."

"You can't make a grand a throw anymore. It's the young ones get that."

"But you can find me something?"

Mrs. Grenville looked hard at her visitor. "It'll be the kinky end, pet."

"Kinky?"

"You know, two girls, three girls. Fetish stuff. S and M."

"Oh."

"Even then, you'll be lucky to get two hundred and fifty pounds."

"That's all?" Mara was horrified. She had been hoping not to have to do it more than once or twice.

"It's good money. Most places pay a lot less."

"*Most* places? Is there a lot of call for . . . you know?"

"It's the older gentlemen mostly. Can't get it up, you see. Need a bit of extra push. Something unusual."

Visions of gray-haired, wrinkled, flabby old men drooling over leather-clad women flashed through Mara's brain. She'd never taken part in a staged performance, never been to bed with other women, never had a man watch her having sex. Her looks had protected her from that end of the business. Until now.

She tried to tell herself that it was just another job, that it made no difference what she was expected to do, that she had to do it for the girls.

But she knew she couldn't. Not even if it were just her and a client for an evening. She'd managed to bury her head in the sand, persuaded herself that what she had done once, she could do again. But she'd been wrong. Eleven years had passed since she'd last had sex for money. Eleven years of Jake and the girls, eleven years of a normal life, eleven years of love. She was no longer the Mara who had sold herself to man after man. She might be a dreadful mother, she might be tossing away her best chance of keeping her girls, she might be letting her beloved Jake down, but there was no way she could return to her old life and then go back to Moo and Tilly and carry on as normal. Though she knew the girls would never know, knew they wouldn't even see her until she had scrubbed every vestige of what she had done from her body, she felt she would be soiling them as well as herself if she sold her body again.

Worse, should she cross that line and prostitute herself once more, all the things the Moores had said about her would be true. And they would be fully justified in taking Moo and Tilly.

Mara put down her plate and teacup and saucer and stood up. "Thank you for the tea," she said. "I'm afraid I've wasted your time. I . . . I made a mistake. This isn't for me."

"That's right, pet. Leave it to the young ones."

Mara looked down at the old woman who had played such a huge role in part of her life. Who had recruited her, trained her, and sold her. And felt an odd sense of release. As if only now had she truly gotten free of her. "Goodbye, Mrs. Grenville," she said, then turned and left.

fifty-two

"Lily?"

"Hi. I was just thinking about you." Lily was sitting at her desk at home, in front of her computer, trying to work on an idea for a new sitcom. Though Channel 4 was eager for another series of *We Can Work It Out*, she felt she'd taken it as far as she could for the moment and wanted to try something different. And while a small part of her was still tempted by the idea of a countrywide stand-up tour, she had decided against it for now. Even though Sean hadn't heard her the other night, and so his reaction meant nothing, Lily couldn't forget it. Or how lame and embarrassed she'd felt standing there, listening for laughs and hearing none. And that had been in her own home, in front of her own lover. It would be magnified a thousand, a million times if she were to fail in public. Hence the new sitcom. But it was turning out to be easier said than done. Inspiration was scarce and thoughts of Sean, flashes of him making love to her, kept intruding. "We're still on for tonight?"

"That's what I was calling to say. I'm sorry, I'm going to have to work. The new specs on the building, er, Terry and I found have just come through and I need to go over them before this meeting in the morning. Can I take a rain check?"

"Oh. Okay. No problem. Saturday, then?" Lily sounded as if she were fine about it but underneath she was seething. Seething and worried. Sean's excuse sounded lame at best, as if he were only going through the motions and couldn't be bothered to think up a good story. She was beginning to think he had lost interest.

"Yes. Of course. Saturday."

"Here at eight?"

"Fine."

"I'll think of something interesting for us to do."

"Whatever you like."

"Something in the bedroom."

"Right. Wherever."

"Something like the Royal Oak." Lily had amazing memories of the nights the two of them had spent there. If suggesting they repeat that didn't rouse him out of his strange semi-stupor, nothing would.

"Okay. No problem."

"No problem? Did you hear what I said?"

"Um . . . Sorry. I'm on-site. Delivery truck just arrived."

"I was talking about when we went to the Cotswolds."

"Oh."

"And what we did there." They'd hardly left the bedroom. No way he could mistake that reference. Or have forgotten what it was like. "How it was. How we can make it like that again."

"Good. I'll see you in a few days, then?"

"Good. That's it? That's all you can say?"

"Well, yes. What should I say?"

"Oh, nothing. I'll see you Saturday." And Lily slammed the phone down, furious with Sean and with herself. What the hell was she doing cajoling him like that? Shit. There was nothing more humiliating than trying to entice a man who was uninterested. And Sean had definitely appeared uninterested. Okay, he was on-site, he was distracted, but even so she'd have expected him to pick up on the reference to the Royal Oak. The fact that he hadn't, even though she had underlined it—she hadn't really said they could make it be like that again, had she? Fuck, how undignified—suggested that she was losing her appeal. That he no longer cared the way he had.

And that thought hurt much more than was comfortable. Little by little, piece by piece, day by day, Sean had become important to her. She still didn't want him all the time, but she didn't want to lose her allotted nights either. And it was beginning to look as if she would.

Okay, it wouldn't be a complete disaster, of course she'd find a replacement and probably pretty quickly too, but she didn't see why she should have to. Barely a month ago he'd been crazy about her. And he could be again. She wasn't going to lie down and just accept this. She'd fight back. She'd show him what had attracted him in the first place. And seduce him all over again.

fifty-three

Clive drove at around five miles an hour down the street, the noise of his car's slow engine fading into the surrounding hum of the late-night city. It was dark and cold, rain dripping from wrought-iron balconies onto the mounds of black plastic rubbish bags left neatly stacked outside every house. Opposite Jules's door, he stopped the battered old Ford that he kept for such excursions. He'd left his real car, a Porsche he'd bought with the bonus he'd been given after his exclusive story about a cabinet minister's three-in-a-bed romp had raised his newspaper's circulation by over 100,000, at home in newly fashionable Clerkenwell. He might regret his lost TV career, but no question there was a lot of money to be made in the tabloid world. And the power to make or destroy careers; the cabinet minister in question had been forced to resign.

He jumped out and grabbed the three bags that had been piled up in front of Jules's house. He hurled them into the back of the car to join the two other bags he had already collected from behind Lily's home in Hampstead, got back in the Ford, and drove off.

Technically it was an offense, stealing trash, but Clive had been doing it off and on for years and had never come close to being caught. People seemed to want to ignore the existence of their garbage the moment it had been laid out for the bin men to collect. And it was amazing what you could learn from a few bags of old rubbish.

Yes, you had to have a strong stomach. Particularly in the summer. The smell of things like fish heads and chicken bones and prawn shells left to rot in the sun tended to linger long after the garbage itself had gone to the dump. But Clive had had wonderful success delving in what celebrities threw away. He'd been the first to know when a soap star was pregnant because he'd found the successful test amongst her vegetable peelings and coffee grounds. He'd scooped the rest of the tabloids when he'd found a good-bye letter from a certain TV presenter detailing his breakup with his pop singer girlfriend of two years' standing.

So he took the risk that no one was going to be upset if their black bags mysteriously disappeared. And usually they weren't.

He still had no idea what the Sean story was. He was spending as much time as he could trailing the builder, but things seemed to have gone quiet. Since storming out of Jules's office about two weeks earlier, Sean had seen Lily once. Gone to her house, stayed the night, left the next morning. Nothing there. But he hadn't seen Jules, or Terry. At least as far as Clive knew.

And he was running out of time. So far, Nigel, his editor, had been relatively patient, giving him as much time as possible to pursue the Sean thing, but he was getting restless with the lack of progress and had begun to make noises about calling him off. Okay, Clive could still go after the story, but it would be on his own time and he didn't have a great deal of that.

Hence the garbage. He'd already been through Terry's—nothing at all interesting apart from more boxes of soothing chamomile tea than he could imagine anyone consuming in a week, but though Clive wanted that to mean that Terry was in some kind of emotional state, he had to admit that it was nowhere near conclusive evidence and, in any case, didn't help him find out why.

Sean's rubbish had been a bit more of a challenge. Because he lived in an apartment building, he tossed his trash into a Dumpster and it hadn't been that easy for the journalist to distinguish between Sean's garbage and that of his fellow tenants. But he had managed to isolate two bags because of the envelopes contained within them. Judging by the number of empty beer cans and cigarette packets, Sean also seemed far from happy, but again, it didn't help Clive much.

So now he was trying Jules and Lily.

He drove home to his penthouse in a converted 1920s warehouse, carried the bags inside, spread a large plastic sheet over his wooden living room floor, and tipped out the contents of Jules's three. It seemed to be mostly paper and plastic. Tissue paper, carrier bags from baby stores, cardboard boxes that apparently had once contained a changing table and a sterilizer and a Moses basket. Interesting. It seemed Jules was expecting a child. Interesting but no real help. Unless the baby was Sean's, and there was no indication that that was the case. Although the idea of Jules playing around with Lily's squeeze and getting pregnant appealed to him a lot; he loved the notion of his ex-wife being made a fool of in that way. And it would make a great piece. He could see the headline now: "Lily's Lover Lays Away."

But his editor would demand at least some evidence if he were to run with the story, and all Clive had was supposition. He set to work on Lily's bags. He wasn't expecting to find anything. Other people might not know that he stole garbage, but she did. He'd gotten his lead on that bitter ex-lover of hers that way, and since then she'd been very careful about what she threw away. So he was surprised to find a carrier bag from a shop in Soho amongst all the anodyne bottles and newspapers and eggshells.

A sex shop. Clive hadn't been for some time, but as he remembered it, the Pleasure Chest sold everything from handcuffs to harnesses, from vibrators to Viagra. What would Lily want from there? It could be a joke, of course, a silly gift for one of her friends or coworkers. But what if it weren't? What if Lily had developed a fetish for leather or become an S&M freak or discovered a taste for dressing up as a French maid? That wouldn't explain what Sean was doing with her friends, but it would be the most wonderfully humiliating story to print. Britain's latest celebrity, in chains.

So where to go from here? Well, he could try the shop, but they were unlikely to tell. Those places needed people to believe that they kept confidences. And there was no point in asking Lily, although the idea of doing so at a gala evening or open press conference made him salivate. He was going to have to try to get close to Sean.

fifty-four

"Hi, this is Terry. Leave me a message. Or I'll never call you back. And that's a promise."

"Hello, Terry? I hoped you might be home. I just wanted—"

"Hi, Sean. Mum's not in."

"Oh, hi, Paul. How're things?"

"Great. What about that massive game on Tuesday?" And Paul was off, his enthusiasm for Charlton and the Worthington Cup win in midweek absolutely unstoppable.

Sean stood in the supermarket aisle, next to the packets of pasta and beans and half listened, murmuring appropriate yesses and nos whenever he felt they might be needed, but his mind was on Terry. He'd been determined to leave her alone for a full two weeks after his first call. To give her a chance to contact him when she was ready. And hard though it had been—and it had been, very—he'd managed to resist phoning her for eight days.

Until he went to the supermarket. He'd never have imagined that something as simple as buying a few tea bags and a pot of jam would set him off, but he kept passing things that said "Terry" to him. He'd kept his resolve past massive signs advertising Mr. Sainsbury's latest organic produce, large packets of tofu, and rows and rows of herbal teas, but when he'd reached the pasta, he had crumbled. Dried couscous might not be everyone's idea of romantic, but Sean found it irresistibly evocative of her flat, her kitchen, that night, and the kiss. He'd grabbed his mobile and dialed her number, knowing it by heart. Only to get Paul.

". . . and Rufus's goal. Did you see that? I thought it was going wide, but the way it snuck in round the keeper, that was awesome. Awesome . . ." And Paul continued on his favorite subject. Any other time, Sean would have entered into this wholeheartedly, but not today.

"Paul, Paul, hold on a minute. Listen, I'll call you later or tomorrow, we can talk about the Cup, okay? Only, I'm in the supermarket and a lot of people are looking at me as if I'm some kind of nut, hanging around the lentils and talking on the phone."

"Sure. No worries. Tomorrow."

"Can you tell your mum I called? I'd just like to talk to her for a moment. And no, before you ask, it's not about you."

"About you, then? And her?" Paul hadn't mentioned it to either of them, but he was hoping that Sean and his mam would get together. On bonfire night, he'd deliberately left them alone and he had a feeling something had happened. But then nothing. He'd been expecting Sean to be around more often, but instead he hadn't seen him for almost two weeks.

"None of your business, young man."

"Aaah, come on. You going to ask her out on a date?" Yes, yes. Go on, Sean. You can do it, mate. If I can ask Sally, you can ask my mam.

"Just get her to call me, okay?"

"Okay."

" 'Bye, then."

" 'Bye."

Sean turned off his phone and began to wend his way to the checkout. Maybe he'd done the wrong thing, maybe she'd think he was hounding her, but he didn't think two calls in as many weeks could be seen as hounding. Anyway, he'd done it now. He crossed his fingers, hoping she'd call back. He needed to apologize to her, and he couldn't do that on a machine or through Paul. He was desperate to see her, to say he was sorry face-to-face. To judge how she reacted. And somehow make it up with her.

He piled his shopping on the conveyor belt. The magazine rack in front of him was loaded with *OK!* and *Hello!* magazines, all full of celebrity weddings and parties and openings. Even though one of the covers was emblazoned with a picture of Lily, taken by a paparazzi as she was coming out of a restaurant, and a headline hinting that her companion, Jerry, the director of *We Can Work It Out*, might be her latest lover, Sean looked right through them, his thoughts still on Terry.

"She's amazing, isn't she?" a voice behind him said.

"What? Sorry?"

"I said, she's amazing. Lily James." It was a tall, good-looking man with slightly graying hair and dark blue eyes who was standing in line behind him, buying a large pack of water. He had a copy of the magazine in his hand and was pointing at the image of Lily on the cover.

"Oh. Yes. Yes, she is."

"That *We Can Work It Out* is incredible. I wonder if she can be that funny in real life?" The woman in front of Sean finished paying. He moved up to stand opposite the till. The man behind him carried on. "I mean, how wonderful it would be to come home to her after a long day's hard work. They say a good sense of humor is the most important thing."

The young woman behind the counter rang her bell for help; Sean's carton of milk was leaking and needed to be replaced. They were going to have to wait. Wanting to be polite, Sean said, "Yes, yes, I hear it is."

"I once met that actress out of *Brookside*. Can't remember her name. I'd love to meet our Lily. Wouldn't you?"

Finding the whole conversation bizarre in the extreme considering that he was at that moment going out with the woman his unsought acquaintance seemed so keen on, Sean managed to mutter a noncommittal, "I suppose so," while praying for the boy who'd gone to get the milk to return on the double.

"Yes, she's really something. Really something."

"Here. Sorry for the delay, sir."

The milk arrived and in the bustle of paying his bill and refusing a loyalty card and bagging his groceries, Sean was able to escape the conversation about Lily.

Clive stood at the checkout counter, furious with himself. What on earth had made him think he was going to get anything out of Sean that way? Of course the man wasn't going to start telling the family secrets to someone he met in a queue at a supermarket checkout. Clive thought of himself as a true professional, but that was the most amateurish attempt to get information out of a target he'd ever heard of. He'd been way too eager and so had blown his one chance to get close to Sean. Now he'd have to think again. Even though they'd had only a brief conversation, Clive was convinced the builder would recognize him if he tried again in a more auspicious place and in a more promising fashion. Damn. Back to the beat.

fifty-five

"Are you all right?"

Jules was leaning against one of the Corinthian columns that stood on either side of the main entrance to her father's club. All day she had been feeling weird at times, slightly off balance, with an odd sort of griping in her stomach. She had put it down to nerves at seeing her mother, and the fact that it had flared up again just as she was about to walk through the swinging door of the club suggested to her that she was right.

She pushed herself away from the column and swung around. Her Conservative MP brother, Philip, was coming up the steps, his beautifully dressed, beautifully manicured wife, Carolyn, on his arm. Jules made an effort at a smile. "Philip. How nice to see you. I'm fine. Just a momentary stagger at the idea of Diana."

Philip, a tall, well-rounded man with a red, country-squire's face and a loud, cheerful voice, leaned forward to kiss his sister. "We're all here. We'll look after you."

Jules couldn't help but smile at that. Over the years, her siblings had tried again and again to protect her from her mother, but Diana was like a hurricane or a landslide, absolutely unstoppable once started. But she said nothing, accepting her brother's support in the spirit in which it was offered.

Jules and Carolyn air-kissed. Philip's wife was the perfect Tory MP's helpmeet. She made a keen cup of tea, gave very, very good charity balls, and looked great in hats. She was never anything but charming whenever the two women met, but Jules was always slightly suspicious that the warmth had more to do with Carolyn's interest in the eventual destination of a childless sister-in-law's money than it did in genuine affection. Still, right now, she'd take anything she could get.

AN HOUR later, all her worst fears had come true. Lady Dunne was at her most appalling. When Jules had first seen that they had a private room, she had been relieved not to have to go through the ordeal of the evening in front of other people. The idea of her mother saying cutting things whilst the rest of the tables in the communal dining room strained to hear her words filled her with the deepest despair. It had happened before, time and again, and Jules had hideous memories of the half-hidden smirks and snickers on curious strangers' faces as Diana reviled her daughter in public as an unfeeling, ungrateful prima donna who had been nothing but an embarrassment to her family since she was born.

However, almost immediately Jules realized that she would have been better off in the main dining room. There being no one but the family around removed the few curbs that the presence of strangers might have placed on Diana's knife-edged tongue and gave her the freedom to say anything she wanted. And say it she did. Right from the moment they arrived, she attacked her daughter with all the subtlety of a spitting cobra.

Jules had been determined to do nothing to provoke her. Though she knew from past experience that what she did meant very little, she still tried. She dressed ultraconservatively, in an irreproachably plain dark navy suit that she'd bought in Peter Jones for just such an occasion, kept as far away from her mother as possible, never ventured an opinion or made an unnecessary comment. In short, she tried to be invisible.

But it never worked. As far as Diana was concerned, Jules was a Day-Glo lime green and orange exclamation mark of a person, an unavoidable insult to anyone of taste and discernment. Anyone like Diana. No corner could hide Jules, no dull clothes could veil her, no reserve could mask her presence.

Ian Dunne had tried his best. He'd arranged the table very cleverly. Or so he thought. He and Diana were supposed to be at opposite ends, with Jules on his left, as far from her mother as possible. Except the club had put them in the room with a round table. It was a beautiful chamber, its walls hung with antique, hand-blocked wallpaper, its table and chairs a rich, glowing mahogany, its curved bow windows looking out onto a tiny rose garden. But it meant that Diana was just across the table from Jules. Close enough to kiss. Or bite.

And she bit. On the way into the club, she had seen Michael Hungerford, Jules's one-time fiancé, at the bar, and that one quick glimpse of the man she had longed to boast of having as her son-in-law had been enough to arouse her fury. Over the starter, a platter of smoked salmon, something even the club couldn't burn or overcook or turn to mush, she started to lay into Jules.

"It is unforgivable. He should be here, with us, a member of our family, not downstairs. It was a perfect situation. Perfect. Until you jilted him. The future Lord Ashcliffe, and you decide the day before the wedding that he is not good enough for you." Lady Dunne's high, sharp voice dripped with contempt for her daughter's decision.

"It was a long time ago." Alice, Jules's older sister, tried to deflect some of the poison. Married to David, who was a wealthy gentleman farmer in Wiltshire, Alice was the mother of two strapping, healthy, privately edu-cated sons. She was a conservative woman, happy with her country house and her family, uninterested in London or city society or the latest thing. She and Jules were as different as tea and champagne, but they had been close as children and Alice always tried to help. Even though she risked bringing her mother's wrath onto her own shoulders by doing so.

Tonight, however, Diana was not to be deflected. "Even worse, he then marries Rose Holland. Allowing Jemima to crow over me for all those years."

Lord Dunne got to his feet. "I'd just like to say how delightful it is to have you with us tonight. We see each other all too rarely nowadays. Let's hope this is the start of many more dinners like this." And he raised his glass of white wine. "To the family."

"The family."

"The family."

Jules ignored the wine that had been put in front of her, picked up her glass of water, and took a small sip. Typical Daddy. He just wouldn't let go of his idea of how they should all behave. His resolve was admirable in many ways—most other people would have given up long before in the face of such discouragement—but Jules couldn't help wishing he was just a little less determined. And thus more willing to accept reality.

It was over the main course of overdone roast beef and soggy Yorkshire pudding that Diana started to go on about Jules running her own business.

"It's not feminine. A little job before marriage, of course, that's accepted, but to run your own company? My grandmother would have died of shame."

"Juliet is a great success. We should be proud of her achievements," Philip said. Jules held her breath. Diana was not going to like that suggestion.

"Proud? Proud? Of a traitorous little show-off like that? I am surprised you could suggest such a thing, Philip. Very surprised indeed."

"How are the children, Alice? Is Rupert still taking shooting lessons?"

"Very well, Daddy. Rupert is good, isn't he, David? We're thinking of buying him his own gun this year."

And Diana was sidetracked again. But not for long. Over the dessert, a disgusting steamed currant and suet pudding, called for some long-forgotten reason spotted dick, she began again. This time on Jules's divorce.

"No one in our family has ever been divorced before. Ever."

"Mummy, I'm sure Juliet didn't know she and Will would split up." Jules's younger sister, Elena, happily married to Charles, a successful architect, made a stab at defending her sibling.

But Diana was having none of it. "Nonsense, Elena. We told her when she married that man that it would be forever and she had better think more carefully, that he wasn't our sort, but she made her bed and then refused to lie in it."

"It is all in the past. I know Juliet suffered—" Philip chimed in.

Only to be cut off. "Juliet suffered? Juliet? What happened to her exactly?"

"Mummy. You know what happened. He . . . he hit her. . . ." Alice was still deeply disturbed by Will's behavior. In her comfortable world, men didn't do that. It only happened to working-class women with drunken husbands and too many children and no money. Not to people like Jules. Having to accept that she was wrong, that there were abusers everywhere undercut her vision of life and made her feel insecure.

"I have sympathy for him."

"Mummy!"

"Mother!"

"Diana!" Even Ian couldn't ignore that.

"No need to shout at me. I know what I'm talking about. She probably deserved it. I read a book once that suggested that the woman is always to blame."

Jules stopped herself from expressing her surprise at her mother having ever read anything that wasn't *Tatler* or *Country Life*. She was proud of herself. She'd managed to get through most of the evening without addressing a word to her mother. She'd heard her pour out her venom and, for the first time, found she didn't care what Diana had to say. It was tedious to have to listen to her and she could think of many things she would have preferred to be doing, but she wasn't upset. Previously, she would have been on the verge of tears, concerned that Diana's vitriol had a basis in fact. That she indeed was a stupid little show-off, a traitor to her family and her class. That she had deserved Will's abuse.

But tonight, she was able to let it all pass over her. Because of the baby. Ultimately, that was all that mattered. She was going to supersede all her memories of Diana with memories of her child. She was going to replace her mean, bitter, dysfunctional mother with the family she was creating right now.

"I've never had this pudding done quite as well," lied Ian Dunne. Jules found herself hiding a smile. The pudding was as undercooked and tasteless as ever, and the custard had curdled. She thought it might be a good time to excuse herself and go to the toilet; Diana would never forgive her for smiling.

She got up, murmured to her father to explain where she was going, and walked to the door. Halfway there, she felt a sharp pain in her back and staggered for a moment.

"Drunk, I suppose," said Diana, who was watching this.

Still hurting but determined not to show it, Jules ignored her mother and continued out of the room. Outside the door, she doubled over as her stomach began to cramp. Half-bent with the pain, she inched along the corridor and down the half landing, to the ladies' room. She pushed the door open, lurched through into the empty, impersonal, white-tiled room, and collapsed on the floor. The pains continued to rip through her and she started to cry. Not because she was hurting but because she knew what was happening.

She was losing her baby.

THE DOOR to the toilet swung open. Still on the floor, her chest shaking with sobs, Jules opened her eyes a crack, praying that it would be Alice or Elena. Or even a stranger. But the elegant tan shoes, shapely legs, and gossamer-fine stockings told her that she had been unlucky. It was Diana.

"What on earth are you doing there on the floor?"

"I think . . . I'm . . . having a . . . mis . . . carriage," Jules said, struggling to get the words out. It was bad enough that she had to admit it out loud, to herself, but to have to say it to Diana?

"A what? Speak up, Juliet."

"A mis . . . carriage."

"Rubbish. You're just trying to draw attention to yourself as usual. Miscarriage, indeed. Now get up."

"Mummy. I'm losing my baby." Jules hadn't called Diana Mummy in years. Not since she had managed to banish her childhood longing for a real mother. Or thought she had. But one last remnant must have still lurked in her mind somewhere. And decided to surface now. Jules found herself praying that Diana would offer her some comfort. Would play mother, at least for a few moments.

"You're pregnant?"

"Yes."

"Pregnant?" Diana's voice went up an octave. "Pregnant? You're not married."

"I know." If she hadn't been crying so much, Jules would have been tempted to laugh. It was so typically Diana. Social standing mattered more than anything else. And having an unmarried mother in the family was unthinkable.

"I thought you had done everything you could to hurt me, but obviously not. In the club too. Everyone will know. Everyone."

"Please, Mummy." Jules hated the idea, but she was going to have to ask her mother for help. She had to get to a doctor as soon as possible. Just in case he could save her baby. That was all that mattered now. Not her pride. "I need your help."

"Help?"

"Call an ambulance. A cab. Please, hurry. I've got to get to hospital."

Lady Dunne looked at her daughter lying on the cold, hard floor of the ladies' room, at her hand clutched over her stomach, at the tears streaming down her face. "I'll get the girls," she said, and walked out.

Barely a minute later, she was back with Alice.

"Now, Alice, you hold one side of her. I'll take the other. We've got to get her out of here. Elena's gone to get a cab."

"Mummy, she's not well."

Diana grasped Jules's right arm and tried to lift her limp body into a sitting position. "Alice," she shouted sharply. "Help me."

"Don't you think we should get a doctor first?"

"Here? Don't be stupid."

"No, Alice. I need to go to hospital. Now. Please."

"See? She wants to go." Diana managed to lift her daughter enough so that she could prop her against her legs.

"We should call an ambulance. Look, she's bleeding." Lady Dunne had moved Jules enough to allow them to see a smear of blood on the floor.

"No. The whole club will know."

"Mummy!"

Diana stared at her oldest daughter. "Don't 'Mummy' me. I'm thinking of Juliet. An ambulance in London can take up to half an hour to arrive. I saw a piece on the news about it."

"A taxi is fine. Really. Don't argue about it. Just get me there. Please."

Alice had to accept that. She knelt down, put her sister's left arm over her shoulders, and together she and Diana pulled Jules to her feet. She swayed, staggered, leaned on her sister for support, but she stayed upright.

"Come on, Juliet," said Alice, trying to encourage her sister. "Can you walk a bit?" Jules put one foot in front of the next. Then again. "There. We're here. Just lean on us and we'll get you there."

As Diana held open the door to the ladies', Alice helped Jules walk out of the room and into the corridor outside. Then, with her mother supporting her on one side, her sister on the other, Jules inched her way down one flight of stairs and along a narrow passageway to the main entrance hall of the club. It was empty. Diana breathed a massive sigh of relief.

The sound of men's laughter drifted out of the open door to the bar off the lobby.

Jules lurched forward, half supported, half dragged by her mother and sister, toward the exit.

"Quickly, now, Alice," muttered Diana. "Anyone could come out of the bar and see us."

"Hush, Mummy. I'll take her from here. Why don't you get the door? Come on, Juliet. Just a few more steps. That's it."

Lady Dunne went to hold the door open for her two daughters. And Michael Hungerford walked out of the bar and into the lobby.

By now, Alice was almost carrying her sister. Michael, looking deeply shocked, backed up against the wall, leaving as much room for the girls as he could. Without saying anything, the two staggered out of the club, into the taxi that Elena had found. And away to the hospital.

Diana turned to Michael. "I do hope you won't say anything to anyone about this regrettable incident," she simpered. "So embarrassing. So typical of Juliet."

Michael looked at her. And looked at her, seeing for the first time the full nightmare of what Jules had had to cope with all her life. Finally, he nodded. And walked on into the depths of the club.

fifty-six

Jules opened her eyes to see unfamiliar blond-wood furniture, a small television perched on an elevated platform, and an enormous vase full of yellow
roses. She was in a hospital. Sitting next to her was Lily, on the end of the
bed was Mara, and in an armchair in the corner was Terry. Jules looked at
her friends, at their concerned faces, and she burst into tears. She'd lost her
baby.

The night before had been horrendous. Her sisters had brought her into
the emergency room, but it had been five hours before she was seen. Five
hours of that bright, neon world of green curtains and beeping machines
and the mixed smells of strong disinfectant and human waste. Five hours
of Alice and Elena holding her hands while her cramps slowly decreased
but she continued to bleed heavily. Then, just before two o'clock in the
morning, it had all been over. She'd lost her baby. Exhausted and expecting
her to sleep for the rest of the night, Alice and Elena had gone home.

But Jules hadn't slept. She couldn't. Instead, too beside herself to think of
asking to be transferred to a private clinic, she'd had her first experience of
being in a National Health hospital. The place was full to the seams, the staff
was harassed, and the patients were expected to take what they could get and
be grateful. She had lain on a trolley in the emergency room until four
o'clock, when the young, overworked intern who'd been given her case finally
wangled her a proper bed and she'd been taken to a ward for observation.

The hours passed. She knew that. Every time she glanced at the institutional clock hung at one end of the room some time had elapsed. Ten, once even fifteen minutes. But more often it was only one or two as the night crept past, second by miserable second. Apart from an occasional cramp, there like a hollow echo of what had gone before, the pain had disappeared. The physical pain, that is. The other hurt grew and grew as Jules listened to patients cough and snore and struggle for breath and came face-to-face, over and over, with the realization that she had lost her own child.

Finally, when bedraggled light began to seep into the ward, signaling the start of another cold, wintry day, Jules had managed to drag herself out of her bed and to a phone and called Lily. Half an hour later, Lily bustled in and used a combination of her charm and her celebrity to magic up a private room and peace and quiet and blessed sleep.

But nothing had changed. Jules had escaped from the public ward. She was more rested. Her sisters had called. Her father had sent flowers. She had her friends with her. But she had still had a miscarriage.

Lily leaned over to hold her. "There, there, sweetie. It'll be okay."

"No it won't. It can't. I've lost my baby. All that work, all those schemes, and now nothing."

"It's a setback, that's all," Lily said.

"A setback." Jules's voice was empty.

"I lost my first, remember? And then three months later, I was pregnant with Moo. The doctor said it often . . . often . . ." Mara began to cough, a deep, rasping cough that sent spasms through her chest. Days spent in her cold, drafty, damp house, the smoke from the fire, nights in the icy bedroom she couldn't afford to heat, the stress of not knowing what was going to happen, when the Moores' ax was going to fall, was taking its toll. She'd caught a cold a few weeks before and had not been able to shake it off. She struggled to finish her sentence. ". . . often . . . hap . . . pens."

Terry came over to the bed and rubbed Mara's back, "Are you okay, love?"

"Sorry. It's just . . . just the end . . . of a cold." She reached into her bag, pulled out a packet of lozenges, and popped one in her mouth. "I'll be fine."

"Doesn't sound like just a cold to me."

"Please don't worry about me. It's Jules needs our . . . our he . . . help . . . ," Mara said as she bent over, coughing again.

"We do worry," Lily said. "Have you been to see the doctor?"

Mara shook her head. How would a doctor help? Could he make her house water- and windproof? Could he mend her central heating? Could he stop the Moores from taking her girls away?

"Don't you think you should, sweetie?"

"There's no . . . need. It's getting . . . better. Really." Mara's coughing fit eased off a bit as the lozenge did its work. "There, see? I'm fine."

"Mara." Horrified by the chesty, hoarse sounds that had been coming out of her friend, Terry was about to argue. Until she saw Lily winking at her and mouthing, "Later." And so held off. If Lily had a plan . . .

"Mara's right," Lily said to Jules. "About the baby. You just give your body time to recover and, wham! you go at it again."

"You'll be pregnant in no time. Honestly." Mara's voice was husky from the coughing but her breathing was getting easier.

"No I won't. Not unless I find someone else to donate the sperm."

"What's wrong with Sean? He'll do it again. No problem." Lily didn't like the idea, but she wasn't going to deny her friend in her time of need.

Terry said nothing. What could she say? The others had no idea what had happened between Jules and Sean. He hadn't even told Lily. But he'd told her. And she knew there was no chance of his agreeing to give Jules another child.

"He won't. I doubt he'd even take my phone call."

"Why? What happened? He didn't say anything."

"He bought me this gorgeous rocking horse a friend of his had made. I told him I didn't want it. To take it away. I said he had no further place in my or my baby's life. That he was just a man who provided me with some sperm. He was furious. I thought he was going to hit me."

Lily and Mara were silent for a moment. Both of them looked shocked.

"Um, perhaps that was a bit harsh," Mara said.

"It was worse than that. My father had just left after getting me to agree to last night's dinner with the family and I wasn't at my best, but that's no excuse. I should have let Sean down more gently. I owed him that at least. Instead, I was mean and cruel and horrible."

"You were tense and upset," said Lily.

"Surely he'd understand. If you explained? Wrote and told him why you'd been so hard on him?"

"You think that might help?"

"Maybe it wasn't your manner that upset him?" Terry couldn't keep silent any longer. Although she was reluctant to talk about that night when Sean had come to her house to pour out his woes, she couldn't stand around and listen to Jules get things so wrong. "Maybe it was cos you told him he wasn't going to play a part in the baby's life?"

"Do you think? But she told him that was the way she wanted it right at the start. Didn't you?" Lily turned to Jules.

"Yes, of course I did."

"Well, then."

"Maybe he thought you didn't mean it?" Terry suggested.

"No. He couldn't have. I was quite clear."

"But if he believed you'd changed your mind? After all, from where he's sitting, you'd done it before. Remember, at the beginning, you said you only needed his sperm and then you decided to have sex with him."

"I suppose that's possible. Now I think about it, he did say something like that. Lily? You know him best."

Lily didn't want to upset her friend any further. But it did sound like Sean. He'd done that with her. Ignored what she said. Built up a whole fantasy about them living together even though she'd been adamant about not wanting that. "Maybe. It does make some sense."

"Then writing a letter won't help, will it?"

"No. It won't." Terry didn't want to upset Jules either, but she felt an obligation to Sean to tell the truth. He deserved so much more than he'd been offered, and part of Terry wanted Jules to realize how unreasonable her expectations had been.

"Not if that's the problem, no, babe," Lily said as gently as she could.

Jules started to cry again. "It's all my fault. If I hadn't been so selfish. So shortsighted. I just thought I could have everything I wanted. My own baby. No father to bother me." Jules's sobs got louder. "I never thought about Sean. Or even the child. Just me."

Terry looked down at her small feet in their sensible, bus driver's boots. She had wanted to provoke some reaction, some remorse, but not this storm of weeping.

"Come on, sweetie. You'll make yourself sick." Lily stroked Jules's sweat-darkened hair off her forehead.

"You'll find another donor," Mara said. "There've got to be lots of men out there who'd jump at it."

"Of course there are." Lily reinforced Mara's thought. "A nice young fertile girl like you, they'd be crazy to turn you down. Wouldn't they, Ter?"

"Sure they would." Terry still had her doubts, but for now, her friend needed reassurance, not a lecture. Time enough for that when she started to look for a new target.

Jules appreciated her friends' attempts to cheer her up, but it didn't help. It wasn't only that she knew her chances of finding another Sean were slim. In the time she'd known she was pregnant, her child had become real to her in a way she hadn't imagined before. And now he or she was gone. She'd never know it, never feed it or change it or cuddle it or watch it growing up day by day. And she couldn't bear it. Her baby was dead.

She realized she needed to be by herself. To mourn in her own way. But Lily and the other two would never leave if they thought she was still desperate. So she made a huge effort, muted her sobs and turned off the tears.

"I'm sure you're right," she said, pretending to stifle a yawn.

Mara took the cue. "Poor Jules. You must be exhausted, and here we are wittering on and on."

"Not wittering. But I am tired."

"Come on, you lot. Time to go. Leave Jules to have a nap." Lily bent over to kiss Jules's cheek, followed by Terry and Mara. And all three trooped out, leaving Jules alone. To cry.

"IT WASN'T just the cough. She looked like she hadn't slept for weeks," Lily said, her hands cupped around a mug of hot tea. Once the three women had left the hospital, Mara had said good-bye to her two friends and rushed off to catch a bus so she could be home in time for Moo and Tilly getting back from school. Lily had steered Terry into a nearby café.

"Or eaten properly."

"Or eaten properly," Lily agreed.

"I knew I should have forced her to see a doctor. Why did you stop me?"

"You can't make her take medical advice if she doesn't want to. Anyway, we need to remove the cause before we deal with the symptoms."

"What cause? She's ill."

"We've been being fools. It's winter, isn't it?"

"Yes."

"And it's cold?"

"Yes. So?"

"Well, we know Mara's roof leaks, right? Suppose that's not the only thing? Suppose the windows are damaged?"

"God, yes. Or worse. Suppose the central heating's broken?" Terry said.

"It'd be like living on the streets."

"And she'd never tell us."

"No."

"Silly girl. Too proud for her own good."

"I think it's time we had a word with Sean."

"We promised Mara we'd give up. Not force him on her anymore."

"We're not going to force him on her. This isn't about getting her back into dating. This is about us sorting out her house."

"She'll never accept help. You know that. We've tried often enough."

"She won't get the chance. This time we're not going to offer. We're going to do it."

fifty-seven

"There's something there, I tell you."

"Fine, Clive, fine. But what is it?"

Clive paced around the large, book- and video-filled office of Nigel, the newspaper's editor-in-chief. His boss. It was late afternoon, already dark outside. He was being grilled about the Lily story. Or the Lily nonstory. "I don't know that yet," he was forced to admit.

"Yet? You've been on this story for weeks."

"I've got a lot of stuff. Like Jules, you know, the upper-class one, was rushed to hospital in a taxi last night; she's still there now. The girls have all been to see her, but not Sean."

"Yes? And?"

"I think she had a miscarriage."

"So?"

"So I just haven't found out what it all means yet."

"Clive, dear, I'm sure it's all fascinating, but there's no story if you can't connect up the bits. Who is he? Why is he seeing all three friends? What are they doing together? Where's the beef, love? Where's the beef?"

Clive gritted his teeth. Nigel could be a patronizing bastard. But he had the power to keep Clive on the story. Or order him to forget it. "I'll find it. I will. I just need more time."

"I don't know."

"Please, Nige. This could be really big. Front-page stuff."

"Hmm. You're very keen, aren't you? Perhaps you're too close, what with Lily being your ex? Maybe I should put someone else on it?"

Clive held himself back. Better not to say anything. Nigel liked to make his underlings squirm. It was part of what made him a good editor, they said.

"So what is it between you two, then?"

"Nothing. I'm just interested in what she does. She's a new kid in town. And you know how people eat up stuff about the latest thing."

"Hmm. I'm not sure."

"I know this is something big. Come on, Nige, I've got great instincts. You know I have. When have I ever been wrong about a story? Remember, you all laughed at me about Scott Lineham. And there he was, fucking his coach's wife. You said after that you'd never doubt me again."

"Did I?"

"Yes. You did."

"All right, drop everything else you've got going, concentrate on Ms. James. I'll give you another week. But no longer. If you don't know what's going on by then, you've got to forget it. Completely. Agreed?"

"Agreed," said Clive. What need to mention his determination to carry on on his own time? With any luck, it wouldn't take more than a week to connect the dots and paint in the details. . . .

fifty-eight

Sean turned off Chiswick High Road onto Mara's street, unaware that he had been followed by a man in a late-model Porsche ever since he'd left King's Cross. The builder found a parking space in front of the railway memorabilia store; Clive drove past and turned into the next street. He had no need to see where Sean was going; ever since they had reached the edge of Chiswick, he'd been pretty sure his target was going to Mara's. And their arrival in Elliott Road had only confirmed that. The journalist parked and looked back, waiting to see the builder pass by before he got out and followed.

Sean locked his car and turned to walk to Mara's but was distracted by the railway-shop window. He stared at all the displayed toys and couldn't help but think how the boys would have loved an old-fashioned train set. He could have set it up in the attic, arranged the miniature rails and the tiny signal boxes and the little stations, and let them play with it to their hearts' content.

For a moment, he let himself dream: of himself and Mark and Ben, back together, watching the perfect replica of a 1920s steam train go around and around, the boys' voices piping their excitement as it passed through a tunnel or over a bridge. . . .

Sean shook off the fantasy. And told himself that it was just that. A daydream. Nothing more. It wasn't going to happen. Even if he did ever find

Mark and Ben, they would probably be past the age of train sets by then, preferring things like skateboards and music and football. Even girls.

He left the shop window and walked along the road to Mara's house. God, it was in terrible shape. The windows looked rotten, the walls were in desperate need of repointing, and even from the ground he could tell that there were holes in the roof. No wonder Lily had asked him to sneak a look at the place and tell her how much it would cost to fix it up. If Mara carried on like this, soon she wouldn't have a house left.

MARA HAD been horrified to see Sean on the doorstep. She'd thought her friends had promised to let her alone, to stop forcing him on her. But when he explained that he had been in the area looking at a job, had just wanted to say hello, and so had gotten her address from Lily, she'd relaxed and let him in.

In response to his request to see the house, she'd given him the grand tour. Just as they were finishing, Moo and Tilly had come home from school and he'd ended up trying and failing to help them with their homework, then playing video games with them, laughing at himself as he went out at the first level over and over. Delighted to see her girls having such fun, Mara had asked Sean to stay for dinner; now it was eight-thirty, Moo and Tilly were in bed, and the adults were sitting by the fire, finishing the bottle of wine Sean had run down to the off license to buy.

He hadn't said much for the last half hour. Whilst the girls had been there, he'd been animated, joking with them, teasing her, telling them funny stories about being a builder. But since Mara had tucked them up in bed, he'd seemed totally lost in thought. Not that she minded; she was happy to sit and look into the flames. The room felt properly warm for once—maybe it was the extra person—and she hadn't had a coughing fit for hours.

But now he seemed to be on the verge of talking. A couple of times, he had opened his mouth, apparently about to speak, but had then thought better of it and said nothing. Mara had received enough confidences in her time to recognize a man desperate to discuss something but not sure of how to introduce the subject. Or whether he ought to do so. She settled in to wait. Sooner or later he was going to tell her what was on his mind.

"Mara?" Sean finally said five minutes later.

"Yes?"

He was silent again. For another minute. Until:

"Mara?"

"Sean."

"I . . . Can I ask you something?"

"Of course you can."

"It's about Terry."

"Oh. Okay." What was this? Terry?

"This is in confidence, okay?"

"Of course."

"You see, I had this fight with Jules. About the baby. And then after, I went to see Terry. Only I got a bit wasted and . . . and I kissed her."

"You kissed Terry?"

"Yes. And she pushed me away. But I can't just leave it like that."

And all Sean's feelings came pouring out, his undeniable desire for Terry, his attempts to understand her apparent attraction to, then abrupt rejection of, him, his need to see her, to talk to her, to explain, to try to persuade her to forgive him for making a move on her while going with her best friend.

Mara listened. And heard a man in love. Whatever Sean might call it— liking, desire, attraction, guilt—Mara was convinced it was love. And judging by his description of Terry's reaction to him, it sounded as if at least some of those feelings were mutual. But what should she do? The only way to explain Terry's actions to Sean would be to tell him the truth about her. Her past experiences with men, her inability to enjoy sex, her determination to remain celibate rather than continue hoping. But that would mean Mara betraying her friend's confidence and she was not prepared to do that.

Still, she couldn't just say nothing. Some instinct told her that, despite all the sharing, despite Lily's and Jules's involvement with Sean, he might be the man for Terry. There was nothing obvious there but she sensed a similarity in them, of outlook maybe or background or beliefs. Something, anyway. And if Terry had reacted to Sean's kiss the way he described . . .

At heart, Mara was a romantic. She'd had her great love and she wanted the same for her friends. For Terry. Maybe she shouldn't interfere—she could hear Jake telling her not to meddle, that it never paid to get involved in friends' love lives—but for once she ignored her husband's advice. She couldn't help herself. Sean wasn't for Lily or Jules, but he might be for Terry. Lily wouldn't mind—in the end one man was much like another to her—and Jules had already pushed him too far. But Terry was another matter. Maybe it would be a disaster, but Mara decided the possible gain was worth the risk.

"You need to persevere."

"Persevere?"

"Yes. Go round. Make her see you."

"How? If she won't speak to me on the phone."

"Ask Paul to help if you have to. Get into the flat. Talk to her."

"Suppose she still despises me?"

"I don't think she does. Or ever did."

"But I made a move on her. She's got to."

"Why?"

"Because I'm her best friend's boyfriend."

"Ah." She hadn't thought about that. Of course, from Sean's point of view, with no knowledge of the friends' scheme, it would look that way. "I wouldn't worry too much about that. Terry's never been the judgmental type." Well, it was the best she could come up with on short notice. And after all, it was true. Terry had always believed in letting people make their own decisions.

"But Lily . . ."

"Is a very strong person. She can look after herself. She always could."

"I betrayed her." Twice, but he wasn't going to mention that. Even though this conversation did seem oddly like a confession. "I feel like such a shit."

"Don't. Please. There's no need." Mara couldn't bear the fact that Sean was eaten up with guilt, convinced he'd betrayed Lily when all the time he'd been used by her and the others. She had to help him. But how to put it without letting slip that she knew all about his and Lily's relationship? She might feel desperately sorry for poor Sean but she still didn't want to be disloyal to her friends. "You and Lily aren't exactly permanent partners, are you?" she asked.

"No. We see each other only a couple of times a week. Lily wanted it that way."

"And you're free to do what you want the rest of the time?"

"Yeah. Yeah. She insisted on it. No commitment, that's what she said."

"Then there can be no betrayal. Can there?"

"No. No, I guess not."

"You know not. Go and see Terry. Talk to her. She won't hate you. She won't even be angry with you." Mara crossed her fingers behind her back. There was a chance of course that Terry would be both those things, but Mara was convinced it was an outside chance. "The worst she'll be is confused."

"But what do I say?"

"What you've just told me. Tell her how you feel."

"Really?"

"Really. Only take it slowly."

"Slowly?"

"Terry's very sensitive."

"She doesn't come across like that."

"I know. But she is. Just try not to pressure her. Physically, I mean. I can't say any more, so please don't ask. I shouldn't have said this much."

"I won't." Sean leaned over and gripped Mara's hands. "Thank you. You're amazing."

"I'm not."

"You are. One hundred percent amazing." Sean found himself smiling for the first time in weeks. Nothing had happened yet, he knew that, but Mara had given him the reassurance and the hope he'd needed.

Sean looked around him at the dingy room, the smoke stains on the ceiling, the patches of damp in the corners, the slight bow in the front wall. The place was in a terrible state. Lily had been right when she'd sent him here, Mara did need help. But he didn't think the kind of simple repairs Lily had in mind would do. The house needed almost complete rebuilding. "Now, in return for the fantastic food and the clever counsel, would it be okay if I gave you some advice?"

"If you like."

"It's your house." Sean looked at Mara, trying to decide just how much to tell her. "I'm afraid it's in pretty bad shape."

"I know the roof needs work."

"It's not just the roof. It's an old property. And they take a lot of upkeep."

"I'll manage somehow."

"I'm not sure you will." Sean paused, trying to decide what to say. And came down on the side of the truth, even if it was not what Mara wanted to hear. She deserved honesty in return for her kindness to him. "Mara, you don't just need a new roof. You need new windows, new brickwork in places, your chimney needs rebuilding, that illegal fire of yours looks like it smokes, and you've got to do something about that wall that's out of kilter. Not to mention a full damp course and the central heating."

"I thought just the roof and the heating and a lick of paint."

"I'm afraid not."

"But it'll cost a fortune."

Sean nodded. "About thirty thousand pounds at a rough guesstimate. Maybe more if there's any rot upstairs."

"Thirty thousand pounds." Mara was horrified. It was impossible. Much, much more than she had thought.

"Hey, it's not that bad. I can find you guys who'll do a proper job, not rip you off. And I get discounts on materials, that should knock off a bit."

"But I could never pay for all that. I don't have anything like thirty thousand pounds. I don't have five hundred."

"Then I'm sorry, but you've got no option. You've got to sell."

"I can't."

"I know it's hard."

"I bought this house with my husband. We were happy here. The children came here as babies. I can't sell."

"Then it'll fall down round your ears. Guaranteed."

"Surely it won't. Houses don't just collapse. It'll be all right. I know it will."

"Mara. The longer you leave a place like this, the more quickly it declines. Think about it. How many leaks were there last winter? How many are there now?"

"I can't sell. Jake wouldn't like it."

"He wouldn't like you living in a place like this either. Besides, Jake isn't here."

"No. But I know what he'd want. And I owe it to him. He gave me everything."

Sean was tempted to enlighten Mara about her beloved husband. Lily had told him all about the blessed Jake after the evening of the dinner party. But he couldn't. It had to be one of her girlfriends. Not some man she hardly knew.

"He was the best husband. I couldn't, I just couldn't sell the house we shared. Watch someone else come in and change the place, throw out the bath he washed in, the kitchen he ate in." Mara was working herself up into a panic at the thought of selling her memories.

Sean realized that her attachment to her dead husband was so strong that she would not accept the truth, whatever he said. She'd continue to hope that something would turn up, that it would be all right in the end, until she was out in the street, homeless.

"I can't even consider moving. It'll be fine. It's no worse than it was this morning. It's the roof that matters. And the heating. Surely the rest can wait. Of course it can."

For the moment, there was no point in his arguing with her. Maybe it had been her ability to talk herself into believing whatever she wanted that had gotten her through the last few years alone. But now it was in danger of leaving her homeless. He would have to talk to Lily. She, Jules, or Terry had to come clean with Mara, and soon. Otherwise the house would be uninhabitable and worth not much more than the land it was crumbling upon.

For now, though, he took the line of least resistance. "I suppose I could be wrong. It was getting dark when I arrived, I didn't see the house in the daylight."

"Yes. You haven't seen the whole place properly. It's just the roof. Just the roof."

fifty-nine

"So what do you think he'll say?"

"Nothing. He won't talk to you."

"But why not? I agree it'll be difficult, but if I wrote a nice letter to explain?"

"I thought we covered all that last week. A letter won't do it."

"Then I'll wait in his office. If I'm there for long enough, he'll have to see me."

"Jules. Knock, knock. Anyone home? He doesn't want to hear from you."

"How do you know that? I'm different now. I learned my lesson."

"Did you?"

"Yes. I did. I won't ask him to disappear. He can see the baby every now and again if that's what it takes."

"Feeling generous, are you?" Terry dug her fingernails into her palms, struggling for control. Once again, Jules had managed to respin events to her benefit. So that she didn't have to face any unpleasant truths.

"Don't be nasty."

"I'm not being nasty. I'm being sensible."

"You don't think I could persuade him? Not if I tried very, very hard and was very, very contrite?"

"It's not that you couldn't. I think you shouldn't."

"But why not?"

"Because you used him. He knows that. You know that."

"And I'm sorry. I am. What more do you want me to say?"

"You just don't get it, do you?" This was not a conversation Terry wanted to have. The girls were getting together—apart from Mara, who was at home, hopefully letting Sean have a look at her house—to try to cheer up Jules, and though Terry wanted her friend to be less depressed, she didn't want it to be because she thought she had found a way to exploit Sean again.

Jules walked across her living room, took a bottle of wine out of a cooler, and poured some more into her's and Terry's glasses. "Get what? Why are you making such a fuss? All I'm asking for is a little bit of sperm."

"Then get it from somewhere else."

"But he's perfect."

"No, he's not. He's the worst person you could choose."

"But why? He's healthy, handsome, potent. He's just a little bit unhappy with me. But I can put that right. I know I can. It's just a matter of persuasion. It's got to be. If I can forgive him for almost hitting me, he can forgive me for what I did."

Terry drank down half of her wine in one go. "Fucking hell, Jules. Can't you see? You hurt him. A lot."

"I didn't mean to. And I'm sorry. You know I'm sorry."

"Do I? Does he even know you lost the baby?"

"I don't know. I didn't think . . . Lily must have, surely?" Jules didn't want to talk about the baby. After a week of tears and regrets, she desperately wanted to block out all thought of what she had lost. Hence her resolve to approach Sean. If she could just convince him to help her again, perhaps she would be able to look ahead rather than back.

When she'd first thought of the idea, she'd dismissed it. She kept seeing him advancing on her, shouting at her, threatening her. But then she remembered their nights together. His tenderness in bed, his easygoing friendliness, his willingness to help. That was the real Sean. The incident in her office had been a onetime thing. She had shattered his illusions, told him he wasn't going to have anything to do with her baby, and he had snapped. It wouldn't happen again.

"See? You haven't changed at all. It's still you, you, you. How the hell can you think he'll come back for more?" In an attempt to hold on to her temper, Terry walked over to the bottle of wine, refilled her now-empty glass, and gulped most of it down.

"But I need him. Surely there's a way I can win him over?"

The beseeching tone in Jules's voice, like a child wheedling for a treat, sent Terry one notch closer to losing it. "Don't you care about anyone but yourself? I thought you said you'd learned your lesson. It doesn't sound like it. It sounds like you're so desperate to have a kid that you're prepared to use and abuse a great guy to get one."

"I just want a baby."

"And that's all that matters, isn't it? What you want. Sean's feelings don't come into it. God, Jules, what the hell makes you think you should be allowed to have a kid?"

Jules was shocked by her friend's words. She stared at Terry, unable to reply for a moment. Until she managed to stammer out, "I'd . . . I'd be a good mother. I would."

"Not with Sean's baby. Not if I've got anything to do with it."

"I told you, I'd let him see it."

"That's kind of you."

"It's what he wanted."

"Then. It's what he wanted then. Who knows what he wants now? But I bet it isn't to give a selfish cow like you his baby."

Jules's mouth dropped open. She found it hard to believe that Terry was saying such things to her. Yes, there had always been some tension between them, but not like this. This was more than tension. This was deep-seated resentment finding its way into the open for the first time. Of the four friends, Jules and Terry had always gotten on least well, and Jules had never felt that she could relax with Terry in quite the same way she did with Lily and Mara. She had always been a bit intimidated by Terry's forthright manner, and often felt distinctly mediocre in comparison. For while her upbringing had trained her to mouth unconvincing and unexciting social platitudes, Terry's had made her sharp and funny and true to life. But even though the two had never been all that close, Jules had had no idea that Terry had such hostility stored up inside.

"I told you months ago this was a mistake, didn't I?" Terry continued, unable to stop the angry words. "But you didn't even hear. You just carried on, like anything you wanted had to be right. Stuck-up, spoiled, self-indulgent bitch that you are."

"Me? Me a bitch? You're the one." Jules's shock was wearing off. "Where's your compassion? I lost my baby."

"Don't give me that. If you were still all that upset, you'd not be obsessing about getting Sean back in your bed." Terry couldn't believe what was coming out of her mouth. She'd wanted to champion Sean, but that had somehow turned into something very personal. And cruel. "Time you faced the truth. No matter what you do, no matter how much you butter him up, Sean is not going to father another child for you. And if you had any sensitivity at all, you'd leave him alone."

"Why? I suppose you're interested in him yourself." Jules threw out a shot in the dark.

And hit a sensitive nerve. "No. Course I'm not."

"I always knew that celibacy thing was a joke."

"It wasn't. It isn't."

"Anyway, why should you have him? When I can't? Who's the selfish bitch here?"

"Piss off."

"Just the kind of intelligent response I'd expect from a Liverpool slag like you."

"You stuck-up cow."

"Oh, dear. Chips on both shoulders."

"Fuck you. Looking down your superior, snide little nose at me. Well, I've had it. Years and years and years I've put up with that sneer of yours."

"There's a lot to sneer at."

"So I'm from Liverpool eight. So I never finished school. So I drive a bus. Who the fuck cares? I'm better than you any day of the week."

"Are you? When your mother didn't even know who your father was?"

Terry staggered at this assault. Then launched her own attack. "I'd rather have a mother who fucked the whole of the bleeding British Army than yours. No wonder Diana hates you."

Cracks appeared in Jules's scornful facade. "You vindictive little bitch."

"That hurt, did it? Good."

"What on earth possessed Lily to befriend you?"

"Easy. I'm a hell of a lot more fun than you are."

"You are not. You're barely educated. You buy the *News of the World*. When was the last time you read a book?"

"Books. God, you're dull. Dull, dull, dull. It's like spending time with the Queen. Always so reserved. Yuck!"

"At least I enjoy sex."

"You fucking cow."

"Bitch."

"Slag."

"What the hell are you two doing?" Lily's voice broke in on them. She'd heard the shouting from outside the door and had let herself in.

Terry and Jules were standing at opposite ends of the small living room. Terry was breathless, her face red, her fists clenched. Jules appeared more poised on the surface but her face was rigid, her eyes were glittering with anger, and she was holding on hard to the back of a small leather chair. Neither turned to look at Lily or replied to her question, both struggling to contain their rage and resentment.

"Sit down, both of you. Calm down. Have a drink. Whatever it is, it isn't worth this."

Lily's cool voice broke the spell. Terry started to look more embarrassed than angry, Jules's face lost its hard-set look and she let go of the chair she was clutching.

"Good thing I got here when I did. You two looked ready to kill. What on earth happened?"

"Er, nothing," Terry mumbled.

"We just . . . We disagreed about something," Jules muttered.

"If that's what you call a disagreement, I can't wait to see you quarrel."

Terry looked over at Jules. Now that the heat had worn off, she was horrified she had said all those hurtful things. What on earth had possessed her? Even if Jules did rub her the wrong way at times, she'd never wanted to hurt her. Well, not before Sean, that is. She walked over to her and held out her hand. "I'm sorry. I was a monster. I don't know what came over me."

Jules shook her hand. "Or me." She knew she should do more, should hug Terry or give her a peck on the cheek, but she was still dazed from their fight. And though she regretted retaliating, she was also shaken by Terry's attitude. And the apparent depths of her anger.

"Friends?" Terry ventured.

"Yes. Yes . . . of course."

"So what was it all about?"

Jules and Terry both blushed.

"Like that, eh? Let me guess. Sean?" Terry nodded. "Oh, girls. No. This isn't how it was supposed to be." Lily wasn't nearly as disappointed as she sounded. The sight of Jules and Terry going at each other over Sean had been horrifying, yes, but it had also been reassuring. It wasn't just she who found the sharing tough. "It was supposed to solve our problems, not create more."

"And it did."

"To begin with."

"It's got to stop. Right now." The fight would give Lily a welcome excuse to end the scheme without admitting to anyone that she was having a hard time dealing with it herself. "Look at you two. Screaming at each other, dripping with anger, forgetting your friendship. It's too much."

"I didn't forget," said Terry sheepishly.

"Nor did I." Jules looked at the floor.

"And what I just saw was a demonstration of sisterly love? Sure, Sean seemed like a good idea. But it's not working. Maybe it's asking too much of us. Maybe it's just not gone right. Who knows. Anyway, it's time to call it off. I can't deal with watching my friends become rivals. Ter?"

"Fine by me." No question, that was the right thing. They had to stop treating Sean as if he was a commodity to be sliced up and shared, without his knowledge or consent.

"Jules?"

"If you say so. Yes. Of course. It's your decision." What else could she say? It was Lily's choice. He had been hers to give and so was hers to take away.

"Good. That's settled, then."

The thought of another chance at Sean—no matter how unlikely it had seemed—had temporarily held Jules's post-miscarriage blues at bay. But now that she could no longer clutch at that very short and very fragile straw, depression sank back over her. But she didn't want Lily to feel guilty about her decision—after all, she had every right to call time on their sharing scheme—and so, to hide her misery, Jules said the first thing that came to mind. "So what about you? Are you going to carry on seeing him?"

"Yeah. I think so. He's too good for me just to drop like that. And there's Mara's repairs to think of. Besides, I'd miss him."

"And we won't?" The words snapped out before Jules could stop herself. "Jules?"

"Sorry. Take no notice of me. I wasn't thinking."

"Do you want me to give Sean up too?"

"No. Of course not. Why would I want that?"

"It might be fairer."

"He was yours. He still is. What's unfair about that?"

"Nothing. But you don't sound happy."

Jules didn't want to talk about how she felt. What would be the point? She searched for something to distract Lily. "I'm fine. Only, am I allowed to feel just a little bit envious?" she said, trying to make a joke.

"Of what? Or can I guess?"

"I would think you could." She forced a smile. "After all, he is very, very good at it."

"Isn't he?"

Terry listened to her two friends talking. They didn't seem to have grasped the point at all. Maybe Sean wasn't up for grabs anymore, but they were still talking about him as if he was nothing. A body to be enjoyed. A penis, there for their pleasure.

Jules wasn't going to miss Sean. Jules didn't know Sean. And Terry was coming to the conclusion that Lily didn't either. But Terry did. And she was having a hard time coping with the thought that she was never going to see him again.

Four

sixty

Sean scrunched up the tiny strip of paper and threw it at the wastepaper basket. He'd just finished a lunchtime take-away Chinese meal and had cracked open the accompanying fortune cookie in the vain hope that he might get some kind of guidance. But it had been useless. Of course.

After his dinner with Mara the previous day, he'd wanted to rush straight around to see Terry. But it had been too late when he'd left Chiswick; by the time he got to Terry's, chances were she and Paul would both be in bed. Then, in the cold, unforgiving light of a November day, he'd begun to waver. On the one hand, Mara had been very encouraging. She hadn't said it in so many words, but she had hinted that Terry liked him. But what if she were wrong? What if he did what she suggested, told Terry how he felt, and she then laughed at him? Or even worse, felt sorry for him? Half of him wanted to get up right then, rush across the city to Stoke Newington, wait for Terry to finish her shift and come home so he could talk to her. But the other half wanted to linger at work, to put off seeing her and hang on to the hope that Mara had given him.

Then there was Lily. He'd agreed to see her at ten that night. He hadn't wanted to, but he'd had to call her to talk about Mara and she'd asked and he hadn't been ready with an excuse, so he'd said yes. But he couldn't imagine anything he wanted to do less. All he could think about was Terry and going to visit her and making things right. Over the last months, she had somehow become necessary to him. He hadn't noticed it happening. It wasn't as if he'd spent all that much time with her. But now that he couldn't even talk to her, he realized that whenever he'd been with her, he'd been happy. Not just passing the time, not just doing things to stop him thinking of his boys, but happy.

Sean looked at his watch. It was getting dark already and he'd done nothing all day. Just cowered in his office, dithering. Angry with himself, he made a snap decision. He was going around to Terry's that evening. If it went wrong, so be it, but he had to see her, to talk to her, to explain.

He reached out, picked up the phone, and dialed. Lily had said she'd be in a meeting all afternoon. With luck he'd get her voice mail.

The phone rang twice in his ear. Then her message machine picked up. Sean breathed a sigh of relief.

"Hi, Lily. Sean. Listen, something's come up. I'm sorry, I, um, won't be able to make it tonight. Er, see you. 'Bye."

LILY STOOD in Mara's front yard, looking up at the window she knew was the girls' bedroom. The lights had just gone off. The signal she'd been waiting for. Moo and Tilly were in bed. She could tell Mara what she had to without them overhearing. Lily had been waiting outside the house for ten minutes, pacing up and down, trying not to make herself obvious but too nervous to stand still in the shadows. She wasn't looking forward to the next hour or so. Destroying a friend's illusions about her loved ones ranked high on her list of least favorite things to do. But now Moo and Tilly were safely out of the way. And she had to go in.

Looking at the house through freshly opened eyes, Lily had realized that the place was almost a ruin. She'd not noticed before, the deterioration had been so gradual. But now, observing it anew, even in the dark, she could see what Sean meant. Mara had to sell. That or pour a fortune into the property. And Lily was sure that even if she and Jules could raise the amount needed, Mara would never accept it. They could perhaps have railroaded her into accepting a couple of thousand as a gift, but £30,000? Never.

No, Mara had to sell before the place was worth nothing. And if she refused to do so because she and Jake had bought it and lived there together, then she had to be told about Jake.

Lily picked up the bottle of wine she'd brought with her in the hope that a drink or two might make this a little easier, reached out, and pressed the doorbell. She listened to the sound of that happy tune ringing through the house and was very sure that Mara would find it hard to see a bright side to what she was about to learn. But much as Lily dreaded it, much as she longed for another solution, she knew that there was none. Mara's cough might be better, according to Sean, but if she insisted on staying in her house, it was only a matter of time before she'd be ill again. She had to be told that her perfect husband had actually been a womanizing jerk.

ON THE other side of the road, Clive, concealed behind an overgrown hedge, watched Lily as she dithered on the doorstep for ten minutes until she finally rang the bell. He'd decided to hang around Mara's house for a while. As far as he was aware, Sean hadn't been near her before the previous day. Maybe, just maybe, something was about to happen. He had certainly not got what he needed from watching the others. So he'd taken a chance and stayed in Chiswick, waiting.

And he wondered if he was about to be rewarded. Lily visiting her friend wasn't unusual, but her hovering on the doorstep, apparently reluctant to go in, definitely was.

Still, when Mara appeared at the door, all smiles, it looked as if nothing was wrong. Clive thought about returning to spy on Sean but decided against it. Maybe Lily had just been distracted—thinking up a new joke or choosing fabric for her disgustingly expensive house—but it hadn't seemed like that. Clive's bloodhound nose scented trouble. He'd stick around a while longer.

TERRY STIRRED two large dollops of yogurt into her spicy mushroom and lentil casserole. It had always been one of her favorite meals, a warm, comforting stew that she made for herself when she was feeling down. And it almost always did the trick. But tonight Terry had a feeling it wasn't going to work. She needed something more than a tasty dinner to cheer her up.

She needed Sean. But she wasn't going to get him. Even if he called again, she'd still have to say no. Because no matter how much rejecting him might hurt at the time, it had to be better than allowing him to find out how useless she was in bed. And see his liking for her turn into disappointment. Or worse. In the end, she'd prefer to protect her fantasy of his being the man who could make it work for her rather than suffer the grim, bitter reality of another failure.

She chopped some parsley, scattered it over the stew, and shouted, "Paul! Dinner," just as the doorbell rang. "I'll get it," Terry yelled, and went to the door. Probably someone delivering pizza to the wrong address. Although Minnie, bizarrely, wasn't barking but was running around and around in circles in apparent delight. Strange dog. She'd not been the same since Sean had stopped visiting. Well, none of them had been, had they?

Terry pulled open the door, oven gloves still in hand. Minnie ran past her and leapt into the air. And into Sean's arms.

He grinned. "You're a mad dog," he said, and she licked his face in delight. He was back.

Sean looked at Terry. "Can I come in?"

Terry didn't move. She couldn't. The moment she'd seen Sean, she'd felt the same way she had the night he'd kissed her. Excited and breathless and sort of desperate. And all of that without him even touching her.

"Please, Terry, I need to talk to you."

Terry snapped out of her coma. And stood back to let Sean in. Paul, on his way down the stairs to the kitchen for his dinner, stopped the moment he saw who was at the door. He didn't want to get in the way if there was a chance that Sean had come to ask his mam out. "Hi, Sean," he called out. "Mam, I don't need dinner, okay? I'm going to stay up here, do some work, maybe go to bed early. Leave you and Sean alone to enjoy yourselves."

Terry stared at her son. It wasn't like him to choose work over food. "Are you okay?" she asked.

"I'm fine. I ate when I got in from school. See you, Sean." In fact, he had had only a bag of chips and was ravenous, but the sacrifice would be worth it if his mam and Sean got together. As he walked back to his room, his stomach growled at him but he ignored it. He had a bit of a Mars bar left in his school bag, that would have to do.

Terry walked down the corridor to the kitchen. Sean's arrival had blown away her certainty. Part of her still yearned for safety, for the simplicity of her long-celibate life. But another part was screaming for her to take a risk.

Sean and Minnie were right on her heels. She had mere minutes, if not seconds, to make up her mind. No chance to reread her stars in the evening paper for a bit of guidance. She tried to think back but her mind seemed incapable of concentrating. Was it a good or a bad time for change? Was she due for a lucky break? Was Venus rising?

"WHAT DO you mean he wasn't the man I think he was?"

"Just that there are things you don't know about Jake."

"I was his wife. How can there be things I don't know?"

"Do you think any of us ever truly know anyone?" Lily cringed at her *Woman's Own* words. She took a deep breath, then another. Facts. That was what she needed. Facts. Not this nebulous, cod-philosophical, there-are-things-you-don't-know crap. Facts. Give Mara something to hold on to. "After he died, you remember we cleared all his stuff out for you? When you couldn't cope?"

"You were wonderful."

"You may not think that in a couple of minutes."

"Of course I will, silly."

Lily looked at her friend sitting opposite her, looking as worn down as she had the other day but smiling slightly, sure of the love of her dead husband. Shit, this wasn't difficult, it was well-nigh impossible.

"We found some papers. Letters."

"Letters?"

"Yes. From girlfriends."

"Girlfriends?"

"Yes."

"Jake didn't have girlfriends."

"I'm afraid he did. And lots of them."

"No."

"He did, sweetie. I'm sorry."

"I don't believe it."

"Mara. I know it's hard. But it's true."

"It's not. It's not. I know it's not. Why are you lying to me like this? You're supposed to be my friend."

"I am your friend. And I'm not lying."

"Lies. Lies. Lies." Mara put her hands over her ears. She would hear no more.

Lily took a deep slug of her wine. Then looked up at her disbelieving friend. "I didn't want to have to do this. I was hoping you'd take my word for it." Lily put down her glass on the rickety old kitchen table, reached into her pocket, and pulled out a sheaf of letters. "We couldn't decide whether or not to destroy them." She held out the letters to Mara, who ignored them. "Mara. You've got to stop burying your head in the sand. Here."

Mara shrank backward. "No. I won't listen. This is not true."

Lily scrabbled around for a way to persuade her friend to face the truth. "Go on. One look. If I'm lying, there's nothing to be scared of, is there?"

Mara stared at the letters lying on Lily's outstretched hand. She didn't want to take them. She shouldn't have to check up on Jake. He had been faithful to her. He had. She knew that. Lily was lying. And yet her hand moved and took the sheaf. She opened and read first one then another then another.

There was no doubt. These were love letters. And they were written to Jake. Mara tried to stop reading, tried to protect herself from all the details of where and when and how, but things kept springing out at her.

Jake spending the night with a girl when Mara thought he was away driving a client.

Jake with another one the day Mara brought Moo home from the hospital.

Jake using their house, their bed while she was out at play group with the girls.

Mara started to shake and the letters fell from her hands, onto the floor around and under her chair. She made no effort to pick them up. Instead, she slumped forward, her head cradled in her hands.

Lily let her cry for a minute. Then she reached out to put her arm around Mara's shoulder. "I'm so sorry, sweetie." She knew this was inadequate but she couldn't think of anything else to say.

"Sorry?" Mara's voice cracked.

"Yes. But we had to tell you. We had to."

"We?"

"Jules and Terry agreed. We hoped we'd never have to say anything, but now Jake's stopping you doing things and we thought—"

"You all got together and decided what to do?"

"We talked, yes."

"With my life?"

"We didn't want to hurt you. . . ."

"So you lied to me."

"It wasn't like that."

"It looks like it from here. My best friends hide the fact that my husband was fucking around on me for years and that's not lying?"

"It wasn't lying. Just not telling."

"And I'm supposed to see the difference? You three have spent the last four years watching me worship a man who you all knew was no good. Did it make you want to smile when you heard me go on about how faithful he'd been? What a great husband I'd had? How'd you manage to hide the laughs when I went on and on and on about how I wished you all could find someone like him?"

Lily stared at Mara in shock. She'd never seen or heard her calm, gentle friend so angry. "I never laughed. Nor did the others. It was terrible."

"But you never told me. Never. It was terrible, but you still kept your secretive little mouths shut." Mara heard herself shouting and forced herself to lower her voice. She mustn't wake up Moo and Tilly, they mustn't know about this. "I suppose you enjoyed jeering at the silly girl who couldn't even see what a pig her husband had been?"

"No. Of course not." Lily was horrified. This wasn't Mara.

"Or was it the pity you liked? I can hear you now. 'Poor stupid little Mara. Poor, deluded girl, swallowed Jake's line and wouldn't let go.' Aaaah." Mara stood up and walked over to the kitchen window to look out. But her eyes didn't see the darkened garden, its neat empty beds waiting for the spring. She was blind to everything but the fact that her great love had been a mirage, something she'd created, all in her head, to make herself feel special.

"It wasn't like that. I promise," Lily said. "When we found out we just thought it was better not to tell you, you were so destroyed by Jake dying. After that, well, there never seemed to be a right time."

"I think I'd prefer to be laughed at than pitied." Mara took no notice of Lily. All she could hear was the voice in her head that kept repeating, "Jake cheated. Jake cheated. Jake cheated."

Lily got up, went to the window, put her arm around her friend's shoulders, and gently turned her around so they were face-to-face. "Mara. Listen. It wasn't like that. We didn't want to hurt you. So we said nothing. And hoped you'd grow out of it."

"Grow out of it? Like a child with a bad habit?" Mara pulled herself away from Lily. "Get out."

"What?"

"Get out of my house. Now."

"But . . . can't we talk about this?"

"You've just destroyed everything. J . . . Jake. My marriage. My memories. And you want us to sit round and *discuss* it? Well, fuck you. Get out." Part of Mara knew she was being unreasonable, shooting the messenger when the person she should be blaming was long dead, but she couldn't stop herself. She had to lash out, and Lily was there.

This was the first time Lily had ever heard Mara swear. She wasn't a prude, didn't object to her friends' sometimes terrible language, but never did it herself. Not even a mild "bloody" or a gentle "damn." And now she'd said "fuck" twice in one night. Lily looked at her friend, aware of how miserable she was, and tried desperately to think of something, anything, to say to make it better. But nothing came to mind.

"Get out!" Mara shouted, the girls forgotten for a moment. "GET OUT!"

And Lily got out.

THE LENTIL and mushroom stew sat, uneaten, on the top of the stove, a thin wisp of steam rising from it. Terry stood, her back to the sink, her face tense, her body stiff. Sean, Minnie still in his arms, leaned against the propped-up dresser, looking easy and relaxed. From a distance, that is. Close up, he was as on edge as Terry. His eyes never left her for a moment, his jawline worked as he clenched and unclenched his teeth, and he held on to Minnie for dear life.

First there was silence. Now that the moment was here, neither of them was ready to start. Sean was hoping for some kind of signal from Terry, some hint as to how she felt and what he should do to make her want to see him again. And Terry was scared. In the time it had taken to turn off the stove, put down her oven gloves, and turn to face Sean, she had made her decision. She was going to tell him the truth. Explain to him about her frigidity and how she had been celibate for years. Be honest with a man about her problems for the first time in her life. It might scare him away, but if it did, he was not the person she thought he was.

Terry took a deep breath and opened her mouth to speak. At the same time as Sean.

"There's something I need to explain—"

"Terry, I need to talk to you—"

"You first."

"No, you."

"I . . . I . . ."

Terry tried to think how best to put it. Every phrase she could think of— "I am frigid"; "I have never had an orgasm"—either sounded too clinical or too alienating. So she drew a deep breath, ignored the sick feeling in her stomach, and rushed in.

"You see, I haven't ever enjoyed it. Sex, I mean. So I gave up years ago. I was just tired of it all. Pretending I was having fun when I wasn't. Or of not pretending and being attacked for it. Or it not being noticed."

"Terry—"

She held up her hand to stop Sean's interruption. She needed to get through this in one piece. "So when you kissed me, that's why I pushed you away. I hadn't touched a man in ages, had I? And I wasn't expecting . . . wasn't expecting . . ."

Sean put Minnie on the floor, walked over to Terry, and stroked her cheek. "Wasn't expecting what?" he asked.

Terry flinched away from Sean's hand. If the attraction was strong when he was on the other side of the room, it was overpowering when he touched her.

Hurt, he pulled back and started to walk away.

"No, don't. I'm sorry. I just . . . I can't concentrate when you touch me."

Sean turned back, his face split by an enormous grin. "And why do you have to concentrate?"

"I need to tell you. To explain."

"No, you don't. You don't need to say a thing. Not one word." Sean leaned over and kissed Terry. Kissed her eyes, her ears, her nose, then at last her mouth.

And she forgot everything. Forgot the stew sitting on the stove. Forgot the ironing she had intended to do after dinner, the evening walk that Minnie hadn't yet had. Forgot the years and years of pleasureless sex. And for the first time in his life forgot her son waiting upstairs in his bedroom.

Sean took her by the hand, led her out of the kitchen and along the corridor to her room.

On the stairs up above, Paul watched the door close behind them, then jumped up and punched the air in delight. His mam was with Sean. And he could have his dinner.

CLIVE LOOKED at his watch in the light of a nearby street lamp. Three quarters of an hour and nothing. He must have been wrong. Lily and Mara were just visiting, talking girlie talk about whatever it was women discussed when they got together. Tampons and chicken casseroles, for all he knew.

No question, one-man surveillance was a boring, lonely job. He couldn't even go and get himself a coffee, for fear that he'd miss something important. Although that was beginning to look less and less likely. Maybe his nose had misled him for the first time. Mara seemed to lead a very quiet life. Apart from Sean the night before and the kids coming back from school, Lily had been her only visitor in twenty-four hours. Not exactly Euston Station.

And then the front door opened. Lily flew out and Mara slammed the door shut behind her. Lily stopped on the street, right opposite Clive's blind, and burst into tears.

Clive just stopped himself clapping his hands together in delight. Now, this was more like it. It appeared Mara and Lily had fallen out in a big way. Clive had no idea over what, nor did he much care so long as he could exploit the situation to his own benefit.

He waited while Lily walked along the shadowy street to her car, got in, and drove away, then crossed the road to Mara's house and knocked on the door.

Inside, he could hear footsteps marching to the door.

"What are you doing back? I told you to get out," Mara said as she flung the door open. Then she saw Clive. "Oh. I thought you were . . . um . . . right."

"Hi, Mara. Sorry to bother you. But you wouldn't be a darling and let me use your phone? My car's just broken down and my mobile's on the blink and I'm supposed to meet a friend in town. Then I remembered you were here and I thought, Mara won't turn away an old pal in trouble." Clive shrugged his shoulders and smiled sheepishly, turning on the charm. Years of experience had taught him that even the most suspicious source could be tricked into talking if he could just wheedle his way into their house.

"Well, I suppose. . . ."

"Thanks, thanks. You're a great lady." Clive walked past Mara and into the living room. "Lovely house you've got here."

"It needs some work."

"Adds character. How about some tea?"

"I don't know. It's not a great time."

"Sorry about that. Maybe I can help? I'm a very good listener."

"What about your friend?"

"You put on the kettle and I'll give him a quick call."

And before Mara knew it, the two of them were sitting in the kitchen with cups of tea in front of them. She knew that she didn't want to be with Clive, didn't want to be with anyone, but she couldn't seem to bring herself to say anything. It was as if her brain were stuck in neutral, unable to summon up the energy to move one way or the other, to do anything. It was shock, of course, Mara knew that, but knowing it didn't help her avoid its effects.

"So what's wrong?"

"Nothing." She wasn't going to discuss Jake and the letters with Clive.

"Must be something. Come on, we're old friends."

She wouldn't have put it like that. But she didn't have the mental strength to argue.

"Come on, love. You can tell me."

Mara cast about for something she could talk to him about. And told him about the house.

"Can't that chap of Lily's help? That builder. What's his name?"

"Sean."

"Yeah, that's it. Sean. Well, can't he mend things for you?"

"No."

"No? He looks a decent sort of bloke to me. Isn't he?"

"Oh, yes. Of course."

"So there you are. Get him to do it. He's helping Terry and Jules, isn't he? Why shouldn't he help you?" Clive took a punt, hoping he was heading in the right area. "Helping" seemed a general enough word. And Mara seemed dazed by something. If she'd been herself, chances were she'd have shown him the door.

"You know about that?"

Bingo. "Of course."

"Lily told you?"

"Yeah. We talked the other day. I was very surprised. Shocked, even."

"So was I. When I first heard about it."

"I mean, this thing they're doing with him. What's the word Lily uses?"

" 'Sharing.' "

"Yeah, that's it, sharing. I just didn't see how they could."

"I know."

"Lily didn't say, but I bet it was her idea."

"She thought it would solve all our problems."

"Until it fell apart." That seemed a reasonable guess; certainly, the girls weren't all sweetness and light with each other at the moment.

"Yes."

"Though Lily said Terry was happy enough."

"Maybe. She only wanted a friend for Paul, after all. Nothing messy like . . . you know. No sperm or sex or anything."

Sperm? Sex? Clive made an educated guess. "Unlike Jules."

"Poor Jules."

"It must have been awful." "Awful" sounded a safe bet. After all, she'd been in the hospital.

"She wanted that baby so much. The miscarriage almost destroyed her."

"So Lily said."

"And she's alienated Sean, so she can't use him as a donor again."

A donor. This was getting better and better. Lily had actually lent, no, shared her lover with her friends. He set about asking the right questions to get Mara to let slip all the juicy details. God, what a story. Front page, for sure. And Lily would hate it. Clive struggled hard to repress a grin. He was a happy man.

LILY WAS tempted to ignore the message on her answering machine. It was nine-thirty already and all she wanted to do was take a long, hot shower before Sean arrived at ten, let the six wall-mounted jets of water in her marble walk-in stall wash away the stress of the day. The horror of telling Mara about Jake. But she walked over to the hall table and pressed the red button on the machine. What if it was one of the kids needing help?

Beep. "Hi, Lily. Sean. Listen, something's come up. I'm sorry, I, um, won't be able to make it tonight. Er, see you. 'Bye."

"Fuck. Fuck, fuck, fuck, fuck." Lily slammed her handbag down on the table. "Fuck."

She went downstairs, into the kitchen, and poured herself a very, very stiff gin and tonic. This was not supposed to happen anymore. Having Sean back to herself was supposed to have made him more interested. Instead, it seemed to have made him less so. That message, along with its pauses and ums and ers, was a lie. Nothing had "come up." Sean just hadn't fancied it. Hadn't fancied her. Fuck.

She reached for the phone. This was a case for Terry. If she couldn't have Sean, she could at least talk to her best friend.

"Hi."

"Paul, it's Lily. Is your mum there?"

"Yeah. But you can't talk to her."

"Is she okay?"

"Yeah. But she's busy."

"Paul. This isn't funny. What's she doing? Tell her it's me."

"I can't."

"That's crap. Why can't you?"

"Cos she's in bed."

"What? Is she sick? I'll be right over."

"No, no. She's okay. More than okay. She's fantastic. She's with someone." Paul stressed the last two words to give them extra significance.

"With someone?"

"Isn't it great? It's what I've been hoping. I knew when he didn't come round for a bit that something had happened but she wouldn't talk about it and nor would he but then he turned up this evening and they talked for a bit and then they went off to bed together. Yes."

"He? Do you mean Sean?"

"Course. Isn't it great? Aunt Lily? Aunt Lily?"

But Aunt Lily had already hung up. And hurled her drink at the expensive stainless-steel American fridge.

What the hell was Terry up to? She'd trusted that girl. Relied upon her. And now look. She was fucking Sean.

It had been one thing when Lily had chosen to give her lover to her friends, but now they seemed to be taking the law into their own hands and doing whatever they wanted, with no reference to her. And she couldn't take it. This had all been her idea—Sean was her lover, he was hers to control, hers to organize, hers to say yes or no to.

Lily got another glass out of the cupboard and poured herself an even stiffer drink. He was supposed to be here tonight. She needed him after what had happened this evening. But instead he was with that . . . that bitch. While she was sitting here, alone, longing for a man. For Sean.

Fuck her. Had all that garbage about not wanting sex been just that? Garbage? Lily had always had trouble believing it, but Terry had been so sure, she'd taken it at face value. But supposing it had all been an act? Supposing she'd just been biding her time, waiting for the right guy to come along?

Lily remembered all the days Sean and Terry had spent together. Okay, most of them had included Paul, but there had been some—the trip to look at buildings, the visit with Sean's friends in South London—that even at the time had sounded more like dates. Had Lily been played for a fool by her supposed best friend? All the time she'd been convinced that Terry wasn't a threat, had she been homing in on Sean? Persuading him that the woman he wanted wasn't Lily, but Terry?

And today? What a brilliant masterstroke that had been. To send Lily haring off to Chiswick, then step in and grab what she wanted. Sean.

Fuck. Her friend. Her best friend. In bed with her lover. Lily grabbed the bottle of gin and poured herself another, this time not bothering with the tonic. She took a big gulp and fought back tears. She was not going to cry about this. She wasn't going to give anyone that satisfaction. But it was hard. She hadn't just lost Sean. She'd lost Terry too. For the last twenty years, Terry had been the first person she'd called whenever anything happened, good or bad. The person she'd have entrusted with her life. With her twins' lives. And she had turned out to be false.

Lily picked up the bottle and her glass, took them to her den, and settled in for the duration. She'd worry about what to do about Sean and Terry the following day. Tonight, she was going to get rip-roaring drunk. And try not to think about what was happening right now in her ex-best-friend's bed.

. . .

"THAT WAS . . . I can't think of a word for what that was." Terry lay on her side, facing Sean. She was having a hard time stopping herself smiling. So that was what it was all about. No wonder people were so mad for it.

"Nice?"

"Nice! A cup of tea is nice. This wasn't tea. This was . . . I don't know. Like the best champagne. Fantastic. Unbelievable. Amazing." Terry still couldn't believe it. After all this time, she'd finally managed it. No, they'd managed it. He'd managed it.

Because it was all down to Sean. For the first time in her life, she hadn't felt any pressure. At no point did she sense him glancing at his mental watch, wanting her to hurry up, to move on, to finish. Instead, it had been wonderful. Slow, gentle, easy. She'd been able to forget her past problems and enjoy what was happening. To stop worrying about where she was supposed to be going and whether this would be the time she would get there, and simply live.

"I gather you liked it?"

"Liked it?" Terry spluttered, almost angry with him for putting himself down this way. Didn't he know how incredible he was? But then she looked harder at him, looked beyond his slow smile to the telltale moisture in his eyes. And realized that this had meant as much to him as it had to her. So much that he didn't want to—maybe even couldn't—talk about it. She leaned over to kiss him. "You could say that."

sixty-one

Sean opened his eyes. It was still dark. Slowly, quietly, he edged out of bed and, shivering in the early morning chill, pulled on his clothes as quickly as possible. Terry was still fast asleep. It was no wonder. They hadn't dropped off until it was gone three. He would have given a great deal to stay with her, to wake up slowly, bring her breakfast in bed, and then start in again, but they had decided that, for Paul's sake, he should leave before the boy was up. Chances were Paul would have already realized that Sean had stayed over, but Terry didn't want his nose rubbed in it until she'd had a chance to talk to him and make sure he was all right about it.

The night had been amazing. If anyone had asked him in advance how he would feel if a woman told him what Terry had, he would have said pressured. Pressured to perform, to make things happen at last. But he hadn't felt that way at all. Instead, there'd been a strange sense of release. In the past with women, he'd always had a lingering fear of failure. The responsibility for their pleasure could seem onerous. And the idea of falling short where others had made the grade was hard to take. But with Terry, none of that had been there. He'd been so focused on her that he'd had little chance to think of himself.

Maybe because he was truly in love, for the first time in his life. He'd known from the moment she opened the door of the flat the previous evening and now was even more sure, if that were possible. He loved her strength, her nerve, loved the way she'd told him the truth about herself even though she must have known that many men would have laughed at her for it. More than that, he loved her pretty, roguish face, her wild hair, her idiosyncratic style. Loved the way she came up only to his shoulder, loved her gorgeous, curvy body, her amazing legs, her soft Liverpool voice. Loved her empathy with others, her ability to listen, the way she never took herself too seriously. He loved her.

Sean heard a door opening and Paul's footsteps coming down the stairs and heading for the bathroom. He'd better get going before he was seen. No time to write a note. Terry was huddled under the duvet. He leaned over to kiss the top of her head, then waited until he'd heard the bathroom door close behind the boy, pulled on his leather jacket, and tiptoed out of the flat. He'd call later in the day. And arrange to see Terry in the evening. To talk about their future.

THUMP. THUMP.

"Mam! It's seven-thirty. Time to get up." Paul knocked on his mother's door, then clumped off down the corridor to scavenge some breakfast. He couldn't stop grinning. Last night must have gone well. Mam never overslept on a school day.

Terry stirred at the sound of her son's voice and woke. And smiled. She couldn't remember the last time she had woken up feeling so good. So hopeful. She turned to Sean. And opened her eyes to find him gone. Of course, it was late. She hadn't heard him get up, and though they'd agreed he'd leave before Paul was awake, she couldn't help being disappointed that he wasn't there. She wanted to see him, to talk over last night, to make sure she hadn't been dreaming.

"Mam! Come on."

She got up, felt the muscles in her inner thighs complaining at the unaccustomed exercise, and had her reassurance. It had happened. Wait until she told Lily. She'd be amazed.

Terry sat back down on the bed. God. Lily. Her best friend, the person who'd saved her life when Finn walked out. Who had been nothing but supportive of her from the moment they'd met. And look how she'd paid her back. By seducing her lover after they'd all agreed that the share was off.

So what should she do? She couldn't say nothing, could she? It was tempting—it would be much, much easier to keep quiet about it. But she'd always told Lily everything. Besides, if she and Sean were going to be together, how long could she hide that from her best friend? Maybe for a few days, a week even? And then what? In the end, Lily would have to know, and telling her would get harder and harder the longer she put it off.

No, she had to put her in the picture. And soon, before she chickened out. But maybe there was no need to be worried? After all, Lily didn't love Sean. And she was always saying that one man was much like another, wasn't she? Even if she'd seemed keener on Sean than on some of the others, maybe she wouldn't be too upset at losing him when she found out just how much he meant to her friend?

Well, Terry could only hope. Before she could change her mind, she grabbed the phone and dialed Lily's number.

"Yes."

"Lils, it's me."

"Oh."

"This a bad time?"

"You could say that."

"Sorry. I know it's early. I can call back later? I just need to talk to you for a couple of minutes."

"Do you? How interesting."

"Lils, what is it?"

"Well, I fucking don't need to talk to you."

"Wh . . . wh . . . what?"

"Can't find your own man?"

"I . . . I . . ."

"Have to steal mine, then. Now, now, don't be coy. You see, I know who was sleeping in your bed last night."

"Oh."

"Yes. 'Oh.' "

"Who told you?" Could it have been Sean? He wouldn't have, would he?

"Your beloved son."

"Paul? But how?"

"I called you last night. I was depressed. I'd been stood up. Foolish little me, I thought you might cheer me up. Not that you were the one I'd been stood up for."

"Lils, I don't know what to say. I'm sorry."

"Thieving bitch."

"I didn't mean . . . It just happened."

"Yeah. I bet. I bet it did."

"It did."

"You fucking cow. I suppose you had this all planned from the start."

"I didn't."

"We agreed. No more sharing."

"I know. Only I couldn't help it, could I? I love him."

"Love?" She made the word sound like the strongest expletive going. "What's love got to do with it?"

"Please, Lils. You don't understand."

"Fuck your love."

"But It happened. It. You know. After all these years. I came."

"Oh, goodie."

"Please be happy for me."

"Piss off."

"Don't be like this. Please."

"And I suppose you think he loves you?"

"I don't know. I hope so."

"Well, he doesn't. He loves me. You better make the most of last night. Cos it's all you're getting."

"Lily . . ."

"And don't fucking call me again."

With that, Lily slammed the phone down.

Shocked, Terry looked at the receiver. And then pressed the redial button. Lily couldn't mean it, could she? She needed a punching bag, someone to scream and shout at, an outlet for her rage. But she'd calm down. They just had to talk it out and she'd get over it. Wouldn't she?

The answering machine picked up. "Hi, this is Lily—"

Terry hung up. There was no point. Lily knew who was calling and was refusing to pick up the phone. She'd try again later.

sixty-two

Sean forced himself to ease up on the accelerator. The last thing he needed was a speeding ticket.

Not today. Not now.

In only a few minutes, he was going to see his boys. It had been an incredible twenty-four hours. First Terry, now Mark and Ben.

At about ten, his mobile phone had rung. The number that came up on the LCD display was unfamiliar. If he'd been in the middle of something, he might have ignored it, but he'd just finished overseeing the installation of an outsize bath in the model flat and was on his way to get something to eat in the local fry-it-all café. He was ravenous. Dinner had gotten lost in the excitement of last night, and he'd been too rushed to get breakfast any earlier.

So he answered the call.

"Hello, Sean. Long time no speak."

"Isobel!"

"Yes, Isobel."

"Where are you? Are Mark and Ben okay? What's happened?"

"God, I forgot how you always got so panicky about them. Don't worry. They're fine."

"Promise?"

"Promise. They're big, healthy, bright, noisy kids. But they're growing up."

"Yes. Yes, of course. Of course they are." Sean couldn't stop babbling. It was Isobel. And the boys were fine.

"And missing their father."

"Whose fault is that?" Sean knew it wasn't sensible to jibe at Isobel—here she was, making contact after two years, he shouldn't alienate her—but he couldn't stop himself. This woman had put him through hell.

"Mine."

"Is that really you?" She must have changed. It wasn't like the old Isobel to admit to any kind of fault.

"It's me. And I'm sorry. I made a mistake when I took them."

"Sorry."

"Yes."

It seemed a very small word to make amends for his loss of Mark and Ben. But he had lived with Isobel and he knew how much it must have cost her. Under normal circumstances, apologies were not part of her armory. And after all, they could do the recriminations later. Now there were more important things. "Where are you?"

"Cancale."

"Where?"

"Cancale. In Brittany."

France. France. Why hadn't he thought of that? She was Canadian, she'd studied French at school. And all his many detectives had said that her plumber boyfriend could get a job anywhere in the world. Now that he knew, it made complete sense. "When can I see the boys?"

"Whenever you can get here."

"I'm on my way."

"No rush."

"No rush? Are you mad? I haven't seen my kids in two years and you say there's no rush. Give me the address." Sean hunted in his pockets for a scrap of paper, came up with an old credit card receipt, and scribbled down the directions. "I'll be there as soon as I can."

"Good. And, Sean, I want you to take them."

With that she had hung up.

Now it was close to five. The moment he'd stopped talking to Isobel, he'd called his foreman to say he didn't know when he'd be back, run to his car, raced to the Channel Tunnel, got a train to Calais, and then driven along the northern coast to Brittany. To Cancale. As he came into the old fishing village, down a narrow, high-hedged road, past stall after stall selling oysters and mussels, he could smell the salt tang of the sea, hear the sound of gulls crying in the air, see the oyster beds in shadowy rows far out in the bay. And this was where Mark and Ben had been living. Making friends, going to school, growing up. Speaking a foreign language. Without him.

He found the address Isobel had given him and parked about twenty yards farther on. The narrow street, one block back from the café-lined seafront, looked as if it rarely saw the sun. The homes were small, gray-stone oystermen's cottages, indistinguishable one from each other apart from the color of the front doors and the occasional roadway shrine. Sean didn't know what he had expected; certainly not this quiet, sedate place that looked as if nothing unusual had or ever would happen.

Now that he was here, he found he was reluctant to go in. What if the boys didn't recognize him? What if they resented his absence from their lives? What if they didn't want to go home with him? What if they only spoke French?

A pack of about six kids came around the corner. Some dressed in blue French national team shirts, some in jeans and different colored sweat-shirts, they moved down the middle of the street, laughing and joking, some walking backward, others kicking a soccer ball against the walls. As they advanced, kids peeled off to go into various houses. Until there were only two. Mark and Ben.

Sean would have recognized them anywhere. Recognized the individual ways they walked, how they held their arms, the expressions on their faces. Yes, they'd changed, they were older, taller, and he'd heard them calling out good-byes in French to their friends, but they were still his boys. Mark's smile was still Mark's smile, Ben's frown of concentration still wrinkled his brow.

He couldn't stop shaking. With excitement, with nerves, and with the sudden release of the stress that had been with him, so familiar as to be unnoticed most of the time, for the last two years. Ever since they'd disappeared. He pulled his cigarettes out of his pocket, lit one, and took a deep drag. They were alive and well and safe.

He let Mark and Ben walk past him on the opposite side of the street and go into their house. After all this time, he didn't want their first meeting to be in public. He looked at his mobile, thought about calling Terry, and decided against it. Part of him was longing to tell her where he was and why. To talk to her about the boys, about last night, about everything. About their future. But he also wanted to see Isobel and find out whether she'd meant what she'd said just before she'd hung up. And the extent of what he would be asking Terry to take on.

He switched off his phone, got out of the car, and crossed the road. He walked up to the boys' red front door, reached out to press the doorbell, and heard it echo through the house. And Mark's—Mark's?—voice shouting, "Someone's at the door, Mum." And the realization finally hit him. He was going to see his boys.

sixty-three

The giant bus swung around the tight corner, into the constricted back street, and stopped in front of the tiny hole-in-the-wall pub. Normally, Terry enjoyed this bit of the journey north; Islington was always humming nowadays and she was proud of the fact that she was able to maneuver the bus through the narrow one-way system. But today she couldn't wait to get home. Away from work, away from the passengers, away from her conductor, Fred. And away from the world. She was desperate to see if Sean had called. Or Lily.

She hadn't been able to think of anything else since she'd left for work. At first, it had been Lily. Terry had seen her lose her temper in the past, but never had her friend seemed so consumed with rage. So determined to lash out and hurt. Nor had her anger ever been directed at Terry before. And it had been scary. All morning, as she moved around the city, sitting in her little cab, locked in the world inside her head, Terry had tried to reassure herself, insisting that all Lily needed was a bit of time to calm down and all would be well.

But all wasn't well. Terry had tried to call her on her first turnaround at ten, and then at twenty past eleven, and finally at ten to one. When the recorded phone company message had changed from "The person you are calling is busy. Please try later" to "The number you have called is no longer in service."

Lily had changed her number. It wasn't unknown for her to do that—since the success of her show, she'd done it a few times, to escape some bothersome journalist or a particularly persistent fan who had gotten her personal details from somewhere—but she'd always let her family and close friends know in advance. Usually days before the switch happened. But Terry had heard nothing. And she would have done. No, it felt like Lily had done this on the spur of the moment. To avoid Terry. And to let her know that they were no longer friends.

All she could hope for was that there would be a message waiting for her with the new number when she got home, but she was very afraid that there wouldn't be. She went over and over what had been said on the telephone, and no matter how she tried, couldn't get away from it. Lily's attitude had not been that of someone who is going to forgive and forget in a hurry.

What had she said? "I suppose you think he loves you? Well, he doesn't. He loves me. You better make the most of last night. Cos it's all you're getting. And don't fucking call me again." Those were the words of a deeply angry, jealous woman who wasn't about to change her mind. She wanted Sean. And she believed she had him.

Terry's general uneasiness grew into real worry. Outwardly, she carried on as normal, maneuvering the red bus around the streets of London, returning the waves of people she recognized, stopping and starting on cue, but inside she was on autopilot, her thoughts dominated by Sean, her night with him, and what it might have meant. And whether Lily was right. That he loved her, not Terry.

At no time during the whole night had he said anything about the future. There had been no mention of tomorrow or the day after, no reference to what they were going to do, to how they would be together. Had there? Terry had just assumed, but maybe Lily was right. Maybe it had been a one-night stand?

Terry thought back, tried to remember every word they had said to each other, and realized that Sean hadn't said anything about his feelings. He certainly hadn't declared undying love. In fact, he hadn't even mentioned fancying her, had he? She'd presumed, because of the kiss and his reaction to her rejection of him. But he'd been drunk. Maybe it had been a hasty impulse, regretted almost as soon as it had occurred? Maybe he'd been abrupt when he left that night out of embarrassment, not frustrated desire? Maybe his phone calls had just been to apologize?

When he'd arrived at her door yesterday evening, she'd been so pleased to see him and so caught up in her own internal struggle that she had launched into her speech about her problem. He hadn't said anything about wanting her, had he? Not a single word. She hadn't given him a chance. Suppose he hadn't been interested? Suppose he'd taken her to bed out of pity? Oh, no. No. No.

From worry, Terry now sank into panic. She'd presumed that he'd enjoyed the night as much as she had but there was no proof. Maybe it had been just another fuck. Nothing special. Just being kind to his lover's needy friend. God, how humiliating. There she'd been burbling on about how it had been special and wonderful, and he'd been more or less unmoved.

She'd been so sunk in her own fantasy that she'd even imagined seeing tears in Sean's eyes. Of course there was no way the night could mean as much to him as it had to her. How could it? Chances were, he'd been having and enjoying sex since his teens. Whereas she'd more or less begged him to give her her first-ever orgasm at the age of thirty-seven, hadn't she? Christ, how embarrassing. He'd been perfectly polite, but he must have been laughing at her all the time.

How could she have imagined that he preferred her to Lily? Preferred her old-fashioned, generous curves to Lily's gym-toned leanness? Her wild, rainbow style to her friend's designer chic? God. She'd lain there in bed with him, so crazy happy that she'd not even bothered to try and hide her flabby thighs. Or her droopy tits. And she thought he still wanted her after that?

Terry shuddered in horror at the extent of her naiveté. And stopped the bus. Halfway around Newington Green, in the middle of the traffic, blocking two lanes, she halted. Ignoring the rules, forgetting the trusting passengers, she bent over the steering wheel and howled. If it hadn't been for the tight fit, she'd have tried to curl up into a tiny ball on the floor of her cab. She'd made a complete fool of herself. Unbidden and unstoppable, images of Sean and Lily together crammed into her mind. In bed, in the bath, out to dinner, dancing, sleeping, driving, fucking . . . and in all of them, they were laughing. At Terry. She howled again. And again.

Bang. Bang. Bang. Bang.

The noise made Terry look up. Fred was outside, banging on the side of the bus. "Terry? Ter, love, what's up? What's the matter?"

Slowly, slowly, with a massive effort, she pulled herself out of the vortex. "Sorry, Fred. Just a . . . a sudden cramp. You know," she managed to stammer out. She hated to use the fact that she was a woman, but she didn't want to admit to Fred what was wrong. "I'm fine. Really." The conductor looked very unsure. "Go on, get back on the bus. We're holding up half of North London here."

Fred stared into Terry's white, set face. She didn't look well. Or happy. And that howling had sounded as if she were in real pain. However, if she were determined to carry on, there wasn't much he could do to stop her. With a last, worried look backward, he walked along the side of the bus to the platform at the end.

Waving an apology at the waiting traffic, Terry drove off. She had to hold herself together until she got home. She couldn't allow herself to think about Sean or Lily. Or last night. She had to concentrate on moving the wheel, on changing gears, on stopping at the proper stops. One minute at a time.

sixty-four

The door opened.

Her hair was a little lighter, her makeup a little heavier, the lines around her eyes a little more deeply etched, but in essence Isobel looked much the same.

"Sean. Thank you for coming so quickly." Her voice was different. He hadn't noticed on the phone so much, but it was softer, more resigned. Whatever had prompted her to call him, Sean bet it wasn't because she was happy.

"Belle."

"Who is it, Mum?" And tearing along the corridor came a small, nine-year-old, toffee-haired boy with an infectious grin. Mark.

"Have a look." And Isobel moved back, allowing Mark to see his father.

"Hello, Mark." Sean felt oddly shy.

The boy was silent.

"Don't you recognize me? . . . It's Dad." Sean longed to grab his son, to hold him, to hug him as hard as he could, but he held back. It had been two years. Mark needed time.

"Dad?"

"Yes."

"Really Dad?"

"Yes. Really Dad."

And Mark launched himself into Sean's arms. "I knew. I knew. I knew you weren't dead. Ben said you were, but I knew."

Sean swung Mark around and around. "You knew right. Course I'm not dead." He could hardly stop himself jumping for joy. Mark was here, in his arms, and happy to see him.

After a time, he put him down, though still holding fast to his hand. "Where's Ben?"

And Mark pointed along the corridor. At the far end, standing in the doorway to what looked to be the kitchen, was a small figure clutching a *Star Wars* model, staring at the tall man in the hallway.

"Ben?" Sean started to walk toward his younger son. "It's me. Dad." He crouched down in front of the boy, who literally looked as if he was seeing a ghost. Because, in his mind, he was. "Don't be scared. It is me. I promise." And he reached out to touch Ben, hoping to reassure him that he was here, alive, real flesh and blood. But Ben shrank away from his hand. Sean let it drop. And looked around for inspiration. How could he persuade a child he wasn't dead?

Mark pushed forward to talk to his brother. "Stupid. It's Dad. Look." And he held Sean's hand up, to show Ben that he was solid, no ghost. "See?"

"You sure?"

"Yup."

"Okay." And Ben tentatively reached out to touch Sean. "D . . . Dad?" Sean grabbed him, held him tight. "Ben. Ben. Ben."

"Dad. You're hurting me," Ben said after a few moments.

Sean laughed and relaxed his hold. Everything was going to be all right. They had things to talk about, and it would take time before they were back where they had been two years before, but crouching there in the narrow corridor, Ben held lightly in his arms, Mark by his side, his small hand on his father's shoulder, Sean felt better than he had since he had first heard of their disappearance. He felt normal.

sixty-five

"Why didn't you tell me?"

"I didn't know, dear."

"Not about that, maybe. But you didn't like him."

"Yes I did. He was charming."

"Charming. But a pig."

"No, not that, dear. Just a man. Most of them do it if they get a chance, you know."

"Amy!"

"No point gilding the lily. They're like that."

"Not Archie?"

"Oh, yes, dear, he was. Not at the beginning, I don't think. Not while we thought . . . Not while we were trying to have children. But then after, when we had to give up. I suppose it was consolation for him."

"But not for you. Poor Amy."

"He'd never admit it. Even after I found out. That upset me most."

"Were there many of them?"

"Five or six that I knew of. He was a handsome man, was my Archie."

"It must have been awful."

"I never got used to it. But I tried to understand. I told myself it didn't mean he didn't love me."

"But it does, doesn't it?"

"You mustn't think that. Jake loved you and the girls."

"Not enough to be faithful."

"It's us that want weddings and devotion, dear. They're not that way. Not really."

"Was Archie still . . . at the end?"

"No. Oh, no. That was all long forgotten. He had his pigeons then, you see."

Mara leaned back in her friend's old, broken-spring armchair and took a sip of her wine. It was a stormy night, wind-driven rain buffeting the windows. An hour or so ago, she had set out the bowls, taken the girls for a sleepover at a schoolmate's house, and instinctively headed for Amy. After a night and a day of massive emotional upheaval, her friend's cool acknowledgment of the facts of life had been what she'd needed to calm her down. And allow her to see through the distortion of her feelings to the reality of her and Jake's flawed relationship.

The last twenty-four hours had been like repeating the process of grieving all over again. Mara had gone through shock, anger, denial, more anger, and finally acceptance. Shock that this could be happening, anger at Lily for telling her, denial that what she had learned was the truth, rage at Jake for so betraying her and the girls, and now, at last, some acceptance.

Jake hadn't been a saint. Quite the opposite. He had been a more than usually fallible man who happened to die before Mara could find out—as she inevitably would have—that he was sleeping around on her. And so, faced with a life without him, Mara had put him on a pedestal. Worshiped him and the life they had led together. And refused even to contemplate moving on.

"Amy?"

"Yes, dear?"

"Would you hate me if I told you that I'm sort of relieved?"

"I could never hate you, dear."

"But don't you think it's odd? Surely I should be sad?"

"No, dear. Why?"

"Because I've just found out my perfect husband wasn't perfect."

"I never held much with perfection myself. It's hard to live up to."

"Exactly. Yes, that's it. That's why I'm feeling the way I am. I don't have to be guilty for being me anymore. My feet of clay are fine now Jake's turned out to be mud."

"That's nice."

"In fact, I feel better than I have in years and years and years. I can sell the house."

"Yes."

"I can live a normal life."

"Yes, dear."

"I can do anything. Anything."

"Maybe you can call your friend? And tell her she did the right thing?"

"Lily." Mara stared at Amy, horrified. With the mention of Lily's name came memories of last night. Of Clive. Of what Mara had said. "Oh, my God. Lily."

"What is it?"

"After she left, I . . . I . . . Amy, can I use your phone?"

"Of course, dear."

But Lily's number had been changed. It wasn't all that unusual, but Mara cursed the fact that it had happened today, of all days. She had to get around there, right now. To warn Lily about what she had told Clive. The story hadn't appeared in the paper yet—he would have needed a day or so to do some research and put it all together—but it was only a matter of time.

"GIVE ME another, please, Charlie."

"Are you sure? It'll be your fifth."

"I'm sure. Very, very sure."

"Okay. You're the boss." And Charlie, whose real name was Giuseppe but who answered to anything when working, poured Jules another glass of wine. She was sitting at a large bar in a trendy new restaurant, all leather seats and linen walls. Behind her, the party she had organized was beginning to wind down. Not that she cared. Technically, she was on duty, overseeing a wealthy industrialist's fiftieth birthday bash, but in reality she hadn't taken any interest in what was happening since the arrival of the first canapés. For the past two hours, she'd been at the bar, steadily drinking, leaving the party to run itself.

She had thought that she would feel better back at work. But she didn't. If anything, she felt worse. Spending her days and nights with happy, celebrating people only made her more miserable. All those jolly, smiling

faces made her want to scream. Or get drunk. And as screaming wasn't recommended at posh parties, she took the other option. This was the third
time this week. And she still had the weekend's slate of functions to go.

Somehow, the fine points of her company didn't seem quite as crucial anymore. Jules kept reminding herself of all the years she'd spent building up
Dunne Parties' reputation for attention to detail, that she mustn't toss that
hard work away, but she couldn't help herself. Who cared whether the blinis
for the caviar were the right shape and size? Why did it matter if the quail
eggs were hard- rather than soft-boiled? What was the difference between one
Chardonnay and another so long as it was good and cold and plentiful?

Particularly plentiful. Jules took another long drink of wine. Ever since
the decision to end the Sean time-share scheme, she had been finding it
astonishingly hard to keep up the pretense, to make people believe that she
was a normal, happy person enjoying life. Instead of a miserable, depressed,
childless woman who was already thirty-eight. Years and years of social
training were all that stood between her and the ever-present threat of tears.
That and copious amounts of alcohol.

Behind her, the party was in its last stages. Women were kissing each
other's artificially smooth cheeks, men were making soon-to-be-forgotten
promises to have lunch. A group of about twenty were planning to go on to
a nightclub. And over in one corner, a tall, graying man was sitting by himself, his eyes fixed on Jules as she finished off her wine.

When she held out her glass for the barman to refill it once more, the
man got up and walked to the bar.

"Juliet."

Too far gone to recognize the voice, Jules swung round to face him. And
almost fell off her bar stool. "M . . . Michael?"

"Yes. Michael." He pulled out the stool next to her and sat down.
"Brandy and soda, please."

ONE THING about eighteenth-century windows. They looked pretty but they
did rattle. Lily was curled up in her study, by the fire, huddled under a fur
throw, sipping water, attempting to ignore the remnants of one of the worst
hangovers in creation and trying to forget about Terry whilst listening to the
wind make her house creak at the seams. She was just wondering whether

the only way to feel any better about the loss of her longtime best friend was to repeat the previous evening's performance and get drunk again, when the doorbell rang. And rang.

Now, who the hell could that be in such a hurry on such a night? Lily jumped up and groaned at the renewed pounding of her head. She paced along the hallway and threw open the door. It was Mara.

"I'm sorry, I tried to call."

"I know. I changed the number. Come in. It's freezing out there." Lily couldn't help grinning at the sight of Mara. She'd been wondering how long she should leave her alone before going around and trying to make up. And here she was. "I am so pleased to see you." Lily leaned forward, gave Mara a hug, then took her arm and led her along the corridor. "Come on. Let me get you a drink."

Mara stopped and pulled away. "You'd better hear what I've got to tell you first. You may not want me to stay."

"Have you killed the girls and buried them in the garden?"

Mara giggled, half shocked, half amused. "Course not."

"Then you're safe. Go in the den, sweetie. I'll be up in a second."

Mara was standing before the fire, warming her hands, when Lily returned, complete with glasses and a bottle of red wine.

"Here you go." Lily poured the wine, handed Mara one of the glasses, then took a sip out of the other, grimaced, and set it aside. That had not been a good idea. "Now, sit down, tell me what's happened."

Mara sat. She took a swig of her drink and then started in. "Lily. I've done a terrible thing. I should have told you before, but I only just remembered when Amy mentioned your name and then it all came flooding back. I don't know if we can stop it, it might be too late."

"Hey. Hey. Calm down. It's no problem, whatever it is. I'm just pleased you're okay. You are okay?"

"I'm fine."

"And you've forgiven me for telling you?"

"There's nothing to forgive. It was a shock, but you were right. I needed to know."

"You look exhausted again."

"Exhausted. Yes. But I'm truly grateful you told me. You have no idea how difficult it is always living up to an icon."

"There's no need to be grateful. If we'd been braver, we'd have done it long ago."

"No. I wouldn't have heard you." Mara reached out to hold her friend's hand for a second. "Thank you," she said.

"Is that what you came all this way in the wind and the rain to say?"

"Oh, no. I let you distract me. Lily, I'm so sorry. I told Clive."

"Told him what? That you were angry with me? I don't think even he can make a story out of that. Although I can see him trying."

"No. No. About Sean."

"Sean?"

"And the sharing." Mara expected Lily to explode. When she didn't, she rushed in to fill the silence. "I didn't mean to. He arrived just after you left, saying his car had broken down, and I was in shock and I let him in and he sort of wormed it out of me."

"He would. He's very clever."

"Can we stop it? We could call his editor, couldn't we?"

"No. Oh, we could, but it would make no difference. No self-respecting editor would stop a story like this. He'd lose his job."

"I'm so sorry. I'd understand if you wanted to stop being my friend."

"It's not your fault. Clive's sharp even when you've got all your wits about you. When you're upset, it's no wonder he got what he wanted. And maybe it's not so bad."

"How can it be not so bad?"

A slow smile spread over Lily's face. "Well, I hate being in the tabloids on principle, but ultimately, who cares? Compared to some of the things they print, it's positively positive."

"Lily . . ."

"No. Listen. What we did wasn't terrible. In fact, it was sort of cool. Okay, it didn't work, but we were brave to try it. Not many women would. We were in the forefront of modern life, an advance guard showing the way for others."

"Do you really think that?"

"Yes. Yes, I think I do."

"You're amazing."

"And cool."

"And very, very cool. Should we call the others?"

"Hmm. Yes, we'd better try and warn Jules."

"And Terry."

"No."

"No?"

"She's stolen Sean from me."

Mara couldn't escape a twinge of guilt. It had been she who had sent Sean to Terry. But they looked like an ideal couple. "Forgive me, but is that such a bad thing? You didn't really want him that much, did you?"

"Maybe I didn't. But I didn't want him stolen. It should have been my choice to give him up."

"Yes, of course. But if Terry's happy?"

"Fuck Terry. Let her face Sean with no warning."

"Sean?"

"He's not going to be very happy about this. To put it mildly."

"Lily. She's our friend."

"No. And as penance for having told Clive, you're not leaving here until you promise not to call her yourself."

"Oh, no."

"Oh, yes." Lily waited for the promise. When it didn't come, she advanced on Mara, trying hard to look threatening. "Mara. Mara. I'll lock you in the attic."

Mara laughed.

"I mean it. Bread and water."

"Think of poor Terry."

"I am. She's got what she wanted." Mara looked as if she were about to argue. Lily held up her hand. "No. I'm serious about this. I don't want you telling her."

Finally, Mara had to give in. After what she'd done, she definitely owed Lily. There would be no story if it hadn't been for her. "All right. I promise. But I don't think it's fair."

"I'm sure it's not. But it's the way it is. Terry broke the rules. So she pays."

"The rules?"

"Of friendship. Remember?" Lily reached out, picked up the phone. "Let's try Jules."

. . .

JULES WASN'T in. Jules was in the road outside her house, being helped out of a cab by Michael.

"Here, Juliet. Give me your hands. Good. Now, one foot down."

"I'm not that drunk."

"Of course you're not. One foot down. Good. And the other. There. Right, put your arm round my shoulders. Hold on a moment." He reached behind him and closed the door to the cab. "And forward."

Behind them, the driver put his vehicle in gear and it shuddered off down the street.

"I can walk on my own."

"I know. Of course you can." Michael ignored Jules and continued to prop her up while he looked around the street at the row of nearly identical houses. "Now, which one is yours? . . . Juliet, it's cold and windy and I would be prepared to bet it's about to rain. Which house is yours?"

Jules had had what seven glasses of wine told her was a brilliant idea. And the more her three-quarters sozzled brain thought about it, the more brilliant it seemed. She and Michael should go to bed together. He was more good-looking than ever. He had been so nice to her tonight. And she deserved a treat. Something to cheer her up. Why not Michael?

"Juliet. What's your address?"

"Number 5, Bellingham Road, London SW3 4RJ," Jules answered automatically.

Michael smiled. No matter how far gone, there were certain questions people always answered. He walked Jules to her door, hesitated before rummaging in her bag—there was something about a woman's handbag that was sacred, he could still remember his mother shouting at him for looking in hers—but when Jules made no move to find her keys, he realized that it was up to him. He waded through tissues and lip gloss and diary and mobile phone before locating them in the side pocket. He held Jules upright, squinted to see which key went where, and finally succeeded in opening the door.

Jules stumbled in. And Michael followed her, as she'd known he would. Having seen her safe this far, he wasn't going to abandon her now.

No question, the cold night air had sobered Jules up a little. She wasn't as drunk as she appeared. Oh, she'd had way too much and she was going to feel dreadful the next day, but she wasn't about to pass out. Or to pass up this opportunity. Her conscience had disappeared somewhere around the sixth glass. Maybe she was making a big mistake. Maybe she'd regret it deeply in the morning. But right at that moment, seducing Michael seemed like the most sensible idea she'd ever had.

Deliberately, she swayed a little. "I need to go to bed."

"You do. And you should drink some water or you'll have a dreadful head tomorrow."

"Can you help me? It's upstairs." Jules allowed herself to fall toward Michael. He caught her and lifted her against his chest. She put her arms around his neck.

As they climbed the stairs, Jules laid her head on his shoulder and nuzzled into his neck. If she'd been a cat, she'd have purred. He walked into her bedroom, laid her down on the bed, and tried to move away. But Jules wouldn't let go. She pulled his head down to hers.

"Juliet—"

"Shhh. Don't argue. Just kiss me."

When he held back, Jules raised herself and pulled him toward her. "Kiss me."

Michael knew he shouldn't. Juliet might appear less drunk than she had a few minutes earlier, but she was far from sober. And he wasn't exactly clearheaded either. Neither of them was in any state to be making decisions.

On the other hand, he had never forgotten what it had been like with her. He'd had lots of girlfriends after her and been married and divorced since their time together, but nothing had wiped out his memories of her. Looking down at her, her flushed face, her disheveled hair, her glittering eyes, he realized that he didn't have the strength to refuse her. If nothing else, he had to find out if it had been as good as he remembered.

A COUPLE of hours later, he was lying, wide awake, next to a sleeping Jules. And berating himself for having given in to her. He hadn't even put up any real resistance. She'd asked and he'd jumped. Yes, he'd been drinking, but he'd not been drunk. He should have been able to say no, gently but firmly, and leave. Instead he'd leapt at her offer.

In the restaurant, as he watched her systematically falling deeper and deeper under the influence, he kept thinking of the last time he had seen her, in the club. Of the way she'd staggered out, held up by her sister Alice, her legs bloodstained, her face twisted with pain. Of her monster mother, who was more interested in her own social standing than in her daughter's health. He'd called Alice's husband, an old school friend, the following day to make sure Juliet was all right and discovered that she'd had a miscarriage. Full of sympathy—he could still remember how he'd felt when his wife lost a baby—he'd been tempted to send flowers, even to visit, but had resisted. Had pushed all thought of her from his mind.

Until the restaurant. When he'd seen Juliet so unhappy, he couldn't help remembering what Jocelyn Hannesford-Jones had said to him. It had been several weeks after she had seen him walk away from Juliet at that drinks party that the woman had made a point of searching him out. He had to give her full marks for nerve. No one mentioned his ex-fiancée to him, either unwilling to offend him or unaware that the two had any connection. But Jocelyn had been determined to tell him what she thought. What had the meddling old witch said? "I can tell she holds you in high esteem, and I know how much it would mean to her if she could believe that you had forgiven her."

And so he hadn't been able to stop himself going over to her to do just what Mrs. Hannesford-Jones had suggested. It had seemed little enough, after all, and he'd decided that if it cheered Juliet up even the smallest amount, it would be worth it. And to begin with, it was. But look where it had led him. Here. In bed with the woman who had walked out on him the day before they were supposed to get married. Leaving him to deal with five hundred guests, rooms full of presents, and a passel of eminent bishops. To explain that there wasn't going to be a wedding after all. And to cope with the fact that the woman he loved didn't love him.

He had known when he'd asked her to marry him that it was a mistake. She was far too young. Every instinct he possessed told him that he should wait until she'd had time to grow up, to have some fun and freedom living in London, before he talked marriage. But he couldn't resist. Just like tonight, he had wanted her so much that he had ignored his better judgment and gone ahead. When she'd agreed to marry him, he had allowed himself to believe that she felt about him as he did about her. But she hadn't. And deep down, he'd known it.

In a way, that had made it worse. After his initial coruscating rage and deep embarrassment, try though he might, he couldn't blame Juliet alone. It had been his fault too. If he had only trusted his own intuition. But he hadn't. He'd been weak. And he still was where she was concerned.

Even more so after tonight, after finding out that his memories of them together had faded over the years. Or that they were even better in bed now than they had been then. Either way, it didn't matter. It wouldn't happen again. He couldn't afford to let it.

Jules stirred, shifted, turned toward him, laid her head on his shoulder, her arm across his chest. He waited for her to say something, but she was silent. And still asleep.

He longed to make love to her again. But if he wasn't very careful, he could see what had happened in the past repeating itself. His falling for her, her playing with him for a bit, then moving on, unhurt. Leaving him to cope without her again.

Michael rolled Jules away from him, ignoring her sleepy protests. He knew he shouldn't hold her responsible. Her life was obviously in turmoil, she'd simply gotten drunk and taken comfort where she could, but he found it impossible to forgive her. Not for what she'd done so much as for the hold she still had over him. And the fact that what meant so much to him mattered so little to her.

Jules had curled up on the other side of the bed, still fast asleep. Michael looked at her for a moment, resisting the urge to curl up with her, to stay the night and be there to make love in the morning. He forced himself to turn away from her and get out of bed. He would not let her do this to him. If he couldn't be in command of his own emotions where she was concerned—and he had to admit, hard though it was, that he couldn't—then he wouldn't see her. Ever. It was as simple as that.

He collected his clothes and walked out. Without a good-bye kiss, without a note explaining his absence, without even a backward look.

sixty-six

Sean supposed he would soon get tired of the tinny music and high-pitched zaps and squeals. But right at that moment, the Beatles couldn't have sounded better. He'd spent the night on Isobel's sofa and had got up at dawn, keen to get home, a part of him still afraid that she would change her mind. Now he was back in England, driving to London, his car piled high with clothes and toys and books. And two young boys who were sitting in the back, playing a portable video game.

In the end, there had been no need to negotiate with Isobel. Steve Jones, her lover, had given her an ultimatum. He'd had enough of France. When she'd panicked after Sean had found out about her leaving the boys alone and decided that they all had to flee England, it had been her choice to go to Brittany. She came from Canada, she spoke French fluently, and an old friend of hers from her Vancouver days taught at the high school in Cancale and would help them settle in. Steve had been reluctant at first, but eventually she'd managed to persuade him that moving abroad with the boys would be a bit of a lark.

It had turned out to be anything but. When they'd arrived in Cancale, Steve spoke not a word of French, and though he had picked up a bit here and there, he still needed Isobel to help him communicate. He'd managed the work all right—plumbing terms weren't all that different in French— but he'd missed the banter on-site, missed going out to the pub for a drink with his friends afterward, missed the football on Saturdays, missed fish and chips, and plain roast beef, and curries.

More than that, he'd had enough of living as a parent. Time enough for Saturday nights in and weekends camping when he was closer to forty and ready to settle down.

Finally, desperate to go home, he'd insisted that Isobel had to choose between him and the children. And she had chosen him. Maybe because she was still desperate to hold on to her younger man. Maybe because she too had had enough of life in a small French town. Or maybe because she had wanted to give the boys up all along and had finally found someone to take the blame for her doing so. Sean had no idea. And he didn't care. He had Mark and Ben back. Isobel would come to see the boys once or twice a month, but otherwise, they were his. And, he hoped, Terry's.

He still hadn't called her. He hadn't forgotten her in the excitement of seeing his kids, but he'd pushed thoughts of her to the back of his mind while he spent the evening with Mark and Ben, overseeing their good-byes, talking to them about their lives, their school, their friends, trying to snatch back just a week or two of the years he had lost. Once they'd gone to bed, he'd had to make arrangements with Isobel for the future, and by the time they were finished, it was getting too late to call anyone. Besides, he hadn't wanted to have his conversation overheard by either his ex-wife or her lover. Now he had Mark and Ben with him and he couldn't talk to Terry in front of them. In any case, he had left it so long that he felt he needed to see her and tell her in person. He would get back to London, take the boys to Ray and Babs, get them settled there, and then find her.

Sean swung off the motorway and into a gas station. Leaving the boys in the back to continue fighting the forces of evil, he filled up the car, then went to pay. He didn't even glance at the racks of newspapers. But then, at the counter, he saw one of the other customers reading a tabloid. With a huge, banner headline: "Sharing Sean." And a photo that looked very, very familiar.

Giving up his place in the queue, he went back to the papers and grabbed a copy of the *Daily News*. There it was. "Sharing Sean." And a picture of him. Quickly, unable to believe what he was reading, he skimmed the story, which occupied five whole pages of the newspaper. There were photos of all of them, of Lily, of Jules, of Mara, of him. Of Terry.

Sean slumped against the wall of the shop. God. He felt as if he'd been raped. They'd manipulated him, controlled him, made decisions about his life with no thought of what he wanted. They'd used him for their own ends. All of them.

Even Terry.

No matter how he tried, he couldn't find an acceptable explanation for her involvement. She had been in on this. She'd conspired with the others to get him to be a friend to Paul. He thought he'd made the offer to help her in good faith; in fact, he'd been cleverly manipulated into making it, his every action stage-managed by others. Who was to say Terry hadn't also planned her night with him? Connived to get him into bed with her and lied about her problem just to get him going? The pleasure he'd felt, yes, that had been real, but even so, their night together now didn't feel all that special. What had seemed perfect had turned out to be deeply and irrevocably flawed.

sixty-seven

Jules was ecstatic.

She had finally turned the tables on Diana.

But it had all been very, very different when she'd woken up that morning with the grandmother of all hangovers. Her head had been pounding, she had found it almost impossible to stand up, let alone move, and even the thought of food turned her stomach.

And she had been alone. Sometime in the night—Jules had a vague, fuzzy memory of being rolled over in bed—Michael must have left.

There was very little to show that he had even been there—a small dent in his pillow, a hint of his musky aftershave on the sheets, a touch of stubble rash on her cheeks—and after a couple of cups of coffee and a hot bath, Jules decided that it would be best if she behaved as if he hadn't been. It didn't seem as if it would prove all that difficult. The night had been odd, almost dreamlike; even now, after it had happened, the idea of their ending up in bed together felt unreal.

Making love had been amazing, though. Jules had wiped from her brain any memory of what being in bed with Michael all those years ago had been like; thinking about him had only revived the initial trauma and the massive guilt of jilting him. So the attraction between them had come as a complete and very welcome surprise. For herself, she wouldn't have been averse to carrying on. Not averse at all. In fact, she would have loved it.

And not just for the sex. She had also enjoyed Michael's company. She'd drunk a great deal, and there were a few gaps in her memory, but she would never forget how nice he had been about the past. Even with a hangover, remembering his words of forgiveness gave her a nice warm glow. She had always said that he was the only decent, honest man she'd ever been with. And it looked as if she'd been right.

But she wasn't going to see him again. As she remembered, she had been the one to do the seducing, and though once committed he had entered whole-bodily into the proceedings, he had been reluctant at the start. If he'd wanted more, he'd have stayed the night. Or at least left a note. Clearly, he wasn't interested in her. And the least she owed him was to leave him in peace. So, after one long, lingering look back, she resolved to put all thought of him out of her mind.

Even so, the solid gloom of misery that had been hanging over her for the last weeks seemed to have lifted. Jules still felt sad, and she would always mourn her lost baby, but that overpowering melancholy was gone. She had no idea why—for all she knew, it was hormonal—but she wasn't going to complain. For the first time in ages, she could function as normal.

Apart from the hangover, that is. The coffee and the bath made her feel a tiny bit more like a human being but nowhere nearly together enough to get dressed and go to work. She was just about to lie down and see if she could manage a nap when the phone rang. Jules had yet to listen to her messages from last night and so the machine picked up after only one ring. She lunged for the receiver.

"Hold on. Hold on," she shouted over her outgoing message. "Hi. Sorry about that."

"Juliet. How could you? I have never been so humiliated in all my life."

Rats. It was her mother. What on earth could she want? They hadn't spoken since the night at the club, and it was a little late to be checking up on her daughter's health. Why, oh why, had she picked up?

"How could you even have thought of such a thing?"

"What thing?" Jules asked, confused. This didn't seem to be another of her mother's generalized rants but something more specific. What had she done?

"Davina called me this morning to tell me about it. Davina! She positively gloated."

"But what about?"

"And in such a newspaper. Disgusting. How am I supposed to go out and about now? It's mortifying."

Jules couldn't think what it could be. It was obvious she had upset her mother very much but she wasn't sure how. And she needed to know the details so that she could enjoy this to the full. In the past, anything she had done that had provoked this kind of rage and misery from Diana—her jilting of Michael, her divorce—had upset her also and so she hadn't had a chance to see her mother's despairing fury as a victory. Some sort of revenge for what Diana had put her through. But now she couldn't imagine what she had done. And so she was unlikely to be unhappy about it. "Please. I have no idea what you're talking about. What newspaper?"

"The *Daily News*." Lady Dunne's voice hissed the words. "All over the front page. About you and your friends and a builder."

This time, Jules was convinced she heard her mother spit out the words. Someone must have found out about them sharing Sean. No wonder she had messages on her machine from last night. The others must have called to warn her. For a moment, she wondered how they were feeling, but then put that to the back of her mind as her mother ranted on and on. Time enough to talk to her friends later. And decide how she herself felt about being found out. For now, she had to enjoy the moment.

". . . every detail of your life. Your marriage. Your divorce. This man. Your miscarriage. It's sickening. Sickening. Never, never did I think to see our family name dirtied like this. All my friends will laugh behind my back for years to come. The idea that I could have a daughter like you."

Diana paused. Jules said nothing, hoping Diana was going to continue. She was.

"Well, I hope you're happy. You've upset your father. And you've destroyed me. I was giving a drinks party in two weeks. How am I supposed to stand there and welcome people who are all laughing at me? How? How? Tell me that."

"I don't know. Perhaps you could cancel?"

"Do you think this is funny?"

"Yes, actually. I do."

"Funny? You've ruined my life. Do you hear that? Ruined it. It'll be years before this is forgotten. If it ever is. The *Daily News*! With a builder!" Diana moaned. "Deliberately getting pregnant like that. My daughter, a single mother. How could you? How could you?"

"Very easily." And though part of Jules wanted to stay on the phone, to revel in the sound of her mother beating her breast over what had happened, another part of her longed to be the one to end things. For the first time in her life, she wanted the last word. "Good-bye, Diana," she said calmly, and put the receiver down, her face split by a grin as wide as Siberia. She supposed she should worry about the effect this was going to have on Dunne Parties, but for the moment she wanted to revel in her mother's embarrassment. Besides, wasn't any publicity supposed to be good publicity?

"Yippee!" she shouted. What a great day.

sixty-eight

Paul didn't find out until lunchtime. Newspapers weren't a regular part of his day. If he read one, it was only the back pages.

At about midday, he left the school—he wasn't supposed to, but no one bothered patroling the grounds anymore and it was simple to slip away unnoticed—and walked to the local café. Terry had been too distracted to make him a packed lunch that morning and had thrust a fiver into his hand instead. He'd thought about skipping the meal and putting the money toward his take-Sally-out-to-dinner fund, but he was starving. And the idea of bacon and fried eggs and sausages—rare in his house—was irresistible.

So he'd walked into the greasy spoon café, ordered his full English breakfast, and sat at one of the chipped Formica tables. On one side, there was a pile of discarded newspapers. Absentmindedly, he pulled one of them toward him and was about to turn to the sports pages when the enormous headline on the front page caught his eye. And the accompanying picture. Worried, his fingers crossed for his friend, he started to read. What on earth could Sean have done to make the *Daily News* interested in him?

Paul ignored everything else around him as he read the story. His lunch went uneaten, the waitress's queries unanswered as he read about his mother going looking for a friend for him. About Sean being a dupe of his mother and her mates. About the end of all his hopes for Terry and Sean getting together. At first he was puzzled. Then he was hurt. And finally he was furious. With his mother. He knew that Sean had been in on the plan too but he wasn't as angry with him. No, he blamed Terry. She'd set the whole thing up, she'd manipulated him and Sean, she'd controlled and used them for her own purposes. All the rage and disappointment and misery he'd felt after Finn's death, which had dissipated over the past few months, flooded back, and it had only one focus: his mother.

Paul pushed his untouched, congealed lunch aside, gathered up the newspaper, and left the café. The waitress raced after him, wanting to be paid. He thrust the fiver at her and ran away, with no thought of change or tips or apologies. No thoughts at all apart from finding Sally.

sixty-nine

It wasn't until early afternoon that Terry noticed the odd way people were staring at her. And whispering together when they saw her, as if she were some kind of celebrity figure of fun. Passengers, people on the street, even Sid, her replacement conductor, as it was Fred's day off, seemed to be unable to stop gawking. And giggling. Normally, she would have been concerned. But she had no room for any more worries.

Every scrap of her brain that wasn't required to keep her alive and her bus moving from stop to stop was occupied in thinking about Sean. And why he hadn't called her at home the previous night. The more time that passed, the more she became convinced that she'd been right. He didn't want her, did he? He'd never wanted her. That night that had meant so much to her had just been a one-night stand, a pity fuck for a poor, frigid, lonely woman who had been begging for it. What was it men always said? Gagging for it.

She tried to tell herself that his not calling meant nothing. He was busy. Something had happened at work. Paul had forgotten to tell her he'd rung. There'd be a message waiting for her at home. Men often didn't call immediately afterward. They made you wait a few days. It meant nothing.

But it didn't work. No matter how hard she tried to convince herself that everything was all right, ultimately she couldn't stop her thoughts piling one on top of another, building an edifice of certainty. She'd made a complete fool of herself. Sean didn't care.

No wonder, then, that she wasn't bothered by a few odd looks. All she was interested in was finishing her shift and getting home. Just in case there was a flashing light on her answering machine and a message explaining the silence of the last two days.

She pulled into Victoria Station, slotted her bus into a bay, and turned off the engine. And saw him. Pacing up and down, a newspaper tightly gripped in his hand. Waiting for her. She climbed down from the cab and ran up to him.

"Sean! Sean! I was worried, I hadn't heard from you. . . ." Her voice petered out when she saw his face. No way was this a boyfriend come to greet her after a day's work. His expression held no love, no pleasure, no affection. Instead, his mouth was a thin, grim line, his eyes alight with rage, his features hard-set.

"What's happened?"

"Congratulations." His voice was a deep growl.

"What for?"

"Making the front page."

"Sorry?"

"What did you get?"

"Get?"

"You're a fool if you took less than fifty thousand pounds."

"What're you talking about? Fifty thousand pounds? Where would someone like me get that?"

"Tell me, did you all plan this from the start or was the money just a nice added extra?"

"Plan? What plan? Sean, you're not making sense." Terry couldn't imagine what it was had upset him—all that burbling on about plans and money and front pages—but she was sure it had nothing to do with her. And that it didn't matter. Whatever it was. What was important was that he'd come to see her and that he wasn't doing any of the things she'd imagined over the last thirty-six hours. He was angry, yes, but she could cope with that. Anger meant he cared, didn't it? And anger left no room for contempt or scorn or laughter. Ignoring his stiff, shuttered face, she smiled up at him. "Come on, let's go have a coffee and we can talk and you can tell me what's the matter, and whatever it is that's bothering you, we'll deal with it."

"Will we?"

"Course. The main thing is that you're here. With me." Terry stood on tiptoe to kiss Sean. "Whatever it is, we'll cope," she said. "Together."

"That wasn't much of a kiss."

Terry smiled. "More later, I promise."

"Unless you'd like to give me a better taste now. To put me on?"

Terry looked round at the crowded station, at the passengers thronging the bays, at the group of drivers and conductors who had stopped on their way to or from their vehicles and were staring at her and Sean, wide, leering grins plastering their faces.

"Well, okay." If that's what he wanted. Although later she was going to get the piss taken out of her unmercifully. "How's this?" She leaned into Sean, put her arms around him, and brought her mouth up to his.

They had barely touched lips when he shuddered and jerked himself away from her. "Or perhaps you'd like to get your friends to help?" he snapped.

"Sean?"

"Like I said, congratulations. You managed to fuck up one of the best days of my life."

"What?"

"You and your posh friends. You used me." He thrust the newspaper at her.

Terry stared at Sean with horror. It sounded as if he'd found out about Lily and Jules and the sharing, but how? None of them would have told him.

"Open it." He pointed at the newspaper. She hesitated. "Go on, open it." And Terry opened it. And saw the headline. "Oh, no."

Sean saw the truth in her face and heard it in her reaction. And lost his last, lingering hope. That she'd been as much a victim as he. No, he'd been twisted and exploited and played for a fool by a group of selfish, hard-headed bitches. "Fuck you."

"Sean, I . . . It wasn't like it looks. . . ."

"No? How was it, then?"

Terry looked at him, unable to think of a single thing to say. He was right. They had used him. There was no excuse.

"I thought I loved you. Spent yesterday planning all of our futures. While you four spilled your guts to some tabloid journalist."

"I didn't talk to anyone. I didn't know about this. You know I didn't know." God. He'd loved her. Had planned a future for them. But now? She looked at his face, still iron-hard, heard the past tense in his words.

"Not know about the article? Maybe. But you knew about the sharing, didn't you?"

"Yes. But that was before."

"Before what?"

"Before I fell in love with you."

Sean's snarl told Terry what he thought of that.

"I'm so sorry. Lils made it all seem so sensible, so natural. It was wrong, not telling you, I know it was. But I never planned . . . you and me, that had nothing to do with the others. It was just supposed to be you and Paul. Nothing else."

"That's an excuse?"

"No. An explanation. There's no excuse. I know that."

"You know, I thought I was a complete shit. I reproached myself over and over for fucking Jules and kissing you while I was with Lily, when all the time you planned it that way. Hard to believe, isn't it? How bloody stupid I was?"

"Sean. Love. I'm sorry. It wasn't meant like that. We just didn't think how you'd feel. Please, please don't turn away from me. We can get through this, can't we? I need you."

"And I suppose you'll tell me the others do too. Haven't you girls had enough of me?"

"That's not how it was, you know that."

"Well, fuck you. This time I get to decide what happens. Good-bye, Terry."

And he turned and walked away.

For a moment, Terry was paralyzed, unable to move or speak. Then, as she saw him getting farther and farther away, she shouted after him, "I'm sorry. Sean, I'm sorry. Please. It just happened. I was going to tell you."

He carried on walking.

"Sean! I love you," Terry screamed, completely focused on his shrinking back, indifferent to the four o'clock, early rush-hour crowds hovering around, enjoying the unexpected entertainment.

But Sean paid her no attention. He marched out of the bus station. And Terry's life.

seventy

Paul wasn't sure how to feel when he discovered that Mark and Ben were at Ray's. Determined not to go home, he'd taken refuge with Sally, meeting her after school and going back to her house with her. The two boys came as a complete surprise—he hadn't known that Sean had kids. He'd never mentioned them. There was a part of him that was hurt—why hadn't Sean confided in him about them? There was a part of him that was jealous of the boys—they had Sean for their dad. Something that he'd been hoping to get until he'd read the newspaper story and realized that there was no chance. There was a part of him that resented Sean for being taken in by his mam's schemes. And a part of him that was desperate for reassurance that Sean did care for him, that it hadn't all been a favor to Terry.

So when Sean arrived to collect the boys, Paul stayed in Sally's room. He didn't know what to do or how to act and so he hid, listening to the bustle downstairs as Mark and Ben greeted their father and the younger kids screamed for his attention.

A couple of minutes later, there was a knock on the door and Sean walked in.

"Don't blame Sally. Babs told me. It's time for tea."

"Oh. Right."

"Are you okay?"

"Uh-huh."

"Babs said she wasn't expecting you." Sean didn't know what to do. He suspected Paul had run away from home over the newspaper story, but he couldn't be sure. And if the boy didn't know, it was up to his mother to decide what to tell him.

"No."

"Does your mother know you're here?"

"No."

"Paul?"

"I read the story."

"It must have been a shock."

"I hate her."

"No you don't. You're angry with her. But you don't hate her." Sean might be furious with Terry himself, might be sure he could never forgive her, but he didn't want her son to suffer.

"Do."

"Paul, she was only trying to help you. She doesn't deserve hating." Not by you anyway.

"Everything's ruined."

"No it's not."

"It is."

"You and I can still be friends. If you want."

"Can we? I thought you wouldn't want to. I mean, the story said you only did it to help mam."

"Yeah, well, they didn't get it all right. They often don't. Remember when they said Charlton was going to sign that Brazilian player? For twelve million pounds, wasn't it? As if Charlton knew what twelve million looked like."

"Yeah, I remember."

"Maybe I met your mam cos of all this, but I knew no more about her and her mates' scheme than you did."

"You knew mam wanted you to be a friend to me."

"Yes. I did. But that was all it was. What your mam wanted. I didn't have to do it. Did I?"

"I guess not." Paul desperately wanted to believe him, but the newspaper article had been a huge shock.

"I wouldn't have introduced you to Ray and Sally and Babs if I hadn't liked you, now would I?"

"No. No, I suppose you wouldn't." That did make sense to Paul. He may have been only a kid, but even he could see that Ray and his family were too special to Sean for him to mess around with them.

"Friends, then?"

"Yeah. Course. And you and mam?"

"One rule. I don't want to talk about that. Or her. Ever. Okay?"

"I suppose."

"Good. Now, come have some tea and then you've got to go home."

"Don't want to."

"I know you don't. But you can't hide here forever."

"Sally doesn't mind."

"I'm sure she doesn't. But you need to sort this out. Come on, I'll give you a lift."

TERRY WAS huddled behind the old dark green velvet curtains that covered her front window, Minnie perched on an ancient leather ottoman beside her. She was looking out in the street, hoping to see some sign of Paul coming home. And hiding from the slew of reporters clustered around her door, hustling anyone who went in or came out. If this went on much longer, she was going to have to make major apologies to her neighbors.

She knew she'd be better off ignoring the press and retreating to her kitchen, but she couldn't. She was desperately worried about Paul. The last she'd spoken to him, he was intending to come straight back after school, but it was already seven-thirty and there was no sign of him. Much as she wanted to believe that there was another explanation for his being late, she was convinced that he must have seen the story. And was terrified that he might not come home at all. Losing Sean had been bad enough. What if she lost Paul too? What if he never returned? You heard stories all the time about kids just disappearing, running away from home and never being seen again. What if Paul did that?

Terry knew she was overreacting. Paul was three hours late and here she was imagining him gone forever. But she couldn't help it.

She wished she could cry. But the shock of the confrontation in the bus station and finding the tabloids encamped at her house and then her concern over Paul's nonappearance had kept her tears at bay. They were there, she knew, like a flood just waiting to break through hastily erected sand-bags. All it would take would be one more shock.

Sean's Saab drove up, on the opposite side of the street. And stopped. At the sound of the engine, Minnie jumped down from the ottoman and ran off to the front door, expecting to see her friend.

For a moment, nothing happened. Terry shivered. The car was just sitting there. She pulled back the curtains, hoping she'd get a better view if she wasn't peering out through a thin slit. Hoping she'd be able to see what was happening inside the Saab. The streetlights were just bright enough for her to make out that there were four figures in the car. Sean, another adult-sized person in the front seat, and what looked like two young kids in the back. Could they be his boys? Had he found them at last? He had said today had been one of the best days of his life. Terry crossed her fingers in hope for him.

Then the passenger door opened. Slowly and very, very reluctantly, Paul got out and closed the door behind him. Terry slumped against the window, her breath frosting the glass. He was safe. Sean had brought him home. The reporters, seeing the boy in the street, left their posts and clustered round him, flashbulbs popping. Paul shrank back, his hands in front of his eyes. Terry knew she should go out there and help him but she was unable to move, riveted to the window while she waited to see what Sean was going to do.

The driver's door opened and Sean got out. He walked around the car, waded into the pile of journalists, put his arm around Paul, and shepherded him toward the house. For the first time since the confrontation in the bus station, Terry felt a thin, small thread of hope. When he'd walked away from her that afternoon, it had been clear that he had no intention of ever seeing her again. But here he was. And though she tried to stop herself, to keep calm, she couldn't help getting excited. He was coming to see her.

She watched as the two crossed the road, trailing press and photographers, and forced their way up the front steps and out of Terry's sight. She heard the fumble of Paul's key in the lock and the front door slamming closed. They were in the house.

But then Sean's tall figure reappeared, pushing his way back through the throng. He got into his car and seconds later drove off.

Terry leaned her head against the bitter, wintry glass. He hadn't been coming to see her. He'd been dropping Paul off. He'd gotten out of the car to help her son across the street, to protect him from the press herd. And then he'd left. He hadn't looked up at her, had he? Not even a brief glance. He hadn't changed his mind at all. He'd meant every single word he'd said at the bus station. He wasn't coming back.

PAUL FLICKED on the living room light.

"Turn it off." Terry was still standing by the window, fighting for control. Only now, when she most wanted to be dry-eyed, were the tears that had been brewing all afternoon threatening to overwhelm her. Whatever else happened, she didn't want Paul to see her cry. She was his mother, she couldn't indulge herself in things like weeping.

Paul walked away from the wall and the switch.

"Please, Paul. Turn it off."

"No. Why should I?"

"Because I asked?"

"Fuck you, Mam. Fuck you."

"You saw it." Terry struggled to speak, her unshed tears distorting her voice. Making her sound hard. And uncaring. "I'm sorry. You must have been upset."

"Yeah. You sound sorry."

"I am."

"Right. And I'm Tom Cruise."

"Very sorry."

"That's crap. Anyway, I can find my own fucking friends."

"It wasn't to get you a friend."

"Then what the fuck was it?"

"To get you a father figure."

"A father? I had a father. Remember? I knew him for two whole days. I sat and watched him die. Remember?"

"Of course I remember. I was there, Paul. And I know how much it hurt."

"You don't. You don't know. If you did, you'd never have been with him. You'd never have chosen a drunk to have a kid with. You'd have found some sensible, sober bloke who'd not have died in front of me like that. Who'd be *here*."

"Maybe I made a mistake with Finn, but I didn't know that at the time. I didn't mean it to be—"

"Who the fuck cares what you meant. I hate you, I hate you, I hate you."

Terry had just about managed to hold it together until that moment. But at the point in her life when she most needed support, everyone was against her. Lily wasn't talking to her, Sean never wanted to see her again, and her son hated her. She gave up the struggle, slumped into an armchair, put her head in her hands, and wept.

Paul looked at her, unable to comprehend what was happening. His mother, his invulnerable, indomitable mother, crying? Through all the crises of his life, she had been there, strong, immovable, a constant, supportive presence. He'd seen her irritated, he'd seen her worried, he'd seen her angry, but he'd never seen her cry. And he couldn't deal with it.

He rushed over to her, knelt at her side, and put his arms around her, tears pouring down his face also. "Mam. Mam, don't cry. Please don't cry. I don't hate you. I love you. It'll all be all right. I promise. I promise."

Terry, who felt that without Sean it would never be all right again, nonetheless let herself be comforted. Her son still loved her. That was something. No. That was a lot. And she couldn't sit here weeping when he too was crying and needed her help and support. "I know, love. I know," she said, wiping her eyes. "Don't worry. I'm fine. Really I am."

seventy-one

Mara thought something had changed when she opened the door. The air felt different. More welcoming. Warmer. She walked in and saw the card, the box of chocolates, and the bottle of champagne standing on the coffee table. She rushed over and ripped open the card. It was an invitation to a housewarming party from Lily and Jules. Puzzled, not aware any of her friends were moving, she looked at the address on the card. Her address.

She dashed over to the radiator that had been useless for nine months. It was hot. As was the other one in the room, those in the kitchen and upstairs in the bedrooms. Her friends had had her central heating mended for her.

She grabbed the phone and called Lily. Yes, the card had come from her and Jules, but this coup had her name written all over it. After two seconds she answered, as if she had been waiting for the call. "Feeling warmer, sweetie?"

"Lily, what have you done?"

"What we ought to have done ages ago. Ignored your pride and gone ahead regardless. Are you pleased?"

"No. Yes. I don't know. You shouldn't have."

"Yes we should. You were freezing your ass off in there."

"It was twelve hundred pounds!"

"And well spent. I'd only have bought another unnecessary outfit with it."

"Lily!"

"Seriously. How many designer dresses does a girl need? Much more fun to buy a handsome, chic heating system."

"How am I ever going to pay you back?"

"You're not. Sweetie, doing this has given me and Jules more pleasure than anything else in years."

"It's too much."

"It's not. We're your friends. That's what friends do."

"I don't . . . I can't . . ." Mara couldn't find words. To have a warm house. No more smoke in their eyes and throats, no more danger of being found out lighting illegal fires. Tears were rolling down her cheeks. "Someone was looking after me that day I saw your ad in *Loot*. I shouldn't accept, I know I shouldn't . . . but . . . thank you. Thank you so much."

seventy-two

Lily walked down the stairs to the theme song from her sitcom. She smiled at the packed audience she could just glimpse beyond the bright lights before kissing the revered, pepper-and-salt-haired host and settling into a chair beside him.

Originally, she'd had no intention of replying to Clive's story. She'd ignored his two other barbed attempts to humiliate her. And it had worked well. The other stories had sunk without a trace within a day or two.

But this time was different. First, her friends were involved and she felt a need to defend them. Pretending nothing had happened was fine if it was just her, but when Clive targeted poor, shocked Mara, whose life had just collapsed around her, she couldn't stand around and do nothing. Second, this story felt as if it had legs. It wasn't just another ten-a-penny tabloid tale of an overindulged celebrity behaving badly. It was new. And therefore wouldn't be easily forgotten. For all Lily knew, sociologists were right now writing articles for the *Times* about the new trend in man/woman relation-ships. Third, this time she wanted to talk about what had happened. Because she'd realized that her offhand comment to Mara was true; she was genuinely proud of what they had tried to do. And finally, she'd had enough of Clive. She wanted to fight back, to take his territory out from beneath him. And stop him continuing to grub around for dirt on her.

She had first thought of calling another of the tabloids and giving them an exclusive. But then she'd remembered that she was booked to appear on the BBC's flagship chat show the week after Clive's story broke. She called the producer and applied a little pressure and they moved her forward seven days, bumping an over-the-hill actor, in town to promote his second autobiography. In truth, it hadn't been hard; they'd been delighted to reschedule things in order to get her on-screen while the story was still fresh in people's minds. They might have been public broadcasters, but they weren't averse to a few ratings victories.

So there she was. Dressed top to toe in this season's Prada, her hair newly cut, her face beautifully made up. Ready for battle.

The host sat down, pulling up the legs of his trousers to preserve the pleats. He cleared his throat and was off. "Lily James. You've been called our funniest and cleverest new comedienne, our best sitcom writer since John Cleese, the first series of your show *We Can Work It Out* was the surprise hit of last season. Why do you want to share your men with your friends?"

"Man, not men. We'd never done it before."

"You don't sound at all embarrassed about it."

"I'm not. I'm proud. We tried something new."

"That didn't work."

"It's hard to get things right at the start. Give us a chance."

"Does that mean you're going to try again?"

"I don't know. Maybe. It'll depend on my friends."

"If you're proud of it, why not tell the world?"

"I thought that's what I was doing."

"No. I mean why hide it in the first place? Why the need for a big exposé in the press?"

"Who wants the media dabbling around in their lives? Their business read by millions? Their celebrity harming their friends? Anyway, we didn't hide anything. All we did was lead our lives as we chose."

CLIVE WAS in the office, sitting with a group of other journalists and his editor, watching Lily on TV. The BBC had been promoting the show over and over again. Hinting at new revelations. Suggesting that Lily was about to spill all. It looked as if she were going to try and recover her reputation. A reputation

Clive believed he had tarnished once and for all. Before the program started, he'd been absolutely sure that he'd beaten her. That because of him she'd now be forever known as the foolish, promiscuous woman who'd deliberately shared her man with her friends. He'd gotten his revenge. And it was sweet.

He'd gathered the group of colleagues and rivals together so they could see him enjoy his triumph. He'd been expecting to see Lily squirm. And to be able to revel in it. But she wasn't squirming. She wasn't squirming at all.

Instead, she was being candid, giving her reasons for the Sean episode, talking about her friends, their problems, comparing them to many other women in the same situations, at the same points in their lives, and talking about sharing men as if it were the most natural next step in the shifting balance between the sexes. The audience—and the famous host—were lapping it up.

". . . there's lots of us thirty-somethings have been married. And divorced. And don't want that again. Look at the husband I had."

"That's Clive Morris?"

"The man who broke the original story. Yes. I threw him out years ago when I discovered he'd been having an affair, spending my money taking his lover on a skiing holiday. He's still trying to get back at me." Lily grinned and winked. And the audience laughed. In that one gesture, she'd dismissed Clive as an irrelevance.

"We've all had the love and the dependence and the quarrels and in some cases the violence, and we've come out the other side determined not to get into it again. To stay independent. But we still want men for certain things. Sex. Sperm. An escort, maybe. Help with a difficult son. Household maintenance, perhaps. Just not there all the time, expecting attention and servicing and feeding."

She was fighting back. And she was winning.

"So sharing one man seemed like the obvious answer. Why not? We would get what we wanted. And so would he."

"Did he? Get what he wanted?"

"You tell me. Look at us. We may not be in our twenties, but I think we still look pretty damn good. We're bright, interesting, unusual people. What man wouldn't go for a situation where he got to be with all of us?"

"Are you advocating this for everyone?"

"It's about independence. Me and my friends, we don't need to be looked after by a man. We don't need to be supported. We don't need to pretend to be the weaker half. Maybe if we all weren't so hung up on finding the right partner, we'd all be happier."

Clive's editor jumped up. "Okay. Seen enough. We need to reflect all this. And try to recoup. Too late for tonight, but first thing tomorrow. Brian, get some quotes. Anti. Pro. A vicar, maybe. Anne Widdecombe ought to be good for something if you can find her. Steve, go talk to the friends if you can. Get their side. I know Clive had trouble getting to them, but maybe they won't feel so bad about you. Mikey, you try Lily. She likes them handsome. Maybe she'll share you if you play your cards right."

Brian, Steve, and Mikey scuttled off. Leaving Clive and his editor.

"What about me?" asked Clive.

"Ah, yes. Clive. I've got a very special story for you. It's round here somewhere." The editor riffled through the pile of paper on his desk. "Yes. Here you go. There's a potato on an allotment in Hackney looks like the Pope."

"But . . . but . . . Lily? The story's mine. I found it, I broke it."

"Yes. So you did. Brilliant. I loved the way you so cleverly realized the implications of what had happened. And used the newspaper to pursue your own agenda. You've made us a fucking laughingstock."

"What? But it was a huge success. Circulation went up by a hundred and fifty thousand. I know it did. You told me."

"And how much will it go down by tomorrow? How many people will have been alienated? You're an idiot, Clive. You had the greatest human-interest woman's story in years and you turned it into smut. Lily's a heroine. Every single woman in the country who saw that show will admire her. Hell, not just the single women. Plenty of married ones will also. She's taken what she wanted and enjoyed it. And she's proud of it."

"But men will hate it. Being used like that."

"All fun and no responsibility—I don't know a man who doesn't dream about that. And most of them'll be drooling at the idea of her and her friends all rolling round in bed together. Sure, I know they never did that, and so do you, but this is fantasy time."

"But, Nige. No one would have known if it wasn't for me."

The editor shrugged. "That was then. This is now. You fucked up big time, Clive."

"I can walk out of here and get a job on any paper I want."

"Yesterday you could. Today? There's not an editor on Fleet Street will touch you with a barge pole."

"Think of the stories I've found for you. The scoops I got. I was great. You know I was."

"You're not being fired, are you?"

"You can't send me out on vegetable call. I haven't done that since I was first here." It was the bottom rung of the ladder. New-boys' shift.

The editor held out the info about the potato. The implication was clear. It was that or nothing.

Clive stared at the piece of paper. And finally grabbed it. He needed to keep his job. After this fiasco, he wasn't likely to be offered another in a hurry. Because Nige was right. Editors had very short memories. He'd seen it happen to other reporters on other papers. Their previous triumphs wiped out by a single disaster. In the tabloid world, the past was just that. The past.

seventy-three

"And this is the garden." Mara walked out of the back door, followed by a perky young man with a perpetual smile and wearing a cheap suit. It was a bright, clear, cold winter day. Apart from a number of cabbages, red and green, and some Brussels sprouts, much of the ground was still bare, waiting for spring planting.

"No flowers?" the young man asked, his words an accusation.

"No. No, we've used the space for vegetables. As you can see."

"Self-sufficiency, eh? The good life?" He laughed at his own non-joke.

"Yes. If you like."

"Hmm. No one wants all that work. A patio and a few pots is the thing now."

Mara flinched. The garden was the one part of the house of which she was proud. It was neat, weeded, productive, the result of hours and hours of toil. She might not have been able to do anything about leaks and crumbling masonry and the like, but she had improved the property in her own way. Or so she had thought. But there was no point in her saying anything. He wouldn't listen.

In the last few minutes, she'd found out that all the stories about the awfulness of real estate agents had a solid basis in fact. Not only had he mocked her beloved vegetable patch, but he'd also made rude remarks about her tumbledown furniture and complained about the smell of spices in the kitchen. Anything she'd tried to say to him had passed unnoticed.

She had decided that it was time to sell the house a few days after she'd learned the truth about Jake. There didn't seem any point in hanging on to it any longer. Without her illusions about her perfect marriage, she could see her home for what it was: a badly run-down, old property that was becoming more and more uncomfortable to live in by the day. And that she needed to get rid of whilst it was still worth something. Lily and Jules's incredible gift had made it a more cozy place to live, but there was still the roof and the walls and the damp.

She had been nervous about telling Moo and Tilly, but they hadn't seemed to mind. In fact, they'd been excited at the idea of moving to a new place, a flat with a proper roof and a modern kitchen and, hopefully, a bedroom for each of them. Plus, the daily spectacle of reporters hanging around the door, hoping for a word with their mum, tended to drive all other thoughts out of their head. When the press had first turned up, Mara had been worried that the girls would want to know exactly why, but they'd accepted that it was all something to do with their aunt Lily and concentrated on enjoying the spectacle and boasting to their friends about their famous mother. Luckily, no one had shown them the newspaper. And the talk show was on too late for them or their friends to watch.

The Moores, of course, would have lapped it up. Even though Mara had been treated lightly in the newspapers, they'd have seen the whole Sean story as more proof of her unfitness for motherhood. She'd heard nothing from them since their letter to her lawyer saying they intended to sue for custody, but it could only be a matter of time. Which made the move to a waterproof flat as soon as possible even more important.

"So what do you think, Mr. Black?"

"Can we go in?" Without waiting for an answer, he led the way into the living room. "The property is rather the worse for wear, Mrs. Moore."

"Yes, I know."

"The market is good at the moment, of course, but no one wants to pay any more than they have to. And it would take a considerable amount of work to do this place up. Roof, walls, windows, kitchen, bathroom . . . You're basically starting from scratch. In many ways, it would be cheaper to build new. So you've got to factor that in. A reasonable price, someone will jump at it. Nice street, nice area, opportunity to put their own stamp on the place. I'd say one-eighty. Maybe put it on the market for two, two-ten. See if anyone bites. But be prepared to accept one-eighty."

"One hundred and eighty thousand pounds?"

"Something like that. Maybe a little more."

"A house up the street went the other day for three hundred and forty."

"I heard. In perfect condition. With a loft conversion."

"But it can't be worth only one hundred and eighty thousand. This is Chiswick."

"You may get more, of course. But you said you wanted a quick sale."

"Yes. Yes, I do." But would the price he was suggesting leave her with the money to buy anything close by? It sounded like a considerable sum to her right now, but was it enough? "That's less than I thought. After I pay you and the solicitor, I'll only have about one hundred and seventy thousand. And I don't want to leave the area, you see, my daughters are at school here and—"

"We've got a nice flat for one-seventy. Two bedrooms. On the railway line, but you can't have everything."

The railway line. Okay, the girls were old enough for her not to worry about them wandering out onto the tracks and being hit by a speeding train, but still. What about the noise? However, it didn't sound like she had any choice. Yes, she could go north into Acton or west into Hounslow, but then Moo and Tilly would have to move school as well as home. And she didn't want them to do that if she could possibly avoid it.

James Black walked toward the door. "Think about it. I can show it to you anytime."

"I will. Thank you for taking a look at the house."

"You'll have other agents coming round, but they won't say any different. One-eighty would be close to top whack for a property in this state."

Mara showed the man out. She was sure he wasn't trying to con her; what he said about prices made absolute sense. Unless she found someone desperate to live on her street and willing to pay extra because of that, she was unlikely to get more than £180,000.

But she had to sell. And quickly.

seventy-four

"Paul? Are you home?" Terry shouted as she walked through the door, her hair dusted with melting snowflakes. It had been coming down since lunchtime and the whole of London was now sprinkled with white, like confectioners' sugar on a restaurant dessert.

"Here," Paul replied as he emerged from his room. "Everything okay?" He looked worriedly at his mother. It had been two weeks since the article in the newspaper and ten days since Lily's appearance on TV. Reporters had given up hanging around their door only the previous evening, having finally accepted that they were not going to get anything.

Terry appeared all right on the surface, but Paul sensed that underneath she was still hurting. A lot. But she wouldn't talk about it. Instead, she maintained a sort of forced jollity that might have fooled a stranger but not anyone who knew her well.

And at night, in bed, she cried. Though she tried to hide it, Paul had listened at her door and heard her muffled sobs. But whenever he mentioned Sean and what had happened, she clammed up.

"I stopped and got us some fish for tea." Like that.

"Mam, I don't care about fish."

"It's cod. Your favorite."

"Cod, tuna, what's the difference?"

Terry headed for the kitchen. "Lots. One's white, one's pink, for a start."

Paul knew this was supposed to be a joke, but he didn't smile. "Aren't you going to change?" he asked. His mother had always, always gotten out of her uniform the moment she got home. For as long as he could remember. But now she didn't bother. Instead, she had stayed in the black serge jacket and wool trousers every evening for two weeks. Since that day.

Terry ignored the question. "Roast, I think," she said, and proceeded to bustle about the kitchen, pulling out pans, chopping vegetables, trimming fish. Keeping herself busy.

"Why won't you talk about it?" The question burst out of Paul.

"About what, love? Don't you fancy fish? I think there's some soup left in the fridge and I could make some cheese on toast—"

"Mam, stop it. Fish is fine. Why won't you talk about Sean?"

Terry froze, her knife poised above the board, a carrot half sliced. She was delighted that she and Paul were once more getting on together. Since they'd cried together, they'd felt as close as they had before Finn appeared. And she was touched that her son cared about how she was feeling, but this was not a conversation she wanted to have. Holding herself together in public was hard enough without talking about Sean.

"I know you're upset."

"I'm fine."

"You're not. Look at Minnie." Paul pointed to the little dog, who was just that moment slinking in the door of the kitchen, her tail between her legs. She walked over to Terry, sat down, and leaned against her leg. For comfort. "She knows you're miserable."

"Oh, Minnie." Terry leaned down to stroke the little dog. "You're a love. But I'm fine." She took a deep breath and carried on chopping. Maybe if she said nothing, Paul would give up.

"I want to help. Let me help."

No such luck. Terry put down her knife and turned to face her son, a tear already trickling down her face. "You can't."

"I thought girls liked to talk. That's what they always say."

"Sometimes it's too hard. I'm sorry, love. I know you want to make it better, but some things people've just got to suffer through on their own. I messed up. I know I did. And there's no getting it back or making it come out right. But it'll get better. It will, I promise. In time. Things always do, don't they?"

"Mam. You're just as unhappy as you were when it happened. Look at you."

Terry brushed her tears away with a corner of a tea cloth and dredged up a watery smile from somewhere. "It's only been a couple of weeks. Give it a month or so," she said, privately thinking no way was she going to get over Sean that quickly, but keen to reassure her son. "Just let me deal with it in my own way. All right?"

"I suppose."

Terry leaned over the table and kissed Paul on the cheek. "Thanks, love. I have you, you know. And that makes up for a lot."

seventy-five

Surrounded by dusty boxes, Sean stood in the center of a poky room whose low ceiling and fake oak beams only added to the airless feel. Outside, in a suburban street, a team of men was unloading furniture, pictures, and yet more boxes from a large truck and carrying them inside. Sean had long since given up telling them where to put things—a lot of the stuff had been in storage since he'd moved to the loft in King's Cross, and some of it he didn't even remember having had. Where, for instance, had that hideous overhanging glass-and-chrome floor lamp come from? Had he bought that?

Once he'd gotten Mark and Ben back, he'd had to move—the loft was no place for kids. Besides, he wanted the boys to be close to Ray and Babs and their kids, to have some sort of family outside himself. If he could, he'd have gone back to the large semidetached house he'd bought after he and Isobel split up, but it was leased and so he'd had to find an unfurnished, three-bedroom house in South East London to rent. At short notice. It had not turned out to be as simple as he'd hoped, and this cramped, dark excuse for a home had been all he'd been able to get.

Mark and Ben dashed into the room.

"Dad, Dad, my bedroom's great. It's got its own sink in the corner and there's a fireplace with an electric fire. . . ." That was Ben, talking faster than a speeding bullet.

"And you can see the woods from mine and there's still some snow and there was a fox in the garden. . . ." Mark was animal crazy, determined to be a vet when he grew up.

Sean grinned at his overexcited sons. If they were happy with the place, then he'd live with it. Strange how kids found different things pleasing. It would never have occurred to him to think that a sink in a bedroom—a sign of the tasteless fifties to Sean—was worth getting enthusiastic about.

"Can we go look at the woods?"

"Yeah, can we, Dad?"

"Okay. But put your coats on. And don't go too far." And they were gone, out of the house and off to the woods at their regular speed of nine hundred miles per hour.

Sean smiled after them. Thank God for Mark and Ben. He couldn't imagine how he would have coped without them. They kept him sane, his joy and relief at finding them and the pure pleasure of their company balancing the other side of his life.

No one could be continually unhappy with such whirlwinds around. At least not while they were there.

But when their energy and excitement and noise had gone, and Sean was left to himself, he could no longer avoid his thoughts and memories of Terry. Though her lies had destroyed the relationship, images of them together, bits of conversation, things she'd said and done kept coming to him unbidden.

He forced them out of his mind as soon as they did, refusing to accept that he still felt something for her. But they continued to appear. Giving Terry up felt like giving up smoking had the one time he'd tried it. It was a continual struggle that never seemed to get any easier.

seventy-six

Terry shut the newspaper and added it to the growing pile on the kitchen table. Paul had been bringing all her favorites home for her every day, hoping to reawaken her interest in the horoscopes she had once read so intently. But though she skimmed through them to try and please him, her heart wasn't in it. No astrologer could send Sean back to her, and all their talk of patience and a surprise being around the corner and romance in the air couldn't persuade her that she should be positive about the future.

Halfheartedly, she picked up the next paper. And the phone rang. She jumped. Just as she did every time this happened nowadays. She knew it wouldn't be Sean, knew that there was more chance of her becoming minister for Transport than of his calling out of the blue, but still the little bit of hope lingered. Maybe, just maybe.

She grabbed the receiver. "Hello?"

"Terry. It's Lily."

"Oh, Lily."

"Don't sound so pleased."

"Sorry. I thought you might be . . ."

"Sean?"

"Someone else."

"Still seeing him, then?" Lily couldn't resist a little jibe at Terry. She'd called to try and make things right. She'd hated their not talking and had decided that one betrayal shouldn't erase twenty years of loyalty, but there was a part of her that was still very angry with her friend.

"No."

"Good. Now, all this has gone on long enough. It's been three weeks. And I miss you."

"Oh, Lils. I miss . . . What do you mean, good?"

"Just good. I want us to be friends again."

"Good why? Good because I deserve to be unhappy? Good because I got my just desserts? Good because you want him back yourself? Why?" Terry heard the words pouring out of her mouth and couldn't believe that it was herself talking. She'd missed Lily. Missed her humor and her support and her ability to laugh at misfortune. But she'd kept her feelings bottled up for weeks. And because of that, all her anger, all her misery, all her resentment had backed up and was ready to flood out of her.

"Good because it means we can get over this."

"We? You, you mean."

"Terry. I called to say that I forgive you. It's almost Christmas and—"

"Forgive me? You forgive me? For what?"

"For sleeping with Sean. For stealing him." What was the matter with Terry? She must know their quarrel was not Lily's fault, that she was the villain of this piece.

"I don't need your fucking forgiveness. He was up for grabs. You put him there."

"That was before. At the beginning. Then we agreed to stop it."

"You agreed. You."

"So did you."

"I didn't know then, did I?"

"Know what? Don't tell me you fell for him? Impossible."

Terry struggled to contain her fury. In the past, she'd always found Lily's take 'em or leave 'em attitude toward men amusing. It was so Lily. But right now, her nonchalance in the face of Terry's misery was infuriating.

"Terry. Come on. I'm making the move here. And you were the one who broke the rules. Meet me halfway, at least."

And Terry snapped. Her anger poured out of her, uncontrolled. And uncontrollable. "Halfway? Halfway? Are you fucking mad? We're not negotiating a treaty here. There is no fucking halfway. You screwed up my life. You and your celebrity."

"Hey. I was hurt by this too." Lily felt the unfairness of Terry's attacks but managed to hold back her temper if this was what was needed to get them back on the right footing.

"When did you find out about it?" Terry asked the question that had been bothering her ever since she'd first seen that headline.

"The story? The night before. Mara came to tell me. Clever, calculating Clive had wormed it out of her."

"The night before?"

"Yes."

"So how come you didn't warn me? Give me a chance to talk to Sean before he learned about it in the newspapers?"

"I . . . there wasn't time."

"Liar. There was time. Lots of time. You didn't want me to know, did you? You wanted to hurt me. You set out to get revenge for me going with him."

Lily's own control wavered and broke. What Terry had said hit a very sensitive nerve. "Revenge, crap. You fucked some guy, so what? One night with you, fifty with me. What the hell do I care? Plenty more where he came from. For me anyway."

"Piss off, Lily." Terry jabbed the button to cut off her oldest friend, threw the receiver across the kitchen, and then burst into tears.

Paul, on the hunt for a snack before dinner, opened the door to see his mother huddled over the kitchen table, an array of used tissues spread in front of her. She was crying again. He knelt down next to her.

"Mam? You okay?"

Terry gathered up the tissues. "Take no notice of this. I'm fine." She rustled through one of the newspapers piled on the table. "Anything on the telly tonight?"

Paul wasn't fooled. In a way, he found her crying easier than the fake jollity, but either way, her unhappiness was obvious. It had been weeks now, and if anything, she was worse. He knew she didn't want him to interfere, but he couldn't take standing by and watching her misery any longer. He had to try to do something.

seventy-seven

"This is it? The only offer?" Mara held the telephone in one hand and a letter in the other.

"So far. It's early days. Give it some time."

Mara's house had been on the market for nearly a month. In the end, she had given it to James Black, the first agent she'd seen. He had been right. All of the others who'd been around had given her the same estimate. One had even been tens of thousands worse. So she'd gone with Black. Not least because his agency had the flat on the railway line.

When she'd seen it, she'd been shocked by what her money would buy her. The top half of a 1930s duplex, it was warm and dry and the double glazing cut out a lot of the train noise, but the rooms were small, the bathroom chipped, the kitchen old-fashioned dingy, and the whole place in need of redecorating. On the surface, it didn't look all that much better than her own dilapidated house. But it was waterproof. The windows were brand-new, the brickwork was whole, and the roof had been redone three years previously. And ultimately that was all that mattered. The kitchen would do and she could paint the place whenever she had time. Yes, she couldn't change the dimensions, but there were worse things than small rooms.

So she'd put in an offer of £150,000. And had it accepted immediately. Now all she had to do was sell her house.

But that was proving more difficult than she had hoped. Lots and lots of people had paraded through but no one had made an offer. Not even a low one. Not until now.

"I don't have time." The stories in the papers had spurred the Moores into action. Just that week they had filed suit against Mara, claiming full custody of Moo and Tilly. The court date had been set for two months from now. "No one else is even interested?"

"Not yet."

"But this isn't enough for my flat."

"No."

"Who is this Kevin Morris?"

"A local developer. He's done up a lot of houses in Chiswick."

"And he thinks mine's only worth one hundred and fifty."

"It's a low offer, of course, but you did say you were in a hurry—"

"I am, I am."

"Then you might want to think seriously about this. It's for cash, and he won't be concerned about the state of the house."

The offer was insultingly low, as if the developer had known just how desperate she was to get shut of the place. Mara tried to think the best of people, but the revelations about Jake had made her less trusting than she used to be and she couldn't help wondering if perhaps James Black had been blabbing. Not that she could do anything about it if he had.

"Of course, you could drop the price. See if that attracts someone else? Or just hold tight, wait for the right buyer. It is a bad time of year, just before Christmas. Plus, houses don't sell overnight, Mrs. Moore. We've got some on our books have been there six months or more."

"Six months!"

"You need a bit of patience in this game."

Which was just what she hadn't got. Her options were decreasing by the minute. The developer's offer wasn't enough for the flat on the railway line. And for the money she wouldn't find anything else in Chiswick she could afford. If she accepted his price, she would have to move out of the area, and so take the girls away from their school, their friends, the life they were used to. She hated the idea of disrupting their world like that, but the alternative was to hang around and wait for another, more generous buyer, possibly for months. With the chance that one would never appear and the court date getting ever closer. If, on the other hand, she took his offer, they could definitely be in a waterproof flat before the Moores' case against her came up. It would have to be a cheaper place, in another part of London, but in the end that had to be better than running the risk of losing the girls. Of seeing them for only a few hours a month. They'd have each other, they'd settle down soon enough . . . and who knew, they might even prefer the new school she'd have to find for them.

"If I accept, how soon can the deal go through?"

"A few weeks. Just a matter of the solicitors doing their thing."

Mara could see no way out. In a perfect world, she would wait for the right person to come along. But this wasn't a perfect world. Far from it. And she needed to be out of Elliott Road in under two months.

"Tell Mr. Morris I accept."

seventy-eight

"Happy Christmas, love."

"Mam. Mam. It's . . . it's massive. Where'd you get it?"

"Friend of a friend of a friend. This guy's got a job somewhere in Europe—Portugal, I think—for the next six months and wanted someone to take over the second half of the season. Are you pleased?"

"Pleased? I'm over the moon. It's wicked." Paul looked at the little booklet in his hand, "Fifty-five J. Wonder where that is."

"You'll find out tomorrow, won't you?"

"Tomorrow! Mam, you're amazing. A season ticket."

Terry smiled at her son. Sometimes, like when he was trying to cheer her up, he seemed a real adult, and other times, like now, he was back to being a little boy. She knew she couldn't have bought him anything he'd like better. At least one of them could get what they'd asked Santa Claus for.

"Lunchtime. Come on."

Terry had been determined to make Christmas a happy occasion in spite of how she herself was feeling. Or even because of it. There was no reason Paul should suffer because she was miserable. Other years, they'd spent the day with Lily and her kids—Jules always escaped to Barbados, to soak up some sun and evade her parents, and Mara had a quiet family day with Amy—but this year they were on their own. After her telephone quarrel with Lily, Terry had longed to apologize, but she was too ashamed of the way she'd behaved. Lils had taken the first step toward a reconciliation, and instead of ignoring her best friend's lingering bitterness and welcoming her offer to make up, Terry had shouted at her, insulting her, telling her to piss off, then slamming the phone down on her. She couldn't see any easy way back from that. Maybe time would do its job.

To make up for the two of them being alone, Terry had put more into the holiday than usual. She'd got a bigger tree, had decorated the flat with so much holly and fir and mistletoe that the place looked more like a winter wood than an apartment, and had bought way, way too much food. Massive boxes of chocolates, enormous dishes of nuts, and giant, huge, heaping bowls of fruit were ranged about the living room, just waiting to be eaten.

The turkey was colossal. Paul carving off their two portions hardly seemed to make any impact. They were going to be eating it for weeks. Along with the sausages, bacon, bread and cranberry sauces, roast and mashed potatoes and three vegetables that came with it. It looked as if there were twenty for lunch rather than two.

But in spite of all her preparations, the gifts, the decorations, the food, in spite of all her determination to be happy for Paul, the day was a real struggle. She hadn't thought she'd miss Sean more than she did the rest of the time—after all, they'd never spent Christmas together and so there were no happy memories to be blocked out—but she did. Maybe being off from work for four days gave her all the more time to think about what she had tossed away. Maybe everyone else in the country being with their nearest and dearest made her feel extra lonely. The day after Boxing Day couldn't come quickly enough. . . .

"Here, Mam. Pull." Paul held out a black-and-white cracker, banded in silver. More extravagance. Terry had bought them in a posh Islington boutique. Apparently they had useful gifts inside them and special fortunes written by Magical Mo.

Terry pulled. The cracker broke and out tumbled a green-and-red hat, a tiny diary for the new year, and a curl of paper.

"It's yours, Mam. Go on."

Terry reached out, unrolled the hat, and put it on. "Now you." And they pulled again. When Paul was similarly kitted out in a blue-and-yellow paper cap, he picked up his fortune. " 'Fate leads you south.' Well, that's true enough. I'm off to Charlton tomorrow. Though how can they tell when they don't know who's going to open the crackers?"

"It's just a bit of fun, isn't it? Not serious." Terry uncurled her own. And burst into tears. And ran out of the room.

Paul leaned over and picked up her fortune. " 'Fate introduces a builder,' " he read out loud. "Oh, Mam."

LILY SLOWLY maneuverd her supple body into the next impossible position. She'd been doing yoga for years and was aware that the unhurried movement from one pose to the next showed off her long, lean body to its best advantage. Which was exactly what she wanted to have happen. Particularly for the tall, sun-streaked blond man at the back of the class who she'd had her eye on since she'd arrived at the Haven the day before. And who she was sure was interested. In fact, she suspected he'd only joined the class because she was taking it.

Lily moved easily into the next position, a difficult headstand. She had never been by herself at Christmas before. The last few years she and the twins had been with Terry and Paul. Before that there'd been Clive, and Lily's mother until she died. But now she was alone. Jack and Bella were still in Australia, and it was a long, long way to go for a few days. Plus, they had planned to spend the time with friends they'd made since they'd gone out there and, as much as they loved their mother, would likely find her more intrusion than welcome guest.

Thus, when her attempted rapprochement with Terry had imploded, she had decided to do a Jules, to give herself a treat. She had booked into the most expensive, exclusive health spa in the country for a long weekend of constant pampering. Days full of facials, body wraps, and mud baths. Of delicious but healthy food, of aromatherapy massages, of peace and quiet away from "Jingle Bells" and fake snow and tinsel-covered trees.

Best of all, there were the men. Lots and lots of unattached men. Apparently, the place was always heaving with singles over the holidays. And while Lily wasn't ready to throw herself back into the hunt for a part-time, twice-a-week lover yet—memories of the failure with Sean were way too fresh—it had been weeks since she'd last been to bed with him and she could certainly do with a fuck.

The moment the teacher called a halt, she went over to her blond guy, put her hand on his arm, and smiled into his eyes.

"Hi, I'm Lily," she said.

"WHO PUT you up to this?"

"No one."

"Ray."

"No one, I said."

"Don't lie to me. I've known you since I was five and you nicked my lunch at school."

"Did not nick it. You'd finished. You hate tomatoes."

"Did."

"Did not."

"And so on. Come on, who was it?"

"Well, Paul did mention that she was very unhappy."

"Good."

"You don't mean that."

"Maybe I don't. But that doesn't mean I'm going to forgive her."

"Just talk to her."

"No."

"Sean, you were in love with that girl."

"Was, Ray. Was. Not any longer. You want another?"

"Why not?"

Sean picked up their two glasses and walked to the bar. It was Christmas Day. They had nipped down to the pub for a couple while Babs looked after the kids and made the dinner. He should have known something like this was coming; playing football in the icy garden with the boys before a few beers at home was more Ray's kind of thing. He supposed Ray—and Paul—meant well, but he wished they'd mind their own business.

"Here you go. A pint of lager top. Though how a man like you needs lemonade in his beer I'll never know."

"So why not call her?"

Sean sighed. He'd hoped to change the subject. "Okay, I will not call her because she humiliated me. I fell for a woman who cared about me so much she was happy to share me with her friends. You should hear what the guys at work had to say."

"Bet they were envious."

Sean said nothing. Because Ray was right. His men had whooped and hollered at him the day after the story, full of questions about Lily's sexual prowess, requests for introductions, and jokes about four in a bed. And Sean had loathed it. It had made the situation more real, had rubbed in the truth about him and Terry, made him face her lack of real interest in him all over again. They had not been about love at all.

"Listen. Maybe at the start she wanted to share you. But that wasn't how it was at the end. Easy enough to agree to something when you don't know the person involved. She fell for you, my boy. The sharing stuff was all before. And the newspaper said it was Lily James's idea, not hers."

"She went along with it, didn't she?"

"What was she supposed to do? Stop seeing you?"

"She could've told me."

"Maybe she didn't know how she felt till the end. What does it matter? She knows now. Paul says she's incon . . . incon . . ."

"Inconsolable."

"Yeah. That's it. Inconsolable. Just like you."

"I'm perfectly happy, I'll have you know."

"Yeah. Right."

"I am. I've got my boys."

"And your pride."

"It's not about that. She didn't tell me. She could have mentioned it anytime."

"And you'd have been fine about it, would you?"

"Yes. I would. Well, I think I would."

"But you can see why she'd have been reluctant?"

"She lied to me, Ray. Then she let me find out the truth in the newspaper. She's two-faced, hypocritical, deceitful. I can't go back to someone like that. Can I?"

Ray downed the last of his drink. "Obviously not."

"Well, I can't."

"Okay. So you can't."

"Hey. I'm the one in the right here."

"And that'll warm your bed for you. Sean, you're an idiot. Come on, Babs'll have dinner ready."

JULES TWISTED and turned, trying to spread the sunscreen evenly. One hand over her shoulder, the other behind her waist, she stretched to make them meet in the middle of her back, then move from side to side. Last year she had missed a bit and had suffered badly as one spot about an inch in diameter burned and peeled and itched. And in the end left a small but very obvious white patch in the midst of gorgeous tanned skin.

Finally satisfied with her efforts, she lay down on the pale blue linen cushions and prepared for another day in the warm Caribbean sun. She thumbed through her book but found she couldn't remember what she had read the previous day. Over the wall separating her suite from the one next door, she could hear the empty-nest, fiftyish couple who had been there for the past few days joking with each other. They wouldn't have to contort themselves to rub lotion into their backs.

She sighed. She had been looking forward to getting away, but now a large part of her wished she hadn't come. She hadn't had to. She could have changed her mind, canceled her reservation, and remained at home. There would have been no problem about her avoiding her family this year. Diana would have insisted on her staying away from Bevingdon Hall. But she had decided to stick with it. And had been regretting that decision almost since the moment she'd arrived.

Two Christmases ago, still hurting from Will, she had gone to the Virgin Islands to hide. From her family, from the season, from herself. The Gorda Point Hotel had been recommended to her by a client and it had been perfect. Small, luxurious, and so private, the only access was by boat; she had loved the place so much—the warmth, the seclusion, the peace of it—that she had returned the next year. And again this time.

She had expected to feel the same way about it. By now the manager, the waiters, even the chambermaids treated her more like an old friend returning home than a paying guest. She had booked the same suite, a short distance from the beach, with its own small private pool; she'd indulged herself with lots of new shifts and bikinis and sarongs; and she'd picked up all the latest, held-me-from-first-page-to-last thrillers.

She had been determined to enjoy herself. And for the first day or so, she had. Until she'd realized that she was lonely. Everyone else had company at breakfast, at dinner, on the beach, everywhere. And they all seemed to be happy, their arms wrapped around each other, their hands clasped, their bodies touching. The past years, she hadn't cared; she'd been so pleased to be without Will that she relished being alone.

But this time she hated it. The setting was as beautiful, the service as gracious, the food as delicious, the weather as glorious as always, but now it was diminished for her by its not being shared. The sight of all those so-together couples made Jules ache with what felt like a kind of envy. And wonder if she had been wrong about not wanting another partner. Certainly it was true that the only way to guarantee not getting a Will was to remain aloof. But she was no longer sure that security was more important to her than anything else. Looking at the couple next door, seeing them breakfasting on the patio, reading their books, not even talking to each other and yet still so obviously together, she had a telling glimpse of what she was giving up by shunning even the idea of a partner. They had twenty years or more of history between them, twenty years of shared experiences, of jokes and anger and memories. By refusing to get involved at all, with anyone, she was abdicating all chance at that kind of companionship.

And letting Will control her still. Letting his abuse continue to dictate her behavior, even though it was over two years since she'd seen or spoken to him.

It could take Jules a long time to learn things. She knew that. She could be blind, stubborn, and very willful. She hated admitting faults or mistakes to herself. Or to anyone else, for that matter. But occasionally, very occasionally, if she was given time and space and not put under any pressure, she could see through her own pigheadedness to the truth. And when she did, she never tried to hide from it.

Terry had been right. About the donor scheme, about Sean, about Jules's insistence that she didn't need any part of him once she'd conceived. And not only because of the child—although she was able to admit to herself now that she had always known, deep down, that the baby having no contact with the father was far from ideal—but because of Jules as well. She wasn't sure exactly what she did want, but she knew she wasn't Greta Garbo. She didn't want to be alone. Or even like Lily. She needed more of a connection with a man than sex a couple of days a week.

She had a brief vision of Michael. In the last few weeks, since their night together, she had tried her best to wipe all thoughts of him from her mind, but she hadn't succeeded. Every now and then, much more often than was comfortable, memories of him as he had been that night came to her unbidden. And each time she thrust them away. He was not for her.

But there would be someone. In a few days, she could go home and start looking.

"SHE SHOULD be in a hospital."

"Please, Doctor. She hated the idea so much. I couldn't bear her to wake up in the middle of a ward. I know there's not much chance of that happening, but just in case. For the last few hours?"

"You'll stay with her?"

"Of course . . . of course I will. Until, you know." Mara made the only choice she could. The girls would have to manage by themselves for one night. She was only a few doors away.

"All right. I don't suppose it'll make any difference at this stage."

"Thank you, Doctor." Mara held out a heavy wool overcoat. The doctor, a stout, bearded man in his late fifties, shrugged himself into it and wrapped a thick scarf around his neck.

"Good night to you," he said. And slipped out of the door and away into the bitterly cold, hard-frost night.

He had been perfunctory at best, but Mara couldn't complain. It was Christmas and he'd come when called. She supposed it was a miracle that people still made house visits in London, and on a national holiday, but she wished Amy's own GP had been the one on call. Not that it sounded as if he would or could have done anything differently, but the hurried, whispered, businesslike consultation seemed less than Amy deserved.

Two hours before, Mara had just put the girls to bed when she decided to run quickly up the street to check on her friend. She wasn't sure why— Amy had left only a little while before, after dinner and presents and a nap in front of the TV, and had seemed fine, if very tired—but something, some instinct, had made her want to have a quick look. Just to reassure herself. And she had found her lying on the floor, out cold.

Months before, Mara had promised her friend never, under any circumstances, to call an ambulance for her. Even if she was dying. So she had carried Amy upstairs to her bed, amazed by how little she weighed, and then rung for an emergency doctor's visit. And a couple of hours later had heard the verdict she'd dreaded. Amy was dying. It was unlikely she'd last the night. Her heart had just about given up.

Mara went upstairs and into her friend's dark-wood and lace 1930s bedroom. Amy was lying on her back, hardly moving. Mara could only just make out the shallow rise and fall of her chest as she struggled for breath. She sat down next to her and reached out to stroke her pale, wrinkled face. The doctor had said Amy was past feeling her touch, that contact would make no difference, but Mara believed that somewhere her friend would be aware that she was with her. And that she was in her own bed.

Mara had never seen anyone die. She'd never been in the same house, let alone in the same room. She thought she'd be scared. But she wasn't. Amy was still Amy. The friend she'd loved for years. The friend she'd depended on, who'd always been there for her and the girls.

Amy had always insisted that nothing she could do for Mara would be equal to what Mara had given her; at the end of her life, she'd had a taste of the family she had never been able to have herself, of the grandchildren for whom she had always yearned. But Mara knew that what she had done was very little compared to all the unconditional love and endless encouragement provided by Amy. And she had no idea how on earth she was going to manage without her.

It was almost dawn when it happened. For the whole night, Mara sat close to her friend, listening to her slowly lose her struggle for life, hoping for a miracle. But there was to be none. Amy's heart was exhausted. Mara held her hand and talked softly to her about things they had done together, about the time they'd gone to the circus and Moo had been scared of the clowns, about the birthday cake the girls had baked for her last year, about Tilly's appearance as a sheep in the school play. Little things. Family things. And Amy slipped away quietly, without fuss or pain. In her own bed. The way she would have wanted.

seventy-nine

Jules ran to the toilet, leaned over it, and threw up her breakfast.

She'd felt queasy the moment she'd taken a bite of the buttered toast, but she'd dismissed that as hunger pangs and soldiered on. Only to find herself unable to keep anything down.

There wasn't much there to come up, but her stomach kept heaving even after it was empty. Finally, she managed to stand up and half walk, half weave out of the little downstairs loo and into the kitchen. She poured herself a glass of water and sipped it. She supposed she must have picked up a bug somewhere. It couldn't be anything she'd eaten; her last meal had been lunch the day before. But then again, she didn't feel ill. No sweats, no cramps, no fatigue. Just the sudden sickness.

The sudden *morning* sickness. Jules quivered at the thought. And then tried to dismiss it. It seemed very unlikely. It had been just that once and not at the most promising time. On the other hand, her hormones had gone haywire because of the miscarriage. And what about the odd way her depression had lifted the following morning? She took a few deep breaths, trying to control her excitement.

Still feeling weak, she went into the living room as fast as she could manage, scuttled over to her briefcase, and fumbled in it for her diary.

She riffled through the pages, counting back. November 24. The night of Charles Pilkerton's party. All of six weeks ago. Easily time enough for her to be having morning sickness. Or so the books said. She hadn't had it the last time, but she remembered reading that sometimes you did, sometimes you didn't. It wasn't a hard-and-fast thing. People even said it depended on the sex of the baby.

She poked around in her medicine cabinet and found a pregnancy test, left over from the time with Sean. Five minutes later she was holding it in her hand, looking at the telltale, clear blue line. She was going to have Michael's baby.

Ten minutes later, she was in a panic. She didn't know what to do.

Once she'd gotten over the initial excitement of being pregnant, and thought about the situation she was in, she had realized she was facing a major dilemma.

Should she tell Michael?

On the one hand, she'd now realized she'd been wrong before. She wanted a father for her child. She wanted some kind of relationship with a man. And, if she were honest with herself, she couldn't imagine anyone she would prefer in the role more than Michael Hungerford. On the other hand, the way he had left in the middle of the night, without saying good-bye or even leaving a note, the fact that he hadn't called since, told Jules that he wasn't interested in seeing or hearing from her again. Though it hurt her to think it, chances were he only went to bed with her to prove that he could.

So what should she do? Tell him about the baby and so force him into something he wanted like a Sunday-night party? Not tell him and deprive her child of a father? Or wait and see if she carried the baby to term and then decide?

She could see arguments in favor of all three options. Waiting was the easiest choice, as it was no choice at all; it allowed her to put off her decision until later. Telling Michael had definite appeal. Not least because it would allow her to see him again. But also because she knew he wouldn't walk away. From her or her baby. He might be touchy where she was concerned, he might be a bit cold toward her on occasion, and he might lose his temper once in a while, but he was not the kind of person to renege on his responsibilities.

Or she could say nothing. Perhaps that was the fairest option from Michael's point of view. He hadn't wanted to have a child with her. He hadn't even wanted to go to bed with her. It couldn't be right to foist a baby on him when it was the result of a late-night, half-drunken, and mostly one-sided seduction.

In the past, Jules would have done what she wanted and let everyone else go hang. But not now. Maybe it was the effect of the miscarriage, maybe the knowledge of the hurt she had caused Sean, maybe the triumph over her mother, maybe the thinking she had done at Christmas, and maybe a combination of all four, but Jules had changed.

She found herself worrying more about Michael's feelings than her own. And thinking of the baby's needs, putting its welfare and happiness first. Months ago Terry had tried to make her see how important it was for a child to know both its parents. At the time, she hadn't been able to hear. But now she couldn't forget that conversation. And it threw her deeper and deeper into doubt. Something had to give. She couldn't both respect Michael's wishes and do the best thing for her baby. And she couldn't decide what to do.

She needed help.

eighty

"We did what?"

"You borrowed money against the house."

"No. We didn't. I didn't."

"I'm sorry, Mrs. Moore, but you did. I just got the paperwork yesterday."

"But . . . but . . . We can't have. I'd've remembered. I know I would. When did we do this?"

"About six and a half years ago."

"I don't believe it. I don't borrow. I never have. I just wouldn't."

"You had no idea?"

"No. None."

"Forgive me, Mrs. Moore. Would your husband perhaps have done it without your knowing?"

"Jake? I suppose it's possible. But wouldn't it have come out? You know, when he died?"

"Not necessarily. The lien's against the house, not him personally, and because you owned the property in common, his part would have been automatically transferred to you, so whoever did his probate could easily have missed it. It seems to have been a private deal. A colleague of some sort. The agreement was for it to be paid back, with interest, when the house was sold."

Mara slumped in her chair. This was a disaster. "Could he do that?"

The local, inexperienced, cheap solicitor she'd hired to do the conveyancing on the house had never come across such a case himself but he'd asked a senior colleague, who had assured him it was all permissible. Unusual but legal. "Yes. I'm afraid he could."

"But wouldn't I have had to sign as well?"

"You did, Mrs. Moore." He handed a piece of paper over to her and pointed out her signature at the bottom, along with Jake's. "He probably slipped it to you with other things. It's easily done."

Mara would have been busy with the kids. Getting dinner. Doing any one of the hundred things that would have distracted her from whatever Jake was saying. And she would have signed without looking. She would. In those days, she'd trusted Jake implicitly.

"How much?" She might as well know the worst now. If it was ten or even twenty thousand, perhaps she'd still have enough to buy somewhere for them to live.

"Seventy-five thousand pounds."

"Seventy-five thousand? He can't have. He can't."

"Plus interest, of course, set at fourteen percent a year in the terms of the loan, that's about one hundred and forty-five thousand pounds in round figures."

Mara didn't know what to say. When the solicitor had called her in for a meeting, she'd presumed it was to sign papers or discuss dates for completion or something minor. Not that he was going to tell her that she was broke. That the sum total of all she was going to make out of the sale of the house was five thousand. Take away the commission and the money for the solicitor and she would be lucky if she came out of it with anything at all.

She thought back six and a half years but couldn't remember anything significant. Jake hadn't been particularly flush with money at any time. Or especially worried. She tried to imagine what he could have done with 75,000 pounds, and supposed it must have been gambling or drugs or both. Not that it mattered. He had borrowed it. She had to repay it.

And she'd thought finding out that Jake was a serial adulterer was hard.

eighty-one

Jules stood on Terry's doorstep. She hadn't called ahead because she hadn't known what to say. Instinct had told her Terry was the person to talk to about the baby. Lily would be delighted for her and would tell her to do whatever she wanted. Mara would be hesitant, unable to decide between the baby and Michael, wanting Jules to do the best for both. But Terry would tell it as it was. She always did. And while that kind of honesty could be an uncomfortable trait in a friend, it was what Jules needed.

None of them had spoken to Terry for weeks. Lily out of pride after her attempt at reconciliation had been snubbed. Mara out of shame—she was responsible for the article that had caused all the trouble—and Jules out of a mixture of inertia and intimidation. Whenever she thought of Terry, an image of her screaming insults came to mind. No matter how she tried, she couldn't forget the sheer vitriol that her friend had spat at her and so hadn't been inclined to get in touch. Plus, given that the others were much closer to Terry, she hadn't felt that she should be the one to make a move. Until now.

Nervous, unsure of her reception, but determined to go ahead, Jules gathered her courage and reached out to press the doorbell.

After about twenty seconds, she could hear someone running down the stairs, then undoing the lock. She took a deep breath and stepped back a bit. Terry might be pleased to see her. On the other hand, she might be furious at the intrusion and slam the door in her face.

The door opened. Terry saw who it was and squealed. "Jules!" She reached out and hugged her. "What a great surprise!"

"You don't mind me turning up like this?"

"Do I look like I mind?" Terry grinned.

Jules smiled right back. "No. No, you don't."

Terry reached out for another hug. "It's fantastic to see you. I've wanted to call you guys. I was a real cow with Lily. Did she tell you?"

"A bit. Yes." Lily had just said they'd quarreled, though not what about. And that Terry had rejected her overtures of friendship.

"I haven't known how to make it right. So I've done nothing. Coward, I am."

"No. Not you. Never you."

"Yes, me. But that doesn't matter now. You've come." Another hug.

"Hey. I'm here. No need to keep checking."

Terry laughed. "You are, you are. And I've got just the thing, haven't I?" And she ran off up the stairs.

By the time Jules got into the flat and found her friend in the kitchen, Terry had already opened a bottle of champagne and poured two glasses. "I've been saving this. For a special occasion. Like this. You coming here after the last time at your house and that. I've wanted to talk to you, say sorry again. I was a nightmare. I don't know what came over me."

"It's okay. I wasn't all that nice either. In fact, I was a complete bitch."

"Nicer than me."

"Not noticeably." Jules shook her head. "Am I forgiven?"

"Course. Am I?"

"No question."

"A bit of a celebration, then." She held a glass out to Jules. "Here you go."

"Terry, I'm sorry. I can't."

"You can't?" Terry looked closely at Jules, noticed her slightly swollen breasts, her rounder belly, her shining eyes and clear skin. "You're pregnant!"

"Yes. That's it."

"Jules! Since when?" Terry tried hard to sound excited. And pleased. But it was a struggle. Because she couldn't stop thinking that it must be Sean's, that he had sent Terry here to break the news to her. And shriveling inside at the idea.

"Forty-six days." Jules noticed Terry's forced enthusiasm but put it down to her already stated disapproval of predetermined single mother-hood.

"Congratulations." Terry kissed Jules on the cheek, then turned and poured her a large glass of milk. "Here. I'll have to drink all the champagne myself, won't I?" She took a large gulp. For courage. "Who's the father?" Terry needed to ask. She had to know, even if it were bad news.

"It's the oddest thing. You remember Michael? The man I was once engaged to?"

"You left him at the altar." Terry's voice shook with relief. She felt like leaping up and down and dancing around the kitchen. Michael. Not Sean. Michael. "Wasn't he a lord or something?"

"An earl."

"God, Jules. Will the baby be an earlette?"

"No. He was married until a few years ago. He's already got his heir."

"Oh. All right."

Terry waited for Jules to continue.

But Jules didn't. She'd heard the relief in her friend's voice when she'd said it was Michael, realized that Terry must have thought she was going to say Sean. And been terrified by the idea. She knew Terry had been to bed with Sean—Lily had told her—and had thought it just a fling, a meaning-less one-night stand. But what if it hadn't been? It would certainly put a new slant on their quarrel about him. If Terry were in love with Sean, of course she'd be that angry when Jules tried to restake a claim.

"Well, come on, then," Terry prompted.

"What?"

"Where? When? Why?"

"Not how?"

"I know that. Well, I think I do. If my memory serves me right. Now, spill the beans. Details, girl, details."

And Jules spilled. All about meeting Michael that night, about going to bed with him, about him disappearing and her deciding not to try to contact him, about her discovering she was pregnant.

"You had no idea?"

"None."

"God, after all these years. Your ex-fiancé. What do you think he'll say? Will he be pissed off?"

"I don't know. Possibly. Probably. Terry, what should I do?"

Terry looked at Jules, dumbfounded. In her experience, her friend had never come to her directly for advice and had rejected any that she offered, particularly if it was contrary to her own wishes. Had she changed that much? "You want me to tell you what to do?"

"Yes. Please."

"Well, okay. Sure. Fire away."

"Do I tell him about it? No, wait." Jules held up her hand when she saw Terry about to jump in. "It's not that I want to keep the baby to myself this time. Believe it or not, I learned a lot from the thing with Sean." Jules was watching Terry closely and saw her wince at the mention of Sean's name. "It's just that I don't think Michael wants to see me. And I hurt him so much and I don't want to do it again."

Terry looked closely at Jules, trying to see if she was telling the truth or was attempting to justify her desire to have the child alone. "Is that really it?" she asked.

"I know what you're thinking. That I'm using this as an excuse. But I'm not. I'm not. I want my baby to have a father. I do. But not a reluctant one. And not one I have to hurt to get."

"Are you sure he'll be hurt?"

"No. But he walked out while I was asleep. He didn't say good-bye. Didn't leave a note. He hasn't called. And up until that night, he'd always avoided me like the plague."

"He doesn't sound mad keen, does he? Still, I can't see any way round it. It's his baby too. You can't say nothing. Suppose you don't tell, and then later what do you do when your kid wants to know about his dad? Believe me, you don't want to lie. Anything can happen. I never thought Finn would turn up like that, did I? Suppose he'd talked to Paul before he died? Suppose Paul had found out his father didn't love football and terriers and spicy food and that? Found out I'd been telling him fibs all these years? God knows what he'd've thought of me then. Not much, I bet.

"But telling the kid the truth's no better. Not if you haven't told the father. What if he insists on meeting him and then you have this earl person faced with a child he knew nothing about. Which'll hurt him even more than if he did know. You've got to tell him. You have. And as soon as possible."

"What if he won't see me?"

"Then you have to make him. But he will. You know he will."

"What if he won't accept that my baby is his too?"

"This is the new millennium. You have a DNA test, don't you?"

"What if he wants me to . . . to . . . have an . . ." Jules found it hard to say the word.

"You refuse. It's your body, your choice."

"I couldn't do that. I couldn't. Not even if it means I bring my baby up totally alone."

"Sometimes it's people's first reaction. Shock and that. You hold firm, he'll back off."

"Then what if he doesn't want to be involved but says he will out of duty?"

"Better any kind of father than none."

"Even a cold, indifferent one?"

"Even that. Anyway, who's to say he'll always be that way? Duty can turn into love, can't it?"

"What if he's just not interested?"

"It'll hurt, but you'll have tried. That's got to be better."

Jules forced a smile. And then started to nibble at her beautifully manicured nails.

Terry left her alone for a minute, before saying, "If you're that hungry, there's last night's leftover dinner in the fridge."

Jules whipped her hands away from her mouth and sat on them. "I haven't done that in years."

"Come on. What is it?"

"It's just . . . Suppose he's angry. I don't think I could cope with that."

"Christ, you've run your own company forever. You organize parties for hundreds of people without thinking about it. You travel halfway round the world by yourself. And you're worried about one measly earl."

"You're right. Of course you're right." And she was. Jules had to see Michael and tell him the truth no matter how difficult that might be. No matter how scared she was of facing him. It wasn't only her baby who deserved that. He did also. She knew it was odds-on he would either stalk out or back away from her, with offers of financial rather than emotional support, but there was a chance that he'd be pleased. That he'd want to get involved in some way. And that in being parents they could become friends. She refused to think any further than that. Even their being friends was a long shot. But she'd have said that about going to bed with him and ending up pregnant with his baby. And that had happened.

She beamed at Terry. "Terry, you're wonderful. I knew I had to talk to you. Thank you, thank you, thank you. I'll call him tomorrow."

IT WAS eleven o'clock by the time Jules left the house. She and Terry had had dinner and had talked and talked and talked. And Jules realized that it was probably the first time the two of them had been alone together for that long in the whole time they'd been friends. There had always been Lily, or Mara, or both to form buffers between them.

But it turned out that no buffers had been necessary. Any lingering apprehension caused by Jules's memories of the fight had disappeared the moment she'd realized how strongly Terry felt about Sean; she had been able to dismiss for good her friend's insults that day. A woman in love couldn't be held responsible for her words or actions. For the first time since they'd known each other, Jules hadn't been at all intimidated by Terry's hard-bitten, down-to-earth views, but instead enjoyed the difference between them and their backgrounds. Maybe it was age, maybe the maturity that had come out of the disasters of the last six months, but that night Jules felt Terry wasn't just part of their group, the friend Lily had picked up along the way in a wine bar, but someone she could trust, could tease and laugh with and enjoy.

By the time she left the flat and walked to her car, she was sure of two things: that she and Terry were real friends at last, and that Terry was deeply unhappy. Oh, she'd not complained, in fact she'd said nothing to suggest that she wasn't the most contented woman in North London, but her sense of fun had disappeared like free wine at a private view. And Jules was pretty sure why.

She was even more convinced when a tall, gangly figure ran out of Terry's house to flag her down as she was driving away. It was Paul.

"Hello?"

"Paul?"

"Yes. Can I talk to you?"

"Of course you can."

Jules pulled into a parking space on the other side of the road and leaned over to open the passenger door for Paul to get in.

Jules was the one of his mam's friends that Paul knew least well. And was most overawed by. The society manners, the smart clothes, the confident air had always intimidated him. But he needed to talk to one of them and it was Jules who had turned up. "It's Mam. She needs help. She won't admit it, she keeps trying to pretend things are okay, but I see her. I see her crying when she thinks she's alone, I hear her crying in bed at night. Please do something."

"Sean?"

"He won't talk to me about her. Made me promise not to mention her. I asked his friend Ray to say something, but that didn't work either. And I can't cope seeing Mam like this."

"What do you want me to do?"

"Get Sean to forgive her."

Jules almost giggled at the crazy idea. There wasn't much chance of her getting within five miles of Sean if he had anything to say about it, let alone persuading him to forgive Terry. "I don't think I'll be able to do that."

"But you've got to. Please. Get him to see her. I don't know. Make her stop crying. Make . . . make it right."

eighty-two

Operating on autopilot, Mara pulled another box toward her and continued packing away the girls' books, even though she wasn't sure why she was bothering. The house sale was due to go through in two weeks' time and they had nowhere to go. They and their possessions would be out on the street. They'd be homeless. After everything was paid off, she wouldn't even have enough for a deposit on a rented flat. Not that anyone would accept an unemployed single mother as a tenant even if she did. She'd have to give the girls to the Moores. She'd have no other option. Yes, she could renege on the sale of the house, but then she'd owe the developer forfeit money because she'd already signed a contract. And she had no money to give him.

If only she still had Amy to talk to. She'd have seen through all the brambles, have known what was the sensible thing to do. Mara missed her friend's kind, sometimes acerbic, always calm presence immensely. She couldn't wish her back; her life had been an increasing struggle for years and she had been granted her desire to die at home. But Mara's and the girls' lives were so much emptier without her.

Yesterday, she'd walked past Amy's house and been tempted to let herself in, just to sit in her friend's chair and maybe get a sense of her. Some hint of what she should do, where she should go. She'd started to walk up the path to the front door but stopped when she noticed through the front windows that there was someone inside. For one instant, one half second, she'd thought it was Amy, that her friend hadn't died, that the events of that Christmas evening had been a nightmare from which she was just awakening. But that was only for a moment. Before reality returned. And she turned around and continued on toward her rickety home. Whoever it was in Amy's house—Mara vaguely remembered her talking about a set of second cousins in Dumfries—they wouldn't want her bothering them.

She'd finished the second box and was starting in on another when the doorbell rang. Standing on the step was a man in a suit, briefcase in hand. Another lawyer.

"The answer's no," Mara said, sure it was one more attempt by the Moores to bully or bribe her into a settlement, and closed the door. Maybe she was going to have to give in, but she'd do it in her own time, in her own way.

The bell rang again. And again. The man was not going to go away. Mara pulled the door open. "Go away. I don't want to sign anything or agree to sell my kids or—"

"I don't think you understand, miss. I'm here to talk to you about Mrs. Amy Fenton. My name's Edward Parker. Here." He held out a card and Mara took a look. Well, she had been right in one thing—he was a lawyer. Though on closer inspection he was smaller, weedier, and far less intimidating than anyone she could imagine the Moores using.

Perhaps he was the person she'd seen in Amy's house the previous day. But what did he want with her? Confused, Mara stood back to let him in.

"Can I get you a cup of tea?"

"No thank you. May we sit down? I think you might need to."

Now even more confused, Mara led the way to the kitchen and pulled out the least rickety of the chairs for him before settling opposite.

Parker cleared his throat. "Um, you may not know, but Mrs. Fenton had no close family."

"Yes. I did know that. She was very lonely in recent years."

"Apart from you and, um, your daughters, she said."

"She was a good friend." Mara surreptitiously wiped away a tear.

"Yes, well. I'm here to tell you that you are the sole beneficiary under her will."

"What?"

"Mrs. Fenton has left all her possessions to you. Including her house."

"In . . . including her house." Mara looked stunned. She was stunned.

"Yes. And about thirty thousand pounds from a life insurance policy."

"Thirty thousand! That's . . . that's . . ." Mara couldn't think what to say. Thirty thousand!

"She . . . the will says that you were the daughter of her heart."

Mara stared at Parker. And was unable to hold back the tide any longer. Tears began to stream down her face. They had been saved. "Oh, Amy. Bless her. Bless her."

eighty-three

"So we've got to come up with some way to help." It was Sunday afternoon at Jules's house. She'd called an emergency lunch so they could celebrate her pregnancy, Mara's inheritance, and talk about helping Terry.

"Of course we have."

"Fuck, I was such a bitch to her."

"She said the same thing. That she was a cow to you."

"I was horrible. Angry and self-righteous. Ranting about her having broken the rules when really I was pissed off cos she'd stolen my toy." Time, a few days of pampering, and a quick fling with the blond from the yoga class had allowed Lily to get some perspective on Sean. And her quarrel with Terry.

"You didn't know she loved him," Mara said.

"I did, though. Oh, she didn't say anything then, but I knew. I even mocked her for it."

"So let's make it up to her. Let's sort it out for them."

"How about finding another Sean? To share? She'll cheer up once there's someone else in her bed."

"Are you insane?" Jules shrieked.

"Lily. After what happened with him?" Mara asked.

"Yeah, I know, but it'd be different with another guy. He'd be all of ours right from the start, sort of a joint possession. Not like Sean, who was mine then ours."

"What difference would that make?"

"There'd be no reason for us to get all competitive cos there'd be no me. No person with first call. Boyfriend by committee. Perfect."

"Mara, you try. I don't know what to say to her."

"Nor me. Nor me."

"What's wrong with it? I think it's a great idea."

"We've all just had a communal nightmare and you want us to walk open-eyed into another?"

"It wouldn't be that way."

"I thought I was pigheaded. Didn't you learn anything? Of course it would."

"Besides, Terry doesn't want another man. She's in love. She wants Sean," said Mara.

"Now she does. But if she just met—"

"Lily! Stop it."

"It was only a thought."

Jules and Mara looked at Lily, heads tilted to one side.

"Oh, all right. It was a silly thought. We've got to get Sean for her. But how? He'll never talk to me."

"Or me."

"I'm happy to try, but I don't suppose he'll want anything to do with me either. He knows how close we all are," Mara said.

"True. Okay, babes, we've got to be clever."

"We need to get them in the same room, give them some time together," suggested Mara.

"I hate to be the voice of doom, but do we know how Sean feels? We know Terry loves him, but suppose he thought it was just a fling?" Jules asked.

"Fuck, no. Please. Terry couldn't run into the man of her dreams and find he's not interested in her. It would be way too cruel."

"I'm afraid Jules might be right. When he talked to me about her, I thought it sounded like he was in love, but if he did care, wouldn't he have called her by now?" Mara said.

"He's very proud."

"Still."

"It's only been a couple of months. Less."

"Possibly he thinks she doesn't care?"

"That could be."

"Paul told me that Sean won't let him talk about her. That he threatened not to speak to the boy again if he mentioned his mother. That doesn't sound like someone who's uninterested."

"It doesn't, does it?"

"But should we interfere? If we aren't sure? Terry may be even more hurt if he rejects her again."

"She may be. Yeah, that's true. But we can't let her just cry her life away, can we?"

"Jake always said you should never mess about with other people's lives."

"I thought you'd given up on all that Jake stuff." Lily was horrified. Mara wasn't supposed to be following his lead anymore.

"What's Jake got to do with it?" Jules asked.

"So I think we should go ahead."

Jules and Lily looked at each other in surprise and then burst out laughing.

"That seems as good a reason as any," said Lily, struggling to control her laughter. "So we'll do it?"

"Yes. I think so. We can't just sit here, can we?"

"No. No. We sure can't."

"Um, do what exactly?" Mara said.

"Damn, you're right. We still need a plan."

"I think I might have something."

"Jules. You're a genius. Er . . . what is it?"

"Well, remember how Sean adored all those dilapidated old warehouses and factories?"

"Hell, yes. He was seriously boring about them."

"Well, I did a deal a while ago with some developers to arrange a party for the opening of a new warehouse conversion in Clerkenwell. And I think I could persuade them to let me use the place the night before the real party. . . ."

Five

eighty-four

"Hello."

"Don't put the phone down. It's me."

"Lils. Oh, Lils."

"I was such a bitch. Will you forgive me?"

"Of course. What for?"

"I could have warned you. And I didn't."

"What about me? We'd agreed and I broke the agreement and betrayed you. And then you called and I told you to piss off."

"Yeah, and I'd've done the same if it had been me."

"No, Lils, listen. I'm really, really sorry. I can't believe I—"

"Hey. Hey. How about we agree that we were both unpleasant bitches and call a halt to the guilt fest. Okay?"

"Okay. Of course. Oh, Lils. I've missed you something rotten. I kept wanting to call you, but I just couldn't think how to explain and all that."

"I missed you too, babe. A lot. How's Paul?"

"Fine. No, more than fine. Great. He's been very loving since . . . recently."

"That's wonderful. Truly wonderful. See, I told you it was a phase."

"You did, you did."

"Now, listen, what are you doing on Thursday? Fancy a girls' night out? Mara and Jules are already signed up."

"Did Jules tell you she came to see me?"

"That's sort of what nudged me into calling. Made me realize how stupid it all was. So can you come? We've got a hell of a lot to celebrate."

"The pregnancy?"

"Yup. And making up with you. And Mara's inheritance."

"What inheritance?"

"Course, you don't know. Her friend Amy, you know, from her street, died and left everything to Mara. No more house woes."

"Lucky Mara. Isn't that great? Not that Amy's dead, but that Mara's got a bit of money. She so deserves a break."

"Doesn't she? So can you come?"

"Try keeping me away. Where're we going?"

"We're picking Jules up from somewhere in Clerkenwell, some launch she's arranging, then on from there."

"Okay. Sounds good."

"I better go. See you on Thursday, huh?"

"Yeah. Lils?"

"What?"

"I love you."

"I love you too, idiot."

eighty-five

Sean flicked through his mail. Travis Perkins wanted paying for a shipment of timber. Hackney Council had questions on the plans he had submitted for the renovation of an Edwardian school. Freddie Hecht was considering selling his loft in Battersea and wanted advice as to estate agents. Nothing unusual. Except for . . . Sean picked up an invitation to an opening of a new conversion. It wasn't often he got things like that. Developers tended not to waste time buttering up their competitors. He looked at the address of the building. God, he'd always loved that place, had dreamed of converting it himself, but had been beaten to it by another company.

He didn't feel much like going to any party. Any normal invitation he'd have tossed in the bin. But he did want to see what had been done to this building. And no matter how much he might like to, he supposed he couldn't stay hiding at home forever. Besides, what was the point of his having hired a housekeeper to be there for the boys when he had to be away if he never went out?

Ignoring his sudden thought that it would be a perfect party to take Terry to, that he should call and invite her, what an excuse, she loved old London as much as he did, he scrawled "Please accept for me" over the invitation, put it on the pile of things waiting for his secretary to deal with, and got out the plans for the school to see if he could satisfy the council.

eighty-six

Jules played nervously with the cocktail napkin that had come with her glass of Perrier and lime. She was sitting at one of two small, round tables placed by the window of an Indian bar/restaurant in Covent Garden she'd chosen at random out of the Zagat guide. She'd wanted somewhere neutral, somewhere she was unlikely to meet anyone she knew. Most important, somewhere with no history for her, or, as far as she knew, for Michael.

He'd been reluctant to see her. In fact, he'd been reluctant even to return her calls. But he was very well mannered, and eventually, after she'd thrown around words like "urgent" and "vital" and eventually "matter of life and death," he did call and she did persuade him to meet her for a drink.

She had been half dreading, half looking forward to the evening. Now it was here, she was starting to panic. She couldn't remember talking to Michael about kids when they'd been engaged; she'd just presumed he wanted them. Wanted an heir, if nothing else. But she had no idea whether or not he liked them.

His two children were now teenagers. How did he feel about them? Did he love them? Or were they just a necessary evil? Did he look forward to their visits? Or did his ex-wife have to persuade him to see them?

Gosh, where was he? Even taking into account the normal fifteen minutes for London traffic problems, he was very late. Maybe he wasn't coming? Maybe he'd decided that whatever was a matter of life and death to her wasn't so to him? That when push came to shove, he couldn't face dealing with a woman whose life had been plastered all over the tabloids? Jules looked at the door for what felt like the billionth time. And for the billionth time, no one was there.

The restaurant was one of the new breed of Indians; no more flocked wallpaper and many-armed statues, but bright, rag-rolled, modern decor, tandoori oven in view in one corner, complete with white-hatted and -jacketed chef. There were a few early-evening, theater-going diners at the tables, but the bar was empty. Jules had been banking on that; anyone wanting to drink at six-thirty was likely to go to a trendy cocktail bar or a pub, not an Indian restaurant.

But it was beginning to look as if all her planning—she'd even done a preliminary reconnaisance of the place to make sure that it felt right before suggesting it—would come to naught. Michael wasn't coming. He was over half an hour late. Crowds of going-home and going-out workers streamed past the windows, but none of them was tall, graying, distinguished, and reluctant.

She took one last sip of her water and stood up, just as the door to the restaurant swung open.

"Sorry. Sorry. Bloody Trafalgar Square. I got out and walked in the end." Michael was furious with himself. He had intended to be so calm, so in control, and now he was half an hour late and flustered and having to apologize.

When she had started calling him, he'd ignored her increasingly urgent messages. Until it became obvious that she wasn't going to go away and that whatever she wanted, it wasn't just a whim. It had been years since he'd spent any time with Jules, and even back then he hadn't known her all that well, but he was convinced she wasn't the kind of person given to bandying about phrases like "a matter of life and death" unless it was crucial.

So he had agreed to meet her. He'd tried to get her to tell him over the phone what she wanted but she'd insisted on being face-to-face with him. And had given him no clues at all. He'd spent the last few days trying not to get too anxious or excited or be anything other than calm, controlled, and unmoved by Jules's sudden reappearance in his life. He was not interested in whatever she might want. He would listen to her, help her if she was in trouble and he could do so, but not get involved. He was very clear with himself on that point. Over the last weeks, whenever thoughts of her and their night together had come into his mind, he had deliberately and ruthlessly forced them out again. In no way, shape, or form was he going to let himself get emotionally involved with Jules again.

"Don't worry. These things happen."

"But you were leaving."

"It's fine. You're here now. What do you want to drink?"

"What's that?" Michael eyed what looked like the remains of a nice long gin and tonic in Jules's glass.

"Perrier."

"You're not drinking?"

"I can't."

"Oh." That was a strange way to put it. Was she ill? Taking pills? God, was that what this was about? Michael remembered an incident with another girl some thirty or so years before. He'd been in his last year at school and had had to go to the matron about a very embarrassing rash. "Do you mind if I do?" he asked. Right then, a strong drink seemed a necessity.

"Of course not. I'll have another of these if you don't mind." Jules watched him go to the bar, order the drinks, and after taking a long swig from his own glass, return with them to the table. She still couldn't decide what to do. Whether to skirt around the subject, or tell him straight-out.

Michael put the drinks down and sat opposite Jules. He took another gulp of his gin and tonic. Jules stared at her lap, twisted the ends of her loose shirt in her fingers and said nothing.

Michael couldn't help but smile. She looked so much like a naughty little girl about to be told off by a teacher.

"What is it?" he asked gently.

One single, solitary, soon-suppressed sob.

"Juliet? Are you all right?"

"No. Yes. I don't know. I don't know how to tell you. You might hate it, but it's the most wonderful thing and I don't want you to hate it. Or me. I want you to be happy, but you won't be and . . . and . . . and . . ."

"Juliet, Juliet. Calm down. I won't hate you. What wonderful thing?"

"I'm . . ." Deep breath. "I'm pregnant."

"That's nice."

"You don't understand. It's yours."

"Mine?"

"You're the father. No, stop, don't say anything yet. I know you don't want to have anything to do with me and you wish you'd not been with me that night but I've wanted a baby for so long and I lost mine and now I'm having one again and I can't think of not having it. You don't have to be involved if you don't want, but I won't, I won't have an ab . . . a . . . a termination."

Jules's eyes had been fixed on the glistening, well-polished toe of one of Michael's neat black shoes during this speech. It had perhaps been the hardest thing she had ever had to do. She dealt with highly strung, difficult people every day, spent her working life negotiating prices and availability, persuading companies to give her what she wanted even if they were deeply reluctant, and she never had any problems. But this was different. This mattered.

She looked up to see Michael just sitting there, staring at her. Why wasn't he saying anything? Was he so angry he couldn't speak?

He wasn't angry. He was shocked. It had been the last thing he had expected. He supposed he shouldn't be so surprised; they had made love and what was more natural than that it should result in a baby? God. After all these years, Juliet was going to have his baby. Something he had dreamed about as a young man in love. Something he had never imagined would ever happen after she left him at the altar. But what did she want him to do? Was she telling him out of politeness? Letting him know because that's how she believed civilized people behaved? Or did she need something from him? He'd read the stories about her and her friends in the newspapers, how she'd wanted to have a baby alone. Did she still feel the same way now? He played back her speech in his head and latched on to one phrase.

"You said, 'You don't have to be involved if you don't want.' Does that mean you do want me to be?"

"Yes. Please. I want my baby to have a father. A real father."

"And what would that mean for us?"

He didn't want to have anything to do with it. His still-shocked voice sounded cold, uninterested, dismissive. Part of her wanted to give up right now, to walk out and forget him. But her baby was too important for that. She brushed her pride aside and began to plead her case. "No one needs to know about this. It'll just be between you and me. I'm not saying we should be a couple. And you don't have to support me financially or anything like that. I just want the baby to know who its father is and spend some time with him. I know you have other children and of course they come first, but if you could just manage a little bit, just a day here and there. . . ." Jules's words faded into tears.

And Michael's arm was around her, her head buried in his shoulder. "Juliet. Don't cry. Please."

"But you're not interested, I can tell from your voice."

"Of course I want to be involved."

Jules tilted her head to look up at Michael. "You do?"

"I do."

Her smile was sun after rain, multicolored, dazzling.

"I only wanted to know what you wanted. I'm sorry."

"You sounded so cold. So unconcerned."

Michael gave Jules's hair one last stroke and moved back to his own chair. "I was shocked."

"Shocked?"

"You didn't give me much warning."

"I'm sorry. I was afraid if I told you over the phone you wouldn't come. Of course you were shocked."

"And pleased."

"You were? Really? You are?"

"Juliet . . ."

"Jules, please. I know you don't like it, but I can't bear Juliet. It makes you sound like my mother."

"And I'd never want that. Horrible woman." Michael grinned at his companion. "Jules, then. I used to imagine you having my babies all those years ago. Why wouldn't I want to be involved now?"

Jules thought she had gotten over most of her shame about jilting Michael. But the idea of him daydreaming about their having children together while she fantasized about escaping from him reawakened all those supposedly forgotten feelings. Jules felt guilt carve through her. "Michael, I'm so, so sorry. I should never have walked out on you like that, I was so selfish, all I could think about was me and what I wanted."

"Hush. You did what you had to. And you were right."

"How can you say that? I left you with all the guests and the cake and five hundred chicken breasts."

"There speaks the party planner. I say that because you were. You were too young to get married. And I knew it. But I asked you anyway. Because all I could think about was me, me, me."

"You are much, much too nice. I'm not sure I'd feel like that."

"I didn't at the time. But hindsight, you know . . ."

"Were you very upset?"

"Well, I wasn't dancing on the tables, put it like that."

"I wrote and wrote to you. But I ripped them all up."

"Probably a good thing. It saved me the trouble."

"You wouldn't have wanted to get a letter?"

"Not then, no. I was too angry with you to see straight. Too upset. Now all that's gone." Michael was amazed to hear himself say this. And to realize that it was true. All his resentment, all his hurt, all his rage, nurtured for so long, had disappeared. As had his fear of giving in to Jules. Because this didn't feel like either of them was in charge. It felt like a joint venture of equal partners. "Now we're going to have a baby together. Yes?"

"Oh, yes. Yes, yes, yes."

"Instead of the miserable, short-lived marriage we'd have managed years ago. I know what I'd choose."

"Would you? Even when the mother's a notorious man sharer who's been plastered all over the tabloids?" Jules had been wary about mentioning the newspaper stories, but now she wanted everything out in the open. If Michael was upset about Sean and all the publicity, she wanted to hear about it. And deal with it.

"And there I'd almost forgotten you were part of a major new trend in male/female relationships." Michael smiled.

"You don't mind?"

"No. You saw what you wanted. You went after it. It didn't work. The papers capitalized on it. That's what they do. Since Rose and I split up, I've been engaged to two princesses, three film stars, and an Olympic gold medalist."

"All at the same time?"

"Now, that would have been a story. Six at a time. I'd have outdone Sean."

Jules laughed, then reached over and kissed Michael's cheek. She was amazed by his generosity of spirit. Why had she never seen it in him before? Where on earth had he got this amazing ability to let go of old, very justifiable resentments, to ignore past scandal and look ahead? "You're far too good to me."

"And you're far too kind."

"I'm not. But let's not quarrel about it. So what do we do now?"

"Maybe we can see a bit of each other?"

"I'd like that."

"I want to help you through the pregnancy any way I can. And make sure your mother comes nowhere near you."

"I can certainly agree with that. Although given how she feels at the moment, it's unlikely she'll stray within twenty miles of me." Jules hesitated before continuing. She didn't want to pressure Michael. On the other hand, she was desperate to find out what he had in mind. And no one was going to ask him unless she did. "And then?"

"Let's start by being good parents. Anything more than that, well, we have time. Lots of time." Michael's smile grew and grew. He didn't feel like a sober, distinguished earl anymore. Instead, he felt more like the young man he had been when he'd first met Jules. He had no idea whether they would make it together. Or even if they would decide to try. But for the first time in ages, he felt hopeful about the future. He and Jules were having a baby.

Three hours later, Jules lay in bed, Michael asleep next to her. They'd had dinner, talked, come home, talked, and finally gone to bed together. It had been a lovely, sweet, relaxed evening, a healing of past differences, an exorcism, in a way, of the mistakes they'd both made in the past. In the future, maybe they'd only be coparents, friends, and occasional lovers to each other. Or maybe they'd end up partners. Either way, Jules knew Michael would be a good father to her baby. As he had said, anything more than that, they'd have to see. But they'd made a good start.

eighty-seven

Mara lay back in the bubbles. She adored this room. She loved the old-fashioned, claw-footed bath and the original black-and-white-tiled floor. Oh, there were things that needed a bit of work, but it was all cosmetic. Just a bit of paint on the walls, a modern sink, a shower maybe if there was room. Most important, there were no leaks. She could hear rain drumming its fingers on the skylight in the roof and yet the room was completely dry.

As was the rest of the house. Mara and the girls had moved in a week before. It wasn't strictly legal—probate wouldn't be granted on Amy's will for weeks yet—but Mara already had the keys and the lawyer had been sympathetic. She knew some people would think she was showing undue haste, but Amy would have understood. In fact, Amy would have been the first person to urge her to move as soon as possible. So they had packed up their belongings and transferred down the street.

The first thing she had done was write a letter to the Moores. Explaining what had happened and asking them to drop their suit against her. So far, there'd been no response.

She'd also investigated how long it would take for her to train as a therapist. She needed five years; two to finish school, then three at college. Looking at it now, it seemed like ages, but Mara was sure that, given her talent for thrift, she and the girls should be able to survive on Amy's money for that time. She could always work on the holidays to get some extra cash. And after she graduated, she'd be able to earn more than enough to keep them.

But at the moment, her dream was dependent on the Moores' response to her letter. If they insisted on going to court, she would have to continue cleaning and use Amy's money to pay a lawyer.

Mara could have wallowed in the large, deep bath for hours, reading or thinking, but she had to get going. The girls would be awake any minute, needing clothes and breakfast and packed lunches before they left for school. She stood up and got out of the water, dripping. Sitting curled up on top of a pile of towels was Joey, Amy's cat. He had disappeared the night of Amy's death and Mara had presumed that he'd found himself another forgiving old lady looking for a companion to love. But the day they had brought their belongings up the street, he'd reappeared. Over the next week, it had become obvious that he had transferred his loyalty from Amy to her and the girls. And Mara had found herself becoming increasingly fond of him, not least because he was a last, living connection to her friend. She leaned over, picked him up, grabbed a towel, and then gently replaced him so he could continue his early-morning nap.

She, Moo, and Tilly were sitting in Amy's kitchen, the girls wolfing down bowls of Cheerios, Mara nibbling on a piece of toast, when they heard the mail drop through the letter box.

"I'll get it! I'll get it!" And Tilly raced out of the kitchen. Moo smiled at her mother and made no attempt to follow. She was growing up. A few months ago she too would have found the idea of collecting the post exciting.

"Two letters. And a magazine. Oh, no. It's about knitting."

Mara held out her hand. Tilly passed the mail over. One letter was a circular from a cable company. The other was an official-looking communication from the Moores' solicitors. Mara put it aside, not wanting to risk opening it while the girls were there in case the news was bad and she let something slip.

"Aren't you going to open them?"

"No. It's nothing important. Come on. School for you."

HALF AN hour later, Mara was back, and sitting in front of the letter, almost too scared to open it. She so hoped they would have thrown in the towel but had a feeling that it was not going to be that easy. That they would fight on.

She reached out, picked up the letter, and opened it. And read it.

The Moores were not giving up. They intended to drag Mara into court and parade her secret in front of the world. The move to Amy's house had made no difference. As far as they were concerned, her past was enough to damn her as an unfit mother.

If they told the court, there was every chance the girls would find out about it sooner or later. Find out that Mara had sold her body. Had spent years as a call girl, being paid to have sex. And that would be how Moo and Tilly would view their mother from then on.

She was sorely tempted to tell the Moores the truth about their sainted son. Only that would help no one. And, on second thought, they might not be surprised. Maybe they had known Jake better than she had.

Mara stared and stared at the words on the page, as if hoping that they would miraculously disappear and new, more conciliatory, less aggressive ones would appear in their place. But they weren't going away.

And neither was she. She and the girls had been given a real chance at a good life by her friend Amy and she had no intention of throwing that chance away. Somehow, some way, she would fight this.

"GO AWAY."

"I just want to talk to you for a few minutes."

"Well, we don't want to talk to you."

"Yes you do. You may not know it, but you do."

"Who is it, Dorothy?"

"It's her. Wanting to talk to us."

"Please let me in."

Mara stood at the door of the Moores' neat, tidy, Twickenham home. Over the past few days, she had come up with hopeless scheme after hopeless scheme to change the Moores' minds and had eventually rejected them all in favor of simplicity. She'd come to their house to try to make them see just how much their court case hurt Moo and Tilly.

"What are you doing here?" Mr. Moore asked.

"I just want a few minutes of your time. Please. Only a few minutes."

"No. I don't want a piece of . . . I don't want you in my house."

"Maybe we should listen, Dorothy. It can't hurt to listen."

"No."

"But we don't know what she's going to say. Maybe it's good news." Mr. Moore looked at his wife meaningfully. Mara knew what he was thinking, that perhaps she'd come there to capitulate, and she had no intention of disabusing him of that notion. She'd use whatever was necessary to get into that house. And get them to listen.

"Oh. Yes. Well, a few minutes, then."

George Moore led the way down the flowery-carpeted corridor into the bright-white, scrubbed-clean kitchen. He and his wife sat at a round dark-oak table set in a small conservatorylike space overlooking the manicured back garden, but made no attempt to offer Mara a seat. She shrugged her shoulders and ignored the insult. She wasn't there to get annoyed. She was there to talk, to try to make some sense out of this mess.

She pulled out one of the spare chairs and sat opposite the Moores. "It's very simple. I think it's time we stopped concentrating on ourselves and thought of the girls."

"We are thinking of them."

"Please, Mrs. Moore. Let me finish. Now, they don't know anything about this, not yet anyway. I've let them believe that their Nan and Pops are away on an extended holiday. And I think we should keep it that way."

"That's up to you. If you agree to our terms—"

"I'm afraid I can't do that. No parent could."

"Then get out. Now."

"No. I need you to listen to me. For just a moment. And then for you to think about what I'm going to say." Mara was amazed by her own composure. Standing on the doorstep, waiting for the Moores to answer the bell, she'd been a bundle of nerves. But now, somehow, she was calm. And determined to get her points across. "I know you'll never like me, and I don't expect you to, but I am Tilly and Moo's mother and that will never change, wherever they live."

"My Jake should never have married you."

"Maybe not. But he did. For better or worse, he did. And we had the girls. And nothing you can ever do will alter that."

"When they learn what you've done, what you've been—"

"They'll be hurt, of course they will. And confused. But they'll still be my daughters. Even if I die, that'll still be true."

"They'll reject you."

"Perhaps. Perhaps not. They'll certainly want to blame someone. But who's to say that person will be their mother? They're just as likely to hold you responsible for having told them."

"They wouldn't do that. They wouldn't."

"Maybe not."

"They love us."

"Yes. And they love me too. And we all love them. So I think we should forget all this talk about my past and who's the most suited to have the girls and try to agree on what should happen between us. Not bring courts into it. If you insist on that, I'll fight, of course I will. I have the money to fight now, thanks to my friend Amy. But I'd much rather spend it on building a life for myself and the girls than on a long, drawn out, bitter court case where the outcome's in doubt."

"It's not in doubt. You're going to lose."

"Perhaps that's so. But you can't know that. Can you?"

Mrs. Moore was silent.

"Can you?"

"They won't let you have our girls. Not someone like you."

"No. We can't know." Mr. Moore spoke for the first time since they'd entered the kitchen. Mara began to see a little chink of light. Dorothy might be dead set against her, but at least George was not completely blinded by prejudice.

"So here's what I think. I think we should forget all this and concentrate on making Moo and Tilly happy. On giving them what they want and need. Their mother *and* their grandparents. We have to learn to share. Split their time between us. Say you have them every third weekend, half the holidays, and a week every month during school time. Or more. Or less. We can work that out later. But all this fighting needs to stop. Yes, we'll never be friends. But we can be civilized. We can think of Moo and Tilly and not of our own selfish needs and wishes. You don't want them to be brought up by me, and I'd prefer you to have as little time with them as possible, but they lost their father and they need what little family they do have. They need both me and you. And the sooner we recognize that, the sooner we can sort this out."

"You're asking us to give in."

"No. I'm asking you to choose peace over war, Moo and Tilly's happiness over our own." Mara stood up. "Think about it, that's all I ask. Now, I've taken up enough of your time. Good-bye."

eighty-eight

"Claire? Claire?" Jules's words echoed through the cavernous room.

There was no answer.

She was standing on the ground floor of the old gin warehouse that was still virtually unchanged from its original state. There were no internal walls, just rows and rows of ornate iron pillars supporting the high ceiling. Apart from the fact that the place was clean, it felt and looked like a building site. Electrical wires dangled, pipes were exposed, window frames unpainted. The only out-of-place elements were a series of trestle tables stacked against one wall and boxes and boxes of wine and glasses piled up in the far corner.

It was the day of the women's party. The cleaning crew had just been in and the caterers were expected any minute. Followed a couple of hours later by the fake party guests. And, hopefully, Sean.

Jules had expected the warehouse to be closer to completion than it was, but the developers were behind schedule. And, she suspected, short of ready cash. Hence the opening. They could show the one flat they had finished and furnished and from that persuade prospective buyers to choose the one they wanted from the plan. And put down a deposit. Jules thought it an odd way to do business, to sell something before you even had it, but the developers insisted it was normal procedure.

And maybe it was. Just so long as Sean saw nothing wrong with it . . .

Claire came bustling down the stairs from the show flat.

"There you are. Where are the caterers? They're late."

"They'll be here. It's Tylers, remember? The old reliables. You chose them yourself. There's no need to worry."

"I know. I know. It's only . . . I've never given a non-party before." Jules was desperate for everything to go well. Terry had encouraged her to con- fess all to Michael and she felt the need to repay her friend for her great advice.

Claire laughed. "I'd treat it as a real one if I were you. There's not much difference. Same champagne, same waiters, same canapés."

"Just only one guest."

"And twenty or so extras."

"God, what happens if they don't turn up?"

"They will. Didn't your friend Lily organize them?"

"Yes. Of course they'll come. Sorry."

Claire had never seen her employer so tense before a party. Normally, she was as cool as ice. "Stop panicking. Go get a cup of coffee or something. Chill out. You'll set everyone off if you go to pieces like this."

"I know. I know. Usually I don't care all that much about the outcome of a party. Usually there isn't an outcome."

"It'll be fine. Leave it to me."

"I don't know what I'd do without you."

"Nor do I. Go on, off you go. There's a nice café at the end of the street does a great line in cappuccinos. Go on."

THREE HOURS later, Lily and Mara were huddled in a black cab parked in between streetlights on the other side of the road from the warehouse, wait- ing to see if Sean would arrive. And to warn Jules when—if—he did. His secretary had accepted for him, so they could only hope that he would turn up. But they had no idea when. Everything was ready. The party was in full swing. Lily's extras—some out-of-work actor friends she'd paid to come— had arrived, the champagne was flowing, and the canapés were doing the rounds. Now all they needed was the guest of honor.

"Where the hell is he?" Lily was definitely twitchy.

"Lily. Calm down. He'll be here."

"Terry's coming at seven."

"It's only six-forty."

"She might be early."

"She might. I think we just have to trust to luck."

"Luck. I prefer planning ahead."

"Don't worry so much. It'll all be fine." Mara was convinced of it. Nothing could go wrong on such a wonderful day.

"A bit of worrying would do you no harm. What the hell are you so happy about?"

Mara pulled in her wide grin and tried to look appropriately concerned. But it was difficult for her. Earlier that day, George Moore had called to make a deal. He and Dorothy would agree to share the girls. To cancel the court case. To forget about Mara's disreputable past. And she was over the moon about it. However, she couldn't tell Lily without explaining about her history. "Nothing."

"Hmm. Funny nothing." Lily peered out of the window of the cab. "I hate waiting."

"It won't be long."

"Somehow it's worse when it's quiet like this. At least if people were passing by there'd be hope every now and then." The warehouse was in a deserted cul-de-sac, surrounded by disused office buildings and more warehouses, each awaiting their turn with loft developers. "Do you think he'll think it's odd, there being no one coming to the party? We should have had people waiting to walk along as soon as he appeared. To make him think they're guests too."

"Wouldn't that have been very difficult to arrange?"

"Probably. Fuck, it's ten to. This was a terrible idea. Why the hell doesn't he come?"

"I'm not sure, but I think he has. Look, there, at the end of the street." Mara pointed at a tall figure standing under an orange streetlight, peering at a piece of paper in his hand. Presumably the invitation.

"It's him. It's him. Mara, he's here." Lily bounced up and down on the cab seat, her arms flailing around. "He's here. He's here."

"Ow. That hurt." Lily's hand had banged into Mara's cheek.

"Sorry, sorry." Lily tried to smooth the pain away.

"It's okay. Nothing broken. But he'll see us if we don't hide pretty quick."

"It's dark. We asked the driver to turn out the lights, remember? Surely he won't be able to see inside."

"He might. We ought to get out of the way, just in case, don't you think?"

"Okay." Lily hunkered down. "I'd better call Jules." She pulled out her mobile and pressed the green button. "He's here. About fifty yards away. You and Claire need to hide."

And as Lily and Mara peeked out from behind the front partition, the man strolled up to the warehouse and went inside.

SEAN ACCEPTED a glass of champagne from a tall, pretty, dark-haired girl behind the trestle-table bar, waved away a tray with tiny potatoes stuffed with sour cream and caviar, and looked around the room. He was surprised to see so few people; he'd imagined a launch like this would have attracted many, many more than the ten or so he could see hanging around. Maybe they were all in other parts of the building. Or maybe he was early. No matter, he was here now and it did give him a chance to look around without being crowded out. He took a brochure and price list from a young guy who appeared to be the agent in charge of sales and prepared to wander.

"SHE'S HERE." Mara saw Terry, tightly wrapped up against the January cold in her deep-red velvet cloak, turning the corner into the street.

"Quick, out. Act as if you haven't seen her." And the two friends got out, unhurriedly, as if they were just arriving. Lily stood by the front window, paying the driver. Then she turned and pretended to spot Terry. She squealed and ran toward her, followed by Mara. First Lily, then Mara enveloped Terry in a huge hug.

"God, I've missed you lot."

"You've missed us? You've missed us? How do you think we've felt?"

"Mild hankering?"

"Well, I did get a vague sort of twinge three weeks ago last Friday. But I'm better now." Lily grinned. Then she took a closer look at Terry and her smile died. "You've lost weight. A lot of weight."

"All that pining for my friends. Put me off my food, didn't it? Most successful diet I've ever been on. Look, cheekbones." Terry didn't want to mention the real reason her clothes were hanging off her. Sooner or later, they'd have to talk about Sean, but she'd prefer it was later. Much later. "Where's Jules?"

"Inside. Organizing the party." Lily was shocked by the sight of her friend. In two months, she had lost that rounded, pretty, smiley look and become almost cadaverous. Terry might have liked the idea of being able to see her bones but Lily hated it. Her friend didn't look like herself anymore. She was drawn, pale, gaunt. Three words Lily had never thought she would be able to apply to Terry. She longed to chide her and then feed her, but it was clear Terry wanted to leave it alone. So Lily kept quiet. After all, if everything went well tonight, she'd soon start eating properly. "Perhaps we ought to go in and find her."

"Yeah, let's. I could do with a glass of wine."

"Me too, babe." And the three women set off across the road, toward the warehouse.

"So where are we going later?"

"It's a surprise. Jules's party first."

JULES AND Claire were hiding in a small, empty storeroom off the main ground floor when Lily burst in.

"Where is he?"

"Upstairs. Just about to go into the show flat in the penthouse."

"Good. Who's there with him?"

"One of yours. I think she said Mandy. Short reddish hair. Nice figure. Anyway, she seems bright, she keeps texting updates to us."

Jules's phone beeped at her. She pulled it out of her pocket and looked down at the display. "He's in the bedroom. Out on the terrace, looking at the view."

"Right. Perfect timing. Claire, tell her to keep him there if he tries to leave. Any way she can. We're on our way."

THE LIFT stopped at the penthouse. Lily and Mara got out, followed by Terry and Jules.

"But I don't want to see the flat. I want to have a drink with you lot. I haven't seen you for months."

"Course you do," soothed Lily.

"It's just nicer up here."

"Yeah. Quieter."

"And there's a wonderful view of the City from the terrace."

Jules and Mara fell back a bit. Lily steered Terry into the flat, past the high-tech kitchen and open-plan living room, and then ushered her into the bedroom. Which was empty. Apart from a familiar figure leaning against the far balustrade of the brightly lit terrace.

Terry recognized him immediately. Even though he was thirty feet away, even though he had his back to her, even though he wasn't wearing anything she remembered, she knew it was him. Just the way he was leaning against the railing, the tilt of his head, the shape of his body, told her instantly. She stared at him in hope and fear, unable to move, to walk forward, to say anything in case he disappeared.

Behind her, the door whispered shut. A key turned in the lock. Terry's paralysis was over. She spun around and tugged on the handle. But the door wouldn't open. She'd been locked in. No, they'd been. Set up by Lily and the others. She didn't know whether to bless or curse her friends for their interference. She was desperate to see Sean, to talk to him, to explain, but she also wanted to run, scared of his reaction, scared that he was still as angry with her as he had been the last time they'd met.

SEAN WASN'T an envious man. But he envied the Chicago Construction Company their possession of this property. Particularly now that he'd seen what they were doing with it. Oh, it was all right, he supposed, lots of people would love the apartments they bought here, but to his mind they were overdesigned, their windows not original, their old wood floorboards often replaced. The only things that made them lofts were the pillars—in some cases, just one to a room—and the brick walls. If he had done it . . . But he hadn't. And there was no point in getting upset—it wouldn't change anything. It never did.

He shrugged his shoulders. Time to go home to the boys. He took one last look at the truly unbelievable view of St. Paul's, floodlit against the night sky, and turned around to leave. And saw Terry standing at the door, staring, big-eyed, at him.

It had been a hard struggle, controlling his need to see her, to talk to her. But it had been a struggle he'd believed he was winning. Oh, he still missed her, still thought about her fifty, a hundred times a day. But each time he found himself remembering their day out looking at London or the conversations they had had about Paul or their night together, he forced himself to put those memories aside and instead lingered on the way he'd felt the moment he'd first read the newspaper or how angry he'd been when he'd seen her at the bus station. Trying to inoculate himself against her, to destroy the good memories by replaying the bad.

As he stood there, looking at her too-thin face, her stunned expression, the tears glistening in her eyes, he realized that he had been fooling himself. All the vaccinations had been useless. He was no more immune to her now than he had been the night they'd gone to bed together. He found himself fighting the urge to grab her and take her straight to the conveniently placed show bed.

Terry kept her eyes fixed on Sean's face, hoping against hope that he would say something. Would relax his grim expression, ease his mouth's thin, angry line, and let her in. But he was silent. It was up to her.

"I'm afraid we're locked in."

Nothing.

"I'm sorry. It must have been Lily, Jules, and Mara's idea—" Terry stopped abruptly when she saw the fury on Sean's face at the mention of her friends. Idiot. Of course he'd feel that way.

She'd just made it even more difficult. Sean's glare was daunting. His silence was intimidating. And his rage made him close to unapproachable. If she could have fled, she would have. But she couldn't. She was confined in that bedroom with him for as long as her friends chose.

It would have been easier to retreat into herself, to say nothing and save her pride. But she was the one at fault here. And she couldn't forget all those nights when she had longed for just a few minutes with him, for a chance to apologize, to try to make him understand. Well, she had those minutes. And she wasn't going to waste her opportunity. Even if he didn't listen, even if he shouted back at her, even if he lost it completely.

"I've wanted to talk . . . to explain to you. To say sorry. I never meant to hurt you. I didn't think, to start with. I was just so desperate to help Paul, and then Lily came up with her idea and . . . I know it was wrong to use you like that."

Terry paused, hoping that Sean would say something. But he was frozen in place, his eyes riveted on her, his face still set. So she fumbled on with her speech. "I was selfish. We all were. But I had no idea I was going to . . . to care about you. And we'd canceled the agreement before you and I ever . . . I know it's not much, but that night was real. It was for me."

Part of Sean's brain registered what Terry was saying. But only a small part. All the rest of him could think about was that he was standing in a room with her. The woman he had vowed never to talk to again. The woman who had hurt him more than anyone, more even than Isobel.

The woman he loved. As Terry fumbled through her apology and expla-nation, Sean felt all the anger, shame, and resentment he'd nurtured for so long drift away. And decided that he was crazy, standing there, rooted to the spot, when she was only ten feet away.

". . . and I know we'll never be able to go back to that, that I've ruined all chance . . ."

Sean crossed the room.

". . . of us . . . of us being together . . ."

And put his finger on Terry's lips to stop her talking. Time enough for that later.

"Who says?" he asked, and bent down to kiss her.

ON THE other side of the door, Lily, Jules, and Mara were huddled, desper-ately trying to hear what was happening but unable to make out more than the murmur of Terry's voice.

"Hasn't he said anything yet?" whispered Jules.

"I haven't heard him," Mara mouthed back.

"Hold on a second. Was that him?" murmured Lily.

"I think, maybe. . . ."

"Why are these doors so thick?"

"Shh. Listen. Listen."

"There's nothing."

"Exactly. Nothing."

"Nothing."

The friends held their collective breath. Crossed their fingers. Hoped that their strategy had worked. And as every silent second passed, it looked more and more likely. Whatever Sean and Terry were doing, they weren't quarreling. And they weren't trying to get out.

"Mission accomplished, I think." Lily flourished the key and, with a wide grin, slowly, silently unlocked the door.

Together the three women stole out of the show flat, leaving their friend behind with her lover.

Three Years Later

eighty-nine

"You can't wear that!"

"Course I can. Sean'll love it."

"He will?" Jules was incredulous.

"Are you sure?" Mara asked.

"No wonder he went off me." Lily said, laughing.

"Give me a hand with this, someone." Terry was trying to undo the tiny, fabric-covered buttons at the back of her 1920s, Schiaparelli wedding dress. It had turned from bright white to faded ivory over the years, but Terry had fallen in love with it the moment she'd seen it in an antique-clothes store in Chelsea. Jules, horrified by the idea that her friend was going to get married in someone else's clothes, had offered to buy her a brand-new, shiny, fresh designer dress, but Terry would have none of it. She wanted the Schiaparelli. And the Schiaparelli she got.

In the end, even Jules had had to agree that it had been the right choice. Cut on the bias, it was not only beautiful, it was also flattering as it flowed over Terry's restored curves. The bride had looked absolutely gorgeous.

But her going-away outfit was something else. No demure suit, no nice little dress with matching jacket, no chic pastel outfit for her. She'd chosen a 1950s circular pink poodle skirt, an electric blue bat-wing-sleeved sweater, and a pair of high-heeled, strappy, turquoise sandals that showed off her narrow ankles and shapely legs. Her friends might be shocked, but four hours in an ivory dress was enough for Terry. It was time for color.

While Jules held her head in her hands and Lily laughed, Mara helped Terry out of the dress. Five minutes later, she was dressed and ready. Lily went to the window and looked out into the long driveway below.

"Not here yet."

"Time for a private toast, then." Jules looked around the ornately furnished room and spotted the champagne she had ordered sitting on a table beside the canopied bed. The wedding had been a Dunne Parties special. Jules—and her onetime assistant, Claire, now the day-to-day manager of the business—had pulled out all the stops. From the setting—the beautiful eighteenth-century Hartwell House—to the champagne—Bollinger—to the music—the Bootleg Beatles—they had been determined that everything would be perfect.

And it had been. Even the weather had cooperated. The day before, it had rained. The day after, it would rain. But for Sean and Terry's wedding, there were only a few small, wispy clouds way up high. It had been warm, not hot, with just enough breeze to flutter a veil.

Jules waddled over to the wine, poured out four glasses, and handed them around.

Lily raised hers. "To us."

"To us."

"Us."

"I have to drink to that," Jules said, and took a tiny sip. "To us."

"And to you lot. For everything you did."

"We did nothing," Mara said.

"Just what any friends would have," said Jules.

And Lily put her finger down her throat and pretended to be sick.

"Stop it, Lils. I mean it. I do. Without all of you, there'd have been no wedding, would there? No Sean and me, no Mark and Ben and Paul all being best men together, no Minnie marching down the aisle and sitting beside us at the altar, no Moo and Tilly as bridesmaids, no Evie as flower girl. No pretty house in Blackheath, no new life for me." Terry paused for a second or two to swallow away the tightness in her throat. "No happy ending. I love you lot."

"Oh, Terry," said Mara.

"We love you too," replied Jules.

Lily smiled. "That we do, babe," she said, her eyes suspiciously moist.

"Lils! You're not crying?"

"Course not. I never cry. Except when my best friend gets married to the man of her dreams. Be happy, Ter." And Lily held out her hand.

"I will," said Terry. "No problem there." She took Lily's hand and squeezed it, tears running down her own face.

"I thought that was great, the boys as joint best men," Jules ventured after a few moments.

Terry threw off her reflective mood. "Didn't they look good in their morning suits? The three of them spent weeks learning to tie their cravats properly. Every time I came near them, it felt like they were fiddling with little pieces of gray cloth. That was when they weren't huddled in a corner, discussing the speech."

"It was great. Really funny. And sweet too." Mara smiled at the memory of the story Paul had told about how he'd been ravenous but had hidden in his room with nothing but the nub end of an old Mars bar, hoping if he left his mam and Sean alone, they'd get together.

"I have a feeling someone I know gave them a bit of help?"

"Not me. Never. It was all their own work, I promise."

"Lils."

"Well, perhaps I pointed them in the right direction a few times."

"Whatever you did, it was great."

"I know I'm biased, but didn't Moo and Tilly look lovely?"

"Absolutely gorgeous."

"Those two are going to be as irresistible as their mother. Did you see Mark? Couldn't take his eyes off Moo, could he?"

"Or the gold dress. I always thought bridesmaids were supposed to be in pastels," Lily said.

"Be grateful. She wanted purple." Jules laughed.

"I loved Evie scattering her petals all over everyone," said Mara. "She's such a little dear."

"She was so pleased with herself, bless her."

"Where is she?"

"Asleep on Michael's lap. Of course. She just adores her daddy."

"Have you decided?" Lily asked.

"No. I mean yes. I'm not going to do it."

"To spite your mother?"

"No. I thought and thought about it, whether that was the reason, and I realized it wasn't. Oh, there's some of that. But it's more. I just don't want to be a wife. I'm happy as I am, living in the country, looking after Evie, seeing Michael on weekends. And getting ready for the new one." Jules patted her rounded stomach.

"Damn. I was looking forward to boasting about my friend the countess," Terry said, grinning.

"I had a whole sketch almost completely written."

"Lily. You wouldn't."

"Well, no, probably not. More champagne?"

Terry and Mara held out their glasses.

"Okay, so now Jules and me are fixed up, we've got to find someone for Lils and Mara," Terry said.

"If you can find me what I want, I'll be your friend forever."

"You will be anyway."

"Well, yes, but you know what I mean."

"Who's the handsome young chap you brought today? Noel was it?" Jules asked.

"The latest disaster. Asked me to marry him after the speeches."

"Oh, Lils."

"They're getting worse. It was only our third date. Years ago, they used to last a few weeks at least."

"Maybe . . . Maybe there just isn't anyone? Maybe you'd better give up on it and look for something more usual? More real?" Mara might have lost her illusions about her own love but that hadn't stopped her being a romantic at heart.

"No way. I am determined. One day my twice-a-week prince will come. I know it."

"Whatever you say. But I'd've thought experience might have taught you otherwise. How long have you been looking now?" Terry asked.

"Five, six years. Nothing. Think of Sleeping Beauty. She waited a hundred."

"I don't think you'll last that long, Lils."

"That's all you know. The search will keep me young." The friends laughed. "Anyway, I've already got the next one picked out."

"It sounds like you have them all stacked up, waiting, like planes at Heathrow."

"I wish. This one's a bookstore manager I met the other day while doing a signing of the collected scripts of *We Can Work It Out*. Tall, good-looking, only twenty-five, and definitely keen."

"Isn't that a touch young?"

"It's how I like them. Juicy and exciting." Lily knew she was pushing it. Knew that the time was coming when she'd have to retire gracefully, forget the vigorous men of her fantasies, and accept older, less-dynamic guys, who would probably be even more interested in settling down than their younger versions had been. But not now. Not yet. After all, she was going to be old for a long time. "Enough of that. I want to know about you. Tilly let slip something about you seeing some guy."

"Mara!"

"Why didn't you tell us?"

"It's nothing. Just a few dates, that's all."

"You dating isn't nothing. Who is he?"

"What's his name?"

"Is he nice?"

"Why didn't you tell us?"

Mara looked astonished by the flurry of questions from her friends and decided to answer the last. "I didn't think you'd be this interested."

"You are a first-class, number-one idiot. You're going out with someone for the first time in years and you think we won't want to know about it? Now, tell all. Or else," Lily said, issuing her orders.

"Yes, sir. He's called Sam. He lives up the street from us, opposite the old house. He and his wife split up a few years ago. He has a daughter Moo's age. That's how I got to know him. He has Moo and Tilly to stay sometimes. Most days I'm back from college by the time they're home from school, but every so often I have to go away on courses. And I need someone to look after the girls. And he offered."

"They like him?"

"Yes. A lot."

The friends waited for more.

"There's nothing else to tell. We've gone out a few times, that's all. We get a baby-sitter, go to a film or out to dinner. It's early days."

"And you don't want to say any more, do you? In case you jinx it?" Terry asked. That's how she would have felt.

"I know it's silly, but . . ."

"Okay, we'll shut up. For now. But we expect regular updates. Don't we, girls?"

"We certainly do."

"The moment there's something to tell."

They all looked expectantly at Mara. "Okay. Okay. I'll write down every word we say, tell you everything that happens. Is that enough?"

"Perfect."

Lily wandered over to the window. "Hey, guys, the car's here. Sean and everyone are out front waiting."

Jules raised her glass. "One last toast. To Terry."

"To Terry."

"Terry."

"We'll miss you."

"No you won't. I'm only married, not dead."

"I know. It just feels like we're saying good-bye. Why is that?" Jules asked.

"Because it is the end of something," Mara reflected.

"The final act of us and Sean."

"Lily. That was three years ago."

"No. It's now. The last bit of the story. The happy ending."

"For all of us," said Jules.

"Except Lily. She's still looking," Terry joked.

"Hell, I'm not unhappy. I'm still making them laugh, I'm wealthier than I ever thought I could be, the kids are doing great, and Clive is leaving me alone. Oh, and once I make a call, I'll have a date next week. Who just might be the one. What more could I want? Apart from ten less years on the clock, that is?" She tossed back her champagne then put down the glass. "Come on. Sean will think we've kidnapped her."

"He's bound to. Especially as it's us."

"Terry's wicked friends," Mara said, smiling.

"That's crap. And you know it. He gave up on all that ages ago. He likes you."

"Yeah. But I'm not sure he trusts us. I know I wouldn't. Come on. You've only got a weekend of honeymoon, better make the most of it." And Lily ushered the friends out of the room.

"We'll have more later. When school's over and we can take the kids on a proper holiday."

"Even I wouldn't want to take the children on a honeymoon," said Jules.

"I know, we're mad, but it just felt right. To involve them. Oh, shit, I've forgotten my bouquet. Hold on." Terry ran back down the wide gallery that ran the length of the house, past the high windows and gold-framed old portraits, and disappeared into the bedroom she'd been using.

Moments later, she reappeared with the arrangement of white and lilac freesia.

"Just so long as you don't throw them in my direction," said Lily.